Praise for
When the Morning Comes

"Cindy Woodsmall writes *real*—real people, real conflicts, real emotions. When you open her book, you enter her world and live the story with the characters. *When the Morning Comes* is a journey of discovering faith, of overcoming trauma, of learning to depend on God's sustaining strength. I eagerly await installment three of the Sisters of the Quilt series!"

—KIM VOGEL SAWYER, author of *Bygones*
and *Where Willows Grow*

"Harness making and prayer Kapps meet cell phones and photography in this latest Cindy Woodsmall novel blending the old world with the new. Through Amish and Mennonite characters in tension with their contemporary world, Cindy weaves the fabric of all faith communities hoping to be relevant to the world around them—and each other—while not losing the strengths of their forefathers and foremothers. *When the Morning Comes* is a fine rendering of struggle and joy that resonates long after the last words are read."

—JANE KIRKPATRICK, award-winning author of the Change
and Cherish Series, including *A Tendering in the Storm*

Praise for
When the Heart Cries

"Debut author Woodsmall's free-flowing prose evokes emotion while exploring the relational dynamics of the Amish community and its long-treasured way of life."

—*Christian Retailing*

"Hannah's struggles and painful experiences as an outsider in her own home will touch the hearts of those familiar with Beverly Lewis's Amish stories. Woodsmall's style packs a powerful emotional punch."

—*Library Journal*

"[Hannah's] story is both touching and tragic, yet hope shines through every page-turning chapter. A moving and meaningful first novel."

—LIZ CURTIS HIGGS, best-selling author
of *Grace in Thine Eyes*

"*When the Heart Cries* is a compelling and moving beginning to what promises to be a great new series."

—DEBORAH RANEY, author of *A Vow to Cherish*
and *Remember to Forget*

When the
the
Morning
Comes

When the Morning Comes

⊷ A NOVEL ⊷

Cindy Woodsmall

SISTERS OF THE QUILT, BOOK TWO

WATERBROOK
PRESS

WHEN THE MORNING COMES
PUBLISHED BY WATERBROOK PRESS
12265 Oracle Boulevard, Suite 200
Colorado Springs, Colorado 80921

The Scripture quotations on pages 249, 251, and 301 are taken from The Holy Bible: Inter-
national Standard Version. Copyright © 1994–2007 by the ISV Foundation of Fullerton,
California. All rights reserved internationally. The quotation of Galatians 6:7 on page 301
is taken from the King James Version.

The characters and events in this book are fictional, and any resemblance to actual persons
or events is coincidental.

Mass Market ISBN 978-1-60142-713-7
Trade Paperback ISBN 978-1-4000-7293-4
eBook ISBN 978-0-307-44628-2

Copyright © 2007 by Cindy Woodsmall

Published in the United States by WaterBrook Multnomah, an imprint of the Crown
Publishing Group, a division of Random House LLC, New York, a Penguin Random
House Company.

WATERBROOK and its deer colophon are registered trademarks of Random House LLC.

The Library of Congress cataloged the trade paperback edition as follows:
Woodsmall, Cindy.
    When the morning comes : a novel / Cindy Woodsmall. — 1st ed.
        p. cm. — (Sisters of the quilt ; bk. 2)
    ISBN 978-1-4000-7293-4 (alk. paper)
    1. Amish women—Fiction. 2. Amish—Fiction. I. Title.
    PS3623.O678W475 2007
    813'.6—dc22

                                            2007015366

Printed in the United States of America
2014—First Mass Market Edition

10 9 8 7 6 5 4 3 2 1

To my dear friend and amazing critique partner
Marci Burke

Main Characters from Book 1:
When the Heart Cries

Hannah Lapp—age seventeen, Old Order Amish. She left her family home in Owl's Perch, Pennsylvania, in disgrace to start a new life in Winding Creek, Ohio, with her shunned aunt Zabeth. She was secretly engaged to Paul Waddell for several months.

Zeb and Ruth Lapp—Hannah's Old Order Amish parents. In addition to Luke, Hannah, and Sarah, they have four other children: Levi, age nineteen; Esther, age twelve; Samuel, age seven; Rebecca, age four.

Luke Lapp—age twenty-one, Old Order Amish. He is Hannah's eldest brother and one-time close friend, who struggled to believe the truth about his sister's tragedy. He is engaged to Mary Yoder.

Sarah Lapp—age fifteen, Old Order Amish. She is a troubled person and generated rumors about her sister Hannah.

Matthew Esh—age twenty-one, Old Order Amish, and a loyal friend to Hannah. He's in love with Elle Leggett. His parents are Naomi and Raymond Esh, and he has two brothers: David, age thirteen, and Peter, age ten.

Elle Leggett—age twenty-two, not confirmed into the Amish church. She was born to Englischer parents, but Elle's mother died, and her father abandoned her during her childhood. Abigail and Hezekiah (Kiah) Zook—a childless, Old Order Amish couple—took her in and raised her Plain.

Dorcas Miller—age twenty-one, a Plain Mennonite. She is friends with Paul and his family and, before high-school graduation, attended the same Plain Mennonite school as Paul.

Paul Waddell—age twenty-one, a Plain Mennonite, and a college senior. For years he's dreamed of marrying Hannah and using his social-work degree to help families. Then he discovered his fiancée's secret.

Katie [Gram] Waddell—Paul's Plain Mennonite grandmother. She lives a mile from the Lapp home and had Hannah working as a helper until her attack. Paul lived at Gram's during his summer breaks.

Gram, Dorcas, and Paul's older sister, Carol—the only people in Paul's life who knew about his relationship with Hannah. Carol's husband is William, and they have two young sons.

Mary Yoder—age seventeen, Old Order Amish. Mary is Hannah's best friend and is engaged to Hannah's brother Luke. She is still recovering from a horse-and-buggy collision with a car. Mary's parents are Becky and John Yoder, and she has nine brothers.

Eli Hostetler—bishop to the Owl's Perch Old Order Amish families. He told the community to leave Hannah in solitude during a critical point in her pregnancy, attempting to force her to reconsider her account of her tragedy. His wife is Grace Hostetler.

Chapter 1

*H*annah gripped the railing as the train squealed and moaned, coming to a halt. Her body ached from the absence of the life she'd carried inside her only days ago. When the conductor opened the door to the outside, a cold blast of night air stole her breath. He stepped off the train with her bag in hand and turned to help her onto the platform.

"It's bad out here tonight." The man glanced across the empty parking lot, then passed her the traveling bag. It weighed little in spite of carrying all she owned—all she'd begin this new life with. "You got somebody meeting you, young lady?"

Wishing she had a decent answer to that question, Hannah studied her surroundings. The old depot was dark and deserted. Not one sign of life anywhere, except on the train that was about to depart. She glanced the length of the train in both directions. There wasn't another soul getting off.

The conductor's face wrinkled with concern. "The building stays locked 24/7. It's no longer an operating depot, but we drop people off here anyway. When somebody lands in Alliance, they better have made plans."

A few hundred feet to her right stood a small blue sign with a white outline of a phone on it. "I've got plans," she whispered, hoping he wouldn't ask any other questions.

He nodded, grabbed the two-way radio off his hip, and said something into it. Of course he wouldn't ask anything else. He had a job to do—a train to catch.

As he stepped back onto the train, it slowly pulled away, its whistle sounding long and loud. For hours as she'd traveled from Owl's Perch, Pennsylvania, heading for Alliance, Ohio, the train whistle had stirred a sense of hope and well-being within her. But as her haven of shelter and food disappeared around a bend, a deep feeling of aloneness shrouded her.

She turned toward the sign with the emblem of the phone on it. Unsure whether she had enough information to get her aunt's phone number by calling 411, she began to realize how foolhardy she'd been not to make calls during the layover at Union Station in Pittsburgh. She'd been so afraid she would miss her next train that she had stayed on a seat, waiting.

Wrapping her woolen shawl even tighter around her, she made her way to the phone. But once she stood in front of the sign, she saw there wasn't a phone after all. She walked around the pole, searching. She spanned out a bit farther, circling the empty lot. The sign was wrong.

God, what have I done?

She'd freeze before morning.

Walking around the building again, Hannah searched for a nook to shelter her from the wind. Finding nothing, she crossed the graveled parking lot to the edge of the paved road. To her left was a hill with a sharp curve and no hint of what lay beyond it. To her right, down about half a mile, groups of lights shone from high atop poles.

Shivering, she set out for the lights, hoping they would lead her to shelter of some sort. Each step made her abdomen contract in pain.

In her great efforts to keep Paul, she'd lost everything.

Everything.

The word went round and round in her head, draining her will. In the distance to her left, she could make out the backsides of a few homes that looked dilapidated even under the cover of night. It appeared that Alliance, or at least this part of it, was every bit as poor as she was.

She approached the lighted area. Sidewalks and old-fashioned stores lined each side of the street. Most of the shops had glass fronts, and each was dark inside except for some sort of night-light. Desperate for warmth and too weary to worry about laws, she wondered if one of the doors might be unlocked. The door to each store sat back a good six to eight feet between two walls of storefront glass, like a deep hallway. The moment she stepped into one of the passageways, the harsh wind couldn't reach her. She knocked on the door before trying the knob. The place was locked.

She walked to the next store and tried again. It, too, was locked. Moving from doorway to doorway, she grew uncomfortably sleepy.

Too tired to try anything else, Hannah leaned back against the cold plate-glass window of the dime store and slid to a sitting position. She pulled out the two dresses she'd packed in her traveling bag and put one dress over her and scooted the other one under her, trying to get some distance between herself and the icy concrete. She removed her prayer *Kapp,* loosened her hair from its bun for added warmth, and tied her Kapp back on tight.

Sleep came in sporadic measures as her body fought to stay warm. Every time she nodded off, thoughts of the life she'd left behind startled her. Her family's gray stone farmhouse, set amid rolling acreage. The Amish heritage that had once meant roots and love. Memories of her mother teaching her how to sew, cook, and tend to infants. Mary, her dearest friend, standing by her even when it meant she'd lose her fiancé, Luke, Hannah's own brother.

Images of Paul filled her mind, making the thoughts of her family vanish. She chided herself for longing for him. But her inner chastisement did nothing to stop the memories of him from pelting her. She could hear his laughter as they played board games, see the strength that radiated from his hands and arms as they worked the garden side by side, and feel his joy on the day she accepted his proposal.

Stop.

Her body shook harder as cold from the concrete seeped through her clothes, and she wondered if she'd wake in the morning or freeze to death during the night.

From somewhere on the sidewalk came the sound of footsteps. Prying her eyes open, she glimpsed through the dark shadows of night and drowsiness to see the silhouette of a man at the end of the long, glass entryway. Her heart pounded, but waking to full consciousness seemed impossible. Maybe he wouldn't see her.

The next time she forced her eyes open, the broad shoulders and lanky body of a man were directly in front of her. Still unable to get fully awake, she couldn't see any more than his profile.

With no energy or place to run, Hannah waited—like an animal caught in a trap.

He removed something from around him and placed it over her. The miserable chills eased, and she could no longer control her eyelids as warmth spread over her.

Chapter 2

Perry County, Pennsylvania

*G*rumbling to herself, Sarah grabbed her winter shawl off the peg and headed out the back door to fetch a load of wood. Early morning sun gleamed against the fresh layer of snow. As she made her way to the lean-to, the strange events of yesterday weighed heavy.

She tracked snow onto the dirt floor of the covered shed as she crossed to the stacked woodpile. Placing a split log in the crook of one arm, she mumbled complaints about Samuel not getting his chores done last night. *Daed* would hear about this.

The sound of a horse and buggy approaching made her turn. Matthew Esh was driving, and his mother, Naomi, sat beside him. As Sarah stood under the lean-to, watching them get out of the buggy, Matthew spotted her.

He dipped his head to come under the low roof. "Sarah." He nodded his greeting rather coldly, then without another word proceeded to stack firewood in the crook of his arm.

Of course he has nothing to say to me.

He was Hannah's friend. And once a man saw the perfect beauty and poise of Sarah's older sister, he never glanced her way again.

Daed came out of the barn and spoke to Naomi for a moment before taking the horse by the lead. He motioned for her to go into the house. Through the open double doors to the barn, Sarah could see Levi still mucking it out after milking the cows and wondered where Luke was. Before she thought to ask Matthew what he and his mother were doing here, he strode down the hill toward her home. Sarah followed in silence.

When she entered, her three younger siblings were eating at the kitchen table.

Naomi stood in front of the wood stove, warming her hands. "It's awful bitter out there." Her voice sounded different today.

Matthew unloaded the wood and headed out the back door again.

"*Ya*, it is cold." Sarah dropped a couple of split logs into the woodbin and closed the lid. "The potbellied stove has been eating wood like it's candy, and the house is still a little cool."

A few minutes later Daed stalked into the kitchen from the coatroom, looking no one in the eye. Since he'd pulled off his mucky work boots, only his black woolen socks covered his feet. "Sarah, fix a pot of coffee while I fetch your mother."

Matthew came in the back door with wood piled so high in his arms he could barely see over it. Sarah moved to the woodbin and lifted the lid. Then she removed a few sticks off the top of his load.

"That's all right, Sarah. I got it." Matthew's words were void of his usual warmth.

Normally, from the moment Naomi and Matthew arrived, he and her father engaged in easy banter about horses, cows, and such. But this didn't have the feel of a normal conversation.

Sarah decided her best chance of being allowed to stay and hear a few bits of gossip was to get something into the oven as quickly as possible. After putting the coffee on to brew and filling the cups with hot tap water to warm them, she began kneading the batch of sourdough that Esther had made and set out to rise last night.

When *Mamm* and Daed came into the kitchen, they said nothing to her about leaving. But they told Esther, Rebecca, and Samuel to take their breakfast upstairs and stay there until someone called for them.

By the time Sarah returned from helping Esther get their two youngest siblings up the steps with their plates of food and drinks, the coffee was almost ready. She set the cream and sugar on the table before dumping the water from the cups down the drain and pouring the fresh brew. Placing a mug in front of each person, she was relieved that she seemed invisible to them. While they fixed their coffee, she placed a few leftover cinnamon rolls from breakfast on the table. The long, awkward silence in the room made her wonder if any of them would say what was on their minds before she was banned to the upstairs with the others.

Daed tapped his spoon against the rim of his cup and focused on Naomi. "I suppose this visit is about Hannah."

Watching everyone out of the corner of her eye, Sarah stood quietly at the counter, molding a handful of dough into a dinner roll. Her insides quivered. Just the thought of Hannah's fall from on high made her feel guilty as well as triumphant.

Naomi cleared her throat. "I think the community was kept in the dark about the…about Hannah's secret for far too long."

Hannah's secret? The wad of dough in Sarah's hands plopped onto the floor. She grabbed it up.

"Sarah." Her father's voice vibrated the room.

She wheeled around. "Yes, Daed?"

"You shouldn't be in here."

She wanted to beg for permission to stay, but the look in Daed's eyes kept her from asking.

Matthew pushed his coffee cup to the center of the table. "Zeb, there's no keepin' what's taken place a secret. If ya don't share it, your children will have to rely on the rumors they'll hear to try to figure things out." Matthew closed his eyes and drew a deep breath before opening them again. "But this is your home and your family."

Her father clicked his tongue but gave a slight nod, letting Sarah know she could stay.

Naomi smoothed the front of her apron. "I've never seen our bishop so set in his mind against a body like he was Hannah. It was his and the preachers' stand concerning anything she said that made them force her to stay alone…"

Sarah couldn't catch a breath. She'd gone to the bishop and told him things about Hannah, but surely that wasn't what had caused this trouble.

Daed pushed his coffee mug away. "What new actions by my eldest daughter have caused you to come see me?"

Naomi looked to her son briefly. "Zeb, Ruth." She paused. "I hope you can find it within your hearts to forgive me."

Mamm's eyes opened wide. "Forgive you? You've done nothing wrong."

Daed glanced at Sarah. "We all know the tricks Hannah pulls. Don't take on guilt for her."

Sarah turned her back as if she hadn't heard him and washed the dough off her hands, hoping this conversation wouldn't end up pointing a finger in her direction.

He continued. "If you've come here thinking something is your fault, you're wrong. No one can take blame for the birth except Hannah herself."

Sarah turned to face her mother. "Hannah has a baby?"

Her mother stared blankly at the table. "Don't repeat that, Sarah."

Matthew rose from his seat. "None of what's happened is gonna stay a secret." He pointed Sarah toward the bench seat. "I think ya should tell her."

Sarah sat, unable to accept what she was hearing. How could her unmarried sister have a baby?

Daed buried his head in his hands. "Okay, okay. Ruth, tell her, but make it brief. Clearly, Naomi and Matthew have something they need to talk about."

"I…I don't know what to say." Mamm shook her head. "Do I tell her what Hannah said is true or what you think is true or what the bishop says is true?" Her eyes misted. "Tell me, Zeb. What am I to say about Hannah and about my firstborn grandchild?"

"Ruth." Naomi's calm voice cut through the freshly loosened anger. "I was there after Hannah gave birth. I would stake my life, even my son's life, that the child Hannah gave birth to was indeed conceived the way she told you."

Mamm clamped her hands on the table and buried her face against them, wailing, "Oh, God, what have we done?" She looked up at her husband. "What have we done?"

Resentment carved Daed's face as he shook his head. "Naomi has the heart of a mother. Of course she believes what Hannah told her."

Naomi stood, facing the head of the household in his own home. Almost instantly the sadness etched across her face disappeared, and fury replaced it. Sarah had never seen any woman face a man with such anger.

Matthew wrapped his hand around his mother's arm and motioned for her to sit. When she did, he nodded his approval. "Mamm was in the room and overheard Hannah praying about the attack. Hannah didn't even know she was there."

The room fell silent.

Hannah was attacked? Sarah dismissed that idea immediately. Her sister had made that up to cover her sin.

Zeb shoved the teaspoon into the sugar bowl, dumped a scoop into his coffee, and stirred it briskly. "More likely that you heard her repenting for telling us she was attacked when she wasn't."

Naomi rose, pointing a shaky finger at Daed. "Don't you dare spread lies about your daughter, Zeb Lapp, because you can't face the truth." She snapped her shawl tighter around her shoulders. "No wonder she didn't want you to know where she was going. She knew you'd never believe her; that you'd only condemn her." She turned to Matthew. "Get your coat. This man would rather listen to the sounds roaring inside his own head."

Mamm rose, looking horrified. "My Hannah's gone?"

Suddenly it became clear; this piece of information was the reason the Eshes had come here today.

Naomi placed her hand on Mamm's shoulder. "Matthew and I took her to the train station yesterday. She told no one where she was heading."

Daed looked to his wife. "But the rumors about her being out at night," he mumbled. "And I saw her with my own eyes in the arms of that *Englischer* doctor. The bishop saw her kissing that man she confessed to being engaged to—a young man who isn't even Amish. She was sneaking around behind our backs mailing letters and who knows what else."

Stiff and mute on the outside, Sarah was relieved there was a lot of evidence against Hannah that went way beyond the pot Sarah had stirred.

Mamm plunked into her chair, staring at Daed. "Is your list of wrong-doings against Hannah all you have to say about this?"

Her mother's look of disbelief at Daed rattled Sarah even more than this news.

Mamm reached across the table and grasped Sarah's hands. "The baby was born the night Mary came to stay here—" Mamm broke into sobs, unable to say anything else.

In spite of the years of frustration that had built between her and her sister, Sarah needed someone to admit that they were all pulling a meanspirited prank. But the grief in her parents' eyes told her this was no hoax.

A horrid scream banged against her temples, making her fight to hold on to her good sense. She looked to Matthew, hoping he had some words of comfort for her. But he seemed torn between anger and sympathy.

His eyes bored into her. "The church leaders had insisted Hannah spend a night alone to rethink her account of how she came to be pregnant. I went to check on her anyway and realized she was in labor and needed…"

His mother eased over to him and placed her hands on his shoulders. "Matthew and I tried to get help for her, but the phone lines were down because of a storm, and…the baby died within minutes of being born."

Matthew reached inside his shirt and pulled out a small stack of folded papers. "Hannah wrote these before she left."

He started to lay them on the table, but Daed took them.

Dazed, Sarah didn't budge. She hadn't liked it when the whole community put Hannah on an undeserved pedestal, but she hadn't wished for this either.

"Sarah," Matthew said, "don't you have something you need to say?"

Her skin felt as if it were being peeled off. Heat ran through her arms and chest. "N-no, of course not."

But God knew she did. Did Matthew know it too?

Luke waited outside the Yoder home for someone to respond to his knock. The hour was awful early to be making a call, but during the night a desire to apologize to his fiancée for their serious disagreement had nagged at him. He needed to share the conversation he'd had with Hannah yesterday before she left and hoped it would bring Mary some measure of peace.

The door swung open, and Mary's mother, Becky, stared back at him.

She didn't step back or open the door farther. "She doesn't want to see you."

Luke resisted the urge to push past her. "I'm sure of that, but I need to talk to her anyway."

She shook her head. "This thing with Hannah is just too much for us to deal with."

He inwardly winced at the lies people believed about his sister. Sadder still, until Hannah was about to board the train, he'd believed them too. "Mary has to be hurting because Hannah's gone. Don't you think it'd be best for Mary's health if she and I talked things out?"

John Yoder came up behind his wife.

"Go home for today, Luke. Just go on home." He shut the door.

Luke stared at the closed door. He knew it'd be a battle to win Mary back.

He moved to the steps of the porch, brushed snow off them with his boot, and sat down. He propped his elbows on his knees and stared out over the snow-covered land. Acknowledging his prejudice against Hannah hadn't been easy. He was as good at pointing an accusing finger and deciding who was right and wrong as his father was.

The memory of his venom against his sister still haunted him, even in the wake of the forgiveness she'd offered him before she boarded the train. The horrid reality was, she'd been raped. And she had borne the trauma and the pregnancy in absolute isolation while rumors devastated her.

Luke groaned. "Father God, how could I have been so stupid? Please help Mary forgive me."

The prayer crossed his lips, and he rose and walked to the buggy.

Before getting in, he looked toward the first story, where Mary slept these days since climbing steps was still difficult for her. She was standing at the window. He lifted his hand and held it there.

He saw her moving about, but she didn't leave the window. A moment later a popping sound came from the window, and she lowered the top pane. She opened her mouth as if to say something, then stopped.

Luke lowered his hand. "I was wrong about Hannah."

Her pale face didn't change. She did that chin-tilting gesture, telling him that although her body still dealt with some frailties from their buggy accident, her will was not as easily defeated. Mary had a bold spunk he'd only become aware of recently. His sister's influence, he was sure.

As he stood outside her home watching her, part of him wanted to speak up and let her know her place as his future wife. But without Mary's frustration with his behavior, Luke wouldn't have questioned whether he was right about Hannah. He would have pressed onward in his anger, blaming his sister for the horse-and-buggy accident and believing the scandal about her.

"Why, Luke?" Mary wiped a tear from her face. "Why couldn't you believe her, believe me, when it would have made such a difference?"

There was no way to explain things he didn't understand. There had been no proof of Hannah's innocence.

He walked to the window, glad to see Mary up close, even if she was furious with him. He studied her features, looking for signs of strength and health. He wasn't sure he saw any. "Hannah and I made our peace, and she forgave me before she left. Can you please consider forgiving me too?"

Mary shook her head. "Don't fool yourself, Luke. If you hated Hannah when you thought our accident was her fault, you'll hate me now that you see it was my fault." Pain filled her eyes, and Luke despised himself even more. "I'm the one who wrapped the horse's reins around the stob of the buggy. I was supposed to take the leads, but I let the horse meander onto that dirt road. Me, Luke, not Hannah."

"Mary, please. I was so wrong to—"

Mary raised her hand, interrupting him. "Yeah, you and Sarah both. I always knew that girl had problems, but I thought I understood who you were—a loving, forgiving, kind man. But now I see how quick you are to judge. You allowed your thoughts to twist the truth into lies just so you could blame someone." Mary closed the window and then the blinds.

Chapter 3

Alliance, Ohio

$\mathcal{S}$unlight danced off the storefront windows as Hannah opened her eyes. Not only had she survived the night, but she felt reasonably warm. As she rose to her feet, two woolen blankets fell from her. No wonder she was so warm. But where had they come from?

The shuffling sound of shoes against the sidewalk made her look down the narrow entryway. A woman, about her mother's age, came toward the store's entrance, searching through her purse. When she was just a few feet from Hannah, she looked up, stopped abruptly, and gawked.

Hannah could imagine how out of place she must look, standing there with her long hair hanging loose under a prayer Kapp, two dresses lying on the ground along with blankets and a traveling bag. She stooped to gather her clothes. "Hello. I got caught out in the weather, and it was warmer back in this cubbyhole. I'll be out of your way in a moment." She glanced up.

The woman's eyes grew large. "You stayed outside all night?"

Shoving the dresses into her bag, Hannah felt her cheeks flush. "I arrived by train, and the phone at the depot was missing."

"Oh my goodness." The woman took a set of keys out of her purse and shimmied past Hannah. "Come inside. I'll get some coffee going and heat up a pastry while you use my phone."

Hannah grabbed her bag, not at all sure what to do with the mystery blankets. She tossed them over her arm and followed the woman into the store. Warmth, blessed warmth, filled the very air she breathed. An aroma of old wood filled her nostrils. The square clock hanging on the wall said the time was a little before eight. She must have slept pretty hard after all.

The woman set her purse on a shelf behind the counter. "So what brings you to Alliance?"

The heated room and the promise of food suddenly lost their appeal. With so much to hide, Hannah couldn't afford to start answering questions.

"How old are you, girl? You can't be much more than sixteen."

Hannah hated deception, but telling the truth—that she was a seventeen-year-old runaway—wasn't an option. She looked out the glass door, considering whether to bolt or lie.

A long shadow in the shape of a man covered the sidewalk leading up to the door. When she looked farther down the street to see who the shadow belonged to, all she saw was a blur moving away from her. A hazy memory of a man covering her with a blanket came back to her.

"I...I think I see someone I need to speak with." Without another word, Hannah left the store. Once on the sidewalk, she spotted a tall, black, teenage boy walking away from her. He turned his head and stole a glance at her, then kept going.

She strode toward him, holding up the blankets. "Are these yours?"

He stopped and turned before shrugging. "You got them now, so they're yours."

The dark-skinned youth was probably only a year or so younger than Hannah, but she felt considerably older. Maybe she'd never feel young again.

"If you put these on me, I really appreciate it."

He shrugged again. "It was nothing. You looked terrified when you saw me, but you fell asleep the minute I put the first blanket on you."

Hannah sighed. "That seems to be the story of my life these days: terrified or asleep."

He held out his hand. "I'm Kendrick."

She shook his hand, realizing she'd never spoken with a black person before. "Hannah."

He released her hand. "So, Hannah, what's with the odd getup? You Amish or a lost pilgrim?"

Fresh realization of how she looked bore down on her.

"Well, don't panic, or I'll have to put those blankets over you so you'll go back to sleep." His voice carried enough sarcasm that she should feel intimidated, but she didn't. Something about him seemed trustworthy.

"Kendrick, I'm in a fix." Trying to think in spite of the grief that clung to her, she decided to aim for a bit of humor. "But if you could assist me without asking any questions, you'd help keep a pilgrim alive through another harsh winter."

He chuckled. "I ain't never met a pilgrim."

"That's okay. Before today I'd never met a black man."

He studied her for a moment. "Well, I guess I better make a good impression then." He smiled. "What can I do to help?"

Hannah told him the name of her aunt she was looking for and the address she'd memorized from the letter she'd discovered back home.

He pulled a pencil and paper out of his pocket and jotted down the info. "I don't have money for car insurance, so I don't drive. I walk to work and stuff. Guess that's a good thing, since that's why I saw you and brought you some blankets from my house."

She held out the blankets again. "Your mother will be looking for these soon enough."

He nodded and took them. "One of my co-workers at the pizza place has a connection to the Amish. I'll give him a call and see if he can get her phone number. If that doesn't work, we'll find you a driver."

He led her to a drugstore that had a pay phone inside. While he made the call, she went into the rest room, determined to shed her Amish look. If her parents had sent word to the Ohio Amish to search for her, she didn't want them or the police to spot her as an Amish girl.

From the backseat of the car, Hannah watched out the side window. The driver scratched his head. "By the way, I don't really care what you call me as long as you call me for dinner, but my name's Gideon."

"Thank you for driving me around today, Gideon."

He smiled and nodded without asking her name. He was a large man who looked old enough to be a grandfather, but Kendrick said he knew his way around this region of Ohio. While on the phone with Kendrick, Gideon had agreed to chauffeur her around for several days if necessary, but he hadn't asked any questions then either. He'd promised Kendrick they'd do their best to find her aunt today, but because Hannah wasn't willing to chance not having a warm place to stay by nightfall, Gideon had helped her locate an inexpensive motel room before they set out. He'd even offered for her to stay with him and his wife tonight, but she declined. She couldn't imagine staying with strangers and fielding the questions they might ask.

The motel was an awful place, a battered one-story brick building with a decaying roof and peeling paint around barred windows, but she wasn't willing to pay for a better place. If she didn't find her aunt, she'd need to conserve what little money she had.

While the car jolted along the rough roads, grief and hope dragged her first one way and then another. The last six months of her life had been horrible, but if she could find her aunt, everything might change.

The snow-covered landscape was sprinkled with homes and farmsteads. In spite of her heartache, inklings of excitement danced within her as she thought of meeting the aunt she hadn't known existed until six months ago.

The driver's voice broke through the long silence. "Hanover Place should be just a few more miles ahead, miss."

"Thank you."

A beautiful brick house came into sight. Electric lights from inside shone warmly against the grayness of the day. Something akin to desire—or was it coveting?—ran through her. Did people who lived like that ever get cold and hungry or stay in a rundown motel?

A mile or so later Gideon turned right and continued a few more miles before slowing the car. Snow crunched under its tires as he pulled onto the shoulder of the road. "This is it—4201 Hanover Place." He pointed to the faded address on a rusty mailbox that sat near a long, curved driveway covered in untracked snow.

He inched the car along the drive, and they passed a small shed that had seen better days. The scene felt right somehow, like a snapshot of a hundred no-longer-used outbuildings she'd grown up around. It wasn't well cared for, but it matched real life: used and still standing.

Gideon stopped the car in front of a house as worn-out as the shed. The peeling paint on the clapboard house was its best feature. Parts of the roof were caved in, as if something had smashed on top of it. Boards crisscrossed the doors and windows, pinned in place with rusty nails. She couldn't imagine why someone would bother to board up such a dilapidated house.

She pulled the door handle and climbed out of the car. Surely there had to be another house somewhere around here. She made a complete turn, looking in all directions for signs of a different homestead along this driveway. All she saw were gently rolling hills, tattered fences, oak trees, and the old shed. Her focus returned to the house.

"You sure this is the right address?" Gideon's question bounced around inside her brain.

Was it possible she'd memorized the address wrong? The wind sliced through her clothing, making her wish she hadn't tried to hide her Amish roots so much that she'd left her homemade woolen shawl along with her apron and Kapp back at the motel.

"Young lady, we ain't beat yet. I promise you that."

She could hear the man, but she couldn't find her way to answer him.

Since burying baby Rachel three days ago, she'd dreamed of arriving at Zabeth's. This was to be her refuge, her direction, her help.

Hannah searched herself to find some sliver of hope to hold on to. But her dream of finding a safe haven in Ohio appeared every bit as ruined as her relationship with Paul.

Soft cries from nondescript voices floated across the fields, becoming more distinct with each second that passed. *Nevertheless,* they cried.

The whisper grew louder. *Nevertheless.*

Nevertheless.

It was the word that had come to her on the train, giving her hope and strength.

She looked at the house. "Nevertheless," she whispered.

Darkness overtook the afternoon as Gideon headed them back to the motel.

"I don't mean to pry or nothing…" His gravelly voice filled the vehicle. "But I'm gonna stick by you until we find your aunt. Maybe you're remembering that address wrong."

Too drained to respond, Hannah shrugged. "Maybe."

The man glanced back and forth between the road and the rearview mirror. "Just take a few relaxing breaths, and try to think." The skin around his sagging eyes crinkled in a smile. "If you come up with a different address, we can give it a try tomorrow."

Nodding, she closed her eyes and backtracked through time. She remembered discovering the envelope in her parents' bedroom. The realization that her father had a sister, maybe even a twin sister, had caused curiosity to overpower her, and she'd dared to read the letter.

Hannah shifted against the cloth car seat, trying to recall what had been written in the upper-left corner of the envelope. There hadn't been a first name, only a last name—Bender—and the street address: 4201 Hanover Place, Winding Creek, Ohio. She could see it clearly in her mind's eye.

Against her will, a few tears ran down her cheeks. The place was nothing but an unlivable shambles.

In the rearview mirror she saw Gideon avert his eyes to watch the road. She wiped her face and sat up straight. "Th-that's the address I remember."

He nodded. "Well, I was in a bind like this in my younger days. You got a name for this relative, right?"

"I think so."

"Then that's where we'll begin tomorrow." Gideon drove up to the motel entrance and stopped the car. "You sure about staying here? My wife is a wonderful cook." He patted his rounded belly and laughed. "She's got some Plain roots in her childhood." He smiled, as if he knew Hannah's secret.

She pulled from her purse the wad of money Matthew Esh had given her and handed Gideon the portion they'd agreed upon. The money seemed to be dwindling awfully fast.

He hesitated before taking it from her. "Tomorrow, if ya like, we can search for your aunt using the computers at the local library."

Paul had told her he used his computer to find almost any information he needed. She figured there was no avoiding them or the Internet now that she was living as an Englischer. She stuffed the remaining money deep into her purse. "Yes, I'd like that. But I also think I'd best spend part of tomorrow applying for a job."

A startled look flashed through his eyes. "You're not giving up on finding your aunt already, are you?"

"I…no…" After last night, she wasn't ever going to chance not having a place to stay. Even a crummy roof came with a stiff price in her estimation. "I've got to plan for what can't be foreseen. And even if I find my aunt, I'll be paying my own way."

He smiled, as if he understood. "Got any ideas where to start?"

"Not yet."

From the seat beside him, Gideon passed her a newspaper. "Read the Help Wanted section. If you find something that looks like a possibility, I'll drive you there."

She blew a long, slow stream of air from between her lips. She needed a driver's license so she could go places herself, but then she'd need a car. The list of her needs in this Englischers' world seemed to spring up like weeds in a summer garden.

"Thanks." She swung open the car door. "Gideon?"

"Yeah?"

"Could you not tell anyone that you saw me or that you know where I'm staying?"

The big man turned in his seat, looking at her directly. "How old are you, missy?"

She bristled. "Old enough to know what I'm doing."

I hope. Oh, dear Father, I do hope.

He stared at her before he nodded. "I was on my own at fifteen. I don't reckon you're that young, are you?"

"No, Gideon, I'm years past that. I turn eighteen in eleven days."

"Good enough."

"Thank you. I'll call you in the morning and let you know my plans for tomorrow."

When she'd stepped out of the vehicle and closed the door, Gideon slowly pulled out of the lot. Tucking the newspaper under her arm, Hannah dug in her purse for her room key. The on-site manager came out of his office and stood in the frigid air, watching her.

Maybe he knew.

Maybe he'd already called the police.

As she fought to get the small gold key inserted into the lock of her motel-room door, the number eleven filled her thoughts. In eleven days, when she turned eighteen, freedom would become a reality. Fear of being dragged back to a community that hated her would end on her birthday.

Eleven days. Eleven days.

Since before she departed the train, the number of days until her birthday updated daily and hounded her continually. And encouraged her.

While she jiggled and cajoled the obstinate lock, a lightning zap of pain shot through her lower abdomen. She leaned her shoulder into the door for support and silently counted to ten. The pain would go away as it always had, ever since it began the day after she'd given birth.

As desperate as she was to get out of the cold and off her feet, she refused to ask the manager for his assistance—even though he wasn't doing anything but staring at her.

"Mach's schnell, du Dummkopp—" Her angry whisper, "Make it quick, you dumb—," ended the moment the key turned.

She shoved open the door, entered the dimly lit room, and deadbolted the lock behind her. Her breath came in shallow spurts as she made her way to the shoddy-looking bed. Sitting on top of the frayed bedspread, she closed her eyes and tried to fight off the sense of panic.

Images of Rachel's tiny body lying inside that homemade pine box buried beneath the frozen earth disturbed her. If only she'd handled things differently—

Refusing to be plagued by a past she could do nothing about, she opened her eyes, trying to dispel the image. The room might be drab with worn carpet and faded paint, but it was warm.

She slid out of her clothes and stepped into a hot shower. While the hot water soothed her taut muscles, she tried to think of another way to find Zabeth.

After drying off, she put on her nightgown and sat on the side of the bed, longing to curl into a ball and cry the night away. If Paul could see her now, he'd think her irrational on top of his other negative opinions of her. But whatever he thought, at least she didn't have to face him.

Hannah slid between the cold sheets and placed her hand over her aching stomach, refusing to cry. She had little doubt that she needed medical attention. But she couldn't go to a doctor, not yet, not as a runaway minor. Odd, but it seemed that living under the *Ordnung* and the bishop was easier than finding ways around the Englischers' laws. But all that would change the day she turned eighteen.

She thought about when she'd called Paul the night before she left Owl's Perch. After placing the call, she remained in the motel room near the train station for nearly fifteen hours—waiting, hoping he'd call her back. Hoping he might still want her. He never returned her call, letting her know that he wasn't even willing to say good-bye.

How could she have lost his love so quickly?

A sob ripped through her, and she could no longer hold back her emotions. Rolling onto her side, she buried her face in the pillow and let her tears flow.

$\mathcal{P}$aul Waddell paced outside the police station, arguing with himself as to whether he should file a missing person report. Hannah had left of her own accord, and maybe she needed a little more time to choose to return. But he had given her two days.

He'd spent most of yesterday trying to make sense of the missing money from his joint checking account with Hannah. Mr. Harris, an officer at the bank, agreed to begin an investigation—if Paul would sign an affidavit swearing Hannah hadn't taken the money. Paul had no problem doing that. Matthew had told him the account was already empty when she tried to get her portion of the money.

Regardless of who had removed the money, Mr. Harris said the bank would not replace it. Too much time had passed. All Paul's years of working as many hours as possible around his schooling, all his weekends and holidays away from Owl's Perch in order to build for their future and support a child at House of Grace—all of it for nothing. Hannah was gone. And all his time away from her had been spent—on less than zilch.

Brilliant plan, Waddell.

As it stood, the only thing left was to hope the bank's investigation would cause the police to get involved, and maybe it would lead them to Hannah's attacker. In the meantime, Mr. Harris suggested Paul return to his normal life.

Paul scoffed. Normal life?

He'd helped chase into hiding the one person who meant life to him.

And to make matters worse, he seemed to be searching for Hannah by himself. There was no way her family would turn to a government agency and allow it to meddle in their private affairs. So if he didn't file a missing person report, no one would.

Reading the letter Hannah had left with Matthew had given Paul some peace, but it had faded over the last two nights, leaving in its stead a churning anxiety to do something to find her.

But what?

If the police found her and dragged her back to her father's house, that could cause her more complications than trying to live on her own for a while.

Paul shook his head. She was in no position to make it alone. She needed him.

He rubbed the back of his neck as he continued pacing the asphalt lane that ran beside the white masonry building.

Even though he believed she was right to leave her community, he ached to join her and build a life with her. That was only possible if he could find her. He headed toward the police station.

The solid blue door to the station reflected the sun. He backed away, wavering in his decision. He moaned aloud. If only he'd heard her out the night he discovered she was pregnant, she wouldn't be in some distant place trying to survive.

How could he have thought that Hannah, his beautiful girl who didn't even kiss him until after they'd been engaged for months, was guilty of giving herself to a man?

His anger had been a reflex, as if he'd taken a sucker punch and had come up fighting mad.

Now he had to find Hannah. He'd messed up by not being there for her, but from this point on, he would be—if he could find her. If the police became involved, they had the authority to get the train records; they'd know where to start looking. He prayed that the Lord would soften her heart toward him and that she'd trust him enough to give him another chance.

Sure of his decision this time, Paul entered the small police station.

Hannah stared out the car window at another brick medical building. It was the fifth one today she'd gone into and applied for work. If she needed another assault on the fragment of self-esteem she had left, applying for more jobs was the best way to do it. She and Gideon had spent a few hours early that morning trying to track down her aunt using the Internet, but everything led to a dead end.

Pain sliced across her abdomen, reminding her that instead of applying for work at a medical facility, she needed to be a patient. Waiting on the pain to lessen, she promised herself that if she wasn't better by the time she turned eighteen, then she'd go.

Longing for life to give her a break, Hannah eased her fingers over her mouth and whispered another plea for God to help her. She had no idea whether her prayers would be heard since she was without her prayer Kapp. Maybe God would never listen to her again until she came under the authority of the church.

Her pinned-up hair had a bit of a stylish, puffed-out look to it, with curly wisps escaping here and there. The solid blue caped dress resembled the Plain Mennonites much more than she wanted it to, even though she'd made a belt by cutting the ties off her discarded black apron. When there was money, she wanted a new styled dress, one that didn't set her apart so easily.

"Miss?" Gideon interrupted.

"Oh. Sorry." Hannah opened the car door.

"I got some other errands to run, and since you said you're not hungry, I'm gonna eat while you're puttin' in applications in that building. I'll be back for ya in a couple of hours. Okay?"

She nodded and got out of the car. The large building loomed in front of her, daring her to think she had any qualifications to work there. She stood on the front sidewalk, staring at the place. Maybe her strong emotional pull to and fierce thirst for the medical field were signs of her mental instability. Rather than looking for employment at a place where she couldn't possibly get it, perhaps she needed to seek psychological help.

Drawing a deep breath, she ignored the negative thoughts. She could wallow in the misery of her stubbornness and stupidity later as she spent another long night in the motel.

Half a mile in the distance, down in a small valley, smoke rose from the chimneys of a few homes. Voices of children playing in a patch of woods, climbing trees a couple hundred feet away, danced across the snowy fields. Desire to see her three youngest siblings burned within her. She wanted to help them scale trees and to hear them tease one another about who would reach the highest point.

Feeling like homemade taffy being pulled in two directions at once, she drew a deep breath and headed for the building. She'd chosen a path, and there was no sense in looking back.

She walked through the foyer, past a packed waiting room, and went to the front desk. A sliding glass partition separated her from the office staff. A thirty-something woman with smudged eye makeup and a short crop of fuzzy blond hair glanced up before she turned her attention back to her computer screen. Using a phone headset, she talked while she typed. Behind the woman sat several other women, all busy with phones, computers, or paperwork. A fresh charge of intimidation ran through Hannah. She knew she had few skills to offer a place like this, but she wanted a job at a medical facility of some type, where she could put to use all she'd learned from the nurses who trained her to take care of Mary for all those months. That was her plan, unless she had no other choice.

Without removing the phone headset, the woman behind the counter opened the glass partition. "Can I help you?"

Hannah swallowed, trying to brace herself for another rejection. "Hi, I'm looking for a job."

The woman motioned to the worker behind her. "On a day like today, any one of us would give you ours." She chuckled and pointed to a door at the far end of the room. "Go through that door, pass the first set of counters, and turn right. Human Resources will be the first door to your left."

"Thank you."

A woman named Mrs. Lehman seemed to be the entire department. Mrs. Lehman said they were looking to fill a few entry-level positions as soon as possible, and she asked how quickly Hannah could start work. When Hannah said, "Today," the woman passed her an application, then told her to fill it out and wait for an interview. Hannah wasn't sure what "entry level" meant, but she was hopeful.

Before long she was sitting in a chair outside the Human Resources office doing her best to fill out the application. Her hands shook as thoughts of lying on the application tempted her. She had no desire to be dishonest, but she couldn't list her real name after all she'd been through to get this far. Besides, she might change her last name just as soon as she was eighteen, had the money, and knew how to do it. With her decision made, she filled in her name as Hannah Lawson.

The office door beside her opened. "All set?"

Hannah stood. "Yes."

Mrs. Lehman took the clipboard that held the application. "Come on in." She entered the room behind Hannah, leaving the door open, and read the application as she walked to her desk. "Do you have any computer skills?"

"No."

Mrs. Lehman frowned. "None?"

Hannah shook her head. "I was at the library this morning, working with someone who showed me a few things about connecting to and searching the Internet."

"Oh." Mrs. Lehman took a seat and flipped the application over. "You haven't graduated from high school?"

Hannah shook her head. "No."

The woman took a deep breath. "You didn't fill out the year in which you were born."

Hope began to dwindle. "Is that really important?"

The woman raised her eyebrows. "Yes, I'm afraid it is, along with schooling." Mrs. Lehman tapped the application. "Or lack of it. We need someone with office skills. I'm sorry. We do need help, but you don't meet the qualifications for any of the available positions."

Hannah blinked, trying to dispel the tears that threatened. "I see. I...I learn pretty quick."

"I'm sure you do. Did you take keyboarding in high school?"

"Excuse me." A man's voice from somewhere in the building interrupted them. "Does anyone here speak German?"

Hannah rose. "I do." Without waiting for Mrs. Lehman to respond, she walked in the direction of the voice. A boy about five years old stood in the middle of the waiting room, looking panicked.

A man wearing a white lab coat was squatting in front of the boy, holding on to his shoulders. "Don't you speak any English yet?"

"Dabber schpring! Dabber schpring!" Tears fell from the boy's eyes.

Hannah crossed the room and knelt in front of the boy. *"Shh, liewer. Es iss net hatt."*

The boy jerked air into his lungs, and the panic across his face eased a little. She took his trembling hands in hers. *"Was iss letz?"*

He let out a sob and opened his mouth to speak, but all that came out were a few broken syllables.

Hannah smiled at him with a calm she didn't feel. She gently rubbed his cold hands between hers, as her mother had done for her when she was little. *"Seller Kall will hilfe."* She nodded at him, assuring him he was able to say what was on his mind. *"Du muscht schwetze."*

Her words of encouragement, mixed with a touch of firmness, seemed to settle him a bit more. Through his sobs he shared broken pieces of what had taken place.

Hannah glanced at the doctor. "His sister has fallen from a tree, and she's not moving." She patted the boy's chest, assuring him they would help his sister. *"Gut."*

The man turned to a woman wearing scrubs. "Get our coats and my medical bag." He pointed to another woman. "Call an ambulance. Watch what direction the boy leads us, and send them that way." He gestured at Hannah. "Where to?" He slid into his coat and clutched his medical bag in one hand.

Hannah asked the boy if he could show them where.

He grabbed her by the hand. *"Kumm! Kumm!"*

They ran out the front door, made a sharp left toward the patch of woods, and crossed over fields that lay covered in untrodden snow—except for the deep, small prints the boy had made on his way to the medical building.

Determined not to fail in this task, Hannah forced her aching body to keep moving.

As they entered the woods, she saw a little girl about six years old on the ground, lying faceup and perfectly still.

The doctor knelt beside the girl and shoved his fingers against her neck. Then he started pushing on her chest. He told a woman to get things out of his black bag. Within ten seconds, she had some kind of apparatus over the girl's mouth and was squeezing a bag. The boy screamed at them to stop.

Glancing at Hannah, the doctor pointed to a different area of the woods. "Get him out of here."

Without hesitation, she reached for his hand. The boy kicked and flailed against her, screaming that they were killing his sister.

Understanding his distrust, she whispered in Pennsylvania Dutch that the doctor was trying to help his sister. When the boy tried to pull away from her, she lifted him onto her hip. Pain ripped through her, causing her knees to almost buckle.

"Du muscht schtobbe!" Hannah spoke firmly.

The boy obeyed and stopped fighting her.

She walked with him on her hip, getting him out of eyeshot of what was taking place. He wrapped his arms around her neck and cried.

All her physical pains seemed to quiet under the tenderness this child stirred within her. Spotting a recently fallen tree, Hannah plodded to it, dusted snow off a small area, and sat down. She rocked the boy and sang to him, ignoring the screeching sounds of the ambulance when it arrived and the distant voices of the medics as they worked with the boy's sister some two hundred feet behind her.

In spite of the mysterious break from the pain in her abdomen, nausea and lightheadedness mounted within her.

Through a series of gentle questions, she learned the boy's name and where he lived. As he relaxed, exhaustion took over. Before long he dozed off.

Blinking, Hannah tried to keep her eyes open as blackness tinged her peripheral vision and closed in. She grabbed a handful of snow from the log and drew it to her lips. The woods spun, and she was no longer sure which way was up.

Had she fallen?

"You okay?" an agitated male voice said.

Pretending she could see clearly, Hannah nodded. "Yes. How's the girl?"

"We don't know yet. She went quite awhile without oxygen, but the cold temperature and lying in snow may have slowed her body's systems enough that she could fully recover."

The man in front of her was shrouded in a thin black veil, and the woods appeared cloaked in dusk, causing Hannah to wonder if night had fallen.

The man lifted the boy from her arms. "I'd like your help to find the girl's parents and explain this to them in the language they are most comfortable with."

"Sure." Hannah forced the word from her lips in spite of the strong urge to lie down and sleep. "But anyone in their family past the first grade will speak English." Hannah stood, using a tree to steady herself against.

"Yes, I know." The doctor nudged the little boy, trying to wake him. "Did he tell you where he lives?"

"Yes." Hannah closed her eyes and reopened them, trying to focus as the trees danced and jiggled like half-set pudding. Feeling an internal darkness pull at her, she grabbed a handful of snow off the log and rubbed it over her face.

When she opened her eyes, the doctor had shifted the boy to one of the uniformed women and was directing his intense stare at her. "I'm Dr. Lehman, and you are…"

Aware of the risk, she didn't answer his question.

"What were your symptoms when you came to the clinic today?"

"I didn't come in as a patient." She tried to stay upright, but her legs folded under her.

She heard Dr. Lehman's frustrated voice. "She's hemorrhaging. Get my bag. Call for another ambulance."

She fought against the dark hole that was trying to consume her. "The boy's name is Marc."

"She's going into shock."

Hannah narrowed her eyes, trying to see something besides darkness. She looked down and saw red snow. "The boy lives at 217 Sycamore. It's half a mile behind...your clinic, past the ridge—"

"Yes. Yes. We can find it. Give me information on how to contact your—"

Something more powerful overtook her, and she had no choice but to go with it.

Chapter 5

A chill ran up Paul's back.

"So." The police chief tapped his pen on the legal pad holding his notes. "What I have so far is that there's an almost-eighteen-year-old girl named Hannah Lapp who's missing. Her parents won't file a missing person report, and if the police show up to talk to them, they are likely not to admit she's gone or even that she exists, for that matter. There are no photos of her, and none of your friends have ever met her."

Paul barely remained in control of his tone. The man's sarcasm was not appreciated. "She does exist. My grandmother can vouch for that."

At the thought of how alone and desperate Hannah must be, a sense of panic stirred within him. But fear would do him no good. He needed a lead, a direction…a miracle. "Hannah's a minor, and she's been traumatized by—"

The man glanced at his notes. "…an attack that took place at the end of last August." He looked up. "The question is, does she want to return?"

"She's a minor, and she needs help. And I need your cooperation in order to find her."

"Look, I agree with you. She got a bum deal, and she deserves a break. But she's less than two weeks from turning eighteen, and she has a friend who says she left of her own accord with money to live on and some sort of a plan. Those details make this a low priority for us. By the time we get the info out on her and anyone has a chance to recognize her, she'll be a legal adult." The man shrugged. "We'll do what we can, but I can't guarantee anything."

Paul clenched his forehead with his fingertips. If the police weren't going to help, he had to get out of here and do something himself.

Grabbing his coat off the chair, Paul headed for the door.

The police chief rose. "You could try hiring a private investigator."

Pausing for a moment, Paul nodded. "Thank you."

He hurried out the door of the police station and hustled down the asphalt alleyway toward his truck. As he reached for the door handle to his old vehicle, he spotted a red brick church with a bell tower two blocks up the street. The place stood resolute, inviting him to come search for peace within its walls. Deciding he needed to pray before trying to figure anything else out, he sprinted toward the aged church.

Dear God, please. I don't know what to pray. Please help.

He whispered his pleadings as he climbed the concrete steps, opened the oversize wooden door, and walked through the sanctuary. Thankfully the place was empty. Paul went to the altar and began quietly praying.

As the panic of the last few days quieted underneath the blanket of prayer, anger at the man who'd attacked Hannah pushed to the forefront of Paul's mind and heart, but he was clueless what to do with it, what he should do with it.

If I could get my hands on him…

Yet, even as the fury caused sickening feelings, he knew he had to let the desire for revenge go. Not only was the desire against everything he believed, but it had no power to help. Only God could help. Only He was stronger than what any enemy could dish out. Paul's and Hannah's families would never agree on much, but all Plain folk had one thing in common: they believed in nonresistance, that forgiving and letting God take vengeance was the only way to live.

"Help me focus on You, God. Not on what's been done, but on what can be done to restore," Paul whispered.

Voices from somewhere inside the church caught Paul's attention, and he glanced at his watch. He needed to go.

Driving toward Penn State, in Harrisburg, he spotted a pay phone and pulled his truck into a parking spot. There was a phone at his apartment, but if he stopped by there, his three roommates would bombard him with questions he didn't want to answer—couldn't answer. He called Gram to see if she'd heard from Hannah or had learned anything about her from Luke or Matthew. She hadn't, but she told him that Mr. Harris from the bank was trying to reach him. He assured Gram he'd make contact with the man and then be home as soon as he could.

Hours later, in the dark, he drove into Gram's driveway. His time with Mr. Harris had been totally discouraging. He got out of his truck and made his way around the side of the house. Stomping the snow off his boots, he climbed the few steps to his grandmother's back porch. The starless night air was bitter cold and the darkness so thick it seemed to smother life itself. He crossed the threshold of the enclosed porch, haunted by its memories. He and Hannah had spent many a long summer day shucking corn or snapping beans right here on this porch.

He plunked onto a padded wicker chair, wondering what his next move should be. Every possible hint of a way to locate Hannah had become a dead end. Aside from Matthew, no one in her community would even talk to him. Maybe a private investigator was the answer.

Through the porch window, he caught a glimpse of his grandmother's silhouette as she entered the kitchen. A dim light flicked on inside the house, and then the door to the back porch opened. Gram tightened her thick terry-cloth housecoat around her as she stepped onto the porch.

She knew why he chose to live here in Owl's Perch with her during the summer and on school breaks rather than spend time in Maryland with his parents. She'd hired an Amish girl to help her around the house three years ago, and after Paul met her, he spent as much time here as he could manage. Gram had reservations about his future with an Old Order Amish girl, but she had come to care about Hannah too.

Gram grabbed a blanket off a nearby rocker and draped it over her shoulders. "Any news concerning the missing money?"

Paul sighed. "The footage of the person who withdrew the money from our account shows a young woman, either Amish or dressed like one."

"What? How did she get hold of the bankbook?"

"We don't think she did. Our best guess is that somehow Hannah's attacker got it, and he either tricked an Amish person into withdrawing the money, using a photoless ID, or he hired someone to act the part."

"Now what?"

Paul shrugged. "It's another dead end, Gram."

Faint streams of light filtered through the kitchen window onto the dark, cold porch. He knew Gram had a meal inside waiting for him; she always did. But Paul didn't want to enter the warm, familiar home. He wanted Hannah.

She needed him, if he just knew how to find her.

"Paul." Gram's voice trembled.

Realizing it was too cold for her to be out here, he nodded toward the door. "Go on inside, Gram. I'll be in later."

She shifted from one foot to another. "I don't want to get your hopes up, but…"—she shoved her hands into her pockets—"a letter arrived in the mail for you today." She pulled out an envelope. "I don't think it's from Hannah. The handwriting doesn't look like hers."

Paul took the envelope and held it in the dull light that streamed from the kitchen window. "That's Hannah's writing. It's more wobbly than usual, but it's hers." He studied the envelope. It had no return address, but it'd been mailed from Pittsburgh two days ago. He ripped the envelope open and removed the letter.

At the sight of his name scrawled across the top of the letter, his eyes clouded. Light flooded the porch. Gram had turned on the overhead lamp and gone inside.

He read the letter.

Dearest Paul,

I wrote a letter to you and left it with Matthew, but then I realized you would not receive it unless you came looking for me.

I'm on the train I boarded in Harrisburg, and I needed to share a word that has caused such hope to grow within me that my strength for life is returning.

Nevertheless.

It's a great word. Ya?

Paul nodded as tears blurred his vision. He wiped his eyes with the palm of his hand.

> If all our dreams lie shattered before us—nevertheless, God can sustain us and even build new dreams.
>
> I conceived a child because someone did not place his desires under God's authority—nevertheless, God's power over my life is stronger than that event.
>
> Rachel died—nevertheless, she is now with God.
>
> You and I are no more—nevertheless, God is not without a plan.
>
> Ach, what I feel in my heart is so much stronger than I can manage to put on this paper. But I laugh as I think—nevertheless, God will give you understanding.

He closed his eyes and could hear her soft, gentle laugh. She was growing in ways that were good for her, and he was thankful for it.

> I know you had to walk away and start a new life without me. I think I'll always miss who we once were. I'm guilty of Rachel's death. I tried to hide that she existed when I should have sought medical help. Nevertheless, God speaks to me. Let Him speak to you too.
>
> In hope forever,
> Hannah

He shot out of the chair, off the porch, and into the yard. He gulped in a lungful of frigid air. Closing his eyes, he felt the burden of confusion ease a bit as it tried to give way to acceptance. A snippet of hope took root, and he sensed that Hannah must have experienced a similar feeling when she discovered the nevertheless idea.

Paul folded the letter, assured that if anyone could make a success out of this mess, she could. He lifted his face to the heavens. "I need to hear from you again, Hannah. I need to know you're safe and have found someone to help you. God, please."

As he stared into the vastness of the jeweled sky, he wanted more from God than just this note.

He sighed.

Nevertheless, he'd heard from her, and it was a good note.

"Thank you, God." He whispered the words and tucked the letter into his shirt pocket. In that moment, all lingering desire for vengeance against her attacker melted. Whatever the destruction, God would not let the story end there.

$\mathcal{S}$et on seeing Elle Leggett first thing today, Matthew climbed into the buggy and pulled to a stop in front of his home to wait for his brothers. If he didn't get some time with Elle this morning before she began teaching, his heart might fail him—right there in the schoolyard in front of everyone.

"Peter! David! *Loss uns geh!*" He should've have ridden there by himself rather than let Mamm talk him into giving his younger brothers a ride to school. He pulled a pair of work gloves out of his coat pocket. So it was cold. If they didn't hurry up, he'd let them walk.

"*Kummet mol!*" he bellowed.

David moseyed out the front door, pulling on his winter coat. "We're coming. Hold your horses. I mean horse."

Nothing was the least bit humorous to Matthew right now. He wanted to see his girl.

David knelt on the porch and tied his shoes. Peter ran out the door, panting, carrying two brown-bag lunches. "Sorry. I didn't realize you wanted to leave this early today." He dropped one of the lunches next to David. "Forget this?"

"Oh, ya. I'd miss that about lunchtime, huh?" David climbed into the buggy.

Peter jostled into his spot on the bench seat. "Elle would share her lunch with you. She's a real nice teacher."

Matthew tapped the reins against the horse's back and clicked his tongue. "Geh."

The horse plodded forward.

David shoved his lunch bag between his feet on the floorboard. "Yeah, she'd share it with any student. Can't say she'd do the same for you, Matthew."

David squirmed around to face him. "So, why's our teacher so frosty whenever your name comes up lately? I thought ya were her beau."

"Just ride." Matthew flicked the reins, stepping up the pace of his horse.

The chaos that had led to Hannah's departure made him unable to keep up with what was happening in Elle's life, but he'd bet she'd heard plenty of rumors about him and Hannah. He slowed the buggy and turned right, entering the long dirt road that led to the one-room schoolhouse.

His last exchange with Elle played through his thoughts. They'd argued over where his loyalties were, with her or with Hannah. He'd ached to climb into the buggy with her and go for a long ride, talking until everything was aired out. But he had agreed to help Hannah leave Owl's Perch and had to keep that promise first.

Today he had time to talk, if she would listen. Pulling the buggy to a stop beside the schoolhouse, Matthew took note of the smoke coming out of the chimney. Elle's driver had already dropped her off. He pulled the brake and wrapped the reins around the stob before climbing down. "Get wood from the shed, and stack it on the porch, but don't come inside until someone else arrives."

"You and Elle feudin'?" Peter asked.

Without responding, Matthew gathered an armload of wood and strode toward the school. He tapped on the door, giving her warning someone had arrived early, then went inside. Elle was sitting at her desk with a pencil in hand and looked up when he came through the door. She pursed her lips and returned her attention to the papers in front of her.

Matthew made his way to the woodbin. Stalling, he unloaded the split logs one by one, hoping the right words would pop into his head. Brushing the dirt and moss off his hands and into the woodbin, he studied her.

"Elle." He walked to her desk and waited for her to look up again. She didn't.

"You got something honest to say, say it."

"Could you look at me, please?"

She slammed the pencil onto her desk, folded her arms, and looked him dead in the eye. "What am I supposed to think of you never having time for me? Could you just tell me that?"

"Han—"

She rose, toppling her chair backward. Her porcelain skin and reddish hair radiated beauty, even in her anger. "Could we manage one conversation without mentioning Hannah? Just one?"

Matthew had no idea what to say if he wasn't supposed to mention Hannah's name along with a list of apologies. He fidgeted with the edge of the student's desk behind him. "I had to help her, but I care for no girl but you."

She moved to the side of her desk, just a foot away from him, and sat on it, leaving the toe of her shoe on the floor. Her eyes of lavender mixed with blue, a combination he'd never seen before he met her, were a regular reminder that she hadn't been born to Amish parents. She played with one of the ties on her prayer Kapp. The way her eyes probed him, looking to understand things she wouldn't ask aloud, left him no doubt that she still cared deeply.

"See, neither me nor Hannah meant to cau—"

Elle rose and placed her fingers over his mouth. "I don't want to hear about her." She whispered the words as her fingertips slid across his lips. Her warm hands moved to his cheeks, and she gently pulled him to her until their lips were a mere inch apart. "I was hoping…"

Matthew clasped his hand around the back of her head, feeling the lump of her hair bun under her prayer Kapp. An image of her without her Kapp, her strawberry blond hair flowing over her shoulders, flashed in his mind's eye. Of course, for him to see her like that they'd have to be behind locked doors and have taken their marriage vows.

He closed the gap between them until her soft lips brushed against his.

The sound of children approaching made Elle dart from his arms and retreat behind her desk before he had time to react. The door to the schoolhouse flung open, and several children scurried in, chatting feverishly.

Elle ran a finger over her lips. "Yep, that's what I was hoping for." She turned to the children and motioned to the pegs on the back wall. "Please put your coats on the pegs and lunches near the stove, and take your seats."

Matthew chuckled. She went from sounding like his future wife to a schoolteacher as fast as the speed of that opening door.

Aching for another kiss, he moved to the opposite side of her desk and behaved like a visiting adult should, but it wasn't easy. "How about if you have the driver bring you by the shop after school? I'll see to it you either get home later or can stay at the Bylers'."

She picked up her teacher's attendance book, avoiding looking at him. "Okay. I'll bring David and Peter with me."

He turned to leave.

"And Matthew?"

He wheeled around, hoping to see a warm smile, but she was still fiddling with things on her desk.

"The girl we're not talking about—she left me a letter. It sounds like there was something you haven't told me." She lifted both eyebrows, waiting on him to answer.

He gave a slight nod. "We'll cover *everything* tonight."

With the bacon frying, coffee perking on the stove, and a huge batch of sticky buns in the oven, Sarah glanced at the kitchen doorway and whispered, "Mamm?"

"Hmm?"

Although she had responded, Sarah knew her mother hadn't fully come out of that faraway world she lived in lately. Mamm had called Sarah to her bedroom last night, shut the door, and explained things about how a woman conceived and what had taken place that caused Hannah to become pregnant. Her mother's voice had been but a whisper as tears trailed down her face through the explanation. Then she'd dismissed her daughter without answering the one question that tormented Sarah.

"Mamm." She said the word more firmly, hoping her mother would break free long enough to talk to her.

"What?"

"Do you really think Hannah's baby died?"

Moving eggs from the basket to a small container, Mamm answered, "Yes." She opened the refrigerator and set the eggs in it.

Dread so thick it seemed to be suffocating her wrapped around Sarah. As much as she'd hated her sister, it was too horrid to think she'd given birth to a child who hadn't survived. That couldn't be true. It just couldn't.

It was your own words, Sarah Lapp, that turned Daed and the bishop against your sister.

She rubbed her temples, trying to clear her head. "But how do you know? I mean, couldn't she have taken the baby with her?"

Her mother faced her. "I know it's a nightmare, Sarah, but it's all true."

Thoughts tripped one way and then stumbled another, all leading her where she just couldn't accept the story the Eshes had told them yesterday.

Why, Sarah had seen how that oldest sister of hers had everyone jumping through hoops and doing her chores while she lay around pretending to be sick. With Sarah's own eyes she saw Hannah climb into a buggy with some man, going off for a joyride at midnight in her nightgown!

Sarah turned the bacon over in the skillet, trying to keep the hot grease from spattering. If Hannah was so sneaky as to use Mrs. Waddell's place to meet her beau and had sent and received letters for years without anyone in her family knowing, what else was she capable of? Maybe she'd never boarded that train. Was she hiding out right here in Owl's Perch with her baby?

"Just how trusting are we supposed to be?" Sarah mumbled under her breath.

"Did you say something?" her mother asked.

"Are you sure she buried the… I mean, did you see the baby before…"

Mamm shook her head. "We saw the casket that Matthew made being lowered into the ground." Mamm sat in a chair, looking too tired to remain on her feet. "Just as well, I suppose."

"Do you think Naomi saw the baby?"

"I imagine. I know this is hard to accept, Sarah, but—"

"Can I go see Naomi after breakfast?"

"You've got chores. Just because you're done with your schooling days—"

"Please?" Sarah interrupted her. "I just need to see her."

The back door opened, and Sarah heard the menfolk stomping around as they pulled off their work boots.

"Okay, after breakfast you can slip out," Mamm whispered. "But be back before Esther and Samuel are home from school."

Sarah knocked on the Eshes' door and waited. A moment later the door popped open.

Naomi's eyes widened at the sight of her. "Why, Sarah Lapp, what are you doing here with everything your Mamm's going through?"

"I brought you some sticky buns."

Naomi accepted the plate from Sarah and walked toward her kitchen. "My guess is you've got more on your mind than sharing food."

Sarah shut the door, peeled out of her cloak, and followed her. If anyone would give her straight answers, it'd be Naomi. Why, she'd been awful outspoken with Daed yesterday. Sarah bet she was aching to spill all she knew.

Naomi set the plate on the counter. "Take a seat, and tell me what's on your mind."

Laying her winter cape beside her, Sarah climbed onto a tall, swivel-backed counter stool. "I was hoping to understand a little more about what happened with Hannah."

"I really don't think we should talk about that. Your sister had a baby out of wedlock. How your parents want to address that with you children is up to them."

Outspoken indeed.

"Did you see the baby that night?"

"Yes. She was a tiny thing."

A pitiful noise, like a baby crying, came from somewhere outside the house. The sound made Sarah's insides jolt, but Naomi didn't respond a bit to the cries.

The awful sound repeated with no reaction from Naomi. Was she just pretending not to hear it? Was she hiding the baby?

Realizing Naomi wasn't going to tell her anything and ready to search for what was making this noise, Sarah rose. "I was hoping you'd say something that could help me understand."

Naomi straightened her pinafore. "I'd like to know some things too, like where she was heading when she boarded that train."

Wrapping her cloak around her, Sarah asked, "Did you see her get on the train?"

"Oh, honey, I sure did. You don't need to worry about that. She got on that train safe and sound with her tickets in hand."

Sarah nodded. So Hannah did leave Owl's Perch. That actually brought Sarah a measure of relief, although she couldn't figure out why. She excused herself and slipped out the door and listened for the sound. It was coming from Matthew's shop.

Hoping Naomi didn't look out her window, Sarah scampered across the yard to the shop. After looking everywhere on the first floor, she climbed the ladder to the storage loft. She looked behind every crate for signs that someone was hiding Hannah's baby. She found none. But it had to be alive somewhere.

When the front door swooshed open, Sarah jumped.

A moment later it closed. She tiptoed in the direction of the ladder, cringing with every moan the wooden floorboards made.

"Hello?" Matthew called.

No way around it, she was caught. With her heartbeat going wild, she hollered down, "Hi, Matthew." Her voice sounded guilty, even to her. Navigating each rung of the ladder carefully, she made her way to the ground floor.

"I saw Old Bess hitched to a buggy out front. I figured it'd be you that came over here, but I guessed you were in the house."

Shaking the dust from her dress, Sarah refused to look at him. "I was. I brought your family some sticky buns, but then I came out here to see you."

"In the attic?" he scoffed. "What are ya really lookin' for, Sarah? Peace?"

"That's ridiculous. I'm not the one who's done anything wrong."

Folding his arms across his chest, Matthew rocked back. "Ah, now I see how you're living with yourself."

She brushed dust off her black cloak. "Well, aren't you just cheeky and rude when you're by yourself?"

"Sticking with Hannah's wishes, I ain't told anyone what I know. But don't let that piece of information make you think it'll stay that way."

"What're you trying to say?"

"Your sister was better to you than anyone. You can mark my words on that. She saw you for what you are and loved you anyway—until you ruined her whole life."

His words stung something horrid, but she wasn't about to let him know that. "And to think I held you in such high esteem. It's clear enough that Hannah has cast her spell over you just like she did my Jacob."

"It ain't like that between me and Hannah. But I'd like to know one thing from you, and then maybe I won't tell your secret."

The shrieking cry filled the room. Sarah jumped, a gray eeriness settling over her. "What was that?"

Matthew rolled his eyes. "A tomcat killed all the mama cat's babes. She ain't quit hollering over it yet."

Sarah swallowed hard. A mama cat?

The baby's not dead. It's not.

An image of a tiny coffin lying in a grave with dark soil being tossed onto it flashed through her mind. She sucked in air and scrunched her eyes closed, trying to free herself of the sickening thought.

"You okay?"

"Of course," she snapped. "I need to go."

"Not before you've answered my question."

"What?"

Matthew leaned against the planked wall, blocking her exit. "I'm not going to ask why you told everyone about Hannah going out for a late night ride. It happened. You told—out of jealousy is my guess. But why did you lie about how long she was gone?"

"I'm not jealous!" she fumed.

"Answer the question."

"I didn't lie." She just wasn't sure, that was all. Most of her life she'd lost track of time easily. Had she lost track that night?

"Wrong answer."

"Well, if you're so smart, how long was she gone?"

"Less than five minutes, and we never left sight of the house, just like she said."

Sarah drew back "We? You were with her? That can't be. I saw her in a tourist buggy with a horse I ain't never seen before."

"Look around you, Sarah. Part of what I do is take old buggies and re-finish them, some of them for touristy places. I go to the racetrack and buy horses and train them, sometimes for those same places."

The screaming returned, banging against her temples and shrieking at her. "But—"

"There are no *buts*. I'll put my hand on the Bible and say how long we were gone that night. Will you stick by your story that well?"

Beads of sweat rolled down her back, and suddenly the door loomed in front of her. Pushing it open, she gulped cold air and ran to her buggy. Shaking like a leaf, she flicked the reins and started toward home. As the horse lumbered onward, guilt inched into her thoughts, feuding with the fear of what would happen when the community found out she'd been wrong.

Her thoughts suddenly became dull and confused, as if a tornado had deadened a path through her mind.

Matthew met Elle at the car and took the books from her hands as she got out. Peter and David wasted no time heading inside the house—for food, he was quite sure.

"Come on." Matthew led her into the privacy of his repair shop. Once they were sitting on the couch, he drew a deep breath and told the whole story of his and Hannah's buggy ride, how she came to stay at his repair shop overnight, and why he'd kept secrets for Hannah.

Elle rose. "That buggy ride everyone talked about… It was you she was with?" She gaped at him in disbelief.

"The rumors are lies. We weren't gone no thirty minutes. I bet it wasn't even five."

"Every time I think things are straight between us, something else concerning Hannah comes up." She rolled her eyes. "If it's all so innocent, why keep it a secret from me?"

"Hannah asked me to, and I was afraid you wouldn't believe me."

"And keeping secrets was your way to win my trust?"

Matthew stood. "See, Hannah and—"

She rose on her tiptoes and pushed her finger against his chest. "If you don't quit talking about Hannah, I'm going to scream."

"You are screaming."

She narrowed her eyes and growled at him. "Make the point, Matthew—without Hannah's name being mentioned—before I show you just how loud I can scream."

"Elle, none of the rumors are true. I don't know what else to tell you."

She propped her hands on her hips. "It's just all so infuriating. I want to believe you. You know I do."

Matthew inched closer, fearing she'd step farther away, but she didn't. "Elle, there was a time when I thought maybe I'd enjoy taking Hannah home from singings. It was just a thought, no real emotions or desires attached to it. Then I met you."

"So I have two choices: believe you and maybe play the fool for life, or believe the rumors and go find someone else."

"For life?" Matthew smiled.

"Oh shut up." She stormed off to the far side of the room.

"You know, you're a mite easier to get along with in the morning than in the afternoon."

A short burst of laughter escaped her. Matthew had the sneaking suspicion he'd hit on a truth about her that she already knew. He crossed the room and pulled her into his arms.

"We're not finished arguing." She pushed against him, but he didn't let go.

He ran his finger over her lips. "Could we take a break and return to arguing later?"

Expecting a snippy remark, Matthew was caught off guard when she slowly kissed his finger.

He lifted her chin and kissed her the way he wished he'd had time to do that morning. "Marry me, Elle," Matthew mumbled between kisses.

Someone banged on the door, making them both jump. A moment later the door swung open.

"Dad," Elle whispered.

Chapter 7

*D*eep darkness became a reddish black as Hannah tried to open her eyes. Papers were rustling somewhere close by.

"Can you hear me?"

A machine near her head made little bleeps faster and faster.

"It's okay. Stay calm. You're in Alliance Community Hospital."

A wave of nausea ran through her. She couldn't be in the hospital. How would she pay? They would find her, and her father would come. Her eyes refused to open. The dark world tugged at her, and she struggled to stay awake. She tried lifting her arms, but they barely budged.

She forced enough air into her lungs so she could speak. "I won't go back. I won't."

Plastic wrap crinkled right beside her. "Well, I don't know where 'back' is, but if you're angry with somebody at home, you just might change your mind when you realize how close you came to not surviving."

She heard water being poured. Licking her dry lips, she commanded her eyes to open. They didn't obey.

"Good thing for you that your body started responding positively. You gave us a scare for nearly twenty-four hours. Then your vitals improved, letting us know you would survive. That took place around this time yesterday." A straw touched her lips. "Take a drink."

Sipping the cool water, Hannah began to come out of that dark place. She pulled away from the straw, scrunched her eyes, and managed to lift her eyelids for a moment.

Standing over her was the doctor from the last clinic that wouldn't hire her. Fragmented thoughts sprang to her mind, too disconnected to make sense.

The straw pressed against her lips again. She drew cool water into her mouth, feeling more clarity with each swallow. She tried shifting in the bed.

Parts of her body were working now—her arms, shoulders, and legs. But with her torso feeling like dead weight and the soreness across her lower body, she couldn't move. "You may not remember, but I'm Dr. Lehman. How are you feeling?"

Forcing the correct response, Hannah whispered, "Okay. The girl…at the clinic, how is she?"

"She made a complete recovery and went home yesterday. You, on the other hand, are still quite sick. You're in ICU. You had what's called a retained placenta. Our best guess is that when that boy kicked against you, the pool of internal blood broke loose from its clot. It was merciful timing to happen near the clinic, that's for sure. The surgeon did what he could to repair your uterus. Until yesterday you were on a ventilator. You were given a ten-pack of platelets and a unit of fresh frozen plasma. Now that may not mean a whole lot to you, but trust me, you should read up on it and thank your lucky stars you survived."

Embarrassed that an entire surgical team knew her secret, Hannah closed her eyes. She didn't want to know what they'd done. The only question she wanted answered was how she would pay for this.

He cleared his throat. "Okay, I've covered all that a doctor is supposed to tell you. Now there are some things I need you to tell me. We'll start with your name."

"Hannah," she answered, hoping he wouldn't push for more information than necessary.

The man drew a deep breath. "That's a start. On the application, you gave Lawson as your last name. Is that real or made up?"

Hannah shook her head without opening her eyes. "I've got money to cover part of the bill. I'll pay the rest when I get a job."

The doctor didn't respond.

Hannah pried her eyes open. The doctor was perched on the edge of a chair next to her bed.

He ran his hands through his thick gray hair. "An older man named Gideon came looking for you the day you passed out. He says he's been driving you around since Tuesday morning, but he knows nothing about you other than you pay in cash and you're staying in a motel." He shifted in his chair. "I know you're Amish—otherwise, you wouldn't know the language so well. You're underage, or you would have put your date of birth on the application. Since you're staying at a motel, you're probably a runaway."

Hannah winced as fear rose within her. He'd figured out a lot about her.

"I also know you've recently given birth to a baby, and you're lucky to be alive, considering the amount of blood you lost when you began to hemorrhage." He drew a breath.

Wooziness washed over her. She closed her eyes, drowning in the awareness that this wasn't the life she'd expected to find. Loneliness. No safe harbor. A cheap motel. Constant fear of getting caught. And now this.

God, please.

Uncertain what else to say, she ended her prayer at two words.

"The surgeon did what he could to repair your uterus. I think you'll recover nicely, but due to the extensive damage…" He paused. "Hannah, I'm sorry to have to tell you this, but it seems unlikely that you'll ever conceive again."

Panic choked her. "Unlikely?"

"The damage was quite severe. It's highly unlikely, probably impossible, that you'll ever have another child."

The words rolled over her. She covered her face with her hands. Was her dead child truly the only one she'd ever have? As if a hidden part of her had just worked its way free, she realized she'd still been harboring hopes of a life with Paul. Somewhere inside, dreams of one day bearing his children were fading.

Something touched the backs of her hands, causing her to lower them. Through teary eyes she looked at the doctor.

"Here." He shoved tissues into her hands, staring at her. "I'm sorry this happened to you, but you had to know you needed medical help long before you passed out."

Accusation pointed an ugly finger at her. He was right—she'd known.

"Where's the baby you gave birth to?"

She shook her head. Her life was none of this man's business. And if he knew the truth, he'd try to send her home. She couldn't go back. She just couldn't.

He shifted. "I need to know that you haven't abandoned your newborn somewhere. If you don't convince me, I'll call the police right now, and you can finish recuperating wherever they take you."

The sternness reflected in his eyes matched his tone. There was no doubt he wanted answers. His motives for prying into her life were sound enough, but she couldn't make herself answer him.

"Fine." He stood.

Hannah tried to lean forward. "Okay."

He turned to face her. "Where's your baby?"

She wondered what the authorities would do with her after she explained what happened. "She died. We buried her."

"How far along were you?"

Hating not knowing, Hannah closed her eyes and wished he'd just go away.

"When did you conceive?"

Hannah fidgeted with the sheets. "I don't know how to figure that."

"Were you sexually active?"

"No!" She stared at him. "How can you just blurt out such wrongdoing at someone?"

Dr. Lehman returned to the seat beside her bed. He sat in silence, as if waiting for her to volunteer information. "Hannah,"—his voice was barely audible—"when were you raped?"

She pursed her lips as tears worked their way free against her will. That day would linger with her forever. "August thirtieth." A sob escaped her. "Paul asked me to marry him that morning." She closed her eyes. "On my walk home a man in a car came up and…"

The doctor patted her hand. "Take a breath, Hannah. I understand enough. According to the surgeon, you gave birth less than a week ago. That means you had a miscarriage, Hannah. The child was not developed enough to survive—unless born in ideal circumstances—and even then it probably would have had serious complications if it had lived." He passed her a few more tissues. "Where are your parents?"

She wiped her eyes. "When rumors started spreading, they thought I was lying about how I became pregnant. I couldn't take any more."

"So you are a runaway."

"I turn eighteen soon."

Dr. Lehman drummed his fingers against his thighs. "How soon?"

"March ninth."

"You should have waited until then to leave home. You're a minor, which means I have to inform social services. Besides, issues between parents and their children can almost always be worked out. Your folks may not have responded as they should have, but you were wrong to run off."

She wanted to scream at him. He didn't know what it was like to have an entire community set against you or to have your parents trick themselves into thinking you were the problem. If she had stayed, the People would have continued to ostracize her. Then her only choice would have been to work for Gram and live with her or with others close by who weren't Old Order Amish. Then she would have been forced to endure her worst nightmare: having a front-row seat as Paul fell in love with someone else, got married, and had children.

She closed her eyes and covered her head with a pillow.

"I'll contact the authorities, and someone from child services will be here in the next few days. In the meantime you'll be staying here."

She swallowed hard and waited to hear him leave the room.

The glass door made a swooshing sound as it slid open.

"I'm sorry, Hannah," Dr. Lehman whispered.

She flung the pillow off her head, waves of anger replacing her misery. "You're sorry? Then try being right instead of lawful. You can't think it's right to send me back home when I'm just days away from being an adult. My family despises me!" She gasped for air. "I'll have to wear a scarlet letter for the rest of my life because of things that weren't my choice." She paused, realizing she was yelling at the man. She lowered her voice. "I'm begging you. Please don't make that call."

He studied her, and for a moment Hannah thought maybe he'd see this her way. But then he shook his head. "I can't break the law, Hannah." With that, he left the room.

The nurse at the station outside Hannah's room stared at her before returning her attention to her desk. No wonder the Amish avoided contact with policemen and doctors. They followed the law, whether it held any wisdom for the individual or not.

If she had any strength, she'd find her clothes and get out of here. But whatever was wrong with her had left her weak.

Staring at the ceiling, she mourned the loss of something she'd never fully had: freedom.

If she had any chance of winning Paul's heart again, she could endure going back. If she could bear him children, he might forget that she'd once carried a child concealed from him. But the news that she'd never be able to have another child slashed the last threads that might have bound her and Paul together.

Oh God, help me. I can't go back. I just can't.

$\mathscr{S}$itting in the enclosed buggy, Luke tapped the reins lightly against the horse's back as he drove down the dirt road toward his harness shop. In spite of how broken his relationship with Mary was and how much he loved her, that's not what he'd try to repair first. If he could go back and do things over, he would treat his sister right. He'd stand against his father and the bishop, even knowing he'd be frowned upon and ostracized, if not shunned.

He spotted a man about his age tossing loose hay into the snowy pastures that bordered the Waddell and Lapp properties. Considering Mary's description, Luke would've bet this was the guy Hannah had been secretly engaged to. The Lapp and Waddell homesteads were a mile apart, but until now Luke had never laid eyes on the guy. Of course the man didn't live in Owl's Perch year round. He only came here during his summer breaks from college—just long enough to make his sister believe she was in love with him.

Torn between indignation and the reminder of his own mistakes with Hannah, Luke had no idea what to think of the man who had tried to steal his sister from her Amish roots. As he rode closer, the stranger glanced his way. Intending to ignore the man and keep going, Luke looked straight ahead. A scene flashed through his mind, causing the hairs on his arms to stand on end.

The night of his and Mary's accident, a car had rammed into their buggy, and he went sailing through the air. When he woke in the grassy field, he couldn't find Mary. He remembered looking toward heaven and praying, "God, please." Shame had swallowed him. He knew he wasn't worthy of God helping him with anything. When he made his way back to the road and saw what was left of their upended carriage, his legs had buckled, and he'd landed on his knees, begging, "Please, Father, if You will, help us."

It had been a feeble prayer from the lips of a man totally unworthy to ask or receive anything from God, but immediately warmth had run through his body, and he had known what he needed to do to find Mary.

Unable to justify coldness to Paul when God had been so merciful to him, Luke tugged on the reins and came to a stop a few feet from where the man stood. Fighting against his prejudice, Luke wrapped the reins around the stob on the dash of the buggy and just sat there, waiting—for what, he didn't know.

The man stepped forward. "Something I can do for you?"

If Luke was going to do penance for how he'd treated Hannah, this was the place to begin. By an act of his will, he climbed down from the buggy and offered his hand. "I'm Luke, Hannah's brother."

"Paul Waddell." He used his teeth to pull off a work glove and then held out his hand to Luke.

Now that he was standing eye to eye with the man, Luke felt like a game-cock ready to attack. Instead, he shook Paul's hand firmly. "I'm right sorry for all that's taken place."

Paul's eyes bored into his. "Have you heard anything from her?"

Luke shook his head. "No, but I'm sure she's doing fine." He shrugged. "Hannah's not like most girls."

Paul seemed relieved to hear something encouraging about Hannah's circumstances. "She's tender-hearted. Courageous. And…" His voice cracked with emotion.

Dislike for the man drained from Luke. "And stubborn. If will has anything to do with making a success out of her new life, she'll stroll back to Owl's Perch someday just to let the bishop know he didn't win."

Paul studied the fields. "Just as long as she returns."

Luke didn't respond. When his sister did return, he wanted to see her grow fresh roots among her own kind, the people God had placed her with.

Paul shoved a glove into his jacket pocket. "If you hear anything…"

"I'll let you know." Luke buttoned his coat against the cold air.

"How's Matthew doing working things out with the church leaders?"

"They seem to have nothing to say to him or anyone else over the events concerning Hannah. But his life is not what he'd hoped. His girl, Elle, was born English and raised by Amish parents after her mother died when she was ten. Her father had been trying to make contact with her for a few weeks. Since he showed up, he's been pushing her to leave the only family she's known for the last ten years and come live with him."

"Is she going to do it?"

Luke shrugged. "I guess so, 'cause—"

Sounds of a horse and buggy made both men look toward the road. The rig turned onto the driveway of the harness shop. Mary's oldest brother, Gerald, was driving, and his wife, Suzy, sat beside him. Luke hurried to the buggy before it came to a full stop. "What brings you two out this way?"

Gerald glanced at Suzy, but neither one answered him.

"Is Mary all right?"

Gerald gave a slow wave of his hand. "Yes and no." He spoke casually, as if they were discussing plowing fields. "Daed insisted Mary go see her specialist yesterday, with all the stress of this business with Hannah and you."

Suzy leaned forward. "I don't know what that doctor said, but whatever he told her has her acting funny—all quiet and withdrawn like." She spilled the words quickly. "Speak with her, Luke. Make her open up to you."

Luke wanted to talk to her so badly he could barely stand it, but she wanted nothing to do with him.

Gerald released the hand brake. "If anybody asks, we didn't say a word." He clicked his tongue and slapped the reins, continuing up the driveway so he could turn around and head back out.

Luke turned to find Paul still standing beside him.

Paul pulled a set of keys out of his pants pocket. "I can drive you in my truck and have you there in no time."

Luke hesitated. It might not go over well with his or Mary's father—or the bishop—to be seen with the likes of Paul Waddell. But Paul could get him all the way to Mary's in less time than it'd take Luke to go a mile by horse and buggy.

Luke grabbed the reins to his horse. "Just give me time to pull the buggy under the shed and put the horse to pasture."

Within three minutes he was climbing into Paul's truck.

Paul jerked the stick shift into gear. The old jalopy rattled even worse than a horse and buggy, and the fumes stank more than Mamm's old gas-powered washing machine, but it moved quickly, and for that Luke was thankful.

They rode in silence, and within ten minutes Paul slowed the truck in front of Mary's home. Luke opened the truck door and paused. "I'm glad we met, but when Hannah comes back...I can't side with you about her leaving the People. I think our ways are the right ones for her. Our community hasn't handled things right, and we've got some repenting to do and some things to learn." Luke swallowed hard. "But she was born Amish, and I believe she's supposed to be with us."

Paul gave a brief nod. Luke figured it wasn't really in agreement as much as a silent acceptance not to argue. "Will you let me know if you hear from her?"

Luke climbed out. "I think that's a reasonable thing to ask." He shut the door to the truck and headed across the yard as Paul drove away.

The front door opened before he even knocked, and Mary's father stepped outside. "What are you doing here?"

Luke took a deep breath. "I came to see Mary."

John Yoder eyed Luke from top to bottom. "She's been in the *Daadi Haus* since last night, but she said she didn't want no company."

"I'd like to go see her. I'm not likely to be able to make things much worse, but I'll do all I can to help her."

John nodded. "Just leave the front door open, and keep the storm door unlocked."

Within thirty seconds, Luke was tapping on the door to *Mammi* Annie's house. When Mary didn't answer, he stepped inside. "Mary?" He walked through the small house, searching for her.

He found her in a chair in the living room. She twitched when she saw him. A spool of thread fell from the quilt in her lap and rolled across the floor.

Luke grabbed it, noticing how pale she looked. "Is that our 'Past and Future' quilt?"

She didn't answer him.

The quilt had been Hannah's idea, a gift for Luke and Mary's marriage bed. She and Mary had worked on it since Mary was released from the hospital in early October. Hannah had gathered patches of cloth from their childhood for the past side of it. He wasn't sure what they'd done for the future side.

He held the spool toward her. "I guess you're hurting awful bad about now, missing Hannah."

She took the thread from his hand without looking at him.

He sat on the ottoman, his knees almost touching hers. "I heard you had a doctor's appointment yesterday."

She repositioned the quilt and ran the needle through an edge of it. "The basting on the future side of the quilt gave way. I don't know why."

He ran his finger along the sleeve of her sweater. "What did the doctor say, Mary?"

She shoved the quilt into his lap, rose, and walked away from him. Luke resisted the desire to stand in front of her and try to bend her will to his. He stayed on the ottoman, watching and listening. The room was silent for several minutes as Mary rummaged through a stack of material. She unfolded a piece of black broadcloth, her hands caressing it gently.

"Who will you sew a pair of pants for?" he asked, hoping her answer might give him some clue as to what was going on in her heart.

She tossed the material on the chair, her eyes focused on the cloth. "It doesn't matter." She turned her attention to him. "Not anymore. It's all ruined. All of it."

Luke rose and went to her. "It doesn't look ruined to me."

Taking a step back, she gestured toward the quilt. "Parts of it are already sewn into our future part of the quilt." She gasped for air. "And now…"

He was clueless as to why she was so upset but fairly sure he had the answer. "I'll buy you a whole bolt of black broadcloth, however many bolts you want."

Grabbing the material, she mumbled, "You can have it." She picked pieces of lint off the cloth. "Someone else can make pants for you."

Ah, so the material is for making my pants. At least he understood a little more, but the pain that crossed her face when she stumbled over that sentence added to his confusion. She folded the material and passed it to him, staying as far away from him as possible.

Luke eased up to her. "Mary, what's all this about?" When she tried to turn away from him, he stepped in front of her. "I need you to talk to me, Mary. I can't stand what's happening to us. I was wrong about Hannah, but I've already done all I can to fix that. And you have the power over *our* future."

"That's just it, Luke. I don't have the power. The doctor has removed it from me. And you'll up and lea—" She stopped, picked up the quilt, and moved back to the chair. The only sound in the room was the ticking of the clock.

Luke returned to the ottoman, waiting for her to finish her sentence. Doctors grated on her nerves easily. They were quick to give her lists of things she had to do, like take physical therapy and nutritional supplements. They also gave lists of things she couldn't do, like stay on her feet for more than six hours each day. He was curious what they'd demanded of her this time that had her so frustrated.

"I think I'll give Paul this quilt." She grabbed the spool and unwound some of the thread. "From the work Hannah put into it, it has more of her in it than anything else she owned."

Though not thrilled with the idea of her so easily giving away their marriage-bed quilt, he gave a slight nod. "If that's what you want."

Mary looked up from her sewing. "You'd not balk at me giving this to Paul?"

"I met him today. He's not such a bad guy. And I think he's hurting awful bad." Luke placed his hands over hers. "But that's not who I'm worried about."

She lowered her head, her fingers tightening around his. "I'm sorry, Luke. But I can't marry you."

Fighting the urges to argue, walk out, or pressure her for an immediate answer, he rubbed her fingers. "Can't or won't?" In spite of his anxiety, his words flowed calmly.

She shook her head. "It's time for you to go."

"Not yet. First I need you to answer that question. You can't marry me, or you won't marry me?"

"You need to find somebody else—" Her face crumpled with sadness.

"Mary, you're scaring me. I feel like I did during those awful days before you woke in the hospital. Does this have something to do with what the doctor said yesterday?"

"It's not like that." She stood. "The doctor says I'm doing great, just as long as I follow his orders."

Relieved, he took a deep breath. "Then what's wrong?"

Her lips curved down, causing a half-dozen little dimples to develop on her chin. "He said I can't plan on getting married this fall."

Shocked, Luke gazed up at her, hoping she meant what it sounded like. "Does that mean you're still interested in marrying me?"

"Of course I am." Her cheeks seemed to flush. "I mean…"

He raised an eyebrow at her. "It sounds like I still stand a chance of being your husband." He reached for her hand and gently tugged on it.

She knelt in front of him.

He caressed her cheek. "I love you, Mary."

"But…" She tilted her chin back as if she wasn't ready to forgive him.

A bolt of laughter escaped him. "Hannah would be proud of that chin-tilting thing. But she was better at it than you."

She smoothed her apron without looking at him. "Oh, Luke, it's not funny. The doctor said I'm not to get pregnant for…fi—for several years. And you know the bishop won't allow…" Pink tinged her cheeks.

Birth control. Not only was she thinking of marrying him, she was imagining the nights they'd share. "Mary, I can wait. You're a bit young to be getting married just yet anyway. I ought to wait for you. You shouldn't try to rush things for me. Right?"

Her lips pouted. "You could at least want to appeal to the bishop."

He encircled her in his arms. "Oh, I'll appeal, all right," he whispered in her ear.

Chapter 9

With the head of the hospital bed angled upright and a food tray in front of her, Hannah watched as Bugs Bunny paraded across the television screen. She'd been moved from ICU within hours of waking, and this morning she'd discovered that some of her strength had returned. The rabbit popped his head out of a hole, smacked loudly on a carrot, and looked around. "I knew I shoulda taken a left toin in Albuquerque." He'd made the same mistake an hour ago and landed in a whole different set of troubles.

Glad for the way this cartoon distracted her thoughts, she took a bite of her scrambled eggs. Her face contorted at the plastic feel in her mouth. She poked at the eggs on her plate with her fork, wondering if they were real, then pushed away the tray.

For the first time since she'd awakened yesterday, she wasn't trembling like a newborn calf. Trying to mask the taste of the eggs, she took a long drink of her orange juice. Maybe tomorrow the IV could be removed, and she'd be able to slip out of this place and go into hiding somewhere.

The door to her hospital room opened, and Dr. Lehman strode in. "How are you feeling this morning?"

Hannah set her juice down and wiped her mouth. "A lot better. Plenty well enough to take care of myself."

The doctor pushed the juice toward her, silently expressing his will. "That's doubtful. Nice try though." As she finished the drink, he pulled a chair close to the bed and took a seat. "I did a little reading last night on runaways. Most of those who flee home have a reason for heading in a certain direction."

A nervous tingle ran down her spine. Wondering if he intended to help her or work against her, she set the empty cup on the bedside tray.

He rubbed his chin. "So why did you come to Alliance? Was this your destination or just a stop along the way?"

Smoothing her hands across the bedcovers, she answered, "Alliance is the closest train depot to Winding Creek, which is where my aunt lives."

"Ah, so you did have a specific place in mind because you knew someone here."

She grimaced. *"Know someone* might be a bit of a stretch."

"You don't know your aunt?"

Hating to admit that part, she fidgeted with the hem of the sheet. While stalling, she decided her best way of getting this man on her side was to be honest with him. "I didn't even know she existed until about six months ago. But I'm sure I can find her."

Dr. Lehman took off his glasses and pinched the bridge of his nose. "You didn't know she existed? That's odd, especially among people as family oriented as the Amish."

"I figure she's been shunned, but I won't know anything for sure until I meet her. I discovered a letter from her, and that's where I got her address."

He nodded, seeming satisfied with her answer. "There's one question that came to me last night and has been nagging at me ever since." He slid his glasses back into place. "I'd like you to answer it, okay?"

She stared at him, wondering how she was supposed to agree to something without knowing what that something was.

He slid his hands into the pockets of his lab coat. "Why apply for a job at a medical office? Why not apply at a restaurant or at a day care?"

For the first time in too long, Hannah felt a smile tug at her face. Science was the most fascinating subject on the whole planet. While working with the nurses in charge of Mary's recovery, Hannah had learned some specifics about how cells form into organs and how each system has its unique job and needs. The needs part was where medical knowledge could help people get well, could even save lives.

She searched his face. "The desire to work where I can learn medical things is in here." She patted her chest. "Learning about healing and medicine draws me like…"—she closed her eyes and tried to think of an expression that matched her desires—"like a new mother longs for her child." She pulled a long breath into her lungs, feeling embarrassed that she'd just shared so much of herself. "You know?"

After a long silence, he scratched the back of his head. "Look, I'm not sure what the laws are, but your chances of not being sent back home have to be better if you can find that aunt of yours. Maybe I can help you."

Pinpricks of excitement swept through her, and she knew she was gaping at him.

"Clearly you have trust issues." He clasped his hands and laid them in his lap. "But I really do want to help you. I've already run some interference for you with Admissions; otherwise they'd already have contacted the police."

She studied his face, trying to determine his true motives. "Why?"

"Maybe I've just turned into an old fool."

Some of the heaviness she'd grown so accustomed to lifted. "You won't regret it. I'd promise to repay you if giving oaths to man wasn't against God's Word."

"And you don't think disobeying your parents and running away are sins?" The wrinkles across his brow deepened as he seemed to dissect her responses.

Hannah lowered her head. "I've wondered about that." She tugged at a loose thread on the top sheet, drowning in the thoughts that rose within her, thoughts she couldn't believe were hers. "But I've decided it isn't a sin to protect yourself, whatever it takes."

He sighed and pulled a pen and pad out of his pocket. "I'm going to take a chance on you. What's your aunt's name and address?"

"I got that driver to take me to her address. It was an unlivable old house."

"Why don't you give me the info anyway and let me see what I can find out?"

She wanted to answer, but her throat seemed to have closed up.

He stared out the window for a few seconds. "Listen, if we're going to have any type of relationship, regardless of how temporary, you're going to have to trust me, or at least pretend."

A whispery laugh escaped her. "I can do that. Pretend, that is."

He chuckled.

"Her name's Zabeth Bender. Her address is supposed to be 4201 Hanover Place, Winding Creek, Ohio."

He scribbled on the notepad.

"What happens to me if you can't find her?"

"One bridge at a time, Hannah."

She wasn't asking for a bridge. She wanted an escape plan, some trace of hope that this kind man had a backup plan that would save her from having to return to Owl's Perch even if he couldn't find her aunt.

He shoved the pad into his pocket. "If I discover anything solid, I'll let you know. In the meantime, rest. And you ought to call your parents and let them know you're safe."

"They don't own a phone."

Dr. Lehman scowled at her. "Don't misdirect me, Hannah. I know a little bit about how the Amish live. I'm sure you can call someone who has a phone and get them to take a message to your parents."

Her cheeks burned. "I don't mean to be dishonest. But I didn't go through everything I have just to be found."

Pulling a small phone out of his pocket, Dr. Lehman growled. "Use this. The number's unlisted, so no information will show up on caller ID or a bill."

Hannah stared at the strange gadget. "I don't know how to use that."

He flipped it open. "Punch in the numbers, with the area code, then press the button with the green icon of a telephone receiver."

Area code? Icon?

She took the phone from his hand and looked at it, then at him, and back again.

"You'll figure it out. I have rounds to make. I'll be back for it later." He lifted an eyebrow at her and looked meaningfully at the phone. "And a full report."

She watched him leave before turning her attention back to the tiny phone in her hand. The man just didn't understand what he was asking of her. No one wanted to hear from her. Well, almost no one. She had promised Mary, Luke, and Matthew that she would write, but aside from her brother and two friends, everyone else fell just short of hating her. Maybe they did hate her. She didn't know. She didn't want to think about it. Her dream was to start fresh, not deal with old things.

Staring at the phone, she huffed. The doctor had put a task before her, one that had to be done or he wouldn't help her. What had Paul told her about making a long-distance call? She closed her eyes, trying to remember.

He had said to dial 411 if she knew the name but not the phone number. Would calling that three-digit number work for locating area codes? She pushed the only green thing she could see. She put the phone to her ear but heard no dial tone.

Paul had taught her a thousand things over their years of friendship, but he hadn't owned a cell phone, so he'd never showed her how to use one. The ache of missing Paul stole her sense of relief. Hope in Dr. Lehman's words couldn't stop the awful hurt of facing her future without Paul.

After trying several ways to make the phone work, she finally reached directory assistance. It wasn't all that hard—press the digits and then the button with the green image of a receiver. Once she had the area code to go with Mary's phone number, Hannah punched the numbers in. The phone rang.

In her imagination she could hear the shrill ring of the phone echoing across the fields of the Yoders' farm. If someone besides Mary answered, would they hang up when they realized who was calling? Would they pass a message to Hannah's parents, assuring them she was safe? If they hung up or refused to take a message to her family, would Dr. Lehman refuse to help her?

A clicking noise let her know someone had just lifted the phone from its cradle.

Chapter 10

Closing the door on his way out of Gram's house, Paul wondered how to go about finding a reliable private investigator. He headed for his truck, hoping the police might offer him some direction. Money was a problem, but he'd figure something out. He refused to return to school or work right now. It was way past time for Hannah to be his top priority.

The sound of a horse whinnying caught his attention. Coming across the back pasture was a man dressed in the black trousers, coat, and hat of the Amish. Paul hurried toward the cattle gate, not sure if it was Luke or Matthew coming toward him. He knew no other Amish person who would come see him.

As Paul opened the gate, the man lifted his head.

Luke.

Although his jaw was set as the horse trod through the snow and muck of the back fields, he didn't look as downtrodden as he had yesterday. The horse slowed its pace as they approached. "Whoa." Luke brought the horse to a stop.

"We heard from her." He exhaled, causing billows of vapor to disperse into the cold air.

Paul drew a deep breath, taking in the heavens. *Thank You.*

Luke's laughter caught Paul's attention. "You should see Mary. Just knowing Hannah was somewhere safe brought some color to her face and relief to her eyes."

"Who spoke with her?"

"No one. The phone is in a shanty some sixty feet from the Yoders' house, so nobody heard it ring. But they have an answering machine, and she left a message."

"What did she say?"

Luke rode the horse through the opening. "Not much. I mean, she said she's fine and safe. She has a place to stay and someone helping her. That's about it."

Songs of praise silently ran through Paul's mind as he closed the gate. "Did she leave a number where she can be reached?"

"No." Luke slid off the horse, his smile fading. "She didn't leave any information about where she is. But she sounded good, hopeful, and at the same time really tired."

The inward songs faded, like a radio being turned down, as he realized there was no way to reach Hannah. "Can I go to the phone shanty and see if we can do anything to get the number she called from?"

A look of concern covered Luke's face. He pulled the loose ends of the reins through his hands several times. He slapped the leather against his palms, clearly mulling over what to do.

Paul waited, hoping he didn't have to figure out how to talk Luke into something he was set against.

Luke patted the horse's neck. "I don't like the idea of taking you to the Yoders' phone. If we're seen together, it won't help my position within the community any. I've risked being seen with you once, and I'm gonna need the bishop's approval over some things." He studied Paul. "But I've been right where you are, so concerned about Mary I thought I'd die. I can't imagine not knowing where she was or not being able to hear her voice." Luke shrugged. "Even when she's mad as a wet hen at me."

"I'd settle for Hannah's wrath over this."

"Good. 'Cause I figure when she does come back, she'll have been stripped of her somewhat-restrained self, and you'll definitely catch it."

They both laughed.

Luke nodded toward his harness shop, some hundred feet off of Paul's property, and to the small barn beside it. "Come on. Let's put her away for a spell and then use your truck to get back to Mary's. But when we get there, we gotta make it quick. I just hope news of us being together doesn't make it back to the bishop. Mary and I don't need him mad at us."

"I thought you and Mary were in everyone's good graces."

"We are as good as can be, considering the stench of trouble he had with my sister. But we need his permission about something sort of private-like." Luke shrugged, looking reluctant to say more.

Grateful that Luke was less like his father and more like his sister when it came to hearing and responding to the needs of those around him, Paul fell into step beside him.

Paul walked back into his gram's house. He'd heard Hannah's voice on the answering machine, and that was wonderful. But after exhausting every possible way he knew to get the number she had called from, he had come home empty-handed.

Added to that letdown, the message from her was in their first language, the only one they spoke among themselves: Pennsylvania Dutch. Paul longed to hear her speak words he could understand. If he were like most of his branch of Mennonites, he'd speak the native tongue too. But both sets of his grandparents had been Mennonite missionaries in other countries and hadn't taught their children Pennsylvania Dutch, so neither of his parents spoke the language.

Even with the communication barrier, he sensed she wasn't faring as well as he'd hoped. Every word seemed to come from a dark place of grief and exhaustion. He couldn't voice his concerns to Luke, because the moment they stepped out of the truck to go to the phone shanty, Mary came outside and joined them.

According to Luke, Hannah had said she had a place to stay, had made a friend who had helped her the night she arrived, and had been to see a doctor. She gave her word that she would write to Mary and Luke in a few weeks.

She made no mention of Paul. None. Was she starting her life over without him, believing he hated her? Surely not. She had written him a warm letter. But when she called, she hadn't left a number, nor did the Yoders have caller ID. When Mary told him they had the star-69 feature, he had hopes—

until he punched in the code and discovered that Hannah had called from an unknown number.

He was grateful to know she was safe, somewhere. Incredibly grateful. But it wasn't enough. He had to find her and set the record straight. Then if she wanted nothing else to do with him, he'd cope.

Who are you kidding, Waddell? You'll never accept losing Hannah.

Fixed on locating her, Paul went to his room, pulled out his laptop, and connected to the Internet. He figured the Net was the best place to start trying to locate private investigators. After finding the names, phone numbers, and even Web sites of several private investigators in Pennsylvania, he decided to make some calls. He called half a dozen places before he found a man named Drew, who seemed worthy of consideration. Balancing the phone between his shoulder and his ear, Paul jotted down notes as the private investigator rattled off a long list of missing-person cases. "Out of all those incidents, how many people have you actually located?"

"Well…," Drew hesitated. "That's harder to answer than it sounds. Finding someone depends greatly on why they're missing. If they don't want to be found and are smart enough to cover their trail—" A phone rang in the background, causing him to stop without finishing his sentence. "Paul, can you hold on one moment? I need to catch my other line."

"Sure."

Again doubts about pursuing Hannah weighed on him. She had left of her own accord, and she'd called using an unlisted number. Maybe she needed more time. Perhaps he should stick to their dream of his graduating and becoming a full-time social worker. That way, when she did return, he'd be settled in the job they'd always dreamed of—helping children in need of an advocate.

His frustration over the empty bank account surfaced again. It wasn't just the money being gone that bothered him. Something else in all this nagged at him. He just wasn't sure what it was.

As he closed his eyes, understanding dawned. House of Grace. He and Hannah had saved for years so they could sponsor a girl at House of Grace.

From the moment he'd shared about the home for girls, her eyes had lit up. For the first time in days, a smile worked its way to Paul's heart.

Remembering that an envelope had arrived from them a few days back, Paul began searching through the mail. Finding the ivory-colored envelope, he noted the words *Global Servants* stamped in purple on the far left side with an image of Thailand beside them. This was the ministry that had caused Hannah and him to unite in determination to reach beyond their lives and help a girl avoid being sold into prostitution. He slid his fingers into the envelope and pulled out the letter.

In the folds of the letter lay a photo of a young girl with a big grin, holding up a name placard. The white sign had the name A-Yom Muilae written in large letters across it. He could help this girl if he stayed focused on fulfilling Hannah's and his dream. He laid the picture on the table and read the note.

Dear Sponsor,

The words typed across the page shared how thankful they were that Paul Waddell and Hannah Lapp had joined forces to feed, shelter, and educate a young girl. It explained how God provided ways for the organization to acquire the girls, without buying them, before they were sold by their families. The letter gave details of how to prepare and send packages for Christmas, birthdays, and even an "I love you" gift throughout the year.

Remember, it is your willingness to give that makes the girls feel loved. Every gift you send, even the smallest gift, says, "I care about you and your future. I love you!"

It wasn't overly expensive to sponsor a girl. It just took some planning and effort, which he and Hannah had been doing since they learned of the plight of these girls. He'd been nineteen and Hannah only fifteen at the time. Even at just sixty dollars a month, plus gifts, he knew it would require planning and sacrifice to continue this journey until the girl was grown. They'd worked for three years toward this goal, and now they had a girl assigned to them.

The phone clicked. "Paul?" Drew asked.

"I'm here." He lifted the photograph again. Her smile seemed genuine, but her eyes appeared to be begging for someone to truly care. Paul knew he had to keep this commitment for the sake of all three of them.

The sound of car wheels crunching against the gravel driveway caught Paul's attention, and he moved to a window. His parents. One glance at their solemn, upright posture, and Paul knew he'd avoided this encounter as long as he could.

"Drew, I need to go. I'll think about all this and get back with you."

"Yeah, sure. Just remember, the trail grows colder with every hour that passes."

Paul disconnected the call and headed for the front door. His mom, bundled in a heavy coat over her caped dress and wearing a black winter scarf over her prayer Kapp, didn't wait for his dad to get the door for her. The two of them stepped out of the car in unison as Paul walked down the steps to greet them. He gave his mother a hug that she barely returned and then gave one to his father, who squeezed him warmly.

His dad placed a hand on Paul's shoulder. "We need to talk."

"Sure. Come on in." Awkwardness joined the array of emotions bearing down on Paul. He was inviting his dad into his own mother's home.

Without another word, his parents moved up the steps and into the living room and took a seat. Too antsy to sit, Paul shoved his hands into the pockets of his pants and waited for one of them to speak. The tension radiating from his mom and dad made him regret he'd kept everything about Hannah so secretive. Last Saturday when he began searching for Hannah, he'd called them and asked them to remain by the phones in case she tried to reach him there. That's when they'd learned their only son was interested in and even engaged to a girl they didn't know.

His mother intertwined her rough-skinned fingers. "So all your years of ignoring us every summer and coming here were because of this Hannah person."

He chafed at the flippant description of the woman he adored. "I didn't ignore you."

Silence lay thick between them.

His mom gave his dad a look he couldn't decipher. "I blame us for part of this. We've allowed you too much freedom. Your sister told us that she and William have gone to a few spectator games. My guess is you've gone too."

He knew professional sports were frowned on by most Plain Mennonites, but he enjoyed them, and he had always intended to take Hannah to see a game as soon as he could. It was a game, for crying out loud, and if his mother wanted repentance, she was looking at the wrong offspring.

She sighed. "I take it you don't care that your sister, William, and Dorcas had to talk to the church leaders about this."

Did his mother really expect him to care about some minor infraction right now?

She rested her head against the back of the couch. "Your sister, who clearly knew about Hannah before we did, said the girl left here with money and a plan and that she is believed to be completely safe, right?"

He'd answered a few of Carol's questions when she called him earlier in the week, but he hadn't realized she was giving a full report to their parents. "That's what we believe. She called—"

"We?" his dad interrupted.

Taking a seat, Paul counted to ten, trying to calm his mounting frustrations. Contrary to what his folks believed, he was an adult, and they were the ones out of line. "I talked to her brother Luke yesterday, and earlier today he came to talk to me."

His mom glanced at his dad before turning back to Paul. "You've been in Owl's Perch all week?"

"Of course." And he'd be here all next week too. "My fiancée is missing. Am I supposed to go about life as if nothing has happened?"

His parents retreated into silence again.

"Paul," his father began gently, "regardless of how we may sound, we're sorry for the pain you're going through. We really are. This is all quite a shock to us, and—"

"And you weren't honest with us," his mother interrupted.

"Hazel," Dad chided.

"He wasn't," she insisted. "Nearly three years ago you sat at my kitchen table and promised me you'd never get involved with any of those Englischer girls on campus. I've asked you about it since then, and each time you gave me your word. And not once did you mention this Amish girl, not once." Her eyes flashed with anger.

"I know, Mom. But you have to understand—I was trying to protect her."

"From who? Me?" she screeched.

Paul wiped the palms of his hands on his pants. "You have relatives in Owl's Perch. It was best to keep it a secret for her sake."

"I won't mention how well that seems to have worked for you, but I will tell you that you must return to school and work. She's gone. I know we don't sound like we're sorry, but we are. If for nothing else, for the pain this is causing you."

She was right about one thing—they didn't sound the least bit remorseful.

"Let her go, Paul," Dad added gently. "If she'd wanted to stay, she would have."

Apparently they expected him to put aside the fact that Hannah was gone and simply move on with his life. "I've been thinking about teaming up with a private investigator and going to find her." He stared at his shoes, wondering how Hannah would feel about being tracked down when she obviously didn't want to be found.

His mother harrumphed. "You have obligations here."

Standing, Paul rubbed the back of his neck. She was right, and he knew it; he just didn't want to give in to it. Hannah had left everything behind. Couldn't he?

Compassion shone in his dad's eyes. "I never doubted you had someone out this way." Dad cocked his head, with a half smile on his face. "But here's the problem, Son. Against what most of our sect of Mennonites believe, you talked us into allowing you to go to college, saying you had to have a specific college degree to carry out your dream of helping families. I know you've worked hard to pay for your truck and insurance, gas, books, food, dorm, clothing." He made a circular motion with his hand as if the list could go on and on. "But if you leave school now, you'll lose the scholarships that were based on your finishing school and working in state for two years. You can't afford to pay for your schooling without those scholarships, and neither can we."

His mother grabbed a pillow off the couch and pulled it against her chest. "If you want to help families, start with your own. You can't leave us drowning in bills from this educational venture of yours while you're chasing someone who left you."

"The scholarships don't work that way, Mom. You and Dad will not be held accountable if I fail to keep the agreement. It's my responsibility and my problem. But you don't understand about Han—"

"Maybe you're the one who doesn't understand," his mother interrupted. "She hasn't called you. She hasn't let you know where she is. She obviously doesn't want you to find her."

"I appreciate your voice of concern, Mom."

"Do not get smart with me, Paul Waddell."

He stifled a groan. Their adult-child relationship needed help, but now wasn't the time to argue that she was guilty of dishing out sarcasm too. "Don't believe the gossip about her. I know it's not true."

"I have no doubt that most of the rumors I've heard are lies." She shrugged, as if Hannah's innocence was unimportant. "However, what I believe or even what you believe doesn't change anything."

Paul shoved his hands into his pockets. "How can you say that? You never met her, so she doesn't seem real to you. This isn't some silly crush. I want to marry her."

"And because of that, I'm glad she's gone!" His mother rose, anger carved in her face. "How could you think of marrying someone I've never met? Someone who was pregnant for months without you even knowing it? Her whole life has been one secret after another, and when her house of cards fell, she ran—without regard for you."

As his mother sliced him with her anger, it seemed he'd never really known her.

"Hazel," his father scolded before he drew a deep breath and offered her a peacemaking smile, "why don't you go upstairs and wake Mom from her nap. I need to talk to Paul alone."

She turned and strode out of the room. Watching her climb the steps, Paul knew she had no respect for him as an adult. Oh, she loved him dearly—as long as he did things her way. But to her, his feelings were as insignificant as a child's tears over a dropped candy bar—temporary and easily appeased.

"She's hurting, Paul. I've tried to tell her for years that you had someone, but she wouldn't believe you'd hide such a thing from us."

"It had to be that way—"

His father held up his hand, stopping Paul in midsentence. "I get it." He offered a weak smile. "If anyone in this family can understand, it's me, along with your Uncle Samuel."

"Uncle Samuel? How can an old bachelor understand this?"

He motioned Paul closer. "Gram doesn't like anyone to talk about this. Consider it a family skeleton."

Paul moved in and took a seat.

"When Samuel was about your age, he fell for a Catholic girl. Both families were ready to disown their children if they didn't stop seeing each other. It broke both their hearts. Samuel was willing to leave his family over her, but she couldn't do it. In his own way, he did leave the family over it, even though he still joins us for holidays and such. I've watched my older brother carry pain unlike anything I had ever imagined, and he did so for years."

"What happened to the girl?"

"She eventually married someone her family approved of and had children. Your Uncle Samuel's ache turned to stone, and he's never been the same. Your mom was in the family throughout most of it. It's part of the reason you've finagled too much freedom out of us; we've tried to handle your wanting more Englischer-type freedoms differently than my parents handled Samuel. Your mom thinks you never should have spent four years in college rooming with Englischers. You've become self-willed, Son. And expected too many family members to cover for you."

Paul realized afresh the position he'd put Gram in. No wonder she kept waffling between respecting his feelings and putting up roadblocks to Hannah's and his relationship. She didn't want to carry the burden of standing between them, and yet she understood how Mr. Lapp felt about his daughter marrying outside their Amish community.

He drew a breath. "Hannah called."

"Here?" Uncertainty flicked through his dad's eyes.

Shaking his head, Paul glanced at the stairway and lowered his voice. "She called her best friend, Mary. They have a phone shanty and an answering machine."

"What did she say?"

"That she's safe and…" Nothing. She'd said nothing else—not really.

"She's not coming home, is she?"

Paul shook his head. "But I've talked to this private investigator, and—"

"Son," his dad interrupted him, "what are you going to bring her home to? An angry community, family, and bishop? To join your family, which will be another set of stresses to work through. Aren't those the very things she needed to get free from?"

"Dad, I can't just—"

"Can't what? Give her time? Respect that she's in the throes of grief and deserves a little space?"

"What if she doesn't return?" Paul moaned.

His dad tapped his fingertips together, thinking before responding. "Making her come back to this mess isn't the answer—at least not yet. Finish school. Keep your scholarship by working in state for two years. We both know the church leaders may have some concerns if you choose to work for the state beyond your internship." His dad smiled. "I think your job choice is fine, always have. But if it's going to pull you away from your faith, find a different line of work. It sounds like Hannah has enough help. And she knows your phone number, right?"

Paul nodded. "But she thinks I abandoned her."

"That's the toughest part to live with. Still, she has to know what caused you to react the way you did. If she really loves you, she'll reach out again, at least once more before giving up." His dad leaned forward. "There's something else on my mind. The preacher and bishop want to talk with you. That has your mother every bit as upset as your intent to marry a girl we've never met. You need to make plans to meet with them. They're going to question you on points of the church disciplines. They know you joined the faith at fourteen. What they want to know is how faithful you've been. For four years your roommates have been watching television, going to movies, and partying. Our church leaders want to know where you stand."

Paul nodded. He had nothing to hide. It was never his intention to use his freedoms for anything but pursuing Hannah—and maybe an occasional Senators game. Pursuing an Amish girl wasn't against any part of the church disciplines, and even going to a game wasn't considered a huge issue—just things he needed to agree not to do again if he wanted to remain in good standing with his church.

The two men sat in silence until Paul finally rose. "I need more time to think through your advice about Hannah. You might be right about giving her some time and returning to school and work. But even if that's what I do, if she lets me know where she is, I'm out of here."

Without waiting for a response, Paul went upstairs. Feeling as if he'd climbed into the very cage his Lion-heart had been freed from, he went to his room and closed the door. With his mind and heart elsewhere, Paul wondered how he was supposed to cope with the pressure of school and work, especially with the added issue of being a week behind on everything.

When the phone in his room rang, he snatched it up. "Hello."

"Paul? It's Dorcas."

"Hey." He tried to keep the fullness of his disappointment from his voice, but he knew it was a vain effort.

"I guess you heard that we confessed to the preachers."

"Yeah." And he wasn't going to apologize for the choices she'd made. He'd never once invited her to a game. His sister did that. Last time they all went to a game, Dorcas had on a dress with lace and had a ticket in hand, all set to go whether he joined them or not.

"I don't mean to bother you. I just thought you might want to talk." She paused.

Suddenly Paul had an idea. Dorcas was only a few years older than Hannah. She hadn't been raised as strictly as Hannah, but the similarities could be useful, and she definitely had the mind-set of a female. His parents knew what they wanted. Paul knew what he wanted. But maybe Dorcas could help him figure out what Hannah might be thinking and feeling. "Now that you've called, I'd like your opinion on something."

Chapter 11

Hannah lay still as the nurse removed the IV needle from the back of her hand. Soon she wouldn't have to wait on Dr. Lehman's plans, all of them relying on various ifs. If he found something solid, if he could locate her aunt—if, if, if. As soon as the nurse left, Hannah would get dressed and sneak out.

The nurse put a Band-Aid in place. "All done."

"Thank you." If Hannah had realized removing the needle was that easy, she'd have done it herself last night and been long gone by now.

"You're welcome." The nurse removed the needle from the IV bag and placed it in the small, red plastic container that hung on the wall behind the head of the bed. She wrapped the tubing loosely over the IV stand before grabbing the thermometer off the table she'd set it on when she entered the room.

While the nurse took her temperature and pulse rate, Hannah thought about what the doctor had said yesterday. His offer to help was nice, but she'd already ridden to her aunt's place. It was abandoned. There was no sense in waiting for the doctor to come back with that news and bring social services with him. No one was going to make her return to the land of persecution—no one. She owed the hospital money, and she'd pay them, but not today. Right now she needed to slip out of this place before—

"Temp's good. Pulse is good." The nurse gathered the pieces of tape, Band-Aid wrappers, and the thermometer's sheath and threw them into the trash. She removed the bed coverings and gently pressed on Hannah's abdomen. "Any pain?"

"No."

"Good." She replaced the sheet and blanket. "You're healing remarkably well. Keep it up, and you'll be out of here in no time. Probably within a few days."

Oh, I'll be out of here in no time, all right. The minute you leave—

The door to her room swung open, and Dr. Lehman strolled in, carrying a short stack of papers. Hannah chafed at the interruption.

Lifting the almost-empty IV bag off its perch, the nurse glanced up. "Your patient is doing much better today than yesterday."

"The benefit of youth…" Dr. Lehman took a seat as the nurse left the room. He raised both eyebrows before closing his eyes and sighing. "I'd bet money on what you're planning, Hannah. Don't do it."

A prickly feeling, as if she'd been caught stealing eggs from the henhouse, ran through her body. This man seemed to know her thoughts and feelings as soon as they came to her.

He rolled his eyes, clearly frustrated at her lack of trust. But if she couldn't trust her own parents or even Paul, she wasn't about to give this stranger a chance to ruin her future. He sat there, skimming his papers. She wished he'd hurry up so she could get dressed and go.

He turned his attention to her. "Hannah, I think it's a great idea for you to pursue this dream of learning about the health field. But getting a degree in any area will be difficult. It's hard enough for honor students who have graduated from high school, but as a seventeen-year-old with an eighth-grade education, you'll have years of learning to make up for."

She bristled. "Every summer for three years Paul brought me his college textbooks and taught me things from them. I can do this. I know I can."

He cocked his head, studying her. "Is this the same Paul who asked you to marry him?"

Hannah nodded.

"If he was in college, then he's not Amish." A troubled look crossed his face. "You weren't planning on remaining among the People, were you?"

She tilted her head up, irritated by his grilling. "No."

Dr. Lehman tapped the papers in his hand. "With all that's happened to you, I can understand why you left the way you did. And I can't see asking you to return—not until you're emotionally, physically, and financially on your feet enough that you can walk away from your parents, if need be."

He's not going to send me back? Suddenly she wanted to jump out of bed and dance around the room.

Dr. Lehman sighed. "And I certainly can't ask you to try to work things out with Paul. What can a seventeen-year-old girl possibly know about choosing a life mate?"

Something defiant in her quaked under his attitude. She'd been so sure about Paul, who he was, who they would be together for a lifetime. But it all changed in the length of time it took him to brush against her rounded stomach, run to his truck, and then take her portion of their money before she could get to it. If that wasn't enough to break her, he'd had some girl in his apartment the one time she'd tried to call him before she boarded the train.

Dr. Lehman showed her the first page of the papers in his hand. In bold letters across the top were the words "Stark State College, Alliance Satellite, State Street." The very idea of attending college raised thoughts of failure, causing a disconnect from all joy.

He glanced at her and then at the papers, a frown creasing his brow. "You can go to classes to study for a GED. It's equivalent to a high-school diploma as far as qualifying you to begin the process of getting into college. Then you'll need to attend college classes in science and math to qualify for whatever medical field you intend to enter. That may take years longer than you're thinking, but your future will be in your hands." He scratched his brow. "You haven't been using your best asset in trying to get a job. You speak Pennsylvania Dutch. Look for work and training at clinics based on that. Why, I might hire you myself to help in my usual line of work if I needed someone and you knew how to log info into the computer."

"What do you usually do?"

He rolled the papers up and tapped them against his leg. "Well, I don't work at that clinic you came to. I was just there filling in as a favor." He stifled a yawn. "Aside from managing a women's clinic for the poor, I'm the doctor at two home-style Amish birthing clinics. I work in conjunction with some nurse-midwives. With a little effort, I could learn the language, but I always have one Amish woman on staff so I'll know what's being said when a patient is talking to a family member. That way I can address some of their fears or concerns they might not ask me directly. And the Plain women are willing to ask them questions in private. The assistant then comes to me, I answer, and she shares that answer in their native tongue. It's the best way I've found to spread medical advice to the Plain communities. You understand the need for that kind of information. You came close to dying because of the lack of it. Well, that mixed with your stubbornness."

"I can't work at an Amish clinic."

"Sure you can. You think you're the first girl not to be baptized into the faith? And give the Amish community a little respect, will you? Even if they learned the truth about you, most wouldn't want to make you go back. Actually very few would dare meddle in such a decision."

"Says who? I'm the one who kept receiving letters upon letters begging me to repent or be ready to pay the price."

"That was different. Members of your own household and your church leaders were probably instigating the letter writing to stop you from sinning. Besides, here no one has to know who you were."

The man was crazy. She wasn't jeopardizing her freedom in order to become some type of public-service announcement over medical advice she knew nothing about.

Dr. Lehman tossed the rolled-up papers onto her lap. "It's my best guess that with enough time and training, you'd be a first-rate midwife, Hannah—regardless of how far you're able to go in school. But that idea is pretty far into the future—" His pager went off, interrupting him. He took it off his hip and focused on it.

Midwife?

Words her mother had spoken as far back as Hannah could remember tugged at her. *Someday you'll make a good midwife, Hannah.* But she herself would never again conceive. How would she stand helping other women bring their babies into the world?

He clipped the pager back onto his belt. "But for now there are family clinics for the Plain, and there are Plain folk who go to Englischer clinics. Those will be good places for you to look for work. Just tell them you speak the language and are willing to go to night school to become trained and that you'll learn how to use a computer."

Not at all sure she liked his plan for success, she laid the scroll of papers on the side table. His leathered wrinkles softened into a smile. "I'm willing to arrange things where you don't have to go back."

Goose bumps ran up her arms. He'd hinted at this a minute ago, but did he really mean it?

He leaned back in his chair. "But I'll expect you to agree to a few terms."

"What kind of terms?"

"You'll need to attend counseling for victims of rape."

A rush of embarrassment swirled through her.

He cocked his head. "There won't be any men at the meetings. And every woman there has been a victim of the same crime—a lot of times even the counselors."

Disbelief at his request surged within her, but somewhere inside she knew she needed the kind of help he was talking about. Just an aroma like one from that day or a sound or a glimpse of blueberries, like the ones she'd been bringing home in a bucket that day, made her chest constrict and her mind cloud with confusion and panic. "Okay."

He patted her arm. "Now that we've got all that settled, there's someone I want you to meet." He opened the door.

A thin woman using a wooden cane came to the doorway. She was about the age of Hannah's parents and looked much too young to need a walking aid. A silky, navy-blue scarf covered her whole head, leaving no strand of hair in sight. Her eyebrows were very thin, and Hannah wondered if she had any hair under her head covering. She wore a matching caped dress, and she looked amazingly familiar, though Hannah couldn't place why.

They soaked each other in before Hannah broke the silence. "Are you Zabeth?"

The woman dipped her chin, looking disappointed. "Your father must not have ever spoken of me, or you'd know how to pronounce it." She lifted her head, looking determined not to care.

Dr. Lehman chuckled. "Well, there's no doubt you're related. Not only do you two favor each other, but you have some of the same gestures. I noticed that when I met your aunt last night."

Indignation nipped at Hannah. "You met her before you had me agree to go to counsel—"

Her aunt stepped forward. "It's pronounced Zuh-beth. It's short for Elizabeth. So it's said just like the name without the first three letters." She smiled and shifted the cane to her other hand. "Hannah, once I was able to prove to his satisfaction that I am indeed your aunt, he talked with me about you going to counseling and getting an education. We decided that you need to make your own choices about your future. I sew curtains and bedspreads for a living, and you're welcome to join me in that."

Hannah wanted to set her aunt's mind at ease. "I'll pull more than my weight, and I'll—"

Dr. Lehman pointed a finger at her. "Not for a while you won't. You need to stay off your feet and rest for at least three weeks. During that time you can decide what you're going to do—go on to school and train at clinics or go to work for your aunt. While you're recuperating, you'll use the money you arrived here with to cover food and such. When your surgeon gives the go-ahead, you can find a job and start paying off your hospital bill."

She'd always worked as hard as she felt like, without anyone telling her otherwise. Then again, she'd barely survived her last round of stubbornness. She nodded. "Okay."

Dr. Lehman offered a brief smile. "Good. I need to go. Bye, ladies."

When the door closed behind him, Zabeth propped the cane against the bed and gingerly walked to the window. "How's Zeb?"

Her mouth suddenly dry, Hannah licked her lips. "I don't know. He's physically well enough, I suppose. Aside from that, he's angry and unreasonable."

Turning from the view to look at Hannah, Zabeth sighed. "I was hopin' he'd changed." Sadness filled her eyes. "Dr. Lehman said you were determined not to return home. But he didn't say why you're in this hospital or how you came to arrive in Alliance."

"I came hoping to find you."

Zabeth toyed with the blinds. "How did you know about me?"

"I found a letter from you hidden in my parents' bedroom."

"Ah, now things are making more sense." Zabeth eased to the side of the bed and sat down. "What happened to make you leave?"

Hannah liked the woman. Her mannerisms said she was reserved, but her words were laced with honesty and gentleness. Unable to stand the idea of keeping any more secrets from those she lived with, Hannah began sharing the events of her life in almost a whisper. Before long she was speaking in a normal tone, summing up what her life had been like since last August.

When she had finished, tears ran down both their faces. Zabeth passed her a box of tissues before grabbing a handful herself.

"And now Dr. Lehman says I'll never have babies."

Zabeth wrapped her frail arms around Hannah and held her. She didn't try to offer any words of comfort. For that Hannah was grateful.

Zabeth pulled away and smiled at her. "I'm glad you've come to be with me, Hannah-girl."

Hannah nodded. "Why were you banned all these years?"

"I wouldn't repent." Zabeth scrunched the tissues in the palm of her hand. "I can't. I'm not wrong."

A laugh broke from Hannah along with fresh tears. "That's exactly how I feel. But what did you do?"

Tossing the tissues into a trash can, Zabeth took a deep breath. "I fell in love." She bit her bottom lip, smiling. "His name is Music." Zabeth's gray blue eyes locked on Hannah's. "I was a baptized member of the faith when I began baby-sitting for a woman while she taught music lessons." Zabeth covered her heart with her hand, and serenity covered her face. "The first time I heard her play the clarinet, I was swept away by the rich melodies. Oh, Hannah, there's nothing like the pleasure of music. Nothing."

Hannah couldn't imagine anyone leaving the fellowship of the People over something like music.

Zabeth paused, drawing a deep cleansing breath. "My teacher, Lauraine Palmer, understood my need for secrecy. She taught me how to play a few songs on the piano, and I did really well. Later on, I snuck off to play in recitals and such. What a glorious feeling! Then one day news of my playing at a recital got back to the bishop. He confronted me and insisted I repent and follow the oath I'd taken before God. I stood my ground, insisting there was nothing wrong with music. The community shunned me, but I kept taking lessons and playing in recitals. It wasn't until your father started hating me that my life took a hard turn."

There was a lot Hannah could say against her father, but it'd take more strength than she possessed. "Did you marry a Mennonite or an Englischer?"

Zabeth shook her head. "Things happened within the Palmer household, and I never married. I just stayed busy with them."

"Then why is your last name Bender?"

Zabeth wiped her forehead with the back of her hand, reminding Hannah of her father. "It seemed important at the time. Zeb was dogging my every step, determined to make me—"

A tap on the door interrupted her.

"Come in." Hannah tucked the sheet around her upper body.

A skinny woman with short black hair, bold makeup, and tight blue jeans opened the door to the room. "I'm going to the parking lot for a smoke. You can just meet me at the car when you're done."

Zabeth motioned for her to come in. "Hannah, I'd like you to meet my music teacher's daughter. Faye was just a child when I baby-sat her, and her baby brother came along some twenty-six years ago. Now she has two adorable children of her own, a three-year-old girl and a four-year-old boy. Faye Palmer, this is my niece, Hannah Lapp. "

The woman's features looked cold and uncaring, but there was something more than just that about her. She seemed different somehow, and not a good kind of different—if Hannah's gut reaction was right. And why, if she had two children, did she have the same last name as her mother?

Faye pulled a piece of gum out of her purse as she sank into the chair.

"Hi, Hannah." She unwrapped the gum and popped it into her mouth without ever making eye contact. "Care for some?" She held out the package.

"No, thank you."

She offered it to Zabeth, who took a piece.

"Hannah's going to move in with me."

"Really?" Faye chewed hard on the gum and glanced at Hannah. "Hope you're used to roughing it, 'cause Zabeth's idea of living fancy falls a bit short." She blew a quick bubble and popped it. "She came out of the Old Order Amish lifestyle to live semi–Old Order Amish." The sarcasm bothered Hannah, but Zabeth didn't look a bit frustrated.

Zabeth placed both hands on her hips. "Hey, I have electricity, a piano, and a clarinet. What else does a person need?"

Faye smacked on another bubble. "She has two outlets and two of those hang-from-the-ceiling-type light bulbs. No phone, no computer, no radio, no television, no air conditioning, no electric dryer, and she says she's not Old Order."

"I have four outlets—one in each room of my house—and indoor plumbing." Zabeth's eyes danced with humor.

"Sounds good enough to me," Hannah said. The news that Zabeth was planning to take her home sounded like freedom's ring.

Faye sighed. "After all you've sacrificed for our family, Dad ought to have you living in a mansion."

Zabeth removed the gum wrapper. "That's enough, Faye." She folded the gum into fourths before placing it into her mouth.

"Well, good grief, when Mom died, you gave up everything." Faye elongated the word *everything,* and Hannah wondered what all Zabeth had given up. Faye rolled her eyes. "And took over running the whole household and raised Martin before he went off to college, while Dad went right on making money, money, money."

"Faye." Zabeth angled her head, trying to catch Faye's downcast glare. "Hannah has no need to know all this. None."

Faye shrugged. "Somebody ought to know it."

"Look at me, please." Zabeth waited. "I don't want you talking about family history. Not now. Not later."

Faye huffed and then nodded her head. A jingly piece of music shot through the room. Faye opened her purse and grabbed a two-inch-long oval thing that looked like a fat beetle. She opened it and stuck it on her ear, making it light up blue. "Hello." She wrinkled her nose. "Hi, Martin." Faye studied her chipped, burgundy-colored fingernails while listening. "Hang on and I'll find out." She lowered the object. "Zabeth, my little bro has had his fill of watching the kids. He wants to know when we'll be home. Seems his niece and nephew aren't as important as the date he has tonight."

Hannah pointed at the odd thing in her hand. "What is that?"

"It's a phone piece, for talking and hearing."

"You're kidding."

"Nope. Here, say hi." Faye passed it to her.

"You mean somebody's still on the line?"

Faye laid the odd thing on the bed beside Hannah. "Yep."

She shook her head. "I couldn't."

Faye held up both hands, backing away from Hannah. "You have to say hi, or he'll be on hold all day."

Feeling silly and curious, Hannah picked it up and put it to her ear. "Hello? Is someone there?"

"Wow, Sis, your voice sure has changed. Your accent too."

"This isn't Faye. I…I'm just checking out this beetle thing."

"I object to being called a beetle thing—at least before you've seen me."

Hannah laughed. "Not you. This thing I'm talking into."

The deep voice resonated with laughter. She could hear the gentle chatter of a preschooler in the background. "Can I talk to my sister again? I—" Hannah heard a *ka-thump*. "Whoa, young fella, you can't dump the can of peaches on the floor until after Mommy gets home. Listen, uh, phone girl, tell my sister if she doesn't get home within an hour, she can pick her kids up at the local orphanage. Do they have orphanages anymore?"

"I wouldn't know."

The man chuckled. "Tell her I have a date, an important one. Bye, phone girl."

"Bye." Hannah held the device toward Faye. "He said he has an important date, and he said something about an orphanage."

"Brothers. And to think this hot date will be convinced he's cool." She shook her head. "But we do need to go. You ready, Zabeth?"

"I'm ready." She pulled a card out of her purse. "We'll be back when you're released from the hospital. Until then, here's Faye's phone number. Call if you need anything. She'll get me any message from you right away."

Faye pulled a set of keys from her purse. "That's me, a carrier pigeon."

Zabeth gave Hannah a hug. "You take care." She kissed her cheek. "You done right to come here, Hannah. It won't be a picnic, but I'll take as good care of ya as I can."

As Zabeth followed Faye out of the room, Hannah realized she still didn't know where her aunt lived. She had a thousand questions, but the pieces of what she did know bothered her. The illness Zabeth had written about in the letter along with her lack of hair and frailty of body said her aunt was probably fighting some type of cancer. Hopefully one she could win against.

And Faye? She left uneasiness in her wake. Or was that Hannah's imagination?

Chapter 12

𝒮tudying Mrs. Waddell's house in the distance, Sarah hoped the woman was gone to church. She tugged the reins and made a right turn onto the driveway that led to Luke's harness shop. The midmorning chill sat heavy on her, and she pulled the lap blanket tighter. Sometimes having church only every other Sunday was the most freeing part of living Amish. It reminded Sarah of slipping into a warm pair of lace-up boots that didn't pinch her feet. As a matter of fact, if it weren't for being able to watch Jacob across the way in the men's seating area, church Sundays would hold nothing for her. But the few words she shared with Jacob during the after-services meal made the going bearable.

Pulling under the huge lean-to designed as sheltered parking for Luke's customers, Sarah had other things on her mind besides trying to share a glance or a word with Jacob Yoder.

Hannah's baby.

It wasn't dead. Sarah knew that. Not one thing in her doubted that the infant was alive somewhere. Clearly her sister had given birth and left, but no one had directly confirmed that the infant had died—not even Naomi, who was there that night. So far, Sarah hadn't seen any hint of a new baby in anyone's home, and she'd spent plenty of time this week looking. She'd baked items and used that as a reason to make visits to people's homes. And for her efforts, all she knew for sure was the community was grieving something fierce over what had taken place with Hannah. Sarah clicked her tongue in disgust. Why should she grieve when she knew it wasn't true? She'd never seen the likes of such guilt as she'd encountered this week. But when she proved to them Hannah's baby wasn't dead, their grief would disappear, and rejoicing would return, not to mention a renewed dislike and distrust for Hannah.

She pulled to a stop and removed the blanket from her lap. Feeling confident she'd find signs that Mrs. Waddell was keeping Hannah's baby, Sarah trod across the mushy, snowy fields that separated the Lapp and Waddell properties.

She tiptoed up the steps and across the back porch of Mrs. Waddell's home. Rapping on the glass, Sarah peered through the window. The large farmhouse was quiet inside, with no signs of movement. As she waited, her excitement grew—just as she'd expected, no one was home.

Without wasting any more time, she went to the storage cabinet and searched for the spare key. Mrs. Waddell kept it in here somewhere. After shifting baskets, tools, and some junk around, she finally found it.

Triumphant, she unlocked the door and stepped inside. The warmth of the place surrounded her, filling her with hope. She was close to finding Hannah's baby. She could feel it.

Mrs. Waddell had some really nice things—fancy things—but she couldn't let them distract her. Sarah looked in the refrigerator and pantries for any signs of infant formula or bottles. When she found none, she worked her way through the living room, looking in drawers and closets as she went. Upstairs she searched through each bedroom and its closet.

Nothing.

She sank onto Mrs. Waddell's bed, wondering where else Hannah might have left the baby. Her fingers danced over the lace-patterned coverlet, the softness triggering some recollection. She'd seen this print, these yellows and purples, elsewhere in this house. But where?

Her mind jumped to the guest room. There she'd seen a baby crib and diapers. Maybe…

~~∽❀~~

Paul helped his grandmother up the steps before he unlocked the front door. They entered the warm house and slid out of their coats without speaking. The fact that lately they both seemed to live in their own worlds nagged at him.

He put his hand on her shoulder. "Can I fix you a bite to eat before you lie down?"

"I didn't ask to leave Sunday school so we could eat." She pointed to the steps. "I'm tired."

As Gram made her way up the stairs, Paul went to his place of refuge—the back porch. It faced the dirt roadway, and if Luke or Matthew were to come visit him, he'd spot them. He'd sat out here for hours, even in the cold, and remembered the dozens of times Hannah had walked across the pastures up to Gram's.

He'd just opened the back door when he noticed someone had tracked snow and mud across the porch. Walking to the edge, his eyes followed a fresh set of prints from the porch to Luke's property. From the size of the marks, they appeared to have been made by either a woman or a younger boy. Wondering if someone had come to see him when he wasn't home, Paul headed toward Luke's shop.

He heard a window open. "Paul!" Gram whispered loudly and motioned for him.

He ran back to the house and up the stairs. "Gram?"

He went to the room she'd called from. She wasn't there. Hurrying through the place, he glanced inside each bedroom door as he passed it. When he came to the guest room on the far end of the second story, he stopped short. Gram stood near the foot of the daybed. An Amish girl was on the floor, sitting on her heels, with her back to him. Every piece of baby clothing his Gram had held on to over the years seemed to be scattered around the girl.

Hannah? Elation soared. Fear raced. But his body wouldn't budge. If it was Hannah, sitting in the middle of the room strewn with baby clothes…

Concern shone in Gram's eyes. "It's Sarah."

The girl turned to face him. Unlike the family resemblance that Luke shared with Hannah, the girl's face bore no similarities to her sister's.

"Sarah?" Paul stepped into the room.

With each fist holding one end of a cloth diaper, she yanked it. He figured if she'd had any strength, it would have ripped. "Where is she?"

Paul crouched. "I don't know, Sarah. I wish I did."

She lifted wild eyes to him. "She isn't here?"

Uneasiness crept up Paul's spine. Did her father realize how unbalanced this poor girl was?

"I've been searching for her all week. She's safe. That much I know for sure." Paul stood and held out his hand to help her up. "Does your family know where you are, Sarah?" He repeated her name as he spoke to her, hoping to help center her.

Shaking her head, she took his hand and stood upright. "I came looking for her by myself."

He glanced at his Gram and nodded toward the door. "Come on, Sarah. Let's get you home."

With Paul in the lead and Gram behind, they walked downstairs and through the house. Once on the porch, they paused.

Gram ran her hand over her chest. "I'd better be the one to take her home. If Zeb sees you—"

"Then what, Katie Waddell?" Zeb Lapp came around the side of the house and stomped onto the porch.

Gram jumped and tightened her hand against her chest.

"Easy, Gram," Paul assured her. "Go on inside and rest. I'll talk to Mr. Lapp."

The man opened his mouth to speak, but Paul raised his hand, signaling him to stop. Surprisingly, he hushed and waited.

Paul opened the door and helped Gram inside. "Go lie down, Gram."

She nodded, and he closed the door.

Mr. Lapp pointed a wrinkled finger in Paul's face. "Stealing one of my daughters ain't enough?"

"It's not like that."

The man wrapped his hand around Sarah's biceps. "Stay away from my family."

Sarah trembled, but the faraway, glazed look only seemed to deepen.

"Mr. Lapp, Sarah needs help. I think she's struggling with—"

"Yeah, she's struggling," Mr. Lapp interrupted. He pulled himself to his full stature, which was about four inches shorter than Paul. "Just like the rest of us. We're all living in the wake of you messin' in my daughter's life."

As the man breathed threats on his grandmother's porch, Paul struggled to control his tongue. "I know you blame me for Hannah's troubles. But if you ignore what's going on with Sarah, you're going to lose another daughter."

"Whatever happens, it'd be best to make sure you are not involved in that process. Do I make myself clear?"

Paul stepped back. "Are you saying you don't care if you lose a second daughter as long as I'm not the cause?"

"I'm saying my family is none of your concern! If you'd kept your hands off my Hannah, none of this would be going on. None of it!"

The man's face turned purple, and he shook all over, making Paul wonder if he might have a heart attack. Did he remember enough from his CPR courses to keep Mr. Lapp alive until an ambulance arrived? Paul flinched at the dark thoughts of not performing CPR if the opportunity presented itself.

"Mr. Lapp, set aside your resentment toward me for just a moment, and look at Sarah. Truly see her, please."

Mr. Lapp hesitated, then he studied his daughter. Some of the anger drained from his face. Placing his arm around her shoulders, he bent his head toward her. "Let's go home, child."

Chapter 13

*J*t made no sense to Hannah. After all her determination to get here and find Zabeth, her elation had settled, and now she felt oddly uncertain. She eased onto the side of the bed, combing her wet hair. The shower had dispelled the bit of chill that clung to her each time night fell. But all her thinking during the long shower brought her no answers.

Dr. Lehman and Zabeth had put her future into her own hands. Unfortunately, neither one could see into the future to know what she ought to do.

What if she did go to work at an Amish clinic and her Daed and bishop found out? Or what if she wasn't smart enough to pass the GED and go further with her education? What if, after all her hopes for the future, the best thing for her was to work with Zabeth in the solitude of her home?

In some ways, it seemed easier when others made the decisions for her.

This approach of your-life-is-in-your-own-hands was uncomfortable territory, for sure. How could she have been so confident as to arrive in Alliance by herself and now, with life looking more hopeful, be completely unsure of what she wanted?

She went to the bathroom mirror and wiped off the steam. Looking past her features and into her eyes, she wondered who she really was. And she wondered how she could find out before she needed to give Zabeth and Dr. Lehman her decision.

There was a tap on her door before it swooshed open.

Hannah peered around the bathroom door. "Gideon!"

He held up her traveling bag. "The motel called me."

She moved to the bed and sat down. "It's good to see you."

He set the bag on the bed beside her. "I've come a couple of times, but you were asleep."

She pulled the bag into her lap and unfastened its latch. "Yeah, I was unconscious for a few days, and then I slept a lot. I get to leave tomorrow."

"Where to?"

"A man named Dr. Lehman found my aunt."

A broad smile shifted his deep wrinkles and loose skin in different directions. "That's great."

Hannah dug through her bag until she found the anatomy book Dr. Greenfield had given her. She pulled it out, glad to have it in her possession again. "Gideon?" She opened the book and slid her hands across the slick pages. "How do you make decisions? I mean, you said you were on your own really young. How'd you know what to do next?"

He chuckled. "Ain't much to decide when you're tryin' to survive. Each day sort of decides for you."

Hannah nodded. He was right, although she hadn't realized it until he said it.

He tugged at his baggy pants before sitting in the chair across from her. "But when there is a choice, trust what you know about yourself. What do you know about Hannah?"

She shrugged.

Gideon crossed his arms over his large chest. "Well, let me tell you what I know. You know how to take blind steps and trust you'll have what it takes to face whatever is ahead. You're strong enough to pay the price of your decisions—even if it means staying in a run-down motel by yourself." He paused. "What has you so spooked that you're confused about everything after you've gotten this far?"

That was what she wanted to know. His words about taking blind steps and trusting she had what it took to face the next step seeped into her thoughts.

She drew a deep breath and whispered what was really nagging at her. "Every decision has a price."

He gave a hearty nod. "Every lack of decision has a price too." His gravelly voice rumbled through the room.

She traced the image of the respiratory system with her fingertips. "I was raised Amish, Gideon."

"Had that one figured out the first moment I saw you. It's part of the reason I was interested in helping you even if you weren't eighteen yet. The Amish are exacting people, so I understand needing to get free. You came here looking for more than just your aunt. If you hadn't found her, you were determined to find a job and get by. What's so different now?"

She pulled the book to her chest. "Before I left home, I told myself that, if need be, I'd carry my fears with me, but I wouldn't let them stop me. But it's not that easy."

"Oh, so it's *easy* you're after. See, now that you know what you want, you'll know what to aim for."

She studied him, feeling a little less confused. That wasn't what she wanted. She wished for guarantees, and there were none. She tapped the book. "I want knowledge, Gideon, medical knowledge. I think it's what I've always wanted, but…"

Gideon raised his hand, motioning her to stop talking. "No one else may ever understand how scary this is for you, a young girl facing her dreams with little money and even less formal education. But what do you want from life in five, ten, or twenty years from now?"

She knew the answer to that. "I think I need to talk to Dr. Lehman. If I'm gonna go to school while taking a chance on working with the Amish, I want it to be with him at the birthing centers—whether he thinks he needs me or not."

As Faye drove along the back roads toward Zabeth's place, it was hard for Hannah to believe how things had turned around for her, and she said a silent prayer of thanks. Across from Hannah in the backseat of the beat-up vehicle, Zabeth chatted with Faye. When they passed the same fine brick home Hannah had seen the last time she was out this way, an eerie sensation slid up her spine. It was only last Monday that Gideon had driven her down this street in search of her aunt.

She'd called Dr. Lehman last night. At first he said he didn't have the need or the time to train her, but when she laid out all the coincidences that had brought her across his path, the phone line went completely silent, as if he needed time to absorb it all. Finally he spoke, agreeing to hire her. Of course he had concessions she had to agree to, like using some of her recuperation time to train on his office computers. The decision she'd made about stepping into the medical field to work with the Amish felt good, and she could only hope it was right.

But she knew she'd never really feel free unless… "How hard is it to change a last name?"

Zabeth's eyes grew large for a moment. "I can help you do that."

Faye glanced back at her. "You'll need your birth certificate though."

Her heart skipped a beat as she turned to her aunt. "I didn't bring it."

Her aunt reached across the seat and patted Hannah's hand. "A good lawyer will know how to get a copy of that through a courthouse without your Daed or anyone else knowing a thing. Trust me."

Faye slowed the vehicle and turned right onto the same long driveway Gideon had taken her on. "I wouldn't suggest changing your first name. That's too hard to get used to. But women are pretty comfortable changing their last names. My boyfr—husband, Richard, can put you in contact with people who can help."

Faye passed the dilapidated house Gideon had brought Hannah to last week. A few hundred feet beyond, after a row of thick hedges, she slowed almost to a stop before turning right. Hannah couldn't believe how close she and Gideon had been to her aunt's place when they gave up and left.

Zabeth's forehead wrinkled. "What would you want your last name to be?"

"Well, I wouldn't want it to be the same as yours. My parents might think of that—" She lost her train of thought as the car topped a knoll and a small log cabin came into sight. Smoke swirled out of its chimney, reaching toward the heavens before it dispersed. A porch ran the length of the cabin, and there was a clothesline with dresses shifting under the frigid breeze. Her eyes misted at the sight.

When the car came to a stop, Hannah climbed out, never taking her eyes off the view before her.

Faye slammed her car door shut. "I told you there wasn't much to it."

Around the side of the yard Hannah could see a place where the snow lay in neat rows. A garden was buried there, just waiting on spring.

She cleared her throat and turned to tell Zabeth it was perfect. *"Es iss fehlerfrei."*

Zabeth nodded and wrapped her in a hug. *"So denk ich aa."* She drew back, looking into Hannah's eyes. *"Des iss aa alleweil dei Heemet. Ya?"*

Hannah's emotions were too thick for words as Zabeth told her this was her home now. She fell into her aunt's embrace. "Ya."

"Okay, guys, the least you could do is insult the place in a language I can understand."

Hannah stepped back, too surprised at Faye's words to respond. Her eyes moved to Zabeth, and they broke into laughter. Obviously Faye didn't understand Zabeth's love for this place.

"Come on, child." Zabeth led her up the front steps while talking over her shoulder to Faye. "Perhaps such a fancy Englischer as yourself can get Hannah's bag out of the trunk and join us in our fine abode…if you can stand it."

Faye huffed, but she went to the trunk of the car.

The front door was made from three vertical planks of rough-hewn wood and had a tiny peephole drilled in it. Zabeth opened the door, and they stepped into a small, scantly furnished room. One lone bulb hung from the middle of the ceiling. Nothing hung on the walls but a plain, round clock. A tiny kitchen sat off to the left, too small for even the dining table to fit in it. The table and chairs were in the main room. To her right, two open doors led into what Hannah figured were bedrooms. The place was more plain than Hannah's own home—except for a shiny piano. She stared at the instrument.

Zabeth shrugged. "I guess that does look a bit out of place." She gestured across the room. "I have a stereo and stacks of CDs in my bedroom that fit no part of this landscape either."

Faye closed the door with her foot and dropped Hannah's bag in front of a couch that had clearly seen better days.

Zabeth slid out of her coat. "So, Hannah, you will need to have a last name. What will you choose?"

Hannah's cheeks burned. She'd put the name on the application, but saying it out loud was asking a lot. "I like the name Lawson, although I don't know why. It just came to me when I was filling out an application."

"Well, Miss Lawson, your room is right there." Zabeth pointed to one of three rooms directly off the living room. "The room next to it is mine. The bathroom is the only other door, and it doubles as a coat closet. That's the whole place." She chuckled.

Faye sat and propped her feet up on the coffee table. "You know, Richard works construction and travels a lot for business. So if you want to write letters home now and then without revealing your whereabouts, he could drop them in the mail for you from different cities and states."

"I did promise to write to Mary, Luke, and Matthew, and I'd like to do that without worrying about being traced."

Zabeth set her glass in the sink. "And by this time tomorrow, I hope to know who Mary, Luke, and Matthew are."

Hannah cocked her head. "And I'll know all sorts of things about you too, right?"

Zabeth paused. "Sure." Grasping the scarf at the base of her neck, she tightened the knot.

Hannah swallowed. "What illness were you referring to in your letter to Daed?"

Zabeth shook her head. "It doesn't matter. You turn eighteen soon enough, and I'm here now."

Hannah took a sip of her water. She only had *now*?

Chapter 14

Heavy-eyed from a long night of wrestling with her fears and her conscience, Mary placed the "Past and Future" quilt onto the brown paper and folded the sides around it. Having come to some decisions, she was grateful for the rules of privacy over her medical charts. Unfortunately the reason for her thankfulness boiled down to one goal: deception.

Just a tad—nothing major like Hannah had done.

But Mary wasn't going to lose Luke—no matter what it took.

The doctor told her that she appeared to be healing quite well, although he wanted to read the results of her next CT scan before he allowed her to resume all her previous duties as the only daughter of a large family.

He'd been quite firm about her not marrying unless she was very careful for several years not to get pregnant.

Easy for him to say. He believed in using birth control.

After explaining a hundred things that sort of made sense and sort of didn't, he'd looked her in the eye. "The baby would be fine, but a pregnancy for you, specifically the labor and delivery, could be very dangerous. I don't know how to make it any plainer, Mary. You either need to use birth-control pills or not get married for at least five years. Okay?"

She grabbed a piece of scrap material and wrapped it around each side of the package. No, it wasn't okay. Thoughts of the latest news she'd learned pressed against her. It was a bad enough indication of her future that Hannah had up and left two weeks ago. Now Mary had learned from her father that Zeb Lapp had done the same thing some twenty-two years ago—abruptly moved away from his Mamm, Daed, and all his siblings. All her father remembered about Zeb's arrival here was that something had happened in his old community that didn't sit well, so he left. When he decided to settle in Owl's Perch, the bishop verified he was in good standing with his old church and welcomed him into their fellowship. That information, along with knowing how quickly and easily Hannah had decided to leave on her own, had opened Mary's eyes to what could happen. She didn't think Hannah knew what her father had done. She doubted if Luke knew it, but pulling up stakes and leaving everyone behind was in their blood. Had to be.

Luke was so frustrated with his family and the church leaders for how they'd handled Hannah that Mary feared if he had to wait on her to marry him, he might just leave Owl's Perch for a spell. Through the grapevine, she happened to know that Mervin Stoltzfus had already offered Luke a job in Lancaster. And while he was working and living there, he might find someone else. But if she and Luke began to make plans to marry in the next wedding season, then he'd be hers forever.

She tied the material into a bow. It was time to give this to Paul and see if Luke had talked to the bishop yet. Maybe he'd give them permission, and she wouldn't need to fudge on the truth.

She suddenly felt flushed.

When the doctor took follow-up pictures of her injuries from the buggy accident, if it all looked healthy and strong, then why should he tell her to wait?

Doctors. Sometimes they wanted too much say over her life. Regardless of what that doctor wanted, she would begin her instruction period in April and join the faith in September—all in preparation to marry Luke the next wedding season.

She grabbed her shawl and the package. Buggy rides made her miserably nervous since the accident, but what was on her mind was more important than trembling hands and an aching chest. Besides, she'd talk her Daed into dropping her off there and then going on. Luke would see to it she got back home.

Paul wanted a chance to talk to Luke before he returned to school and work on Monday. He'd missed two full weeks of school and was no closer to knowing where Hannah was than before. It was time to try to catch up and graduate as planned. Hannah had made her decisions, and if she changed her mind, he was fairly confident Luke would contact him.

He used the newly worn path between Gram's and the harness shop. When he walked inside, an Amish man was at the counter ordering something from Luke.

"Welcome. Be with you in a minute." Luke didn't even look up as he spoke the words.

Taking a moment to look out the window, Paul noticed that Gram had a visitor pulling into her driveway. Oddly enough, it looked like the Millers from his Mennonite community in Maryland. If it was, that probably meant their eldest daughter, Dorcas, would be with them.

The car stopped and let Dorcas out before pulling on up to Gram's house. Dorcas opened the mailbox and checked inside it, then closed it and started walking toward Gram's. Paul was curious but turned his attention back to Luke as he told the customer bye.

"Hey." Luke grabbed a poker and stoked the wood stove, though the place was already way too warm to suit Paul. "Mary wanted to see you. She should be here any minute."

"She wanted to see me?"

Luke chuckled. "You see somebody else I could be talking to?"

Paul shook his head, not at all sure he cared to hear what Mary might have to say to him. He'd met Mary for the first time two weeks ago when he'd demanded to see Hannah and then sped off without hearing her out.

Luke set the poker next to the stove. "I spoke to Matthew the other day. The church leaders are looking for a midyear replacement for Elle. She teaches at the school. If they don't find one, she'll finish out the school year, but then she's going away with her dad for six months. Matthew and I are thinking about using that time to expand our businesses by joining under one roof—E and L Buggy, Harness, and Horses."

Paul frowned. "Buggy, harness, and horses? All three? I don't think I've ever seen all three combined into one business before."

Luke wiped his hands down his workshop apron. "It's a hunk to try to pull off, but if it works out, we'll add three new rooms onto his place, and this building will become storage."

"But can't you do just as well separately without such a big gamble?"

"See, as it stands, when one of us needs to travel to get supplies or drum up business—like when Matthew needs to deliver things to an out-of-state customer—the shop has to be closed for several days. But if we work together, one of us can mind the shops while the other travels for business. Plus we can combine our energy and creativity and really make a go of this business."

"Sounds like some long days of hard work ahead."

"Yeah, if Mary isn't well enough for us to wed this season, I might rent out our upstairs apartment and even spend a bit of time in Lancaster. Mervin Stoltzfus needs some help and is willing to pay good money and give me a place to live while I'm there."

"But if you're trying to build a new business here, why would you take that on too?"

Luke moved behind his work counter. "A new business needs money. I can make good money working part-time for Mervin and sink that money into E and L. Besides, the new business shouldn't require both of us to be here all the time. Just don't tell Mary about the Lancaster deal. It's something I'm only thinking about."

"Sure. I can keep it a secret…" Paul rubbed his fingers and thumb together. "For a price."

Luke laughed. "Renting out my apartment upstairs will be a good source of income, but the idea of living at home when I'm not in Lancaster is a miserable one."

Through the small window to his left, Paul saw Dorcas walking toward the shop. Gram must have told her where he was. He appreciated Dorcas's opinion on certain things, but she seemed to have taken on the powers of a bounty hunter of late. Though tempted to moan and complain to Luke about her, he resisted.

He turned his attention back to Luke. "Maybe while you're enlarging Matthew's shop, you should build yourself a place to sleep there. You could take your meals and showers at the Esh place or with Mary's folks."

Luke's face lit up. "That's a good idea." He slapped Paul on the shoulder. "I knew you college boys were good for something."

Paul chuckled. "Thanks."

The door popped open, and Dorcas entered with a smile. "Sign says you're open for business. Should I have knocked?"

Luke turned. "Knocking isn't necessary when we're open. Can I help you with something?"

"Luke," Paul said, "this is Dorcas Miller. She's a friend of my mother's, and she's not in need of any leather." *Unless we can use it to strap her to a chair in her house in Maryland.*

Dorcas entered the shop, but before she closed the door, they saw Mary getting out of a buggy.

"Mary,"—Luke went to the front door—"come warm up by the stove."

Mary had a package in her hand as she paused just inside the door. "Did you speak to the bishop?" Her voice was hushed, but Paul heard her clearly.

Luke put his arm around Mary's shoulders. "I tried, but before I got started, he said there's too much going on right now for him to make any more decisions. He'll talk to me in a few months."

Disappointment covered Mary's face before she looked at Paul and held the package toward him. "I brought you something."

He felt nailed to the floor.

"Hannah and I made it, but she did most of the work, and it was her idea."

Paul's mouth went dry. He slid the brown paper off, letting it fall to the floor.

Running his hand over the thick, textured quilt, he couldn't believe Mary was giving him anything.

Mary smiled as a tear trickled down her cheek. "It has more of Hannah in it than anything else we own. Luke and me wanted you to have it."

He stared into Mary's eyes, wondering how she could so easily forgive him. He looked to Luke, who nodded his approval.

"I don't know what to say."

Skimming her delicate hands across the fabric, she whispered, "It'll keep you warm until Hannah returns."

The realization that Mary hadn't given up on Hannah's marrying him sat well with Paul. Suddenly the quilt meant even more. "Thank you."

Dorcas stepped forward. "This is amazing. Did you say Hannah made this?"

Mary stroked the blanket. "Yes. She called it a 'Past and Future' quilt. It has patches of cloth from our childhood and patches of material from fabric we plan to use for our clothing in the future."

A car door slammed, breaking the spell of the moment. The front door opened, and a man strolled in.

"May I help you?" Luke asked.

The man pointed toward his car. "I'm thinking about getting a leather cover for my seats."

"Sure." Luke went behind the counter and pulled out a catalog.

While Luke prepared to assist the newcomer, Paul turned to Mary, touching the edging of the quilt. "I can't believe you're giving this to me. Just saying thank you doesn't seem like enough."

Chapter 15

*I*n spite of the whispers inside her head that made her feel crazy, Sarah refused to give up on her quest. Hannah's baby was alive and well, and someone had to know where. She tugged on the reins, guiding the horse to slow down. Since she had baked some goods for others in the community, Mamm had said she could go out visiting for a while as long as she didn't go on foot or by bike. Clearly Daed hadn't told her where he'd found Sarah during her last trip out *visiting*.

She pulled the buggy off the side of the snow-and-muck-covered dirt road just before the knoll. On the other side of this hill, maybe two hundred feet away from her, sat Luke's shop, and not far to the side of that was Mrs. Waddell's place.

John Yoder had come to the Lapp place, saying that he'd dropped Mary off at Luke's and that he thought he saw Paul Waddell inside the shop too. Sarah would bet next year's garden that the whole lot of them were meeting to discuss Hannah's baby. She needed to know where the child was, and they weren't going to tell her, so she'd just have to eavesdrop. Looping the reins around the fence, Sarah shivered. It was awful cold for March, and her wool cloak did nothing to stop the winds from howling up her skirts. Ignoring the constant murmuring in her head, she mapped out the best way to get to Luke's harness shop without being seen. Pulling her cloak more tightly around her shoulders, she followed the side of the ridge that ran parallel to the shop. From the top of the ridge, she saw the roof. She sneaked behind the tree line that went up to the back edge of his place. Hurrying to the side of the shop, she kept a watch on the surrounding yards in case someone was out and about. Then she flattened her body against the side of the building.

If it was any season but winter, the windows would be open, and she'd be able to hear as clearly as if she were standing in the room with them. As it was, she couldn't hear anything. She carefully peered in the window. Mary, Paul, and a young woman she didn't recognize stood around looking at something in Paul's hands. Luke was at the counter, showing a man some leather goods. As she adjusted to get a better angle, the woman beside Mary spotted her. The stranger, wearing a different type of prayer Kapp and cape dress than the Amish, gave Sarah a slight nod.

Sarah jumped back from the window and plastered her backside against the clapboard siding, hoping the girl didn't call attention to her. There would be no way to explain herself, and then everyone would be sure she was crazy.

Sarah heard the door to the shop open.

The girl from inside peered around the side of the shop. "Hi," she whispered, "my name's Dorcas."

A mixture of miserable feelings kept Sarah from finding her voice. If the fields weren't so covered in snow, she'd take off running just so she wouldn't have to answer any questions about her secretive behavior.

"You look awful worrisome over something." The girl smiled and stepped closer. "Anything I can help you with?"

Dorcas's kindness surprised Sarah, and she pointed at the building. "They say anything in there about a baby?"

"Why, no."

Sarah pressed her back against the house, trying to escape her stare. "My sister had one. They told me it's dead."

Dorcas's eyes focused on her, making her feel like the stranger cared what she thought. "Are you Hannah Lapp's sister?"

She nodded. "You know her?"

"I haven't met her, but I've heard plenty about her. Just last week I heard she came up pregnant outside of being married. I also heard her baby died."

Shivers ran up and down Sarah. "It ain't true. I know it's not."

"She wasn't pregnant?"

Sarah trembled. "Yeah, that part's true. But it didn't die. Those who say it did must've made it up."

Dorcas stepped in close and placed her hands on Sarah's shoulders. "Maybe we should talk to someone and tell them what you're thinking."

"You can't tell anybody. Please. If my Daed finds out…"

Lowering her hands from Sarah's shoulders, Dorcas glanced around. "Are you Sarah?"

Sarah nodded. "What are they all looking at in there?"

"Mary gave Paul some kind of quilt. It had a name."

"The 'Past and Future' quilt?" Sarah shrieked before covering her mouth. Lowering her voice, she continued. "She can't give that away to some half Englischer. That quilt's got pieces of Lapp and Yoder family history in it. It even has material from my childhood. It's an Amish quilt for Amish folk."

Dorcas looked distressed before she turned and left without saying anything else. Feeling as if she'd been slapped in the face, Sarah hurried down the snow-trodden path she'd made on her way to the shop. Hoping no one saw her and that Dorcas didn't tell anyone she'd been there, Sarah topped the hill and turned right, then began traipsing back toward the road.

"Sarah." A whispery male voice echoed around her. Eeriness shot through her. The image of a newborn's hand reaching through the snow dominated her mind. She feared she'd pass out from the horror of it.

The voice came again. A hand grabbed her. She screamed.

"Sarah, it's me, Paul."

She wheeled around.

The man was breathing hard, puffs of white clouds filling the air. "I didn't mean to startle you. I've been trying to catch up with you."

"The quilt's not yours. Mary had no right—"

His face reflected no annoyance that she was speaking her mind. "I can see where that'd be upsetting, but the quilt was Mary's to do with as she chose." He shoved his hands into his pants pockets, and she realized he didn't have on a coat. His blue eyes studied her face. "How are you, Sarah?"

Put to silence by his kindness, she folded her arms, feeling like a demanding child. "I'll not accept any part of my sister's past or future being in an Englischer's life. And don't try saying you're not one—your ways speak louder than your sect's name."

He gave a slow nod. "I'm not trying to be Plain or English. My goal is to find the path God wants me to take. If parents or friends or relatives have a problem with that, they need to take it up with Him."

"Where is she?"

A wobbly smile crossed Paul's lips. "I've told you already. I honestly don't know."

The sound of snow crunching underfoot made them both look behind Paul. Dorcas carried something in her arms as she waved a hand and scurried toward them.

Visibly catching her breath, Dorcas held out a coat to Paul. "Mary and Luke think we've gone back to Gram's."

Paul took the jacket and slid his arms into it, then turned to Sarah. "We know Hannah is safe. She left a message on the Yoders' phone the other day."

Sarah kicked a patch of snow. "I wasn't asking about Hannah. I want to know about the baby."

Paul took a step back, looking baffled. "Is that who you were asking about when you were at Gram's?"

Sarah huffed. "Of course."

Concern crinkled his forehead. "I assumed you were asking about your sister. Every answer I gave you was about Hannah. I didn't mean to confuse you."

Paul glanced at Dorcas before looking at the horizon. His eyes lingered there, and then he ducked his head. "I'm sorry, Sarah, but Matthew and Luke buried the baby just a few hours after she was born."

The silence that filled Sarah lasted only a moment before the horrid shrieking started again. All she had wanted was to put Hannah in her place, and now she was guilty of shedding innocent blood.

Sarah tore out toward the horse and buggy.

"Sarah, wait," Paul called after her.

She ran faster, crunching new snow underfoot. After crawling between the slats in the fence, she grabbed the reins and climbed into the buggy. Releasing the brake, she hollered for the horse to get moving. By the time she settled onto her seat, the horse was in motion. "The baby can't be dead. She can't be."

Paul was briefly tempted to try to stop Sarah, but she needed much more help than a few minutes could give, especially from an outsider.

Hannah loved her deeply; he knew that. Still, he doubted if either sister realized how much of a connection they had with each other. A lot of Hannah's letters over the years had centered on Sarah and how to help her cope with her anxiety. But he could only guess at all that had happened between these two young women in the past year.

Dorcas cleared her throat. "We probably better head back before we're missed."

The buggy moved farther down the road and closer to Sarah's home. Poor girl, she lived under Zeb Lapp's roof, with no safe place to share the pain she was carrying.

Dorcas tugged at his coat. "You okay?"

He turned and looked into her green eyes. "You did right to come get me, and I appreciate what you said to Sarah." Paul sighed. "It's such a mess, Dorcas. Everyone needs to see Hannah and set things right. Maybe I'm wrong not to go after her."

"I'll say it again, Paul. If I were Hannah, I'd never forgive you if you made me return to this situation. She knows how to reach you."

Paul nodded. "I've told myself all that over and over."

She gave a nod toward the narrow, snow-trodden path. "Can we go back to the shop to get your quilt and then go on to your gram's now?" She turned and started down the trail.

As he fell into step behind her, resentment welled. Hannah was intentionally covering every trail, and she was good at it.

But maybe by the time he graduated in May, she would relax in her determination to use untraceable phone numbers and to send letters without giving a hint as to where she'd gone.

Or maybe she'd return by then.

Chapter 16

The warm May air buzzed with insects. Under the shade of a black oak, Matthew held Elle's soft hands and listened as she tried to convince herself she was doing the right thing.

Her father sat in his idling car, waiting for her. Although Matthew refused to say it aloud, it irked him that the man who had abandoned his daughter and left her in the hands of Amish neighbors more than a decade ago had returned wearing an air of superiority and hoping to keep his daughter from joining the faith. Matthew feared that Sid Leggett dished out more pain and confusion than he knew. Matthew had concerns about what this could mean for Elle and him, but her removal from Abigail and Kiah Zook's home, for even a few months, meant far more than Sid understood.

The back door of the Zook home opened, and Abigail came out carrying a basket of home-baked goodies. The Zooks were childless, and their years of raising Elle had brought them untold peace as they slowly came to accept they'd bear no children of their own. Elle's desire to be baptized into the faith and take an Amish husband had filled them with a hope nothing and no one else could have given them.

Sid stepped out of his car, took the basket from Abigail, and placed it in the trunk.

Matthew released Elle's hand. "I'll be here when you get back." He didn't ask for reassurances from her that she would return. What could she possibly say—besides promises she might not want to keep by the time the agreement with her father was up? Sid had told her that if she'd come away with him for six months, he would honor her desire to join the faith and marry Matthew.

Sid had wanted her to leave with him when he showed up in March, but the school board had been unable to find a replacement until last week, so Elle ended up almost finishing the school year. Sid had been determined to pull her away as soon as possible, probably afraid that, given more time, Elle and Matthew would connect so strongly she might refuse to go. Because Sid had managed to need Elle regularly over the last three months to help with his newly owned bakery, she'd spent most of her weekends with him in Baltimore.

Matthew thought it unfair to Elle to show his displeasure, so he had kept his mouth shut and been as supportive as he could.

Kiah came from the barn and walked to Elle. He wrapped her in his arms. "This is the right thing to do, Elle." He pulled back from her, looking into her eyes. "You were born English. If that is your destiny, then embrace it. If it is not, then you'll be glad for the proof this time away brings you." He kissed her cheek.

Abigail moved forward. "You'll always be welcome here, Elle. If you choose not to be baptized in our faith, you'll be just as welcome then as you are now."

Elle squeezed her tight. "I'm coming back." She looked to Sid, who stood at the back of his car, watching her. "I'm coming back. I'm joining the faith and marrying Matthew."

Her father closed the trunk. "We need to be going, Elle."

She turned to Matthew. "I'll talk him into allowing me to come for a visit, maybe two, between now and then. I agreed to no phone calls, but we can write each other."

"He just wants you to be sure about your decision, Elle. I don't much like it, but I understand it."

Elle kissed his cheek. "I love you, Matthew." She whispered the words against his skin before going to the car.

She waved as Sid pulled out of the driveway.

"Care to come in for a spell?" Kiah asked.

Matthew wasn't in the mood for visiting or eating, but he nodded. "Abigail, did you save any of those goodies for a couple of hungry men?"

She smiled. "You know I did."

It was late afternoon when Matthew climbed into his buggy to head for home. It'd be quite a long drive back to Owl's Perch, but he needed the time alone. The rhythm of the horse's hoofs against the pavement seemed to echo: wait, wait, wait, wait. The phrase beat against his temples, making him even more restless.

Matthew had a sudden urge to chop several cords of wood. He drew a deep breath. But what could he do? Sid was her father, and he'd begged Elle to give him a chance, saying he was sorry he ever left her. If she did this his way, he'd give his blessing on her decision to join the Amish faith. He'd even agreed to return for visits regularly as she raised her children right here, near Abigail and Kiah.

Matthew rode toward home in silence as the horse's hoofs beat out the tempo. Wait. Wait. Wait. Wait. But he wasn't sure whether he was waiting for Elle to marry him or to find out she never would.

Paul sat in the large auditorium, dressed in his blue cap and gown. Navy banners with gold tassels hung behind the department heads, who sat on stage facing the graduates. Rows of seats held what looked to be more than a thousand excited family members. His family was here, but they were far from thrilled. When he tried to hold a conversation with them of late, his voice seemed to echo back to him, unheard by his family.

He studied the rows of people in the stands until he spotted Dorcas. She waved, grinning broadly. He gave a slight dip of his head. She was excited enough to make up for his whole family. The work it had taken to get to this point hadn't bypassed her understanding in the least. Tonight had been long awaited, although he'd just as soon not participate in the ceremony. They could have mailed him his diploma. But he was here because missing it would have caused continual hassles from his college friends.

His meeting with the preacher and bishop had come and gone and would come again in a few months. He was honest, and they found little fault in the way he'd lived his college life. But his secret relationship with Hannah caused them to bristle. It wouldn't have bothered them to bring an Amish girl out of her community and into their fold—except she gave birth to a child before disappearing. Her pregnancy issue aside, the men expressed displeasure in Paul for keeping Hannah a secret from his family. He should have been more open with them.

The meeting ended with both men strongly requesting that Paul never attend another game and that he repent quietly in front of them. Paul said he'd consider their words. His lack of hearty agreement to do as they requested didn't earn him any respect within the church or his family. The men prayed with him before they left, hoping he'd get on the right path to avoid his name going before the church.

But Paul had something else on his mind that his church leaders would be worried about. He wanted to continue his education and get a license in counseling. If families knew how to really talk and listen to each other, they'd bond rather than rip apart. He hadn't had this desire until his life exploded and he saw how easily relationships were damaged and how hard they were to fix. He wanted not only to understand more about family dynamics and counseling, but he wanted to help others learn how to communicate. So while Hannah worked her way back to Owl's Perch, he'd stay busy taking more classes and serving umpteen hours as an intern. Hopefully he'd come to understand more of what had brought such destruction to Hannah's and his relationship and how to help them rebuild.

Life's journey involved so many changes and winding roads that it was often hard to tell which direction was the right one. He'd never have imagined Hannah and he would end up like they had—separated when they were finally capable of being together. He wondered what Hannah was doing and if she realized what today was—or if she cared. It was hard imagining Hannah these days. He'd only seen her as the Amish girl next door, and he couldn't envision who she was now.

She'd been gone two and a half months. How much longer would it take before she ran out of the money Matthew had given her and realized she couldn't make it by herself? No one could. He considered himself reasonably independent, paying for his own education and living expenses, but he had a home in Maryland and at Gram's place in Pennsylvania, not to mention his church as well as Gram's—all filled with people who were there to help him.

Who was there for Hannah?

Standing barefoot in the budding garden, Hannah scraped the hoe along the soft dirt, ridging the potatoes as the last rays of sunlight danced on the toiled earth. Pausing, she gazed out over the fields. It was no wonder Zabeth didn't mind living with such sparse niceties; the setting made up for any possible lack.

At the edge of the knoll sat a long wooden bench where she and Zabeth spent the evenings when Hannah was home. Each morning Hannah joined Zabeth at the piano, where she was learning praise songs she'd never heard before. She liked starting out the day hearing music fill the home and then carrying the tune with her wherever she went. They'd also spend a few minutes reading a Bible verse and saying a prayer. Zabeth looked at life differently than anyone Hannah had ever known, and she enjoyed learning from her.

Closing her eyes, she listened to the songbirds' low tones as they began to settle for the night. The two and a half months she'd spent in Ohio had been beyond her wildest hopes—in spite of her heart yearning for things that could never be.

Zabeth's health.

Paul's love.

A memory of Paul surfaced, and she shuddered at the ache it caused. Hoping to find more peaceful thoughts, she jabbed the hoe into the dirt again. The counselors at the rape center said thoughts and emotions that ran in opposite directions were normal. They also said it helped to work through a wide variety of thoughts and feelings until a person could settle on something, like reading through a menu of meal options.

Though she found it hard to believe, she almost liked going to the center for the group-therapy sessions. Sometimes when they talked, a piece to her life's puzzle seemed to float right into her hands. A lawyer Zabeth knew had taken care of getting a record of Hannah's birth certificate and changing her last name.

The pleasure of the warm soil against her bare feet and the rich scent of earth filtering through the air faded as her latest round of frustrations with Faye crossed her mind. It was becoming clear that her first impression of Faye had been too kind. The woman seemed to think Zabeth ought to baby-sit for her at any time. When Faye had brought her two children by a few hours ago, Hannah had to insist she not leave Kevin and Lissa for the night. Thankfully the whole scenario took place out front, before Faye even got her children out of the car and while Zabeth was down for a nap. It was ridiculous for Faye to assume the children could spend the night when Hannah was on call and might have to leave. There was no way to know whether Zabeth would have the strength to tend to Kevin and Lissa or not. It wasn't something Faye should be willing to test—for Zabeth's or her children's sake.

The screen door creaked, and Zabeth held up a glass of ice water. Hannah propped the hoe against a tree and went to her aunt.

Zabeth smiled. "The garden has never looked better, even in my best days."

Hannah took the glass and helped her aunt down the steps. "Did you love gardening or just need the produce?"

Zabeth dipped her head. "Love is for people and music, not for plots of dirt." She whispered the words conspiratorially while chuckling.

Hannah laughed. "Yeah, but without that dirt, it'd be hard to feel anything but hunger."

Zabeth wrapped her arm around Hannah's waist. "You're too practical to be just eighteen." Her laugh joined the rustling of the leaves, and Hannah took in the moment.

They slowly made their way to the bench. Here, with her beloved aunt, Hannah's world was sewn together with the most delicate of threads. But it was a seam that could begin unraveling at any point. A second round of combination treatments for epithelial ovarian cancer had severely weakened Zabeth's heart. How long it would be before the illness grew more powerful than Zabeth was anyone's guess.

But five weeks ago the doctor had given Hannah permission to take on as much as she felt up to. Since then she'd done her best to juggle her time with Dr. Lehman and with Zabeth. She hadn't begun studying for her GED yet. Every spare minute not working with Dr. Lehman was spent at his clinic learning how to operate the computer, how to use the Internet, how to log patient info into the computer, and how to answer patients' health questions.

A peaceful silence settled between them as they watched the last rays of sunlight make shadows that turned and flipped in the breeze that shifted the leaves of the huge oaks. Darkness took over, and the birds slowly grew silent while the crickets and frogs picked up the chorus.

Zabeth drew a deep breath. "Did you get that letter to your parents written and sent off like I asked?"

Hannah gave a slight shrug. "I wrote it. It's basic and not worth much, but I gave it to Faye, who gave it to Richard to mail while he's in Columbus this week."

"That's my girl." Zabeth patted Hannah's leg. "Now, tell me how things went at the clinic last week."

"I've already told you. And each time I repeat it, I feel like I'm bragging."

"But I'm so proud of you, Hannah-girl. And so happy you've come to live with me." Zabeth nudged her shoulder into Hannah's. "You're proving how smart you already are without even taking any formal classes. Tell me again."

If her aunt knew she was procrastinating on getting her GED, she wouldn't be nearly as proud. The idea of schooling was intimidating. A one-room Amish school filled with family and friends was one thing. But attending North Lincoln Educational Center for her GED and later going on a college campus—well, she just dreaded it.

Hannah nodded and talked about how well her time at the Amish clinic was going. Dr. Lehman had set her up in a quiet office, and each patient had to meet with her privately before seeing him. Hannah asked a few basic questions and then shared what she'd been taught in a manner fitting the Amish lifestyle. Sometimes a bit of Pennsylvania Dutch slipped into the conversation. Once in a while someone would ask about her background, and although anxiety tried to steal her courage every time, she briefly explained she'd grown up in an Old Order Amish home. Without fail, the women told her they'd pray for her to return to her People and her parents, as she should, but they always assured her they'd not tell anyone but God about the ex-Amish girl who worked at the clinic.

Hannah paused, taking a sip of her water. "The calls to come in and see me have increased so much that we're trying to think of ways that groups of women could come at the same time."

"I've got an idea." Zabeth pulled several patches of fabric from her pocket. "Quilts. One afternoon a week Amish women can gather in a closed room with you at the clinic and ask and talk while working on a quilt. Their husbands won't think a thing about them doing community service work, and once they are there, the conversation can have a specific health topic or just roam onto whatever's on their minds." She bobbed her head up and down. "That way the shyer women who aren't comfortable seeing you one-on-one to ask questions will come to a gathering and just listen while they're sewing. You could even have a box for them to drop in questions, and you could answer those during the gathering without anyone knowing who asked it."

"Zabeth," Hannah gasped, "that's a wonderful idea. Dr. Lehman will love it." She brushed an ant off her foot. "You know, it's so odd. The thing I feared most about this job, that Old Order Amish women would turn my name over to their bishops and eventually make a trail for Daed to find me, isn't something to fear at all. They seem to accept my choice—even if they're praying for me to choose otherwise."

Zabeth reclined against the bench's wooden back. "I think you've underestimated how strong and loyal the Plain folk are. You were ostracized because of a misunderstanding and a set of circumstances no one knew how to deal with. But the People have tons of inner character, even your father in all his stubbornness."

Hannah gave a nod, unsure what to think. She took another sip of water. "I love what I do at the clinic, especially answering questions the soon-to-be-married or young married girls have about women's health, the marriage bed, and having babies."

"Are you still being asked questions you can't answer without talking to Dr. Lehman?"

"All the time." Hannah's body flushed hot with embarrassment even now. Talking to Dr. Lehman about intimate subjects wasn't comfortable. "It seems there's no end to good questions. Why, even Dr. Lehman doesn't always know the answers. Sometimes he needs time to research before he can respond."

She breathed in the evening air and tried to settle her emotions. "Dr. Lehman has received permission from the hospital management for me to shadow him when he goes to the newborn nursery and the neonatal intensive care unit."

"I've heard tell that some of those babies don't weigh any more than a pound."

Hannah nodded. "Because of the hospital's policy, I can't handle the babies, but I can observe and learn. My first time to do that is next week—"

The phone in the side pocket of Hannah's dress rang out, jolting both women. Their laughter echoed off the hills as Hannah answered her phone.

"Hannah, Jeff here."

"Hi, Dr. Lehman."

"I know it's nearly bedtime, but we have three women expected to give birth tonight, and I could use an extra set of hands. And you could use the experience. Do you think it's too late for Faye to give you a lift to the clinic? I'll pay her extra this time, and I'll give you a ride home sometime tomorrow."

"Faye can't, but Gideon probably can since I warned him you might need me."

"The term is *on call*, Hannah. You're on call this weekend."

"Hang on." She looked questioningly at Zabeth. She might be on call, but leaving Zabeth didn't always sit well.

Zabeth smiled. "You go, Hannah-girl. Grab every chance you get to learn."

She nodded. "Dr. Lehman, I'll try Gideon. But if he can't bring me, I'll hitch up Ol' Gert."

"No. I don't want you riding by horse and buggy in the dark. Besides, by the time you get here, all three babies could be born—and celebrating their first birthday." He chuckled at his joke.

Hannah stood. "I'll be there within the hour, even if I have to find another driver."

The freshly cleaned newborn in Hannah's arms seemed to look straight at her, asking where he was and who it was that held him. Wordlessly, she diapered him, wrapped him tightly in a soft blanket, and put a little knit hat on his head. She'd expected dealing with babies to cause her grief since she'd buried her own three months ago and would never have another one, and in many ways it did. But even then her feelings stayed on an even keel better than she'd expected, and she felt good about responding professionally.

The birthing center was once a small, older home, and the residence made a peaceful place to learn about using computers and the basics of midwifery.

Nancy, one of Dr. Lehman's resident midwives, came up beside her. "I've got the blue room. Jeff has the green. Casey just arrived. She's assigned as my RN for the night. As soon as you're done in here, Dr. Lehman needs assistance."

Hannah nodded as she nestled the newborn in his mother's arms.

"Thank you." The mom looked straight into Hannah's eyes, and she felt it in her soul. She stared into Hannah's eyes as if she'd had something remarkable to do with the new life that had, with great effort, moved from the woman's womb to her arms. Dr. Lehman and Nancy had done the remarkable stuff, although just being in the room made Hannah feel like she was part of something as important as the dawning of time. Oddly, seeing how much joy labor and delivery could bring to a family brought no sense of joy to Hannah, only awe at the observable science of life.

"He's a fine, healthy boy—"

"Hannah," Dr. Lehman gently called from down the hall. "Now, if you can."

"Excuse me." She scurried to the green room, peeling off her latex gloves. She tossed them into the trash and grabbed another pair.

"The cord is being a bit of a problem," Dr. Lehman instructed. "Stand on the X, as I showed you last week, and just follow my directions."

A tremor shot through her, and she couldn't budge. "Can't Casey..."

"Hannah," Dr. Lehman's calm voice was a front for the frustration he was trying to hide. "Casey's assisting Nancy right now. Everything will be fine. I just need some help."

She moved forward.

Time passed in odd increments of panic and delight as each person on duty worked most of the night to deliver the three healthy babies. The sun was peeping over the horizon as Hannah finished bathing the newest arrival.

She laid the babe on the changing table and was wrapping a prewarmed blanket around the little girl when her phone rang.

Hannah turned to Casey. "Can you take over for me?"

"Sure."

Hannah removed her gloves while stepping out of the room. She tossed her gloves into a trash can and pulled the phone from her pocket. "Hannah Lawson speak—"

"Hannah, it's Faye." The slurred words interrupted her. "Listen carefully because time is running out. I took the kids by GymberJump yesterday. It's an all-night stay 'n' play, but they close at six. Someone has to pick them up by seven, or they'll call social services. Can you do it?"

"Faye, what's going on?"

Faye broke into sobs. "Can you do it? I called Martin." She sniffed. "He's not willing to get them."

"Why?"

"Please, Hannah. You can't let social services take my children."

"Do you have a phone number for this place?" Hannah jotted down the number as a male voice barked that Faye's time was up. "I'll get there somehow. Where are you?" The line made an odd noise. "Faye?" When there was no answer, Hannah closed her phone.

Without a clue what was going on, Hannah tucked the piece of paper into her skirt pocket and went to find Dr. Lehman.

Inside his office, Dr. Lehman rested in his chair. "Yes, Hannah. He spoke without opening his eyes.

"How did you—"

He opened his eyes and sat up straight. "When you walk, only an occasional floorboard creaks. When it's one of the midwives or nurses, their uniforms make a scrubbing sound." He rubbed his face. "Your dresses continually become more modern though." He pointed to her yellow dress with small flowers and tiny white buttons running down the front. "Maybe one day you'll be comfortable wearing scrubs."

She doubted that. A modest dress was one thing, but pants? "I need to get to a place called GymberJump by seven. Do you know where it is?"

"Never heard of it. Is it in Alliance?"

"I don't know, but I have a phone number."

He let out a long sigh. "We need to add driving to your list of 'must learn.'" He shifted the mouse to his computer. "I'll get directions to this place and take you, but you owe me."

"Owe you?" Hannah laughed. "You took me on when you didn't need me, and you have your trained staff constantly teaching me stuff. I can't possibly owe you more than I already do."

"I think you owe me another apple pie." He grabbed a pen and jotted down some information from the computer screen.

"You didn't even ask why I need to go there."

"I figure if you need me to know, you'll tell me." Clutching the paper in one hand and his keys in the other, he glanced at the clock. "We have forty minutes to get to a place that's supposed to take fifty. We'd better move."

Hannah glanced at the directions and then at her watch. "We've only got six minutes."

Dr. Lehman squinted against the morning sun. "I think it's just up here on our left. Keep an eye out for the sign." He yawned. "When we get there, I've got to doze for a few minutes."

Hannah searched each sign, desperately hoping they'd make it in time.

She spotted one with the right words and pointed to the driveway. "That's it. We found it."

He slowed his vehicle and made a left turn. Pulling to the side lot under a huge oak tree, he pressed a button to lower a window.

Hannah opened the car door before he came to a complete stop. "I don't know how long this might take."

Dr. Lehman drew a sleepy breath and tilted his seat back. "The longer, the better for me."

She got out and closed the door. Trying to gather her confidence, she entered the brick building through a set of glass doors. Anytime she was away from Zabeth's cabin, the strangeness of her new life made her feel awkward and fainthearted. But she did her best to ignore the emotions while she went on about her business.

A thirty-something, brown-haired woman at the counter looked up. Black makeup circled the edges of her eyes. "You here for the Palmer kids?" Her irritation rang out loud and clear.

"Yes."

She got out of her office chair. "This is going to cost extra, five dollars for every minute. The policy clearly states that any child left here for night care is to be picked up by six. It's one minute before seven. I was just about to call social services."

"Five dollars a minute? But Faye didn't—"

"I'll need your ID and a fax from one of the parents stating you have permission to take the children. The signature on the fax will have to match the one we have on file."

Hannah placed her ID on the counter, wondering how Faye would send permission through a fax machine. "Where are Kevin and Lissa?"

"They're in their sleeping bags, snoozing in one of the birthday party rooms." The woman lifted Hannah's ID off the counter and frowned. "This doesn't have a photo on it. I've got to see a photo ID."

"I don't have one. Not yet anyway."

The woman shoved the ID back across the counter. "Is the mother sending a signed fax, giving permission for me to release the kids to you?"

"I don't think so. Does she know she needs to?"

The woman shrugged. "She's supposed to know that if the person picking up the children is not on file, she has to send written permission via a fax."

The glass door swung open, and a dark-haired man stepped inside. The scowl on his face deepened as he pulled his sunglasses off. He stepped forward and slapped his driver's license and a credit card on the counter. "I'm here to get Kevin and Lissa Palmer."

Hannah spoke to the woman. "But Faye sent me."

He turned, as if seeing her for the first time. His green eyes skimmed over her before he turned back to the woman in charge. "My signature's on file. If you could speed this up, I'll add a tip to the late fee."

"Sure. She didn't qualify anyway." The woman took his driver's license to the file cabinet. Hannah swallowed, wondering if this was Richard or Faye's brother. "Um, excuse me, but I just inconvenienced my boss to get me here because Faye said no one else was coming."

The man leveled a look at her. "Of course I was coming. Faye knew that." He spat the words at her like she was stupid.

Heat ran through her, as did a desire to spit back at him. "Who *are* you?"

The woman placed his license on the counter. "Everything checks out. You're cleared to go." She pointed to the credit-card machine. "Credit or debit?"

"Debit." The man swiped his card and punched some numbers. "Since I check out with this place as a viable guardian and you don't, maybe you should tell me who you are."

His arrogance left her speechless.

He slid his ID and debit card back into his billfold.

"But you can't just take her children without her knowing—"

The woman pointed to a door. "I'll go get the kids."

He glanced at his watch. "ASAP, please."

"Faye told me no one else was available to pick up—"

"I heard you the first time." He whispered the words, but his tone clearly indicated that he doubted her intelligence. He studied her. "You look younger than most of Faye's friends, so I'll give you a piece of advice. Find a new group of people to hang out with before she and her entourage drag you down too." With his sunglasses in hand, he gestured from her shoulders down. "And what's with this outfit? Trying to pretend you're well behaved so they'll hand over the kids to you? Or was it retro night at the local bar?"

Suddenly feeling outdated as well as stupid, Hannah fought to keep her composure. "You can't just take her children without telling me who you are."

The man scoffed. "If you were half as intelligent as you are cute, you'd figure out pretty quickly that I wouldn't know the kids were here unless she'd sent me. She sent you for backup." He shooed her away from the counter. "When you talk to her, tell her this is the last time she pulls something like this. I'll call the authorities myself next time."

He leaned toward her. An aroma of musky aftershave offended her senses. "Got it?"

Unable to think of one thing to say, Hannah walked out. He had come to GymberJump, obviously knowing the children were here. He had the ID, a signature on file, and had paid the ridiculous late fee. There was nothing else she could do but leave.

Chapter 17

As one hour drifted into two, Martin's irritation with Faye calmed, and he chided himself for his rude behavior toward the young woman at GymberJump. He was sure she was the same girl he'd had a run-in with once before because of Faye, only it'd been dark the first time. At times his sister's behavior seemed to turn him into someone else entirely. And that girl had been in his path when his tolerance for Faye was at an all-time low. Every time Faye and Richard had problems, she took to drinking or drugs. Or maybe every time she took to using, she and Richard had problems. He didn't know. Didn't really even care. But he hated having the responsibility of his niece and nephew dumped on him, and he hated telling them half truths as he tucked them into bed after feeding them breakfast. GymberJump allowed the kids to play on the trampolines until well after midnight. Kevin and Lissa would probably sleep most of the day.

Taking care of Faye's rug rats when she got all strung out had been Zabeth's job before she got sick. If his sister thought he'd start pulling Zabeth's shifts with the children, she was stupider than he'd given her credit for.

He checked his watch. Nina, the daughter of some friends, would be here in a minute so Kevin and Lissa could sleep while he pulled music duty at church. He was running later than he ever had. Tempted to call Pete and just bail on trying to get there before the service started, Martin wondered if Zabeth might make it to church today. A few years ago she was the one who'd drawn him back into going, but her attendance hadn't been too regular of late. At least she'd had her Amish niece helping for the last couple of months.

He stopped cold. Surely Faye wouldn't pull Zabeth's niece, the visiting teen, into…

He spat a curse. Of course she would.

"Somebody tell me I didn't just insult Zabeth's niece." The room echoed his voice, but there was no one there to answer him.

He had been so sure she was the girl he'd argued with on Faye's front lawn one night a few months back, the one he suspected of getting his sister involved with drugs. He pulled his phone out of his pocket and called Pete to say he wouldn't make it to church. As Nina entered the house, Martin left.

Less than twenty minutes later he was driving his Mazda RX-8 up Zabeth's long dirt driveway. He hated taking his car up this rutted mess Zabeth called a lane.

Since she had someone staying with her, he knocked on the screen door rather than just going in.

Zabeth came into view, walking toward him with a cane. "Hi, Martin." She gestured for him to come in. He hadn't seen her since her niece had landed here, because Zabeth had asked him for six to eight weeks of uninterrupted time.

He hugged her carefully. "How are you doing, Zebby?"

"Not bad. It's good to see you, Martin. What brings you out here?"

"Well, I figure if you can't come to church to see me…" He studied her face. She looked happier and more peaceful than ever—and more frail.

"Is that why you're here?" Her voice held a touch of humor, reminding him just how well she knew him.

"Well, no, but it sounded good." He forced a laugh. Sometimes facing Zabeth hurt. She reminded him of everything his family had once been, before the separation, his mother's death, and his sister's guilt.

She gave him a tender smile, like a mom waiting for the real truth. "What's on your mind?"

He hesitated. He couldn't just ask for a description of her niece or inquire where she had been around seven o'clock that morning. If he did, she'd want to know why. He sighed. This was Zebby. She deserved better than the facade he presented to everyone else. He maintained eye contact. "I had a run-in with someone this morning."

She chuckled. "Ah, that explains everything."

He wished he could join her in the laughter. He didn't want her to know

Faye was strung out somewhere, probably too incapacitated to drive, and he had her children. That seemed like too much for her since her diagnosis, although she'd done all she could in the past to help Faye through her bouts. He glanced to the doorway of what had been the extra bedroom. "Is your niece around?"

Zabeth studied him for a moment before shuffling into the kitchen. Martin followed her.

In spite of how little they had seen each other since her niece's arrival, he and Zabeth usually spent time together. Because he had to be at church early for music practice, he paid a driver to bring her to church, and after services he'd take her out to eat, and they'd spend part of Sunday afternoon together. On Friday nights, Zabeth would come to his house, where a gathering of musicians would hang out. But she was less reliable since becoming ill.

She pulled a Mason jar down from a cabinet. "Funny you should ask. A couple of hours ago, not long after she arrived home, she asked me what Richard looked like. That didn't seem to satisfy her, so she asked what you looked like." She flicked the water on and held the jar under it. "Acted like she was just curious, but I didn't buy it. She worked hard around here all day yesterday and then worked all last night at a birthing clinic, yet she's still awake—working the dickens out of that garden on a Sunday." Zabeth plunked some ice into the glass and handed it to him. "Was my niece nearby when you had your run-in with someone?"

He took a sip of water, wishing he had a different answer to her question. "I think the run-in may have been with your niece."

She folded her arms across her waist and stared at him. "I'm gonna say this once. You'll get along with Hannah at all times. Do you hear me?"

"You're not even going to ask how we met or what caused the blowup?"

"Martin, she's all I'll ever have in the way of a blood relative, and she's the most genuine person you'll ever meet. That makes whatever happened your responsibility to fix. And I mean that."

"Thanks, Zebby." He rubbed his hand across his chin. The girl he had the run-in with wasn't all that remarkable, but obviously bias overruled reality. "Where is she?"

She nodded toward the back door. "I saw her move to the bench a few minutes ago. You remember where that is, right?" She cocked an eyebrow at him, humor dancing in her eyes.

They shared a smile, easing the tension. "Yeah. Most of the blisters from building it turned to scars."

She laughed, and he headed for the back door.

"Martin."

He stopped and turned to face her.

"I appreciate that you dropped everything and came here to make this right." She leaned into her cane and drew a ragged breath. "Your sister might benefit from being on the receiving end of that kind of niceness."

Martin shifted the glass of water he held, trying to think of what to say. "Faye only uses anyone who tries to help her." He searched for something honest yet hopeful. "But I'll try to think of a way that might be possible."

Looking pleased with his response, she nodded.

As Martin went out the back door and across the lawn, he thought about Zabeth's words. He knew she desperately needed to see the Palmer family come together again. He just couldn't imagine how that would happen.

Hannah pulled her feet onto the bench and wrapped her arms around her legs. Stifling the rush of negative emotions, she wondered if all Englischer men were so blatantly disrespectful to females. This morning had been hard, although she didn't fully understand why. There'd been something humiliating about staring that man in the face and realizing how much he knew and understood compared to what she knew. Powerless. That's how she'd felt. Only it had nothing to do with him having authority over her.

She missed Paul more than ever right now. Before their relationship fell apart, he never once made her feel anything but appreciated, smart, and fun to be with. Was this new world filled with people like that man at Gymber-Jump—conceited and educated, with the ability to shoot invisible poison darts at will?

But he knew the ins and outs of life, like Dr. Lehman and those mid-wives she worked with.

Whatever else she'd realized this morning, she was now determined to check into North Lincoln's GED program. No more procrastination. The next time she stared some arrogant person in the eyes, she'd be as educated as she could get. Her fears about going to school had shrunk under her new desire to—

"Excuse me."

Hannah jumped before turning in the direction of the voice. Her eyes lingered on him, as if looking into his eyes might explain why the encounter with him had bothered her so much. Finding no answers, she turned away and resumed watching the fields.

"Look, I'm sorry."

If he was waiting on her to talk to him, he'd have a long wait.

He walked in front of her and pointed at the empty place on the bench beside her. "May I?"

She didn't respond.

He took a seat. "I shouldn't have talked to you the way I did. The call from Faye really made me angry. When I arrived, I thought you were some-one else, someone Faye barhops with." He rocked back as if he planned to be there awhile.

A good ten minutes passed without a word being spoken. Surely he'd up and leave eventually.

"Are you going to talk to me?" He looked out over the fields. "I never expected silence. Yelling, yes. Quietness? What's a guy supposed to do with that?"

Propping her chin on her knees, she gave a slight shrug of her shoulders. She wished he'd just go home.

"It's gorgeous here. I helped build this bench. If you knew my skills as a manual laborer, you'd either be impressed or jump off the seat."

She slid her feet off the bench and looked at him. Her mind was zipping with retorts—"If you were half as intelligent as you are good at gabbing…"—but she kept quiet.

Looking away from him, she wondered how much longer he'd stay. The minutes droned on, but he didn't rise to leave.

The man clasped his hands together and propped his elbows on his legs. "You think you could teach other women this trick? I can think of a few who could use some lessons in silence."

His words made her want to tell him what she thought.

"Just say it," he growled in a whispery voice. "I can tell you're tempted to speak. Whatever it is, just say it."

Sensing a little brashness well up, she nodded. "I can think of a certain man who could use that same lesson."

He laughed. "Wow! You looked all sweet and innocent, and then slam." He continued chuckling and held out his hand. "I'm Martin."

She didn't feel any friendlier than when he arrived, but she shook his hand. "Hannah. And you can't just remove Kevin and Lissa so I can't get to them. I told Faye I'd take care of them."

He released her hand. "Nice to meet you, Hannah..."

"Law...Lawson." She stumbled over her new last name, feeling foolish that it didn't just roll off her tongue like it should.

"I don't think Hannah LaLawson is it. Try again."

Zabeth and Faye said it'd be their secret, that only they and Dr. Lehman would ever know the truth.

He looked around as if spies might be lurking nearby, then whispered, "Phone girl?"

She smiled, remembering how much she'd enjoyed the snippet of conversation that day, but now she was disappointed at the man behind the voice and humor. "That was you, wasn't it?"

"Beetle thing. That's me."

A hawk swooped down in the field in front of them and snatched something off the ground. But if he was the man she'd talked to that day at the hospital, then his tolerance of Faye's children in his life was probably very limited.

"You joked about taking her children to an orphanage."

He gave a nod. "Not very funny right now, I know, but at the time it seemed funny."

"You wouldn't really—"

"No, of course not. It was joke. If I was going to dump them somewhere, I'd have let you, a total stranger, pick them up."

"So where's Faye?"

He shrugged. "No way to know for sure, but I'd guess she went to where Richard's been working lately, argued with him, got drunk or stoned, and then crashed somewhere. When she woke, she was either too out of it to drive or too far away to pick up the kids on time." He sighed. "It happens."

Hannah brushed wisps of damp hair off her neck. "It's my fault."

He chuckled. "What— This should be good. Just how is this your fault?"

"She came by here yesterday, wanting to leave Kevin and Lissa, and I refused to let her."

"Really?" He raised his eyebrows. "Zabeth let you tell Faye no?"

Hannah shook her head. "She was taking a nap, and I hurried out the front door when Faye pulled into the driveway. I knew I might get called in to work, so I put my foot down before she got out of the car."

"Good for you. Zabeth can't seem to tell Faye no." He placed his hands on the bench on each side of his legs. "I'm really sorry about this morning. I thought you were someone else, someone I'd seen for just a minute one time."

"Someone you didn't like?"

He nodded. "When it comes to Faye, things get pretty unfriendly before I realize what's happening."

"Oh."

"But you know, I've not been in trouble with Zebby since I was fifteen and took something of hers that'd been packed away in a box." He propped one leg on the other. His mannerisms spoke of relaxed confidence unlike anything she'd ever noticed in someone before.

"What'd you take?"

He cupped his hands, demonstrating. "Some white net-looking hat thing that'd I'd never seen her wear. It was great for catching minnows at the creek."

Hannah knew her eyes were bugging out as she tried to speak. "You used her prayer Kapp to catch live bait?"

"Only once."

Hannah scoffed. "Yeah, I bet."

"So, you fish much, Hannah?"

"Excuse me?"

"You used the phrase 'to catch live bait,' which means you know something about fishing."

Hearing Zabeth rattling dishes, she rose. "I'd better go help. She's probably trying to fix us dinner."

"You know, phone girl, you're not great at answering my questions."

Hannah gave an apologetic shrug as she entered the house with Martin right behind her. As she helped Zabeth get the meal on the table, she was aware of Martin's presence in the room. She silently speculated about the Englischer tendency to be overly friendly when it suited them and rude when it didn't. Were they all this fickle when it came to their beliefs as well?

The mealtime was a bit stilted as the three of them tried to find subjects they could or were willing to talk about. She learned that Martin was twenty-six years old and lived just outside Winding Creek. He was a civil engineer for a company he owned, but he wasn't a registered engineer yet.

"So where does your father live?"

"He and his wife live in Australia. We own some business ventures together, and he's more than fair to me financially, but I don't see him very often—not since I turned eighteen and went off to college."

Hannah knew firsthand the difficulties of trying to stay bonded to someone who was away at college. "I'm sorry he's so far away. Faye's husband is gone a lot too, isn't he?"

Zabeth's movements paused. "Richard is gone a fair amount, but…he's not exactly her husband."

"Oh, I…" Hannah felt like she had said the wrong thing. She was only trying to make conversation, not pry.

Martin took a sip of water. "He's a common-law husband."

Unwilling to ask anything else, Hannah examined his face, hoping for clues in his expression.

He set the glass beside his plate. "That means they've been living together so long even the law's not clear on whether they're live-in lovers or husband and wife. But Kevin and Lissa are too young to realize their parents aren't married."

A wave of nausea caused Hannah to set her fork down. Drugs, drinking, and a live-in boyfriend. "Why would Faye be willing to live like that?"

A look passed between Zabeth and Martin, one that said they knew but didn't talk about it.

Martin grabbed the salt shaker and shook the granules over the roast. "Faye has issues. Big ones."

Hannah smoothed the cloth napkin across her lap. "Why doesn't someone do something?"

He set the shaker on the table. "Like what?"

"I don't know. Isn't there a group of church leaders who could put limits on her?"

Zabeth reached across the table for Hannah's arm. "No, child. The only people who could be informed are the police, and family members don't call the police because someone gets drunk or uses drugs occasionally. It's just not done."

Hannah took a long drink of water, wondering if there wasn't some middle ground between the Amish church authorities, who sought too much control, and Englischer families and friends, who had no control.

"But I don't understand what would make someone willing to live like she is rather than fighting back."

Martin studied her. "I don't know that the kind of clear-cut answer you're wanting exists. Faye has been trouble for as long as I can remember. When I was twelve, our parents separated, and she got even worse. One day Mom and Faye had a huge argument. I don't know what it was about, but Faye stormed out. After a few hours, Mom went to look for her. It was raining, and the roads were bad."

Zabeth shook her head as if Hannah had wandered into forbidden territory. "Their mother died in a car accident."

Hannah took another drink of water, concerned she'd asked too many questions and determined not to make that mistake again. Martin shared the tragedy, telling just enough facts for it to make sense, but something about his tone said there was a lot more to the story.

He lifted the biscuits toward Hannah, offering her one. When she declined, he took one and set the bowl down. Cutting the bread in half, he asked, "So how long are you visiting?"

Zabeth smiled. "She's going to live here."

"Really?" He buttered his biscuit. "There's no car out front, and someone else was driving when you left GymberJump this morning. Are you old enough to drive?"

Zabeth nodded. "She turned eighteen in March."

Martin's green eyes fixed on Hannah, and he smirked. "Then next on the list is a car and driving lessons, right?"

That's what Dr. Lehman had said too, but Hannah shook her head. "I'm not interested, and from what Gideon told me, I can't afford the insurance, let alone lessons or a car."

Martin propped his elbows on the table. "We'll work something out. Every girl needs a way to help me out." He chuckled. "I mean, needs a way to get around."

Zabeth pushed her plate away. "Yeah, having you here with me, buying groceries and getting me to doctors' appointments, has already made Martin's life easier."

He nodded. "The moment she said you were here and would be helping her for a while, I was able to get to some out-of-town jobs that needed my attention months ago."

Zabeth laid her napkin next to her plate. "Did you get caught up on the Malcolm Crest job?"

"Pretty close. Stayed a night there last week trying to get everything straight and back on track."

Hannah enjoyed how comfortable Zabeth was with Martin, how much they seemed to know about each other's lives. "If anyone cares, I'd really rather hire a driver as needed."

Martin pushed back in his chair. "It's settled, Hannah. You're learning to drive."

"But…"

Zabeth grabbed her cane, which was never far from her, and used it to stand. "I'm going to lie down. You two work this out, but I will say, Hannah, that I think it'd be a mistake not to learn to drive with all you have coming up."

Hannah sighed. "I see how it is with you two."

Zabeth stopped behind Hannah, bent down, and gave her a hug. Hannah gently squeezed her arm. Silence between her and Martin prevailed until Zabeth's bedroom door closed.

Martin tossed the homemade cloth napkin onto his plate. "Zebby needs you. And my life is a ton easier since you arrived, but you'll never be all she needs unless you can drive."

"But cars are so expensive."

Martin smiled. "I'll find you a good used one."

"Can I get a loan for it?"

He shook his head. "That won't be needed."

She stood and started clearing the table. "Yes it is. I'll not take a handout."

He rose, grabbed his plate, and followed her into the kitchen. "Keep your backbone intact for Faye, but work with me, okay?"

She set the dishes next to the sink. "You pay for Zabeth's drivers?"

"Or drive her myself, yes."

"Then find me a used car with a small monthly payment. You can apply whatever would be the normal monthly cost of Zabeth's drivers toward the payment, and I'll pay the rest."

He laughed. "Then I'll end up paying the full car payment, plus all insurance and gas, and you'll get money to boot."

"Really?"

He nodded.

"Does she know that?"

He shook his head and held a finger to his lips. "Shh. There's a lot about finances that Zabeth doesn't know. And she shouldn't have to. I cover certain expenses, and my dad takes care of other stuff."

"Faye doesn't know that, does she?"

"She and my dad haven't spoken in thirteen years. And I refuse to tell either of them what's going on in the other one's life."

Hannah studied the man in front of her. If she'd had to deal with Faye for thirteen years, she'd have been out of sorts at GymberJump too. "I forgive you for this morning."

He laughed. "I had to earn it, eh?"

"Saying you're sorry and meaning it are two different things. I wasn't going to ease your conscience if you didn't deserve it."

"Well, phone girl, you'll be a good protector for Zebby where Faye's concerned. I can't tell you how glad I am that the cavalry arrived." He held out his hand.

"The what?"

"Cavalry. Ah, between your being a girl and being raised Amish, I guess that wasn't the best word choice. It's a military term for soldiers who often arrived just in the nick of time and fought mounted on horses."

"Oh, well, thanks. I guess." She shook his hand, but she knew it was Zabeth who had rescued her. Her aunt had caused her to find a life worth living and was urging her toward the freedom to live it.

Chapter 18

Rays of late-afternoon sun streamed through the broken clouds as Paul drove into Gram's driveway Friday evening. It had been his ritual since he graduated to come to Gram's every weekend, mostly in hopes of hearing something about Hannah from Luke, Mary, or Matthew.

He parked the truck and got out, then headed for the house. This was the summer he and Hannah had dreamed of. Graduation was finally behind him. He would be living with Gram full-time if Hannah were here. Instead, he was entering graduate school next fall and spending thirty-two hours a week as a caseworker in Harrisburg. He no longer lived in the on-campus apartment but rented a one-bedroom place halfway between Harrisburg and Owl's Perch. It made more sense to keep moving forward in life than to spend every moment in Owl's Perch, hoping to hear something about Hannah. Becoming a counselor was heading in a different direction, but the goal was the same—to help others. Rather than spending his life rescuing children from bad situations, he hoped to reach out through counseling before things in a family got that far off track. With all he and Hannah had been through, this new step would fit well into the next phase of their life.

The snows were long gone, and the fields were lush with greenery. The grass grew faster than he could control. It'd take him from sunup to sundown to cut Gram's ample yards tomorrow. A rectangular patch of odd-looking weeds caught his peripheral vision, and he stopped before walking to the edge of it.

Hannah's garden.

It was hers more than his, even though they'd worked it together. She loved it: smelling the soil, working the land, producing a bumper crop from tiny seeds. He always figured it was symbolic of the hope she carried for life, and he loved that about her.

He reached down and pulled up a clump of weeds by the roots. Then another. And another.

A need to plant seeds and watch the fruit of them grow to a harvest nudged him. Hope, from the size of a seed to full harvest—that's what he needed. Dusting off his hands, he headed for the house. After telling Gram he was home and that he'd be in the garden if she needed him, he went to the barn to get the rototiller.

He filled it with gas and cranked it, and his whole body vibrated with the machine as he directed it toward the garden. While walking slowly down the rectangular patch of earth, tilling the soil, Paul wondered if his gift to A-Yom Muilae had arrived and if the little girl liked what he and Dorcas had picked out for her.

When someone called his name above the roar of the machine, he stopped. An Amish woman about his mother's age stood at the edge of the garden. He turned off the rototiller and wiped the sweat from his forehead.

"Hi." He stepped forward.

She stood in silence. His best guess was that he was looking at Hannah's mother and that she thought he knew nothing of gardens to begin planting the first part of June. She cleared her throat. "I'm Ruth Lapp."

"Paul Waddell." He held out his hand, and she barely shook it. He glanced toward Luke's harness shop and saw a horse and buggy parked there—probably hers.

"I…I was hoping to have a word with you—now, if you will."

"Sure." A smile crept to the corners of his mouth. Her reserved but polite succinctness reminded him of Hannah. He motioned toward the porch. "Care to have a seat?"

She shook her head. "I'm needed at home. I got two things on my mind, and I'll tell ya up front, one is sort of a way to haggle for what I want."

Well, this woman seemed to have little in common with her husband. She was calm and forthright.

"You have my full attention." Paul used his hand to block out the sun's rays that were coming from behind Mrs. Lapp.

Her gaze moved over the garden. "Sarah told me a few weeks back that she talked to you the first week Hannah was gone and that you helped her a lot. I want you to know I appreciate that. She has a tougher time with life than any of my other children. I never knew a body to get so nervous."

"How is she?"

Pain seemed to flicker in her eyes. "She keeps…searching for things, making her behavior every bit as hard to explain as it was the first week Hannah went away."

Paul figured Sarah needed more help than the few minutes he'd had with her. "I'd be glad to talk with her again, do whatever I could to help her. Because I'm taking courses about these areas, I know of some good professionals who could help her—"

Mrs. Lapp held up her hand, causing him to stop in midsentence. "Our community wouldn't take too kindly to that idea. Besides, Sarah's always been flighty. It's just her way." She reached into the bib of her apron. "I wanted to show you something." She pulled out an envelope. "Hannah wrote to us a few weeks back. I've been debating whether to share it with you or not, then Sarah told me about your talk with her."

The two months of sleepless nights spent pacing the floors, praying for Hannah, all seemed worth this one moment. Maybe this letter would lead him to her. Maybe she was coming home. Maybe…

Paul took the envelope and noticed it contained no return address, but the postmark indicated Columbus, Ohio. That was about six hours away.

He turned the envelope over and read the words on the outside.

But the words were disappointing.

I gave this note to the husband of a friend to mail while he was on
a business trip.

So Hannah hadn't mailed it from where she was living. He wasn't surprised, not even deeply disappointed. He had come to peace with God on this issue. Hannah needed time. He opened the unsealed envelope and pulled out the letter.

Greetings,

Please tell all who are interested that I'm doing well. I have a job, and
my employer is very kind. He has patiently trained me, and I hope
I'm learning fast enough that he's pleased with me. Life here is inter-
esting. I seem to be sandwiched between the Plain life and the Englischers' life. Day to day is strange among the English, but in many
ways they are much like the Amish, some easygoing, others uptight.
I cannot say more, for I haven't been here long enough to know what
I think about many, many things. I am truly doing well and hope you
are the same.
     Hannah

It struck him how formal this was compared to the note he'd received
from her with "Dearest Paul" written as a greeting and the epiphany she'd
shared with him. Unlike the paper in his hand, she'd revealed parts of her true
self to him, and that gave him hope. Still, her words made it clear she needed
more time away before she knew what she thought about many things. He
refolded the letter, grateful for every word.

"Thank you for sharing this with me, Mrs. Lapp." He slid the note into
the envelope.

She pushed a clod of dirt with the toe of her shoe. "I figured it was only
right to share it. But to be honest, I'm hoping to use it to get what I want."

A little amused at her boldness, he held the letter out to her. "If it's your
leverage, you shouldn't have let me read it first."

She searched his face before they shared a small laugh. "I guess I won't
make a good businessperson anytime soon."

"Mrs. Lapp, I haven't heard from Hannah other than a letter she left for
me with Matthew and one she mailed within a few hours of leaving Owl's
Perch. The second letter was much like this one, no return address. Its postmark said it was mailed from Pittsburgh."

"Do you think that's where she is?"

"No. That's a hub for Amtrak. I think that's probably where she changed
trains before heading elsewhere."

She gave a solemn nod, looking pained beyond what her lack of tears showed. "Thank you. If you hear from her, you'll let me know, right? You'll come to the house and…"

He didn't mind going to the house, even if he was not welcomed by Hannah's father. "I'll let you know. But if she doesn't want to say where she is, I won't tell that part."

She clenched her lips and drew a deep breath. "I understand. But if she does contact you, please tell her to write to her Mamm and give me an address where I can write to her. I can keep it a secret if she needs me to…just like you and she did." Her voice broke, and a sob escaped her before she clenched her jaws and gained control.

"Yes, Mrs. Lapp. I give you my word."

She pointed to the rototiller. "I'll let you get back to your work."

Paul held out his hand, needing some way to make physical contact without daring to lay a hand on her shoulder. "I appreciate that you came here and let me read the note. It helps."

She shook his hand, and without another word she strode toward Luke's old harness shop, where her horse and buggy stood waiting. He was glad she'd come to see him, and her note made him more sure than ever that Hannah just needed time away from her family. She had a job and wouldn't return as soon as Matthew's money ran out, but she would return. He felt sure of it.

Chapter 19

*G*ideon got out of the car at the same time Hannah did.

"You're staying?" Hannah's nerves were bad enough without an audience.

Gideon shut the car door. "Last time I dropped you off at some unfamiliar building, you wound up in an intensive care unit, fighting for your life."

That thought did nothing to calm her nerves. She headed for the DMV building. What she wanted to do was stand in the middle of the DMV parking lot and just scream at the sheer frustration of constantly battling to catch up with everyone else her age in this Englischer world.

Well, that was silly. She'd never stand somewhere and scream. That'd be downright useless—not to mention embarrassing, although her boundaries of what was embarrassing kept expanding.

Ignoring the rogue thoughts, she entered the building with Gideon right behind her. She had all her papers in order, including a statement from her doctor that she was in good health. Martin had explained that not everyone needed papers from a physician, just those who'd been hospitalized or unconscious in the past six months. He'd wasted no time bringing a driver's manual by Zabeth's place for Hannah to study. She had to wonder how many rituals she'd go through before the events of each day stopped molding her into someone unrecognizable.

Gideon took a seat. Hannah stepped behind the last person in the shortest line, hoping she would leave here with her learner's permit.

Sometimes she missed the routine of everyday life among her people. Aside from her garden at Zabeth's, nothing in her life was similar to before. Right now a day of doing laundry by a wringer washer and rinsing the items by hand sounded like a pleasant escape. It was what came with those tasks that kept her rooted in this constant storm of newness—that and the fact she'd never leave Zabeth.

When it came to being pushed into the fullness of the Englischers' life, Martin was the one behind her, shoving. She hadn't been there when he'd dropped off the driver's booklet, but that didn't stop him from making it clear he wanted her learning how to drive—yesterday.

That'd been nearly two weeks ago, and she'd been at North Lincoln, talking to Rhonda, the office manager, about what had to be done to earn a GED. North Lincoln was an old elementary school, a three-story, red-brick building snuggled in the midst of an older neighborhood—not nearly as intimidating as she'd expected.

Rhonda was probably twenty years older than Hannah and really nice. By the time Hannah had toured the building and asked way too many questions, she didn't feel so hesitant about trying to get her GED. It was all a matter of taking one step at a time and studying until she was ready for the next step. There was no set timetable for achieving her goal. Rhonda said whether it took her two years or two months was nobody's business but Hannah's— and her instructor's. There was no way Rhonda could know how much her words meant. For a brief spell in her life, Hannah had stopped feeling like an oddball—until Gideon pulled in front of the DMV building. She drew a deep breath, hoping she wouldn't have to face Martin tonight and tell him she'd failed her first test in the Englischers' world.

And, pass or fail, she'd have to see him tonight. Zabeth woke with a bit of energy and wanted to be at tonight's music gathering at Martin's place. There would be fifteen or so people Hannah didn't know, all playing musical instruments and singing songs she'd never heard. She'd hoped to get out of going by being on call, but Dr. Lehman had insisted she take the night off.

The world she now lived in and the one she'd been raised in seemed to battle within her constantly. Each pulled her in an opposite direction, as if she were the rope in a tug of war. She wanted to experience new things, and yet the moment she did, she questioned if it was the right thing to do. Sometimes her only reprieve was during the Bible study time with Zabeth each morning and evening.

When she read the Word, life made sense. When she went out to live it, confusion dogged her. Among the Englischers, everything was subjective: modesty, stewardship, needs, wants, and even honesty. Nothing seemed to be black and white—just a hodgepodge of folks trying to figure things out as they went, depending on the situation.

"Next," a man called without looking up.

The person in front of Hannah stepped forward. A nervous tingle ran through her. She would need to move forward in a few minutes. If she passed, it'd be another step into the stress-filled world of the Englischers, but there always seemed to be a bit of hopeful news along the way. Like the fact that North Lincoln Educational Center also had a School of Practical Nursing right there in the same building as the GED studies and pretests.

In Rhonda's words, that was way cool.

The man behind the counter gestured for her. His face was void of anything resembling friendliness. Martin and Gideon had both warned her about the DMV staff.

She laid her stack of papers on the counter. "I'm here to get my learner's permit."

He took the papers and read through them. "Do you live at this address?"

"Yes."

"Are you registered to vote?"

"No."

"We can do that here."

"No thank you."

He scowled and slid a paper toward her. "Fill in your Social Security number here."

Hannah wiped her sweaty palm down her dress before taking the pen in hand and following his order.

The moment she was done, he took the paper back. "Look through the eyepiece and read the bottom line." His voice was as empty of emotion as his face.

She stepped over to the vision-testing device. Reading the letters aloud one by one, she wondered if the man was paying any attention to her accuracy or was just going through the motions.

"You pass." He pointed to the sidewall. "Fifth computer. Just follow the prompts."

"The prompts?"

"The screen will tell you what to do. Just do it. It'll make sense once you get in front of it."

Hannah reached for her papers.

He put his hand over them. "I'll keep these for now."

She crossed the room and sat in front of computer number five, hoping she knew enough to operate it without asking for assistance. Following the prompts, she was soon reading questions and clicking on answers. The questions had blanks and multiple-choice answers.

"A broken _____ line separates…"

A broken <u>harness</u> *line separates the horse from its buggy, leaving the driver unable to steer the buggy and yet moving onward, horseless.*

She read the question again, chose an answer, and clicked Next.

"If your car stalls on railroad tracks, you should…"

…have been in a horse and buggy. A horse would never stall on a railroad track. It might bolt at the sound of a train whistle and not slow for a good mile. But stall? Never.

Trying to stop the instantaneous visualization of horses and buggies and think instead about cars and highways, Hannah realized her biggest problem wasn't operating this computer but rather controlling her internal wiring.

Staying on the trodden path surrounded by the ever-growing grasses of the hayfields between Esh and Yoder property, Mary hurried to find Luke. The long-awaited meeting with the bishop was supposed to have begun some thirty minutes ago, so it was probably over by now. She wiped a bead of sweat off her neck, fussing at herself for sitting down in her cushioned rocker, feeling as sleepy as she did. She had fallen sound asleep and had awakened with a start. If she hadn't been so uptight about today and unable to rest well for weeks, she wouldn't have fallen asleep unexpectedly.

As she topped the grassy hill, she spotted Luke, facing away from her with his forearms on the split-rail fence. The bishop stood beside him, talking. Luke nodded, but his stance—with his shoulders drooped—was not that of a man receiving a favorable decision.

Tinges of nervousness rippled through her as she took in the scene. Without having heard the conversation, she was sure the bishop's decision was no.

Of course he hadn't made a decision they wanted to hear. The marriage bed was about trusting God, not about man deciding the timing and delivery of a family's future. This she knew deep within her, and the truth of God's sovereignty within the marriage bed sat well with her, except she intended to marry Luke this coming wedding season—doctor's permission or not.

Paul had lost Hannah—at least for now, maybe forever.

Elle might never return to wed Matthew.

Mary wasn't going to wait and see what lay ahead that might cause Luke and her to suffer the same fate—no matter what it took.

But could she lie to him? The whole idea of lying made her queasy. Surely there was another way.

Bishop Eli caught a glimpse of her as she came near. He smiled. "Hi, Mary."

Luke turned around, his eyes carrying a distant look even though he, too, smiled at her.

The bishop nodded as he used his bony hand to point toward Yoder property. "If I'd realized you were planning to walk the fields in this heat, we'd have met at your place."

Mary eyed Luke, wondering what he was thinking. "It didn't make sense for Luke to lose any more work time than necessary, Eli. How are you today?"

"I'm doing right well. It's my fervent prayer that you do well with the news I brought to Luke." The man paused, watching her intently.

He wasn't a bad man, even if his decision over Hannah had been harsh. The church leaders had no way of knowing that making Hannah spend a night alone would have such consequences. Eli could be strict and sometimes wrong, but Mary never doubted his heart in the matters. Besides, what happened with Hannah… Well, she was quite pregnant and had kept it a secret. Nobody could put that on the bishop's shoulders.

Eli removed his hat, wiped his brow, and put his hat back on. "I was telling Luke that none of us, the church leaders or the community, can allow a marriage, knowing you're too weak to carry a child."

She wondered why it'd taken him so long to say the very thing he'd known from the beginning—the Old Ways did not tolerate birth control. It'd been nearly five full months since Hannah had left. Maybe he'd waited until Luke was calm about the reasons for Hannah's departure and had no desire to blame anyone for the way events had played out.

Eli looped his fingers through the triangle where his suspenders attached to his pants. "Luke's request is a serious matter that goes deep into the heart of trusting God beyond our own understanding."

That was it!

She didn't have to lie. She just needed to trust God.

Luke offered her a lopsided smile before looking at Eli. "I…think you're right. Conceiving a child should be left in God's hands. It's the way things should be, but I appreciate that you considered it."

Eli studied him, as if he'd expected a bit of an argument. She knew better. Luke was asking because she wanted him to. He'd mentioned several times over the last few months that it might be right to wait rather than use some intervention to not conceive…

Eli held out his hand. "You've taken this like a man who's submitted to God. I can't tell you how glad I am to see such maturity."

Luke shook his hand.

Eli focused on Mary. "I'll see you during instruction…"

He left the sentence unfinished, and Mary knew it was more of a question than a statement. He wanted to know if she'd choose to stop going to class. Without the instruction classes, she couldn't be baptized. Without the baptism, she couldn't be wed.

Without Luke, none of it mattered.

"Yes, I'll be there each Sunday until time for the baptism, and…" She stared at the ground, unable to look Luke in the eyes. "And soon after, Luke and I will marry. I…I spoke to the doctor, and…I mean…" She could feel Luke's gaze boring into her. "He said the results of the last CT scan, along with my other progress, shows that I'm all healed." She held on to as much honesty as possible and hoped they didn't hear what she *wasn't* saying. She hadn't talked to the doctor recently, but the last time he'd read the CT scan, he did tell her she was healed and everything looked good.

"Well, how do you like that?" Eli chuckled. "That's why you were late. You were talking to the doctor?"

Her skin felt like it was on fire as she gave a slight nod.

Eli slapped Luke on the back. "I guess this means you won't be partnering with Stoltzfus's Harness in Lancaster after all, eh?"

Mary lifted her eyes, realizing all the rumors about this were true and wondering if Luke would ever straight out tell her of his plans.

Eli smiled. "Well, I'll just leave you two to talk, and I'll see you both on Sunday."

She was still gawking at Luke when she heard the sounds of the buggy pulling onto the paved road.

Suspicion covered Luke's face. "You talked to the doc—"

She gestured toward him, stopping him in midsentence. "What's this about you partnering with somebody in Lancaster?"

Luke's countenance changed. "It was just an idea, a way of making extra money while we waited for your doctor's okay to marry."

Determined to keep him right here in Owl's Perch, Mary whispered, "We h…have permission."

Luke smiled. "So I heard." He stepped forward and took her hand.

The warmth of his touch spread through her. Like the bishop said, this matter went to the heart of trusting God. The CT scan said she was healed. The doctor had given her a clean bill of health, except he'd said…

Never mind what he said.

"Mary?" Luke placed his finger under her chin and lifted her head. She looked into his brown eyes.

There was nothing wrong with trusting God in these matters.

"We can get married this wedding season," she whispered.

Hannah squeezed the steering wheel as she pressed the brake.

Gideon looked out the open window on the passenger's side, acting like he wasn't nervous about Hannah wrecking his older model Buick.

From the backseat Zabeth tapped Hannah on the shoulder. "You think we'll get to Martin's sometime tonight?"

Gideon and Zabeth both broke into laughter. Gideon drew a heavy breath. "I ain't even sure we're gonna get to the end of the lane before morning."

Hannah didn't respond to their playful jests. This machine had real horsepower, about two hundred of them according to Gideon, which made no sense to Hannah. If she had two hundred horses hooked to a buggy, she couldn't imagine it being able to go sixty or seventy miles per hour—although however fast it went, the trip would completely tear a buggy to pieces. She was fairly sure that stopping a vehicle at a red light would be easier than stopping two hundred horses.

Coming to a stop at the end of the driveway, she pushed the lever for the blinker up and waited for a car to pass. Zabeth gave directions as they eased onto the road and sweat inched down Hannah's back. It was quite a drive to Martin's place, and the car seemed much hotter than a buggy.

"We made it...before it's over," Zabeth chirped. "It's that second house on the left. Right there."

The second...

Hannah turned into a paved, circular driveway and stared at the two-story, smooth-stoned home with high arching windows and stacked-rock columns. "Zabeth?"

Zabeth chuckled. "Yeah, we're at the right place. His father taught him how to invest money and gave him a few thousand to invest each year for his birthday since he was twelve. Something about making some savvy choices in the stock market before he even graduated from high school."

She put the car in Park, set the brake, and turned the engine off. She pulled the keys out and passed them to Gideon. "You want to come in for a while?"

"Nah, it's been a long day of driving and…being driven." He smiled. "Since Martin will see to it you guys get back, I'm ready to go on home."

Hannah paid him while Zabeth went to the front door. She made arrangements for Gideon to pick her up the next day and then went up the steps to Martin's home.

Soft, unfamiliar music pulsated through the room as she entered through the opened door. Zabeth was busy talking to people Hannah didn't know. Martin was nowhere in sight as she closed the door behind her. Polished woods and colorful rugs covered the floors. Fancy lights with fans hung from the ceiling, and the walls were covered with photos. Seemed to her the place looked awfully shiny and clean for a single guy.

She meandered into the adjoining living room and stopped in front of a group of pictures on the wall. Her heart palpitated at the sight of photos of family events. Melancholy washed over her as she stared at a picture of Zabeth when she was a few years older than Hannah, holding a one-year-old in her arms and a little girl by the hand—probably Martin and Faye. Another frame had a man and woman standing behind a young boy and older girl. That had to be Martin and Faye with their parents. Several photos had Martin in sports uniforms; one showed Faye wearing a ballerina costume.

"Hey, phone girl." Martin spoke over her shoulder.

She glanced at him before pointing to a photo. "Did Faye take ballet as a child?"

Martin shook his head. "That's a Halloween costume."

"Oh." She touched the silver-framed picture of Zabeth holding a baby. "Is this you?"

His confident nature seemed to melt as he nodded.

Hannah looked around the room. "This isn't how I thought a single man's place would look."

A half smile crossed his lips. "I hired a decorator, who put everything that was worn, torn, or too guylike into the storage room. And I have a cleaning lady who keeps everything shiny and tidy—when I'm not baby-sitting Lissa and Kevin." He rolled his eyes. "So, I heard you inched…I mean, drove here tonight."

She mimicked his roll of the eyes.

He laughed. "Now if you practice that a little, you can tell a person off without ever opening your mouth."

From somewhere she heard Lissa chattering. "Is Faye here?"

Martin shook his head. "The musicians always hire a sitter for our parties. And never underestimate the power of Faye to use any available sitter." He slid his hands into his pockets. "How'd things go at North Lincoln?"

She still chafed under the guilt of pursuing an education, and yet part of her was overjoyed at the opportunity—torn between the ways of her people and the choices offered in the Englischers' world, without a hint of how to pray her way to peace.

She cocked an eyebrow. "You and Zabeth talk too much."

"Nah. Not all that much, but she's a tad interested in you getting on your feet ASAP…" He shook his head. "Sorry. I tend to think about things like they're a business deal and what needs to be handled in what order, and I just saw concern for Zabeth's health flicker through those brown eyes."

Hannah drew a deep breath. "The cancer *is* in remission. Even with the heart condition the treatments caused, she could live for…"

"Yeah, I know." He stepped closer. "And no one wants that more than you and me, but she'd like to see progress made, okay?"

She nodded and opened her purse. "You won't believe this, but the Robert T. White School of Practical Nursing has a program that starts at the first of the year." She pulled a small stack of informational papers out and passed them to him. "Admission testing takes place in time for me to begin the two-year program this January."

He read through the first page, not looking all that impressed. "Are you sure you want to go here?"

"Ya. It's perfect for me. It's close; it's part-time. The classes are at night, so you'd be available for Zabeth while I'm in class. *And* it's even housed in the same building where I'll study for my GED, so I'm pretty comfortable with it." She pointed to the criteria for admissions. "This plan gives me a chance at passing my GED and getting everything in order to begin the two-year course without having to wait until next fall."

He flipped through the papers. "But you won't finish with an associate's degree, just a diploma. There are other schools, nursing schools where you'd have a degree at the end of two years and really good schools where you could earn a bachelor's in four…or a little more."

She took the papers from him. "But I *can* do this one." Clearing her throat, she shoved the stuff back into her purse. "It's only part-time plus a clinical rotation every other weekend. Martin, I've never spent any time in a classroom that wasn't a one-room schoolhouse. Maybe you stepped right into a college campus full-time, but this feels right for me."

His green eyes narrowed. "I didn't mean to…" He held her gaze before offering a smile. "I apologize. This is a huge step, one that makes you happy, and I should've looked at it from your perspective, not mine. So let's try again." Martin pointed to her purse. "That school is perfect, and I think you'll be comfortable there. If you want a better chance of passing the entrance exams, we'll get you a tutor, the GED study book, and whatever else you need to prepare for nursing school. I'll find you a car to drive by the time you get your license. And—"

She held up her hand, interrupting him. "Did you invent the to-do list or something?"

He grimaced. "Sorry. We'll talk about it later." He motioned. "Come on. I'll give you a quick tour and introduce you to everyone."

The kitchen, music room, and open spaces, as he called them, were incredibly lavish. Upstairs he had an entire room devoted to a huge-screen television. He called that the entertainment room. It had leather couches, stained-glass shades on lamps, and bookcases with glass fronts. Lissa and

Kevin were sprawled on the couches, along with some other kids, none of whom even looked up from their show.

She followed him back downstairs and into the kitchen. She'd known he had money because he spent it so freely, but she didn't realize this was what having money looked like on the inside: mahogany cabinets, tiled floor, stainless-steel refrigerator, oak table and chairs, and two granite islands.

Martin opened the fridge. "Care for a bottle of water?"

She looked at the shiny faucet, set in green marble, then back to him. "Is there something wrong with the tap water?"

He closed the refrigerator. "Not that I know of. But bottled water tastes better, and then the container can be thrown away."

"I'm fine, thanks."

"How about some food?" He held a platter of fruits out to her: strawberries, bananas, apples, and red grapes.

She picked several grapes off a vine and popped one into her mouth. Their conversation was disrupted by what sounded like a herd of cattle clomping down the stairs.

Martin propped his forearms on the island. "I guess they got to a part in the movie where they were willing to hit Pause."

"Yeah, I guess so." She held up a grape. "These are really good."

"Hannah," Lissa shrieked and wasted no time jumping into Hannah's arms.

She squeezed her. "Hi, sweet girl. Been riding or feeding any horses lately?"

Lissa's silky black hair and dark eyes were almost a mirror image of her mother's. "Nope. Didja bring Ol' Gert with you?"

Hannah laughed. "I tried carrying him, but he complained."

Lissa giggled. "No you didn't. Ol' Gert's too big."

Hannah glanced at Kevin, who stood back, watching. Until this moment she hadn't realized how much the young boy favored his uncle, in spite of having straight, light brown hair and fairer skin. "Hi, Kevin. How's the bug catching going?"

He poked an elbow into his uncle's thigh. "Uncle Martin ain't much good at catching bugs, but he has no problems squooshing them."

Hannah's eyes met Martin's. "You know, I'd think a beetle thing would show a little respect for his kind…and hope I don't start squooshing all bugs."

He laughed. "Watch it, phone girl."

She turned back to Kevin. "Maybe we can catch some tonight and hide them from the bug squoosher."

"Yeah!" Kevin's face lit up. "She's good at catching fireflies, Uncle Martin."

"Well, then that's one more thing she can do that I don't have to, right?" He set the water bottle on the counter. "We'll begin jamming in a few minutes. You'll enjoy seeing just what Zabeth adds to the group. She's really good and not the least bit shy."

A teenage girl walked into the room wearing skin-tight shorts and a tank top.

Martin lifted Kevin onto the counter. "Hannah, this is Nina. She's doing the honors of baby-sitting for us tonight."

Hoping she didn't look as uncomfortable as she felt around a half-clothed girl, Hannah shifted Lissa in her arms and held out her hand. "Hello."

Nina shook it. "Hi." She turned to Martin. "Dad called and said he's running late but you should get started without him."

Lissa reached for Martin. He lifted her from Hannah's arms. "Nina's parents are Dave and Vicki Slagle. They're good friends I'd like you to meet when they get here." He looked to Nina. "That's fine. I knew he had a lot going on today. Why don't you take the kids outside for a while? That's where we've set up all the band equipment."

"Okay." Nina helped Kevin jump down.

Martin tickled Lissa's belly. "You're going to be good for Nina tonight, right?"

Lissa giggled and nodded, and Martin set her feet on the ground. "Go on." He gave a nod for her to follow Nina, then took a swig of water. "According to Zabeth, you're not interested in coming to church. Is there a reason?"

"I…I've never…" She shrugged.

"Been to church?"

"Not an Englischer one."

"I see. Well, Zabeth had already made those transitions long before I was born, so I guess I hadn't really thought about how you might feel." He backed against the island. "You need to—"

She held up her hand, interrupting him. "I know. I need to put that on my list."

He opened the fridge and grabbed another water bottle. He took the lid off and passed it to Hannah. "I hated church as a teen. Zabeth had Dad's full backing, and I went, even though he didn't go. Then after college, I started going again, but only for Zabeth. It sorta grows on you, but it took awhile to fit in. Maybe because I had to work out some stuff with God before I could really tolerate it." He slid onto the counter, looking relaxed and comfortable with his confession.

His words didn't sit well, although it seemed like they should. "That's... that's not... I don't have a problem with God..."

"So what's the problem?"

She shrugged.

"I saw something in those eyes, Hannah. Just say it."

"The only thing I was thinking is that I don't know why, but I just don't want to be in church. Okay?"

Martin smiled. "It's okay with me. I get the idea it's not so okay with you."

She sighed. "There's a phrase that comes to mind whenever you're around."

"Yeah? Are the words *charming* and *intelligent* involved?"

"Nope." The desire to tell Martin to "shut up" had risen within her since they'd met, but she couldn't imagine actually saying it.

He laughed. "Why am I not surprised?"

The sounds of drums and guitars vibrated through the air. "Palmer, front and center." The male voice echoed through the amps.

"Come on. Zabeth said you have a great singing voice." He grabbed her wrist and pulled her toward the back door.

This was an item he'd put on her list that she wasn't at war with herself over—well, not completely anyway. She'd been looking forward to learning new songs and how to sing with instruments. She'd always loved singing a cappella at the church meetings, but most of the songs were about religious martyrs. Surely that wasn't the only kind of music God enjoyed.

Chapter 20

With everyone settled into bed for the night, Sarah slipped out of the house. Earlier in the day she had seen Daed in the tack room putting a folded piece of paper into a tin box before he shoved the container behind some loose slats on the wall.

She hoped that's where Daed was hiding the letters Matthew had passed to him, the ones Hannah had written and left for them before she boarded that train six months ago.

Six months!

It was ridiculous that Daed hadn't shared the letters with them in all this time. It wasn't his place to be the keeper of what wasn't his. Of course, her sister might not have written to her.

Sarah had been caught on many occasions trying to find these letters, but no one had figured out what she was looking for. Maybe because she wasn't always looking for the same thing. When caught, she'd make up some missing item and say she was hunting for that. They'd look at her funny, but then they'd walk off and leave her alone.

But now she knew right where to go. Walking into the musky-smelling barn, she headed straight for the tack room. Through the darkness she ran her hands along the shelf, gently searching for the kerosene lamp. When her fingers touched the smooth glass, she grasped the lamp and set it on the workbench. After finding the matches on the same shelf, she lit the lantern and slid the matches into the bib of her apron. She held up the light in front of the area where she'd seen her Daed move the boards.

Placing the lamp on the bench next to her, she giggled. Hannah just might have told where she was going and what she did with her baby… Why, the little thing would be sitting up by now.

Instantly she could imagine a sweet little babe growing and happy. That thought seemed to be all that kept her sane these days. The board had a nail at the top, but with some pressure it swiveled onto the boards next to it and out of Sarah's way. The tin box reflected the firelight, and she pulled it from its hiding spot. Her hands trembled as she removed the lid and grasped the papers in her hands. She laid the stack on the workbench and opened the top one.

Day four:
I keep looking for her return. Wake at every sound…

Sarah flipped past that page and several others before reading the last line on the final page.

Six months:
Each night I lie awake, wondering…

Sarah groaned. That wasn't written by Hannah. She tossed the letters to the ground and grabbed one from the bottom of the stack.

Dear Sister,
What has hap—

"Sarah?"

She jumped at the sound of her father's voice. When she turned, he was in the doorway of the tack room.

"I thought we had a thief or something. What are you…" His eyes landed on the papers and then on the gap in the wall as he walked toward her. Concern drained from his face, and anger replaced it. He bent and snatched the papers off the ground and pulled the letter from her hand and the others off the bench. He shook them at her. "Is this what you've been searching for, worrying your poor mother over? Wanting this?" He pulled a handkerchief from his pocket and removed the globe from the lamp.

"Daed, no, please!"

Ignoring her, he held the bundled letters over the flame until they caught fire. He turned them sideways, letting the orange and yellow flames leap. Before the fire reached his fingers, he tossed what was left into a bucket. She watched as the last scripted words blazed and then turned to thin, black ash.

"Go to bed, Sarah." He pointed to the door.

Staring into the bucket, she wondered what had been written before fire destroyed the words.

"Go!"

A thin trail of smoke danced in a circular motion, rising into the air before it disappeared.

Never before had she dared to really look… She lifted her gaze to meet his. It was odd seeing him eye to eye. "Did you see how fire removed what had been written?" She stared into the bucket. "Did it erase the truth with it?"

"There was no truth there, Sarah."

She stooped next to the bucket and smelled the aroma of fresh fire. "Or if there was, it's better to burn it than face it. Ya?"

"Go to bed, Sarah."

Sarah pulled her attention from the ashes, rose, and headed for the house.

~~∞~~

Matthew whistled softly as the horse trod toward the Zook place. The heat of the August day was over, but it'd be daylight for hours yet. Elle had been gone four of the six months she'd promised to her dad, and she was back for a visit, probably arrived at the Zooks' less than an hour ago. She was leaving again first thing tomorrow morning, but he'd been looking forward to this visit since she wrote him a few weeks ago, sharing her plans. He missed her something fierce—from the moment he woke each day until sleep took over. The need to see and talk to her never seemed to lessen.

The upside was the number of hours he could pour into expanding his business. He was working sixteen-hour days, six days a week.

All those hours were paying off too. Really paying off.

But he'd gladly give that up for more time with Elle.

Bits. His mind jumped subjects on him. He had to remember to go by the storage shop and get a package of bits before tomorrow.

Well, he and Elle could swing by there tonight while they were out riding and talking.

Luke was a really good partner, and surprisingly enough, his own brother David was a lot of help. Between him and Luke, they were gaining customers from other states.

He slapped the reins against the horse's back. He could have hired a driver to take him as far as the Zooks', but he was hoping to bring Elle to see his updated and expanded shop. And he wanted to do so in as slow and private a manner as possible. A hired driver provided neither slowness nor privacy.

He hummed for a while and then prayed for a while as the horse clopped along. As he pulled in front of Kiah and Abigail's home, he could smell the feast.

"Hello," he called as he hopped down from the carriage.

The doors and windows were open as they always were when it wasn't winter, but no one responded to his call.

He strode to the screen door and knocked.

"Come on in," Abigail said. A moment later she came around a corner, smiling. "Matthew Esh. Come in, come in."

She sounded surprised that he was here.

He entered the house, looking for Elle. "It sure smells like ya been busy today."

"Busy canning."

Just canning?

"So"—Abigail wiped her hands on the corner of her apron—"what brings you out this way?"

He scratched his head. "Where's Elle?"

"Elle?" Abigail's face was serious. Her eyes narrowed before she winked at him. "Why, I have no idea." She pointed to a door, a closet door from the looks of it.

Matthew walked to it. "Oh, well, I guess I got the days mixed up, and she won't be comin' tonight." He opened the door, expecting to see his fiancée, but what he saw left him speechless.

A huge camera lens stared him in the face as a bright light flashed. He covered his eyes. "What are you doing?"

Elle stepped out of the closet. "An Amish man caught by surprise," she laughed. "Now that should sell." She took the strap of the camera from around her neck, held the bulky contraption away from her in one hand, and gave Matthew a one-armed hug. "Hey."

He laughed. "Leave it to you." He returned the hug, thankful she was in his arms.

She pulled away and took another photo.

"Elle," Matthew protested, "you do remember you're in an Amish home, right?"

Elle made a face at him as if he was making a fuss over nothing.

Her hair was pinned back in a ponytail with reddish blond wisps dangling about her face and neck. Her straight blue-jean skirt and sleeveless knit top gave her a very modern look—a modest one by Englischer standards—but Matthew wasn't comfortable with it.

He looked to Abigail, who pulled a kitchen towel from the bib of her apron and snapped it in the air. "This is my defense."

"You pop her with it?" Matthew looked around the kitchen. "Where's mine?"

"Matthew!" Elle scolded.

"No, it's not for smacking anyone." Abigail frowned at him before shaking the towel. "You've seen the captions that say 'Amish woman avoids camera.' Well…" She draped the towel over her head and face.

They shared a laugh, but Matthew wagged his finger at Elle, not sure how amused he really was. She lifted one shoulder, angling it toward him while raising her eyebrows. But rather than looking like a shrug, her move looked like a dare. Abigail removed her towel just as Kiah came in covered in a sheet with two holes cut out for his eyes. Everyone broke into laughter. Kiah looked like an Englischer kid, a really tall one, dressed as a ghost on Halloween.

Matthew held out his hand. "Elle." He said it firmly.

She harrumphed but placed the camera in his hands. "I told my teacher I'd do a complete photo shoot inside an Amish home. Don't know how a girl is supposed to do that if she can't include some photos of real people."

Her voice and mannerisms said she was joking—sort of.

Kiah pulled the sheet off his head and wrapped the camera in it. "I am real, and so is Abigail."

"Uh, yeah, real covered," Elle retorted.

She took a stack of plates out of the cabinet and began setting the table. It wasn't long before they all sat down to eat, talking about the lack of rain and the price of horse feed.

"Matthew's business is doing so well you might've heard of it all the way in Baltimore. He's got customers from at least seven states—Amish, Mennonite, and Englischers." Kiah stabbed another fried pork chop and plunked it onto his plate. "All wanting buggies, horses, and leather goods from E and L Buggy, Harness, and Horses."

All hint of a smile left Elle's features. "Is it really doing that well, Matthew? You've said nearly nothing in your letters."

Matthew wiped his mouth with a napkin. "It's doing good. Just about better than we can keep up with. Rather than writing about it, I thought I'd show you the additions to the old shop after dinner."

She gave a sullen nod. "Seems like you would've told me…"

He pointed to the counter where the camera sat hidden inside the sheet, letting her know she hadn't shared everything going on in her life either.

She smiled. "I was waiting till I saw you in person."

"Yep. Me too." He returned her smile. "So how about a buggy ride after dinner?"

"All the way to your place? No way. I'll drive."

"Drive?" He glanced out the window. "I didn't see a car."

"That's because I hid it behind the barn." She giggled. "Worked too, ya?"

He nodded. "So you have your license now?"

"Oh, good grief, yes. Do you know how difficult it'd be to get to DC's School of Photography regularly without being able to drive myself?"

Each person froze, staring at Elle.

She blinked. "What?" Somewhere between staring at them and thinking about what she'd said, it dawned on her. "Oh." She lowered her head. "I was going to talk to you about that, Matthew, when we had time alone." She shrugged. "Had planned for us to go for a drive."

The meal wrapped up in silence, and Abigail shooed them out the door, saying she'd clean up without their help.

Elle grabbed her camera, its case, and a large black bag of some sort. She pulled a set of keys out. "Why don't you put the horse to pasture, and I'll drive."

That wasn't the way he'd pictured tonight at all, but he led the mare into the barn, unhitched her from the buggy, and put her in the field. Elle slid behind the wheel, and he got in on the passenger's side, feeling a complete lack of dignity.

Over the next hour, as they drove everywhere and nowhere at the same time, she told him all about living with Sid, helping to run his bakery, and taking photography classes. "See, the school teaches classes two ways, through sessions—which is what I've been taking. Or through an actual professional program—which is what I'd like to take." She paused.

Matthew nodded, feeling rather foggy about what she'd rattled off.

She adjusted the rearview mirror. "Well? What do you think?"

"I think it's an odd hobby for someone who's planning on being baptized into the faith."

She nodded. "Yeah, I know. But if I take photos of people who aren't Amish and photos of scenery, the bishop will make an exception."

Matthew propped his elbow on the car door next to the window. "I'm not so sure he will."

"Of course he will."

"Do you ever lack confidence in what all you can talk people into?"

She turned, frowning at him. "What's that supposed to mean?"

He shook his head. "Let's talk about something else."

"Okay, what?" Her tone was clipped.

"How about if I show you the expansion on our shop?"

She nodded, used a stranger's driveway to turn around in, and headed for Owl's Perch. It was dark now, making it even harder for Matthew to gauge her thoughts.

They crossed into Owl's Perch. "Could we go by Luke's old harness shop and let me pick up some supplies first?"

"Sure. I'm glad the business is going so well for you."

"Thanks. It's a handful, that's for sure."

They drove on for miles in silence. He'd never once thought they might have trouble finding things to talk about. They never had before.

She drew a deep breath. "Matthew, I...I've applied for the professional program."

"What's that?" He took notice of the Lapp house as they passed it.

"I told you...didn't I?" She slowed as the road went from pavement to gravel. "It's a course where I can get a diploma in photography."

"In photography?"

"Well, don't sound so skeptical. It's a viable course."

Wondering what she meant by *viable,* he nodded. "I guess."

Dust churned under the wheels until she slowed to enter the driveway. Putting the car in Park, she drew a deep breath. "The program starts next month and takes eleven months to finish."

He just sat there, staring at her silhouette through the darkness. "Eleven months?"

She fidgeted with the steering wheel. "I know that sounds like a long time, but I really want to do this. I'm good at it, and I've never really been good at anything before."

"Yeah, but..." Firelight from inside the shop caught his eye. He studied the place, seeing a flicker inside as if someone had lit a match. Even though the apartment above the shop-turned-storage-room was rented out to a young Amish couple, no one but Luke or Matthew was supposed to go into the storage area—not that they ever locked it.

Matthew opened the car door. "Wait here."

She turned the car off. "But we're in the middle—"

"I know," Matthew interrupted her before getting out of the car and tiptoeing onto the porch. As he peered through the front window, disbelief ran through him.

Sarah?

She had a thin stick held up to the flame.

He tapped on the door, giving her a warning before he opened it. "Sarah?"

She jumped back, dropping the burning twig onto the floor. Matthew hurried over and stomped the tiny flames out. "What are you doing here?"

"I...I was looking..."

He grabbed her by the elbows. "Do you have any idea how easily these boxes and crates would catch on fire?"

She looked around and shook her head. "I...I didn't think... I'm sorry." Tears filled her eyes. "I...I'm sorry."

He released her and put the globe on the kerosene lamp. "Sarah, are ya not any better in all these months since Hannah left?"

She stomped her foot. "I'm fine! Everybody thinks everything is all about Hannah, even after all these months." She mimicked the last part of the sentence, mocking his words. "You got no proof, you know?"

"Proof?"

"That you and Hannah were only gone five minutes." She stretched her neck, like she was looking down on him.

He sighed. "I'm not going to try to set that event straight, Sarah."

"Why not?"

"Because if I do, it'll only cause trouble—too much of it—for you."

"So you think Hannah's the only one with enough gumption to handle trouble?"

"Do you want me to tell, Sarah?"

Sarah stared at him, looking both petrified and defiant—if that was possible. She grabbed the matches off the counter. "Did you know that I heard fire can erase things? As if they'd never happened." She struck a match. "Don't remember where I heard it though. Do you think that's true?"

"No. But what I do think is that it's time for you to give me the matches and go home."

He was part of Sarah's community, and that meant looking after each other, like being members of the same household, but tonight was for Elle, not Sarah. She blew on the match, making the flame disappear.

The front door opened. "Matthew?" Elle called.

He turned. "Come in, Elle. I found Sarah in here, and she was just leaving. Right, Sarah?" Holding out his hand for the matches, he waited until Sarah put them in his hand. "Don't play with matches, Sarah."

She ran out the door.

Elle frowned. "What was that all about?"

"I didn't take the time to find out." He moved to the back part of the shop and grabbed a box of hardware for the leads and harnesses.

Elle looked around the overcrowded shop. "You must be staying awfully busy to afford this many supplies."

"Beyond anything I thought possible." Matthew pushed against the door with his back and held it open for Elle.

"Will you miss me at all while I'm gone for the next year?"

Matthew let the door close behind her, and they walked to the car. "I didn't realize that issue was settled."

Elle gave a slight shrug and opened the trunk to her car.

Matthew set the box inside, feeling frustration mount. "Elle, is it a settled issue?"

Chapter 21

With butterflies in her stomach, Hannah slid out of the driver's seat and locked her car, then crossed the parking lot of Alliance High School. It was the official test-taking site for her GED. Eight in the morning on a Saturday and a beautiful fall day at that. Not a cloud in the sky. She paused, looking at the life-size jet mounted on school property. It seemed sort of… What was that word she learned last week?

Apropos.

That was it. It meant "befitting," and it was definitely apropos to view this aircraft as she entered the building. The day Paul had proposed she'd felt like she was soaring. She remembered thinking that wherever jets took people couldn't be as exciting as where her dreams were taking her.

Now she knew—dreams weren't what took people places. Circumstances were, followed by decisions and determination. Right now her circumstances required her to pass this GED test, or she'd not be able to get into the nursing program anytime soon.

She had to push through her days with the same determination as in her other, Plain life, just with more right to speak up and make her own decisions. She liked the part about making her own choices, mostly. At least, she thought she would eventually like it. If she could figure out what God really thought about education, television, movies, clothing styles, hair, makeup, and all the other fancy things that were part of the Englischer lifestyle.

She walked into the empty building, thinking it would have been easier to concentrate today if the test site was the same as the studying site. She went up the stairs to the second floor and located room 256. One glance said she was the first student to arrive because she was sure the man in the room was the examiner.

He looked up from the papers in his hand. "Ah, the first test taker has arrived. Just show me your ID, and then find a desk that suits you." He glanced at his watch. "We have four more, who should arrive within the next fifteen minutes, and then I'll give instructions and pass out the tests."

She showed him her driver's license and then took a seat, wondering if she'd pass the test. Around four this afternoon she'd be finished, and within two weeks she'd have the results. But tonight Martin would come by the cabin and want to know what she thought about the test; tonight Zabeth would have a cake to celebrate her taking the test, whether she made the grade or not.

The two of them were quite a pair, prodding and supporting. It was an odd family she'd landed in, but they'd taken her in as one of their own—even Faye had, in her semifunctional ways. Zabeth now had a short crop of coarse black hair, and although the damage to her heart was slowly taking its toll, she was still the core of this unit. Martin seemed to be the leader and organizer, Faye was clearly the rogue, and her children made this strange group of people feel like a real team.

Why was it that every family had a Faye? Or at least a perceived one. Hannah filled that role within the Lapp household, so she felt a kinship with Faye on some level.

Zabeth never wavered in her belief that Faye would find God and would change. Hannah was less certain, but her aunt's belief in people was totally refreshing. It wouldn't bother Zabeth if Hannah came home saying she had a new dream, as long as she was willing to pursue it, whatever *it* was. After growing up in a community where members were forbidden to do anything differently from the forefathers, she found that this life was as confusing as it was exhilarating. Zabeth said she'd get used to it and come to a place where freedom meant boldness to follow God, not fear of displeasing Him.

And Faye was always around to challenge Hannah at every turn, offering makeup, new styles of clothing, and nights out with other girls. None of which she had taken her up on. Not yet anyway.

"Hannah." A male voice spoke her name as he laid the test packet on her desk.

A nervous tingle ran through her. The others had arrived while she'd been daydreaming. Now it was time to see if she was as smart as Martin and Zabeth said she was.

Mary tried to remain calm as the preaching part of the church service ended and each youth who intended to be baptized today rose from the benches. Six young people followed the bishop and deacon out of the Bylers' barn, while everyone else remained seated.

It was time.

In a few minutes the bishop and deacon would speak to her privately and ask if she was sure she was ready to take the vow. It was a serious matter, and they would look each person in the eye and ask if they were sure they were ready to take on the full responsibility of laying all worldliness aside and living in submission to the *Ordnung* and the church leaders.

Mary had no doubts—plenty of guilt, but absolutely no doubts. She'd take her vows. And she intended to keep everything in the *Ordnung* down to the least jot and tittle. But she'd keep her secret.

Her faith was in God, not in doctors who said she was healed. If she was healed, then why tell her she wasn't to conceive a child for several years? *Verhuddelt.* That's what those doctors were. Confused.

Within a few weeks she and Luke, along with every other engaged Amish couple across the States, would be published and could begin preparations for the wedding. She quietly waited her turn, hoping neither the bishop nor the deacon saw anything reflected in her eyes but a desire to be the best Amish woman and wife they'd ever known.

"Mary." The bishop motioned for her. She walked the hundred or so feet to the side yard and stood in front of the two men.

"You may raise your head and look at us, child."

Time seemed to trudge ever so slowly as she fought to lift her head.

The bishop's small eyes were targeted firmly on her. "Is something troubling you, Mary?"

She shook her head. "I have no doubts about joining the faith. I want to keep the ways of our people and trust God with all things."

He glanced to the deacon, who nodded his approval. "Very well then. You may return to the others who wait while we talk to a few more."

It wasn't long before the six youths were following the bishop and deacon back into the service. They kept their heads bowed, but she knew Grace, the bishop's wife, and Elizabeth, the deacon's wife, had moved to the front of the church to help their husbands with the ceremony. When Mary and the others sat on the bench, they bent over and kept their faces covered. Soon enough her back ached as they remained in that position while the service continued. She heard words being spoken over the people being baptized ahead of her and water spattering on the ground.

Was she wrong? Was she taking a solemn vow as she concealed a lie from everyone around her, or was she truly trusting God?

She felt Grace remove the pins from her prayer Kapp and slowly lift it from her head. The bishop's hands were now cupped over her head as the deacon poured water into them.

Oh, dear God, I pray this is a step of faith and not deceit.

Water poured down her face and neck, but it didn't carry the cleansing she'd expected. The bishop's wife replaced Mary's prayer Kapp before kissing her and welcoming her into the fold.

She never should have taken such a vow while hiding her lie from Luke.

With Dorcas moving way too slowly, Paul held the door as they entered the mall. He needed a wedding gift for Luke and Mary, so he'd requested Dorcas's help in finding a suitable present.

Surprisingly, he'd received an invitation, although if he went, it would cause turmoil among Mary's and Luke's families and even throughout their extended families who would come from other states for the wedding. Paul seemed to be really good at causing friction these days—even among his church leaders, among the families in his place of worship, and within his own family.

Maybe it was time he branched out and shared his "golden" touch.

Paul sighed, weary of how the conservative beliefs of his people worked to mold his life. The church leaders were still waiting for him to repent over the ball games.

"Any ideas?" Dorcas asked.

Paul shoved his hands in his pockets. "That's what you're here for. I could draw a blank on what to get Luke and Mary all by myself."

Dorcas grabbed his arm. "Slow down. I can't walk that fast."

He slowed. "We're walking at the pace of an old lady as it is. I've got to find something, get it wrapped, and…" For the first time he wondered, if he didn't go to the wedding, where would he take the gift? He only saw Luke on rare occasions. Since it was fall, and he'd begun school again, he wasn't in Owl's Perch very often.

Nonetheless, he'd received an invitation.

"Think I should go?"

"Go where?"

"To the wedding."

"Oh." Dorcas shrugged. "I don't know. Do you want to go?"

"That's a good question. Because Luke and Mary invited me, yes. For the reaction Luke and Mary might experience from relatives and friends because of me, no."

"Hmm. I would go."

"Why?"

"Because it'd give you some insight into what life would be like if you married into that family."

"If? Thanks, Dorcas." There was a store in front of him with all types of timepieces. "A clock would make a nice gift, wouldn't it?"

"I guess. You go look while I sit on that bench."

He frowned. "You that tired because of walking from the truck to here?"

"I just sort of ache all over." She reached for him.

"You weren't moving this slowly when we bought presents for A-Yom and shipped them off."

She shrugged. "I'm just not feeling good today. That's all."

He placed his hand under her forearm. "You want us to get a drink at the food court and rest there awhile?"

She sat on the bench and looked up at him, seemingly surprised by his offer. "I thought you were in a hurry."

"Sounds like it's time to slow down a bit." Paul took a seat beside her, deciding his tendency to use her to help him was self-centered. He hadn't been a friend. As long as she was helpful, he tolerated her.

That's just wrong, Waddell.

As if catching a glimpse of his life from the church leaders' perspective, he began to wonder if they were more right than he'd given them credit for. There were agreed-upon goals for the Plain society, and either you agreed with those goals, or you separated from the church.

He'd done neither.

"Dorcas." Paul rubbed the back of his neck. "I've been really headstrong and difficult, haven't I?"

Her green eyes fastened on him. "I figured it was your more-buried self coming out."

"What's that supposed to mean?"

She shrugged. "You never considered not being Plain, because the step from Old Order Amish to Plain Mennonite was as much as you'd dare ask of Hannah."

Paul leaned back, wondering if she was right.

A group of teenagers passed them, and he took note of how they dressed and behaved. It took about two seconds to see they were rebelling. Tattoos everywhere, multiple piercing with chains connected to half a dozen parts of their body, and ugly, two-word sayings hand painted on their filthy clothing.

Well, he hadn't taken rebellion that far. But the desire to map out his own set of beliefs and follow them had become a good-sized part of who he was. No wonder his church and parents were so displeased with him. He knew the aim of his people but constantly fought it. Sort of.

When he talked them into letting him get a degree in social work, he knew he was pushing the limits—studying subjects that gave his people cause for concern. The word *forbidden* was usually left to the Amish. His people would say the subjects were to be *avoided* or *approached with great caution,* but he'd pursued his dream anyway. Then there was his going to Senators' games—neither stepping away from his church nor yielding to their wishes. It was as if he wanted to remain Plain, but he wanted to mold it into something it wasn't, wanted to do it his own way.

Dorcas rubbed her wrist as if it hurt. "No one at the church thinks you'll come back under the preachers' and bishop's authority. They figure you'll leave."

He nodded. "I guess I'd think that too if I was watching my life from their perspective." He looked about the fancy mall. "Do you think Hannah is living Plain?"

She shrugged. "What I think is that you'll be a good counselor, Paul, no matter where you land—Plain or English. But I just can't believe you wouldn't use your education to help your own people. There are places that offer counseling for the Plain community. With your foundation and education, you could cast a good net for catching and helping our people."

Paul shifted, removing his arm from the back of the bench. "I guess it's time either to follow the church leadership and lay down the parts of my life that don't fit or to decide I'm not Plain after all."

"I can't imagine not being Plain. Not only because it's who I am—who we are—but because leaving would cause a permanent rift with my family and community."

"Hannah was going to leave her family."

"Yeah, but clearly she finds leaving those who love her pretty easy."

Paul wanted to argue, but the evidence was stacked against him.

$\mathcal{D}$avid stood on one end of the wagon and Matthew on the other as they placed another long wooden table in the bed of the cart. With Luke and Mary getting married tomorrow, he and a lot of others were working all day to set up for it. The Yoder place was buzzing, with thirty couples working together to cook a celebration meal for tomorrow. He wasn't part of the teams of couples who would provide the wedding meal. He couldn't help with that part without Elle being around.

The upside was that she was coming tomorrow. She couldn't get away on a Tuesday morning, so she'd miss the actual ceremony, but she'd be here in time for the meal, songs, and games that would last until midnight. Matthew would carry Luke and Mary from the Bylers' place, where the wedding ceremony would occur, to Mary's home, where the meal and the rest of the festivities would take place. After Elle's last visit, nearly four months ago, they could use an afternoon and evening of songs and games. It'd do them good. And all the fellowship and laughter would remind her of the best parts of being Amish.

Then maybe her letter writing would pick back up. She still wrote, but just short notes and not very often.

David brushed his hands together. "Have you heard that Sarah's been found wandering about at night by different folks in the community? I don't mean being with anybody, just by herself, out roaming around. Jacob's done washed his hands of her, says she's weird."

Matthew shifted the benches, trying to secure them. "I've heard. Don't make nothing of it. She's having a hard time, and the quiet evening air clears her mind. And if you ask me, Jacob's washed his hands of her because he's got eyes for Lizzy Miller."

"Yeah, well I heard that her Mamm's trying to cover for her, not lettin' anybody know just how bad she is, and trying to keep her close, so she don't get in any real trouble." David jumped down from the wagon. "Wanna place a bet what month Mary gives birth? I suspect she'll have a baby within a month of their anniversary."

Matthew stepped off the back end of the wagon. "We'll need more chairs. So go find some and a sense of respectability while you're at it." Betting on how long it'd take Luke to father a child. Good grief. Thinking it was one thing, but speaking it out loud? Where did his brother come up with such brazenness?

But David stayed put, watching the house. Matthew studied their home to see if his brother had his eye on something specific. They both had grown up in the farmhouse, as had their father and their grandfather before them.

Seeing nothing in particular, Matthew tightened the rope across the benches. "Is there somethin' on your mind, aside from foolishness?"

"Yeah."

"Well?"

David grabbed a piece of old straw from a corner of the wagon. "You won't get mad?"

"Depends. What'd you do?"

David stuck one end of the straw in his mouth. "Nothing, not yet."

Matthew moved to the last rope and checked it. "Meaning?"

"I haven't done nothing, but I got things stuck in my mind, and they won't leave me alone."

"You and everybody else. So what's weighing on you?"

"Didn't you think Hannah would've come home crying long before now?"

Matthew shrugged. He figured Hannah was finished crying and had no desire to ever return. She'd been treated poorly and given no options. It was a huge part of the reason Matthew stayed so patient with Elle. Demands were not the answer. Some freedom to make choices was.

David gestured toward the paved road. "Maybe it's not as hard to live *draus in da Welt* as we think."

Wondering if his brother had some romantic idea of life "out in the world," Matthew sat on the back end of the wagon. "You do plenty of living in the world right here. Besides, there's nothing out there worth chasing."

"Then why's Elle living there and not here? Something more than her dad is drawing her. And if Hannah can make it on her own, maybe it's worth a try."

"You're only thinking about this from a money standpoint. How about what you believe?"

"I believe there's other ways to live besides this. I don't want to give up riding a four-wheeler and playing my guitar in order to join the church."

Matthew wondered who'd helped David purchase these mysterious items and where they kept them hidden. "Those are temporal things. They aren't significant."

"Well, they must be pretty important, or they wouldn't cause such a stink."

Matthew didn't care to admit that a misshapen shirt collar could cause trouble under the right circumstances. "Our lines are drawn to keep us from going deeper and deeper into the ways of the world. The desire for more never stops if you don't stand against it."

David took off his hat and gestured toward the skies. "Doesn't it drive you crazy to think about living like this forever? No music, television, or cars is bad enough, but I'm sick of being too hot in the summer to sleep and busy year round hauling pews from one place to another. I'm tired of dressing in a way that makes me stick out whenever I go into town. Most days I feel like I'm gonna bust."

"It gets easier. You'll find someone special, and living by the faith will take on new meaning."

"That's what Kathryn said. She even showed me Bible verses about some stuff, but how can ways as old as ours take on new anything? I want to make my own decisions, and if I thought I could make it out there, I'd be gone already." David turned to face him. "Do you think Elle might help me get a job and find a place?"

Matthew's head ached, and he was sorry to find himself in the middle of this conversation. "If Mamm and Daed hear you talking like that, it'll make them despise Elle for sure. She's coming back to be baptized into the faith. She's not interested in helping anyone, including my family members, separate from the Old Ways."

Matthew went to the barn to fetch the horse, hoping David didn't end up breaking Mamm's heart over this.

As Hannah pulled out of Zabeth's driveway, she pushed the knob to the radio and turned the volume up. The stick shift was fun to drive and made her feel free and modern. The car was used and six years old, but it had everything: speed, locks, heat, air, a digital clock, music, and a plug so she could recharge her cell phone if she forgot to do it at home. Amazingly, she could travel home at midnight from the clinic and feel completely safe—although Zabeth said she was a bit compulsive about repeatedly hitting the lock button.

Thirty minutes ago she'd come home from North Lincoln on her way to the clinic to make sure Zabeth ate a few bites of the stew Hannah had put in the Crock-Pot before daylight. Zabeth was well enough to feed and care for herself, but she often skipped meals if Hannah didn't intervene. Faye tried to come by and stay with Zabeth a few hours on Hannah's busiest day, Tuesdays, but as often as not she didn't make it. When Faye couldn't check on her during the middle of the day, Hannah had to push the speed limit to be on time for the quilting group. After that she had her meeting at the rape crisis cen—

"Oh, peaches and bunnies." Hannah held the steering wheel with one hand and grabbed her purse with the other. Rustling through it, she located her cell phone. While glancing from road to phone, she scrolled to the clinic's number, punched the button, and waited. Removing the phone from her ear, she shifted gears. Maybe she needed one of those beetle earpieces like Faye's. She put the phone to her ear, waiting for someone to pick up or the answering machine to get it.

The machine picked up. When it beeped, she began. "Hey, guys, Hannah here. This message is for Dr. Lehman. I was working on Lydia Ebersole's file when you asked for it. I noticed you hadn't returned it last night, so if you could please put it on my desk, I'll finish up the reports before tomorrow. Thanks." She started to close the phone. "Oh, and Emily Fisher's file needs to be on my desk too. Also, remember that it's an afternoon of quilting, so although you'll see my car on the premises, don't forget I'm not available, and my phone will be turned off. Thanks. See you later."

By the time she pulled her car into the driveway of the clinic, there were four sets of horses and buggies already lined up in front of the quilting shop. Since it was a Tuesday during the Amish wedding season, she hadn't been sure anyone would be here this afternoon. But so far, at least three Amish women had made it for each quilting. Some Tuesdays she had up to twenty women and fourteen buggies.

She pushed the button to turn off her radio as she went past the clinic and up to the quilting house—seemed the respectful thing to do. The quilting house was an outbuilding to the clinic. It'd probably been a carriage barn in its day, which seemed befitting to Hannah. She and the Amish and Mennonite women met in this building rather than in a room inside the clinic. Each week when their sewing hours were over, they could leave everything set up. More important than that, the carriage house was very private. Anyone could say anything, and laughter could peal out as loudly as they wished and not be overheard by lurking husbands waiting on their wives to deliver. The room held secrets and tears and vibrated with laughter every session. It was the one place where Hannah's striving to fit into the Englischers' world stopped.

She got out of her car to see Nancy, one of the nurse midwives, motioning for her. So much for seeing the clinic workers later. Hannah shut the car door and walked toward the clinic. Taking care of Zabeth, working for Dr. Lehman, and studying for next month's entrance exam into nursing school all pulled on her constantly. But whatever was going on in her life, this November sparkled like diamonds compared to last November. With the exception of Zabeth's health, everything happening to her was good and freeing.

"I'm not here, Nancy. Remember?"

"Yeah, I know, but this will only take a minute. There's a woman from the courthouse on the phone, and she says she needs to speak with you, something about the Coblentz twins' birth certificates."

"She couldn't just leave a message?"

Nancy shrugged. "She balked, and I gave in when I saw your car pulling up the driveway. She's on line four."

"Okay, thanks." Hannah walked into the clinic and down the hallway.

Of course this new life had a ton of responsibilities and a controlled panic to it that she'd not yet grown accustomed to. Computers tended to crash at the worst possible moment. Babies were born while the office phones rang and e-mails piled into the in-box. There were always stacks of paperwork to fill out at the end of each day. And even more piles of textbooks, waiting for her to make time to open them throughout the day. Oddly, she wasn't very worried about the entrance exam. Confidence said she'd pass it; she'd passed everything so far.

Punching the fourth red button, she tucked the phone between her shoulder and ear, noticing the stack of written messages on her desk. "Hannah Lawson speaking."

After answering the clerk's question about the birth certificates, Hannah disconnected the call and read through the list of voice-mail phone numbers on her computer. She clicked on the number from Martin's office.

Phone girl, I bet you haven't checked your messages on your cell phone, and I wanted to be sure you knew what was up. It's a crazy week at work, so I can't be there for our tutoring session until late on Friday. If you need help before then, call me.

He was right; she hadn't checked her messages today and probably wouldn't until late tonight. She headed out the back door to the quilting shop. Since the building had no phones or electricity and was completely unadorned, it was a comfortable place for the Plain women to meet.

Leaving all her Englischer stuff in her car and office, Hannah went straight toward her haven, where, for just a few hours each week, juggling to keep up with the fancy life was not a part of her world. The soft light of the sun filtering through the windows, the muted voices of the women, and the lack of hurry put Tuesday afternoons high on her list of enjoyable times.

She walked inside and took her place at the table.

Sadie King, a soon-to-be-grandmother, slid the question box along with a quilt patch toward Hannah. "Glad you could make it."

The touch of sarcasm struck a chord with the other women, and they giggled softly.

"Denke," Hannah replied before she opened the box, pulled out the first note, and read it:

Mary and Joseph never had sex while Mary was pregnant. Does that mean it's wrong while pregnant? And if not, is it safe for the baby?

Wondering if the woman who'd written the question was in the room or if the question had been put into the box earlier in the week by someone who wasn't here today, Hannah set the paper to the side and grabbed a needle and thread.

That was one of the nice things about being here: they didn't expect an immediate answer, just an accurate one. Although she was more comfortable answering the medical question than the moral ones, the mixture of the two was the norm, and she was glad the women trusted her enough to ask. Whether they agreed with her answers or not, she didn't know.

She drew a deep breath, enjoying the aroma of the fairly new rough-hewn planking some of the husbands had installed over the dirt floor. The potbellied stove gave off the perfect amount of heat, making the place feel more like a kitchen than a slightly remodeled outbuilding. After the men installed the floor and wood stove, the women helped her clean the place from top to bottom and add some shelving. It was a perfect place to counsel young brides-to-be, women entering menopause, and those who needed medical advice but didn't want to ask Dr. Lehman. And odd as it seemed, it was here that Hannah fit in best.

"Mary was to conceive and give birth as a virgin, so…"

The midnight November air was nippy as Matthew walked from the Yoders' barn toward the road. Voices and laughter echoed from the barn as the games continued. The antics of his friends were amusing, but Elle had never shown up. He knew Elle was safe somewhere inside her Englischer life. She wasn't here because something came up or she forgot or…

He had a catalog of emotions banked. Fear was the first one—fear of what was happening to them. He did not want to lose her. Sure they had things to work through. Every couple did.

The barn doors swung open wide as friends of Luke and Mary cheered. They strolled out, Luke laughing and Mary blushing visibly even in the dark night. Mary's hand was clasped in Luke's as they headed for Mammi Annie's house. It would be their honeymoon place. That way they'd be right here when it came time to finish cleaning everything tomorrow. They were going to live with Mammi Annie and keep renting the apartment to the Millers. It made the most sense. Mammi Annie's was close enough for Luke to walk to work and go home for lunch, much like he'd been doing for the past nine months.

"Matthew?" Luke called.

Matthew jogged over to him. "Hey."

"What are you doing wandering around out here?"

Matthew ignored the question and chose to tease. "I'll expect to see you bright and early tomorrow for work, right?"

Luke pushed against his shoulder. "You can expect it all you want. I ain't coming in until Friday."

Matthew laughed. "Since you'll not be shaving that huge, ugly face of yours anymore after tonight, you should have plenty of extra time for work. Keep him straight, Mary. Don't let him get all lazy on us now that he's king of something besides a shop attic with a bed."

Luke put his arm around her shoulders and pulled her close. "Mary has enough integrity to keep us both straight."

Mary's smile disappeared.

Luke squeezed her shoulders. "Tell him, Mary."

A look of discomfort crossed her face before she smiled at him. Matthew figured she was having a bit of prehoneymoon jitters.

"Ya," she whispered.

"Well, good night." Luke waved and directed Mary toward Mammi Annie's place. "You are going to keep watch on the place and make sure no one pulls any pranks, ya?"

"Absolutely." Matthew nodded before he shook his head. "Not." The three of them laughed. "If you want no pranks pulled, be vigilant yourself."

Luke opened the door for Mary, muttering about the difficulties of having Matthew Esh as a partner.

The camaraderie between Luke and Mary made him miss his girl even more, and he wondered when his and Elle's friends would get to prank their wedding night.

Chapter 23

*H*annah tapped her pen on the form in front of her. It was an application for a loan for nursing school. The entrance exam wasn't until next week, but she needed to make sure she had funding before she took the exam. If she borrowed money, she'd probably be the first in her family for hundreds of years back. In this case the idea of being the first at something wasn't consoling.

But that was only part of what was bothering her—a large portion, to be sure. The real snag, however, seemed to be that if she took this step, she was locking her life into a definite path for the next two years.

Two years?

Zabeth crossed the room one slow thump at a time. Her frame had a little more weight on it than when Hannah had arrived nine months ago, but the heart condition caused a lot of swelling as her body fought for oxygen. She eased into the kitchen chair across from Hannah and set her cane to the side. "You've been in that chair for nearly two hours, Hannah-girl, and you're not one little dot further than you were before you sat down, are you?"

Rolling the pen between her hands, Hannah sighed. "I…I'm not sure about taking out a loan."

Zabeth folded her arms on the table. "We have other sources. I still have some money put back. You're more than welcome to all I got. Vince, Faye and Martin's dad, would give or loan money gladly, and he'd not miss it any more than dropping a penny on the ground. Martin doesn't have money like his dad, but he could pass you the ten thousand you need without it making much difference to him."

Hannah thought about Zabeth's offer, but it just affirmed that the loan wasn't what was bothering her. So what was the problem?

"Hannah-girl?"

Hannah stared at the forms. "Hmm?"

"What ails you?"

"Luke and Mary's wedding was today. I read about it in *The Budget* a few weeks back."

"I didn't realize you were reading the Amish-Mennonite newspaper."

Hannah shrugged. "Dr. Lehman subscribes to it, and I…"

Zabeth reached across the table and placed her hands over Hannah's. "It hurts to miss the events of loved ones. I know." Zabeth's swollen and slightly blue fingertips rubbed Hannah's hand. "Is that all that's bothering you?"

She brushed Zabeth's hands before pulling away. "Remember me telling you about Paul?"

"Yes."

She pushed the papers away from her. "While I was at a hotel the night before my trip here, I called his apartment. Some girl answered and promised she'd give him the message and phone number. I was in that hotel all night and half the next day, waiting for him to call me back." She tapped the end of the pen on the table, slid her fingers down it, and flipped it over.

"And now you're not sure he got the message."

"I shouldn't care. I know that. He deserted me, no questions asked. He took all the money from the bank. He…" Hannah sighed. "Oh, I don't know."

"I do." Zabeth slid the cell phone from its spot on the kitchen table toward Hannah. "You should call him. Be sure he got the message. See if he had a reason you weren't aware of for moving your money from that account. Find out if what you had was real or if you'd do better to build a life here."

"But you need me."

"Oh, Hannah-girl. I love you, but Vince Palmer would hire round-the-clock nurses if I asked. I want you here. But I don't need you. And now that we know each other, you could come back to visit anytime."

Although her words sounded nice, Hannah doubted if Zabeth had ever directly asked for anything from Vince, Faye, or Martin. Still, she couldn't see arranging her life to be fastened to payments and schooling for the next two years without making sure how Paul felt.

"He's always at his grandmother's the day before Thanksgiving, helping her get packed to go to his parents' place in Maryland."

Zabeth brushed her unruly, curly locks of black hair away from her face. "That's just next week."

"What if he really doesn't want anything to do with me?"

"Then you're no worse off. You can't wonder the rest of your life if you left too soon. I knew I hadn't. Remember, I told you I stayed for a long time even after being shunned. I knew for sure when I left everyone behind, Hannah. Do you?"

"I'm pretty sure."

"But not positive."

"I don't know if I can stand being rejected by Paul a third time."

"Third?"

"The night he left, when he never returned my call, and now this."

"I thought you were ready to move on without ever looking back, and I quote, 'to the likes of Paul Waddell again.'"

"I was… I mean, I am…" Hannah paused, unable to understand the multitude of emotions assaulting her. Paul had betrayed her, yet here she sat, longing for life to be different. Still longing for him.

Zabeth gave an understanding nod. "You'll find he doesn't have the power to hurt you as badly this time. It's the way things work with loved ones. The question is, who are you, Hannah Lapp Lawson? A young woman too afraid to find out the truth? Or a young woman who'd rather suffer the hurt and be sure of her path?"

Hannah laid the pen on the forms and set them to the side. "There's a lyric in one of the songs you sing with the band. It says when we wind up lost and alone, that's when we find ourselves…or something like that."

"Close enough for now. And I think that's true. Bumps and hard places make us both find and face ourselves."

She knew she'd rather suffer humiliation and hurt than hide from her destiny. And she had eight days to find the courage and the right words.

The sun was rising as Matthew rinsed the razor under hot water and stared at himself in the mirror while shaving. Luke would be shaving only part of his face today—his mustache area and his high cheeks, that's all. He'd grow the beard that told all the world he was married. Aching to be in that position, Matthew wondered about his own future.

Through the closed window, he heard a car horn toot. He lifted the green shade and peered out.

Elle.

He wiped the shaving cream off his face, pulled his suspenders on, and finished buttoning his shirt. When he came out of the bathroom, his Daed was putting on his housecoat as he came out of the bedroom.

"It's Elle, Daed."

His Mamm eased around his father, dressed and weaving a straight pin into her hair and Kapp. Concern showed in her eyes in spite of the motherly smile on her face. "I'll have breakfast ready in twenty minutes if you want to invite her to stay."

Grabbing his coat off the rack, he answered, "We'll see." He slid it on and buttoned it as he went down the steps and out the front door.

His first glimpse of Elle was not reassuring. She had on blue jeans and a red coat.

She came toward him. "I'm sorry, Matthew. You gotta believe me. I intended to be here."

"What happened?"

She placed her palms over the breast of his coat. "Don't be mad, please?" She tilted her head, half flirting and half pleading.

"I'll ask again, what happened?"

She played with the button on his jacket. "See, this fantastic opportunity to assist at a photo shoot came in. And I thought I'd be done in time to get here by midafternoon."

"You said you'd be here by noon."

"I know, but..." She pulled her coat tighter around her. "Can we talk in your shop?"

"Sure." He signaled toward the shop, and she turned to walk with him.

They took several steps before she stopped in midstep. "Wow, Matthew. We never made it by here the last time I was home. Look at the additions to your shop. They're amazing."

"We created each shop like a separate building, but they all have either a doorway or covered walkway into the old shop. More like a minicomplex."

She laughed. "A minicomplex? That's a bit too fancy for the Plain life, isn't it?" She grabbed his hand and ran toward the closest building. "Come tell me all about them."

Matthew allowed her the change of topic and showed her each shop and the stacks of orders that kept coming in.

She ran her hand along a row of shelves filled with handmade buggy parts for all the fancy carriages the Englischers were ordering. "Sometimes when you're talking, it's like you're not the same guy who fell off the roof of the schoolhouse the day we met."

Matthew propped against the workbench. "Nor do you look like the Amish teacher I met."

She glanced at her clothing. "I know." She moved in closer. "I hate that I missed yesterday. I'd looked forward to it for weeks. It's my fault. I thought I could squeeze everything in. I drove to Pleasantville, New York, for a photo shoot."

"You drove to New York? How long did that take?"

"About four hours. I assisted at a formal wedding and didn't finish until too late to get here."

Matthew wished he knew what to think, wished he could see into their future and know if he was waiting for her to return or if he was playing the fool. He hoped for the first one, but he was beginning to think the second one was laying a trap for him.

Elle walked to him and stood just inches away. "I know you're not pleased with much of anything about us right now." She looked into his eyes. "But try to see this from my point of view. You get to do this business for the rest of your life, but once I become a wife and mother, stretching my wings is over, Matthew. I look forward to that time—I do. But I need you to understand that you're learning new things and using all your passion to pursue what you want without limits. It's not like that for women, Amish or Eng-lischer. I've found something I can hold in my heart and know for the rest of my life I was really good at it. And I'm hoping you're the kind of man who can understand my needs."

"It makes little sense that your father asked for six months, and ya offer to give him a year and a half."

"He's changing, Matthew. His heart is becoming more tender toward you and me as I stay longer."

"Sid is gettin' just what he wanted to begin with, so of course he's becoming more pleasant. Ignoring that, what's happening with us is because of your choices. You're the one who picked going to photography school. You're the one staying so busy that your letters are just plain-out sparse."

"Yeah, okay, but look at it this way. I missed this year's instruction because my dad wanted time with me. There isn't one next year, so our plans have to follow the schedule laid out by the community. All that's different is I'm not living here while the time passes. That's all." Her warm hands surrounded his face. "Wait for me, Matthew. Give me my time now, and I'll give you the rest of my life." She placed her lips over his.

Every frustration melted, and Matthew wrapped his arms around her, making up for every kiss he'd missed while she'd been gone. Slowly he pulled away. "I'll wait." He sighed. "But you knew that before you arrived, didn't you?"

Her eyes clouded with tears. "I hoped. You won't regret it. I'll make it up to you…if we have to have eight children."

Matthew laughed. "Girls or boys?"

"Yes." She gave him a quick kiss. "How was the wedding?"

"Luke and Mary both glowed. I bet their Christmas present to each other next year is their firstborn child."

"Well, we can't match that, not by next Christmas anyway."

Matthew reached behind her and tugged her ponytail. "I guess I can understand your need to do a few things before the childbearing begins. Just visit more often."

"That's not a good idea, and you know it. Your family is almost as tolerant as the Zooks, but I'll not traipse in and out and tax your parents' tolerance before I join the family."

Matthew didn't like it, but he knew she was right. Because of her heritage, they'd accept her as an Englischer friend or as an Amish prospective wife, but she couldn't maintain regular visits while living in both worlds at the same time.

"Ya, I guess you better save that taxing my parents' thing until after we're a couple. Just don't take too long out there among the Englischers, okay?"

"I won't. I'll be living here by next fall. Promise."

That seemed so far away. "Mamm invited you to breakfast."

"I picked up drive-through on the way here." She glanced at her watch. "I'm going to be late opening Dad's store if I don't skedaddle." She grabbed his hand. "Walk me to my car."

Drive-through? Matthew walked with her, trying to shake off his discomfort at the gaping differences that separated them. All he could do was hope the canyon didn't grow so wide a bridge couldn't be built.

~~∙§∙~~

Pacing the length of her now-desolate garden, Hannah pressed the numbers on her cell to call Gram, stared at the digits written across the screen, and closed the phone without hitting the green icon. Her palms were sweaty, even with the November air so chilly she had on her woolen shawl. She drew a deep breath and redialed it. Again she closed the phone.

Tired of the game, she punched the numbers one last time…she hoped. A nervous tingle ran through her as she hit the connect button. Gram's phone rang.

Once.

Twice.

Three times.

"Hello," a young female voice answered.

Was it the same one who had picked up at Paul's apartment? She didn't know, but she wasn't going to identify herself this time.

"Hi. I'd like to speak to Paul, please."

The girl paused before asking, "Hannah?"

"Yes."

"Have…you reached him…before now?" The stranger's voice quivered.

Hannah didn't think it was any of this woman's business, but she answered, "No."

"Please don't do this. He's just now out of the straits with our church leaders. His mother has finally stopped crying herself to sleep over him caring for…" She inhaled. "He's repented for being stubborn in his own ways and has agreed to stick to the ways of his people. Please, just let *us* alone."

The way she said *us*, Hannah knew there was more to her being at Gram's the day before Thanksgiving than just coincidence. It had been her and Paul's day, one of fun and laughter after being separated from late August until Thanksgiving every year.

"Are you and he…"

"It's what I want, what I've always wanted, and his family is completely behind this union, as is our whole community."

Union?

"Please." The girl sobbed. "He didn't return your call the first time. He's made his choice. It has taken time, but he's happy and content. To hear from you now will only cause more turmoil, but his decision will be the same. He's had to make some changes to line up with our beliefs, but he's glad for the changes—all of them."

Hannah gazed at the cabin, smoke coming out of the chimney, pre-Thanksgiving foods in the oven, and a life that was begging to be chosen. It held love and freedom, but why was it so hard to let go of what was clearly dead and fully embrace what lay before her? It was foolishness. That's what it was. She'd been idealistic beyond reason where Paul was concerned, hoping for a life that was not hers. Even if he'd once shared that dream, it obviously had died an easy death for him.

The girl lowered her voice. "Can't you see? You've left your family. You've got nothing else to lose, but he'll have to break every relationship to be with you."

Hannah felt warm tears slide down her cold cheeks. "Yeah, okay." She disconnected the call.

"Hey, phone girl," Martin called to her.

She was in no shape to turn around. The back screen door slammed shut, and each footfall caused leaves to crunch. The barren trees swayed in the wind. Zabeth had told her he was closing his office today at lunch, but she hadn't realized that meant he was coming by here.

"If a man is alone in the garden and speaks, and there is no woman to hear him," Martin asked, "is he still wrong?" He touched her shoulder. "Hello?"

She turned to face him, and his smile disappeared. "Not now, okay?" She looked at the phone in her hand before sliding it under her shawl and into her dress pocket.

"Yeah, sure. But since Zabeth hasn't felt like getting out much the last few weeks, I've invited the gang to set up the band here tonight. I thought I'd forewarn you."

"For when?"

Martin pushed the sleeve of his leather jacket off his wrist and glanced at his watch. "Um...ten minutes ago not enough notice?"

She laughed and wiped her cheeks.

Martin gave a half smile, watching her intently. "With those hedges, a whole fleet could arrive out front and you'd never know from back here. I brought plenty of snacks, and I knew the place would be spotless, but I guess I didn't figure on everything."

She cleared her throat, demanding the tears to stay at bay. "Me either."

"Anything I can do?"

She looked out over the barren fields, dreading another winter. It felt like just yesterday that she'd survived her first winter's night here in Ohio. "I hate cold weather. I didn't used to."

"The propane tank is full, and there's nearly a cord of wood in the shed. You can burn both at the same time, and if you need more before winter's out, I know who to call."

His sincere concern eased her anxiety. Whenever he tutored her, they always skimmed general topics and shared a dozen laughs, but the need to share her hidden side nudged her. She knew the relationship wasn't one-sided. They tag teamed certain areas of life, like covering Zabeth's health needs, handling Faye, and even managing Kevin and Lissa. On more than one occasion, his *Civil Engineering Reference Manual* in hand, Hannah quizzed him for the professional exam he'd take in two years. She knew she could share her insecurities with Zabeth, and she had begun to feel she could share them with Martin too.

"A few days ago, while filling out forms at the clinic, I signed my name wrong."

Martin's brows knit. "Huh? I can't say I've ever had that problem."

Hannah pulled her Amish cloak tighter. It was all she had in the way of a winter coat. "That's because you've always had the same name."

"And you haven't?"

She shook her head.

Martin motioned to the bench, and they began walking toward it. "Why did you change your name?"

She took a seat. "I thought I was doing it so my family couldn't find me, so my community couldn't write to me and…say things I didn't want to hear."

Martin sat beside her. "What was the real reason?"

"Paul Waddell," she whispered.

"Oh. I didn't realize you… So who's Paul?"

She closed her eyes and took several deep breaths. "He was my fiancé, and I loved him so much that I was willing to separate myself from my family."

"Because?"

"He wasn't Old Order Amish. By the time things ended between us, I'd made enemies of my whole community, and when I landed here, I knew if I kept my last name, I'd keep hoping Paul would come looking for me." She sighed.

Martin laid his arm along the back of the bench. "Really, you changed your last name so you could begin a new life. Is that it?"

She nodded. "I tried to call him today…for reasons that make no sense."

"And it didn't go well."

"Times a hundred." She watched a flock of starlings circle. "There's more to the story, a lot more, but I don't want to talk about it."

He put his arm around her shoulders. "Whenever you do, call me. See, I'm no expert at love, but I bet, with a little time and a few dates here and there, in a few years you'll forget what's-his-name."

"You really think so?"

"Absolutely. The saying is that there are lots of fish in the sea. And I can tell you that's very true. Just find a new fish. And then one day you'll see him for what he was and be grateful you didn't marry the idiot."

She laughed. "I look forward to being glad he's not in my life."

"Yep. And in the meantime, I brought an extra bag of red seedless grapes for the youngest member of the band."

"The youngest member…" She dropped the sentence, realizing she'd been adopted or hoodwinked or something. "I'd like a few minutes, okay?"

"Absolutely." He stood. "The afternoon will be fun. Guaranteed to lessen the disappointment of"—he pointed at her dress pocket that held her phone—"that."

He went inside to join his friends and her aunt, leaving her alone with the barren trees and cold winds. But it didn't take her long to realize where she'd gone wrong. She'd set her mind on a new life and then looked back. That's not where her future was. It was time she took out the loan and prepared to go to nursing school. And just as God had brought her to a better place this Thanksgiving than last, she was sure next year would be even better.

"This life, God. I choose this one."

A blast of off-key music sounded, followed by boisterous laughter. She was sure they'd hit those sour notes on purpose.

She crossed the yard and went inside. Zabeth and about half the band turned in her direction. Some clapped that she'd finally arrived. Others made weird noises with their instruments.

Behind the keyboard, Martin smiled. Her cheeks warmed. He often reminded her of those men she'd seen on advertisement posters in the mall:

thick, dark hair; beautiful green eyes; and a grin that could melt the winter snow.

She returned the smile before peeling off her cape and taking a seat next to Zabeth. "Hey, I'd love to hear that song 'Inside Your Love.'"

"Sure thing." Martin thumbed through his songbook and grabbed the sheet music. He held it out to Hannah. "You have to help us sing it."

Perched behind the electronic drums, Greg held the microphone toward her.

Zabeth nudged her. "Take it."

"Adopted or hoodwinked," Hannah mumbled as she rose to her feet.

Martin pulled his mike close and spoke in a raspy, dramatic voice. "Hannah's life lay before her like a desert, nothing but school, work, and pushy musicians controlling her for years to come." He played the death march on the keyboard.

Greg followed it with the drum roll they always played at the end of a joke. Zabeth broke into laughter. Hannah interrupted the clashing music, laughter, and sarcastic remarks by starting to sing a praise song Martin wrote after he'd started going to church again: "You and You alone are my Alpha and my Omega…"

Martin immediately started playing the tune and joined her in singing. "My life is hidden in You. All I hope to be is kept safe inside Your love…"

Within a few lines, each member had found his spot and joined in playing and singing.

"Inside You we find our path."

Chapter 24

With one hand on the steering wheel while waiting at a red light, Hannah fumbled through her purse, trying to find her sunglasses. She felt the frames just as the light turned green and quickly put them on. Her eyes were light sensitive when driving. Martin said it was because she was getting old. She teased back that, if she was old, what did that make him? Charming and intelligent, was his answer, but for her birthday he bought her a pair of sunglasses.

She merged onto the main road with ease as Kevin and Lissa prattled excitedly about what games they'd play with their Amish friends while the women quilted.

Kevin kicked the back of her seat. "Hannah, will Noah be here today?"

"I don't know. I hope so."

Lissa clapped her hands. "And Mandy too?"

"If Noah is there, his sister will be there too." She glanced at the rearview mirror before changing lanes. At seven years old, Noah spoke some English. Unfortunately for Lissa, Mandy didn't. But Noah enjoyed interpreting for the two of them. Hannah found the warm acceptance of her—and now the Palmer children—by the Amish women quite surprising. Maybe this relationship worked because she came to them as an extension of an Englischer doctor who operated an Amish birthing clinic. She didn't know, but whatever the reason, she found it refreshing.

Martin's iPod lay on the seat next to her. He'd dropped it off at Zabeth's last night while she was at school and had left a message that there was a list of songs he wanted her to hear, but she hadn't had time. Back in November, after her last attempt to reach Paul, she'd begun opening up to Martin, and she wasn't disappointed. Even though he had a tendency to be blunt and sarcastic sometimes, he'd turned out to be a good friend. And for a guy, he seemed pretty much in tune with life. He was definitely right about her getting over Paul. Of late, more days than not, Hannah didn't even think about him. And when she did, it no longer shot pain through her but only caused a dull ache.

She'd turned nineteen two months ago, and before going out to eat with Zabeth and Martin for her birthday, she had walked into the field by herself and told Paul good-bye. He'd told her that through his actions, but this time she told him. At first she'd felt silly talking out loud as if he could actually hear her. But later, when she sat at a candlelit table in a fine restaurant with Zabeth and Martin, discussing her schooling and career possibilities, the euphoric feeling of taking flight once again stirred within her. She knew she was free of what might have been with Paul and had chosen to look straight into the future at what could be. Not only was she hopeful about all of life, but prayer, along with the Tuesday-night meetings at the counseling center, had brought her acceptance without shame concerning the rape.

Acceptance without shame. That seemed to be the greatest sense of peace she'd received this past year. God had cultivated it; she enjoyed it. The beauty she felt each time she prayed told her He wasn't finished yet.

As she pulled into the driveway of the clinic, Kevin unfastened his seat belt. "There's no one at clinic."

Hannah got out of the car and opened the door beside Lissa. "It happens sometimes." She heard a cat meow as she unbuckled Lissa and lifted her from her seat. It had to be Snickers, a stray cat the midwives had adopted. If Snickers knew what was good for her, she'd hide before the children found her. "The clinic is open for appointments every Monday. After that the doctor and midwives come in when they're called."

Kevin shut his door. "Now how's an Amish person who has no phone gonna call if no one's here?"

Hannah chuckled. He was bright for a five-and-a-half-year-old. She thought he should be in kindergarten, but school attendance wasn't mandatory before age six, and, along with a great many other inconsistencies in her children's lives, Faye said she wasn't sending him. "Some Amish have phones, just not inside their homes. But the midwife keeps a cell phone with her, and she gives the patient a cell phone to use. Make sense?"

"Yeah." He pointed to the end of the lane.

Three Amish buggies were pulling in, one behind the other.

"I see Noah!" Kevin reached into his pocket and pulled out two identical plastic horses. "One for me and one for my friend."

Hannah rubbed the top of his head. "He'll like that."

Lissa brushed her hair back from her face. "You gonna pin my hair up like Mandy's?"

"Sure. I have the stuff for it right here in my dress pocket." Hannah ran her fingers through Lissa's hair and twisted it.

Another round of pitiful meows came from somewhere, and Kevin started searching under the car for the animal.

"It's not there, Kevin, but I appreciate your confidence in my driving skills."

Without noticing her humor, he looked around the yard. "Where do you think it is?"

Before the buggies came to a complete halt, Noah jumped down. "Kevin, you're here."

Hannah opened the screen door and held it, greeting each of the seven women as she entered the building. The children set out to find the cat.

Sadie, looking every bit the grandmother, stopped in front of Hannah with a plate of cookies in hand. "I think eating while working on a quilt is just asking for stains, but my daughter said to bring these to you. Said you helped deliver her baby."

"I only helped because it meant you'd bring me cookies." Hannah took one off the plate.

Several children ran into the shop, knocking into Sadie while yelling something about the cat. Hannah steadied Sadie with one hand and grabbed the plate of cookies with the other.

Sadie's hands instantly clasped Hannah's shoulders. "Forget the cookies, girl. They almost plowed me under."

"Yeah, but I saved the important part."

The women enjoyed a hearty laugh. Hannah gave each child a cookie and shooed them outside.

"Clearly, Hannah thinks my cookies are the answer to everything. Does anyone even know what the children were carrying on about?"

"They are happy and outside. Does anybody care?" Lois mumbled around a bite of cookie.

Chatter went in a dozen directions as they settled down to work on their latest quilt, a log cabin star quilt.

Sadie placed her hand over Hannah's. "My Katy was scared when she was in hard labor but not dilating. She said you stayed, assuring her she was fine, for eighteen hours straight. Thank you."

Hannah nodded and squeezed Sadie's hand.

Kevin and Noah ran inside, one prattling in English and one in Pennsylvania Dutch. Neither was understandable.

Noah's mother, Lois, jabbed a needle into the quilt. "Boys, what is going on with you today?"

"The cat's stuck way up in a tree."

Lois's eyes grew wide. "Still?"

"Yes." The boys nodded.

"What do you mean 'still'?" Verna asked.

"I came by here yesterday to leave a box of material, and it was way up in a tree. I figured it'd climb down before now."

Kevin grabbed Hannah's hand. "Come on."

The women hurried out the door and soon were gathered around the trunk of the medium-sized tree. "It must be twenty-five feet up that tree," Verna said.

Lois squinted. "The poor thing has climbed even higher since yesterday."

"Think just looking at it will make it come down?" Sadie nudged Nora with her elbow.

"We could try bribing it with a cookie," Fannie suggested. "It would work for Hannah."

The women giggled, but the poor cat clung to the tree, meowing itself hoarse.

"Think the fire department would come rescue it?" Nora asked.

Hannah shook her head. "There was a write-up in the paper recently, explaining that they stopped rescuing cats long ago."

"So what are we going to do?" Fannie asked.

Hannah rolled her eyes. "Climb a stupid tree. But I can't climb back down while holding on to that cat. It'll scratch me to pieces, and we'll both fall."

Sadie wiped her hands on her apron. "You can drop the cat, and we'll stretch something out to catch it."

"Oh, that's a good idea. Let's get a sheet from the clinic. And I have a set of scrubs in my car that I can put on."

"Scrubs?" Katy asked. "You gonna clean the cat while you're there?"

"It's my nurse's uniform, and it has pants. No one can climb a tree in a dress."

Sadie propped her hands on her hips. "Yes, we know. It's the reason Amish women agreed to wear only dresses hundreds of years ago. Our foremothers banded together and decided if we never wanted to climb up after a cat, we'd better make a dress code."

Lois motioned toward Hannah. "But this is the first time their reasoning has ever come in handy."

The women all nodded in agreement before bursting into laughter. The cat startled at the noise and climbed even higher into the tree.

"You're all a lot of help."

"Denke," the group chorused.

"I'll change. You get the sheet." She gave Sadie a key to the clinic.

Within minutes, the women were showing the children how to hold the sheet for the cat to land in. Hannah climbed higher and higher.

"Hey, Hannah?" Sadie called. "If the fire department doesn't rescue cats, does it rescue girls who go after cats?"

The women's personalities often reminded Hannah of those she'd known in Owl's Perch. Even when Hannah felt overwhelmed in this Englischer world, these ladies—and Zabeth—were steady reminders of her heritage.

She was finally high enough to grab the cat by the scruff of the neck. It writhed and whined, trying to get its nails into her arm. She held it over the sheet. "You ready?"

"Ya."

She let go of the cat. The children looked up at the screeching fur ball as it hurtled toward them. They dropped their portion of the sheet and took off running. The women laughed so hard they could barely stay standing as the cat hit the sheet and darted toward the woods. The children chased after it, screaming for Snickers to come back.

Hannah held on to the tree, her arms scraped, her scrubs dirty, and her body shaking all over as she tried to control her laughter so she wouldn't fall the twenty feet to the ground—all for a stupid cat.

The upside was that the next time she saw Martin, she'd have an amusing story to share. She could hear him laughing already.

Kneeling beside her marriage bed, Mary ran her hand over her flat stomach, whispering words of repentance for the thousandth time. The delay in conceiving should have been a relief to her, but it only reminded her that she'd sinned. Last year she'd bowed before God, receiving the baptism of faith, while hiding a secret. Her first-year anniversary would soon be upon her, and her shame weighed heavy.

A sob escaped her. She alone knew why she wasn't yet with child. No one asked any questions, but every other couple in her community who had married during last year's wedding season either had a babe or would deliver one before the winter's end. This year's wedding season had begun, and she wondered if she'd have to endure seeing these new brides hold a baby in their arms before she did. Right now she wished the wedding season only happened every other year, just like the Amish instruction period did. Then at least there wouldn't be a whole group of new brides coming up pregnant when she wasn't.

Would she not conceive until she told her husband the truth?

In deciding to put matters in God's hands, not once had she considered that she might not get pregnant. Her thoughts had fully centered on trusting Him to help her survive childbirth; that's where the doctor said the problems could come, wasn't it?

Then she should be grateful she didn't have to face that concern. But she wasn't.

Luke cleared his throat, startling her. She opened her eyes to see him in the doorway of the bedroom. He was so handsome in his best Sunday clothes, dressed for the wedding they'd attend today.

Mary rose to her feet, feeling her cheeks burn.

He fidgeted with the black winter hat in his hand. "The buggy's hitched. You about ready?"

She fought tears. "Ya."

With Luke's eyes glued to her, she slid her Sunday apron over her dress and began pinning it into place.

Luke stepped toward her. "We'll have a baby when it's time, Mary." He ran his hands through his dark hair. "If you could just accept that this is God's hand of protection."

Unable to look him in the eye, Mary nodded.

His protection?

What would her husband think if he knew her empty womb was God's hand of judgment—one she might not ever get free of even if she told Luke, her Daed, and the church leaders the truth? How would Luke feel when he learned she hadn't trusted him to keep his vow to marry her, that she'd withheld information so he would marry her? She'd taken her instruction and baptism with a cloud of deceit hovering around her—a fog of self-deception mostly. Tricking herself into thinking she was trusting God for her life when all she was doing was using that *trusting God* phrase to hide her selfish motives. But somewhere inside her she'd known what she really thought…or else she would have told Luke everything and let him have a say as her future head. She'd removed that right from him, not because she trusted God, but because she was spoiled.

Luke stood directly in front of her. "Mary."

The gentleness of his voice washed over her. This was the voice he used when the doors were shut at night and the pleasure of being married lingered. Her resolve broke, and tears welled in her eyes. He drew her close and held her before he kissed her long and deep. Warmth and hope rose in her as his lips moved across her face and he nibbled down her neck.

"I'm sorry." She whispered the words, wishing she could tell him what all she was sorry for.

Luke kissed the top of her head and wrapped his arms around her. "Next week it will only be a year, Mary. Just one year. Try not to take this so hard."

She nodded and pulled away from him. Grabbing the wedding gift off the dresser, she decided it'd be best if she changed the subject. She hadn't meant for Luke to see her kneeling by the bed, brooding under her load of guilt and fear.

Passing the gift to Luke, she straightened her dress. "Will Elle be there today?"

Luke put his hat on. "Last Matthew heard she was still out west, assisting in a photo shoot for some calendar company."

Mary slid into her winter cloak. "I fear she will end up hurting him."

"She broke her word about moving back home this fall, saying she'd be here before instruction time arrived. I can hardly believe it, but Matthew didn't end things with her over it. He doesn't like it, but it seems she's gallivanting all over the U.S. working with some photographer." Luke's words were gruff and had no give to them. "She's already broke his heart, if you ask me. The only thing missing is that she's not told Matthew yet." He took a step back. "She's strung him along so she could have her way, an Englischer life and an Amish man on the hook."

Mary's heart skipped a beat as guilt pressed in on her. She placed her hand on Luke's chest. "Maybe she hasn't broken her word. Maybe she's planning on returning, just like she said, just eight or so months later than the time she and Matthew agreed on."

"I can't believe she stayed a year past the six months her dad asked for. And now she's staying until spring." Luke sighed. "You mark my words, Mary. She won't be here for this spring's instruction period either. Then will she want Matthew to wait through two more summers until the next instruction period?" He grabbed the brim of his hat and pulled it down firmer on his head. "I hate what's happening to Matthew, but our community has a lot more important things to think about than Elle Leggett."

Sarah.

Mary took even breaths, trying to quiet the nervous shiver that went through her every time Sarah was mentioned. Rumors of Sarah not being right in the head weighed on him and the whole Lapp family. Hannah had been gone for more than a year and a half, and Sarah seemed no better. She had weeks, sometimes months, of normal behavior, and then the oddities would begin again. Maybe time didn't heal all wounds. Maybe it just gave the injuries time to fester and turn malignant. A few days ago Edna Smucker had found Sarah asleep in her barn in the middle of the day. No explanation. No excuses. Just there, asleep…with torn quilt patches in her hands.

Sorry she'd let her husband see her despair, Mary took the present from him and set it on the bed. He needed her to help him carry the weight of life, not add to it. She slid her hands under his coat. "Let's forget all the bad stuff and just have fun today, ya?"

Looking down at her, he smiled. "I'd like that."

She pressed her hands against his back and pulled him close. After a long kiss that stole her breath, she backed away. "Maybe we should go and pick this topic up later, ya?"

Luke chuckled. "I'd like that too."

Mary smiled, hoping that maybe this time God would forgive her secret and she'd conceive.

$\mathcal{H}$is arms full of presents, Martin knocked on the cabin door and then opened it. "Man in the house." Christmas music played softly, and the delicious aroma of baked sweets filled the air.

"Martin." Zabeth's raspy voice welcomed him.

He'd spent every Christmas Eve with her since he was born. He would be here tonight regardless of anything else going on in his life, but his friendship with Hannah was a definite attraction these days. It more than made up for the distress his sister would cause when she showed up later in the evening.

"Merry Christmas, Zebby."

From the recliner, Zabeth motioned him closer. "Merry Christmas." The puffiness and paleness of her face and body made her almost unrecognizable as the person who'd sat here last year. He and Hannah had spent a few long nights at the hospital with her since last Christmas. Her heart was failing. The doctors had adjusted her medicines and put her on full-time oxygen, but beyond that there was little they could do.

Her spirit and love remained intact. She still had good days, sometimes a good week, and as often as not she made it to church.

Wondering where Hannah was, Martin set the presents under what he called the neither-Amish-nor-Englischer tree. It was an evergreen inside their home, so that counted for something. The string of popcorn and a few home-made ornaments kept it from looking too barren.

He gave Zabeth a kiss on the cheek before sitting on the coffee table in front of her. "How are you feeling?"

"Fine, just fine." Her breathing was labored even with the constant flow of oxygen through the nasal cannula.

"You warm enough?" He slid out of his coat, glad he'd worn short sleeves. It was always too warm in this place for him.

"Yeah." She barely said the word before she closed her eyes and dozed off.

He tucked the lap blanket around her and moved to the couch. A sound of movement from the bathroom let him know where Hannah was. A moment later the door opened. Her hair was wet and cascading down her left shoulder as she came out wrapped in a thick housecoat and carrying a towel.

Martin leaned forward. "Merry Christmas."

She sandwiched her hair in a fold of the towel and rubbed it while walking to the wood stove. "There's no hot water."

Martin laughed. "That's what happens when you don't wish people a Merry Christmas."

She giggled before putting her hands on her hips. "Uh, yeah, but it happened before then. I knew it was only lukewarm a few hours ago, but it didn't dawn on me there was a problem until I was in the shower. Brrrrr." She shivered. "Can you fix it?" She slanted her head, dangling her hair near the wood stove.

"Not likely. And there aren't any plumbers available tonight or tomorrow."

"Merry Christmas," she said sarcastically before their eyes met, and they both laughed.

This relaxed, genuine relationship added more meaning to his life than any other, although he had no idea how to define it. She stood there with wet hair, her usual look of no makeup, and men's socks—probably his.

"I heard you were called into the clinic today. I wasn't sure if you'd be here until I saw your car."

"It was a doozie of a day. I needed a long, hot shower to wash it off. So much for salvaging a bad day."

"How so?"

"We had two Amish dads who'd been, uh…" She tilted her thumb toward her lips and her pinky in the air, the sign for drinking. "They were in the waiting room being just as loud as they pleased. I asked nicely for them to tone it down. Next go-round I explained the rules. A few minutes later I had to stand eye to eye and try to reason with them while they looked at me like I was some stupid girl, which is exactly how they saw me. Beneath them. Someone to not just ignore, but to prove they didn't have to listen to."

"Where was Dr. Lehman?"

"Delivering a baby. But it wouldn't have mattered if he'd been standing around drinking coffee; he told me to handle it. What those men didn't realize is that I knew their Achilles heel."

Martin had to smile. Sometimes he hardly recognized her as the girl he'd met eighteen months ago. "Yeah, what was that?"

She glanced at Zabeth before putting her finger to her lips, letting him know the story was not to be repeated to her aunt. It was another part of their relationship that he valued. They shared all sorts of aspects of life with each other, just the two of them, things that were too much for Zabeth to know about. "Nancy was afraid I'd come across unwelcoming to the very people the clinic was established for. I don't think so. If they chose to feel unwelcome, it's because they were in the wrong and not my fault. So I told them I'd call the police."

"Hannah Lawson," he chided, teasing her.

"No one hates the police more than Plain men who are breaking the law. They shouldn't have crossed the line of propriety and then pushed my buttons."

"So did you call the police?"

"I picked up the phone and dialed two numbers before they left. When they came back an hour later, they came in quiet and well behaved, although they wouldn't speak or look at me." Her eyes lit up. "Oh, I want to show you a gift I received." She disappeared into her bedroom.

Last year for Christmas he'd bought her an electric blanket to help her feel better about long winter nights. He couldn't spend much on her because she'd made him agree to a limit—a really puny limit. But she seemed to have absolutely loved his gift. When he'd dropped by unexpectedly on a few winter evenings, he'd found her on the couch, wrapped in the blanket while studying.

He just hoped he'd done as well on her gift this year. A couple of years ago, before Zabeth was diagnosed with cancer, he was enjoying a Sunday afternoon with her right here at the cabin. While they talked, he pulled out his digital camera, set a timer, and took a photo of them on the bench—the same bench where he and Hannah had met and talked for the first time, where they still spent time talking every Friday night at the end of her tutoring lesson. Since she really liked the photos of Zabeth on his walls, he figured she'd treasure this gift forever.

For his Christmas last year, she'd given him a gift booklet with several "I owe you" cards for her to make his favorite dinners. He'd taken her up on them too, eating most of the dinners right here with her and Zabeth. But one of his best memories was the time she'd come to his place and prepared a meal. He'd invited his friends Dave and Vicki to join them. They weren't a young couple, yet the four of them could not have had more fun together. It was his favorite memory of the year. After the meal, they went out and played Putt-Putt golf and bowled until two in the morning. Teaching Hannah how to bowl had been an absolute riot, one where they laughed and quipped at each other until it became clear to him just how much this friendship meant.

Zabeth shifted slightly without waking up. The fact that he cared deeply for her niece might have bypassed Hannah's perception, but it hadn't escaped Zabeth's notice. Thankfully she had no objections, as long as he agreed to keep Hannah's best interests above his own. He fully agreed. Aside from an insane desire to kiss her, the relationship was close to perfect.

Zabeth woke, blinking hard and breathing even harder. "How long did I sleep?"

"Just a few minutes."

"Where's Hannah?"

He pointed as she bounded out of the bedroom carrying a leather tote bag. She stopped by Zabeth and gave her a kiss on the head.

"An oversize purse?" Martin asked.

"No, you goof." She sat Indian style on the couch and faced him. "Look." She opened the bag and passed him a small cylinder and something that looked like tongs.

"What am I looking at, Hannah?" He held it up to Zabeth and made a face. The swelling in her features could not block the smile as she watched them interact.

Hannah shifted it. "It's an infant-sized laryngoscope. These are the blades for opening the air passages, and this is the handle." She wiggled her finger through the blades. "The endotracheal tube goes through here." She pulled out another item. "This is a resuscitator." She laid that on his lap and grabbed something else. "And?" She dangled two items in front of him.

He touched each one. "Blood-pressure cuff and stethoscope. Those I know."

"And?" She held what appeared to be a huge set of tweezers.

"Eyebrow pluckers for an orangutan?"

She laughed. "Yeah, that's it, Martin."

He deflected her as she tried to pluck his eyebrows. "So what is it?"

"Forceps. But Dr. Lehman doesn't believe in using them unless absolutely necessary. There's other stuff too. It's a medical bag. Dr. Lehman gave it to me for having a year of nursing school under my belt."

"Belt? What belt? I've never seen you wear a belt."

She sat up straighter, tightening the belt to her housecoat, and even Zabeth laughed. "And…" Hannah pulled a small, wrapped item out of the bag. "This is for you from Dr. Lehman."

Martin hesitated. "For me? Is this a gag gift?"

She shrugged. "I wouldn't think so, not from Dr. Lehman. Open it and let's see."

Her almost-dry hair had become a thick mass of curls, making her one of the sexiest women he'd ever seen—even in a thick bathrobe and men's socks. He removed the red tissue paper. It was a plaque with an inscription that said "Ohio's Best Tutor," plus restaurant gift certificates with "Dinner for Two" printed on them.

Hannah peered over. "Ohio's best? Yep, it's a gag gift."

Martin slapped the top of her head with the gift certificates. "Hey, that's no way to talk to the man who helped you pass math."

"So what's this?" She took the gift certificates from him and glanced at them. "Oh."

"Well you don't have to sound so disappointed. It's a nice gift."

"I have a right to my opinion."

He thumped the certificates. "What's wrong with the gift?"

She shrugged.

When Zabeth was up to it, Hannah drove her to church and stayed throughout the service but rarely went out to eat with them afterward. She usually headed straight for the birthing clinic to either work or study in her office. When he'd asked her why, she said she wanted him and Zabeth to keep their Sundays as they always had been before she arrived. But today he got the feeling there was another reason. In spite of how much they'd come to know about each other, there were still things she didn't tell him, like what those Tuesday-night meetings were about.

He took the certificates back. "I think I'll just hang on to these."

Zabeth raised her hand, and all attention focused on her. "Maybe you should keep them for ten weeks…" She drew a slow, heavy breath. "It'll be Hannah's twentieth birthday. You two could have a great evening out together."

"Yeah, what she said." Martin pointed to Zabeth and winked at her.

Hannah stuck her tongue out at him. "I'm not interested in being one of umpteen dates you take out to eat, but thank you anyway."

He laid his hand across the back of the couch, wondering how long they'd dance around the truth of how he felt about her. It was scary to be twenty-seven and fall for a nineteen-year-old.

Deciding he really didn't want to go any further with the conversation, he dropped the subject. Hannah began putting each piece of the medical equipment back in its exact spot in the bag. He'd been wrong about that nursing school. It fit very well around the other needs in her life. She went to school on Monday, Wednesday, and Thursday nights and had clinical rotation every other weekend. She had to study a good fifteen to twenty hours a week, but that could be done right here at the cabin. Then she worked for Dr. Lehman each Friday and every other weekend. The only other thing in her schedule was whatever meetings she still attended on Tuesdays. Her life was busy but very grounded and focused for a nineteen-year-old. She stayed with Zabeth all day throughout the workweek, sewing curtains for the orders Zabeth wasn't able to keep up with and tracking her intake of nutrition and medicine like a hound dog. Martin kept a check on Zabeth by phone or sat with her when Hannah was gone.

Faye came and went at will, leaving Kevin and Lissa with Hannah regularly. If she didn't seem to enjoy them so much, he'd try to put a stop to it. But she said the house was more like a home since the two rug rats spent three to four days a week here. And then there were times when Faye helped with the in-home care of Zabeth.

His best guess was that his sister was a functional addict, but he had no proof. If not, she was borderline, using whenever it suited her. Using what, he wasn't sure. He only knew she acted very odd at times. There were days and weeks when she had energy to burn and played supermom, so he guessed maybe she used methamphetamine some of the time. Other days she slept round the clock. And still other times she smelled of alcohol. What worried him was that nobody who used part-time to get through the day stayed that way for long. They became hardcore addicts.

Zabeth took hold of her cane, and in a flash Hannah was at her side, helping her up. "Did one of you feed Ol' Gert?"

"We always take care of the horse, Zebby. But I think it's way past time to sell her."

"No way," Hannah retorted. "I take Kevin and Lissa for buggy rides and bareback rides."

Zabeth nodded in agreement. "We're not getting rid of Ol' Gert. I'm going to putter around in the kitchen." She thumped her way slowly, wheeling her oxygen tank behind her.

Hannah sat back on the couch beside him. "Never tell her no when she chooses to go *putter* in that kitchen."

Martin chuckled. "What is puttering anyway?"

Hannah wrapped the blood-pressure cuff around his arm. "Doing little odds and ends in a slow manner."

Martin frowned. "What are you doing?"

"What does it look like I'm doing?"

"Checking my blood pressure."

She put the stethoscope on. "Yep. And your pulse." She squeezed the bulb. "The chest piece goes on the antecubital, and you're to remain still until I'm finished." She took the reading. "Ohhhh, you're one cool cucumber, huh?" She released the pressure in the cuff. "Why am I not surprised?" She patted his arm, letting him know he could shift it so she could get the cuff off. "Okay, I'm done."

He didn't pull his arm away. "Do you have to be?" he teased. "I mean, you could keep checking my blood pressure just for the fun of it."

Her brown eyes locked on his in a way they hadn't before, dancing with mischief. She laid the stethoscope around her neck. "Well, it won't be any fun unless we do something to make your pulse increase." She whispered the words and held her index finger over her lips.

He was sure his heart rate had just increased—substantially. "Mmm, and how do you propose we do that?"

She bit her bottom lip and gazed up at him, making him long to kiss her. "I don't think you're old enough for us to cross that bridge *yet.*" She whispered the words and laughed.

Wondering if she was flirting with him or just being spirited tonight, Martin put one hand on each side of the stethoscope that hung around her neck. "I'm not old enough?" He pulled her closer, within five inches of his lips, and then a horn tooted, ending the moment abruptly.

The noise let them know Richard, Faye, Kevin, and Lissa were pulling into the driveway. Zabeth came out of the kitchen.

Hannah rose, untying the belt to her housecoat. She slid the housecoat off, revealing a typical Hannah dress—stylish and modest. She pulled off his socks and passed them to him. "Slightly used but all yours."

"You're pretty entertaining tonight, you know that?"

She ran her hands through her hair and began twisting it. "Yeah, well, you know how it is. I'm here to please."

"What kind of mood is this?" he asked. "Did those men at the clinic share their booze with you?"

She clicked her tongue at him. "Can't a woman have a little Christmas cheer without being accused of being tipsy?"

Zabeth chuckled. "Obviously not."

Martin grabbed Hannah's clip off the coffee table and held it up to her while she wound her hair into a loose bun. As far as he knew, he and Zebby were the only ones who ever saw her with her hair down. He just sat there, watching and wondering if they'd ever become all that he wanted from their relationship.

Hannah took the clip from his hand. "Maybe if Faye is, uh, void of too much Christmas cheer, we can play some board games like we did last year."

"Board games?" Martin frowned at her, sounding as serious as he could. "That's spelled B-O-R-E-D, right?"

She pouted while pinning up her hair. "I thought I was entertaining."

When her eyes met his, reflecting some of the same feelings he had for her, he knew that Paul Waddell no longer owned her heart.

The door opened. Kevin and Lissa ran inside with their parents behind them.

Kevin held a Matchbox car out toward Hannah. "Look!"

Hannah scooped up Lissa. "I see that. It looks like your uncle's car."

Kevin climbed on the couch next to Martin. "It's not the same, is it?"

"Well, let's take a look at this." He put the toy in the palm of his hand and talked to Kevin while still thinking of Hannah. She'd taken up residence in his soul, whether he fully approved of it or not.

Hannah eased Lissa onto Zabeth's lap, turned and gave Faye a hug, and welcomed Richard before grabbing her medical bag and taking it to her bedroom.

Satisfied with Martin's answers, Kevin moved to an empty area of the hardwood floor and sat down to play. Martin choked out a few niceties to his sister and Richard, recognizing the hollowness in his voice as he tried to find something pleasant to say. When Zabeth struck up a conversation with them, he went to see what kept Hannah.

Hannah's back was to him when he tapped on the open door. Pulling a fleece jacket from the closet, she glanced his way. "Hi." She put the pink jersey on. "You can come in."

He stepped inside the room for the first time in years.

She pointed to the living room. "What do you think?"

He knew what weighed on her mind. "She doesn't look high or drunk tonight."

Relief filled her eyes. "I thought the same thing."

"I know what I want for Christmas."

"Yeah? Did you know Christmas Eve is not the time to have spontaneous wants?" she teased him.

"It is when it's doable."

She sat on the chair, looking up at him—half flirting, half just being friendly. "Okay, as long as this is equitable, I'm game."

"Do you even know when you're flirting?" He hadn't intended to sound so flat and accusing but knew it came out that way.

"Well, that's a mean thing to say. I don't flirt."

"Then I got my answer, didn't I?"

She rolled her eyes. "So for Christmas you'd like us to argue?"

When they were studying together, Hannah knew how to hold her own if they argued. She'd make him apologize for his rude behavior if he threw out some overly snide or sarcastic remark, but she'd never cried or said her feelings were truly hurt. He liked that. Actually, it was a quality he'd always hoped to find in someone special.

"I surrender." He held up both hands. "Whatever you say."

She raised one eyebrow. "Anything I say? Hmm, let me ponder this awhile."

"And yet she doesn't see it," he mumbled, deciding they could discuss the fact that she *didn't flirt* another time. "Tuesday nights. Where do you go?"

All trace of cheer drained from her face. "What?"

"It's what I want for Christmas, please." He teased her, but the smile didn't return to her face.

She lowered her eyes. "The Rape Crisis Center. At first it was mandatory because Dr. Lehman said I needed it. Now I counsel others."

Martin heard the words *rape center,* but he couldn't make himself respond.

Hannah gestured toward her bed. "Need to sit?"

He tried to regain his composure. "I never once thought…" He sat down across from her. "I'm really sorry."

"Me too. I wanted to tell you, but I didn't want you to know. Rape is so embarrassing."

"And you thought I'd think less of you?"

"There's always that chance, but more than that, I wanted you to learn to like me for who I am, not out of pity."

He enfolded one of her hands between his. "Fair enough. But I think you should have trusted me to figure out and separate my own thoughts and feelings, don't you?"

"Is that how you treat me—able to hear the whole story and figure out my own thoughts?"

"That's different, Miss Not-Yet-Twenty-Years-Old."

She pulled her hand away and folded her arms. "Yeah, but I'll always be nearly eight years younger than you."

"I know. You're just going to have to trust me. Okay?"

She shrugged "So are you ever going to ask me out?"

His doubts about the type of relationship they were in vanished. "Give me a break, Hannah. I don't date teenagers."

She whispered, "But you almost kissed one."

"I was sort of hoping you hadn't noticed that."

She caught his eye, and they both broke into laughter. "So now what?"

"We wait…just like I've been doing."

"You call what you do waiting?"

The first thing he'd called it was trying not to care for someone so much younger than himself. Then he labeled it as giving her time to get over Paul, but he couldn't see ruining their moment by sharing too much honesty. He pulled the gift certificates out of his pocket and laid them in her hands. "You hold on to these."

he dreary skies outside Paul's office window seemed to go on forever, only broken up by skeletal trees. It was barely winter, with Christmas just behind him, yet he was tired of the grayness, and he wasn't looking forward to the New Year—although he knew he should be. He lived in a free country and had a loving family, plenty of food, and a good internship at the Better Path. But the holidays had felt empty, just like Thanksgiving and Christmas had last year and this year. It was the year before that where his thoughts always lingered—his last real time with Hannah.

She'd been gone twenty-two months, and he'd survived every day of that time in hope of her returning. He could understand that she hadn't returned yet, but that she hadn't even called? *That* he just didn't get. He'd blown it with her. No doubt. And sometimes in life when you blew it, you didn't get a second chance, but if she'd make contact, just once, they could start to work through things.

While gazing out the window, thinking, Paul saw movement a few hundred feet away. A closer look indicated it was an Amish or Mennonite woman walking here and there in the patch of woods near the mission. He studied the movement, trying to figure out what the woman was doing. She appeared to be gathering brushwood. A bicycle leaned against a tree near her. He eased back in his chair, watching.

The graduate program and internships suited him well and helped keep his mind focused on something other than Hannah's eventual return. Since he really liked working at the Better Path, the facility he was in right now, he volunteered here regularly. It was run by an independent, nondenominational Christian organization that fed, clothed, and counseled people of all ages, races, and religious backgrounds. The place had thirty beds and a dozen different programs to help people, including one of his preferred programs—

after-school care for teens. And best of all, at the end of the day he drove ten miles down the road to Owl's Perch.

The woman carried a huge armload of sticks to the ditch and dumped it. That seemed odd. Deciding to take a closer look, Paul stood. He peered through the window just as the woman turned and seemed to look straight at him.

"Sarah?"

It couldn't be. Surely she didn't bike this far. It was near freezing outside. He grabbed his coat, went down the stairs and out the side door. Jogging across the road and into the woods, he couldn't spot anyone.

Looking about, he called, "Sarah?"

A few moments later she stepped out from behind a tree. Not a trace of emotion showed on her face—no smile, no fear, not even recognition.

"Sarah, what are you doing here?"

She took a step toward the road, not even looking at him. "Have you seen her?"

Paul stood mute.

"She'll come back here, you know. Right here." She pointed at the mission home.

"How did you get here?"

"I saw this house in a dream. And Hannah was inside, looking out that window." Sarah smiled and pointed to the only empty room in the place. "So I set out to find the place, and here it is. She was staring out the window, looking for me. And she still loved you, but you didn't know it. It'll happen, just wait and see."

Paul knew she hadn't needed to dream about this place to be aware of it. She'd passed it dozens of times, and Luke or Mary must have mentioned he was working here. Her imagining Hannah was here was the next natural step. Sarah wasn't delusional; she just got things confused in her mind.

"Sarah, listen to me. You're eighteen years old now. If you want to leave home and seek a doctor's help, you don't have to explain it to your dad or even go back there. There are counselors in the mission." He knew she needed someone different than him, someone who wasn't emotionally invested and who wouldn't stir her community to anger merely by existing. "There's a Dr. Stone, who comes in once a week. She can work out a plan to help you."

Sarah looked him dead in the eye. "Daed burned Hannah's letters, the ones she wrote before she left Owl's Perch. She wrote me one, and he burned it. But he's not the only one with power." She reached inside her hidden apron pocket and pulled out a box of kitchen matches.

Those weren't just sticks she'd gathered; they were kindling. "Come on, let's go inside, and I'll see if I can get Dr. Stone on the phone."

"Everyone's whispering that I'm crazy. I thought so too for a while, but I see things. Just wait. You'll see that I'm right. Hannah will be right there." Sarah pointed to the same empty room of the mission. "And you'll see her, but you won't." She cocked her head, gazing at him. "That's the real problem, isn't it? We see people, but we don't." She waved at him and took off running, then paused and turned to face him. "You got a chance to hear her and didn't. You'll get a second chance, Paul."

Hannah stared in the mirror, wondering if she could actually make herself leave the cabin looking like this. Faye had helped do her hair, scrunching it while using a hair dryer on it. It was awful wild looking to Hannah, but Zabeth said it was classy. Faye said it looked sexy.

Classy? Sexy? In public? Do I really want to do this?

Faye adjusted the inset tie on the side of Hannah's rose-colored wrap dress while Zabeth looked on from her wheelchair. The flutter sleeves and V-shaped neckline were different than anything she'd ever worn, but it was the way the fabric gently molded to her body that gave her reason to pause. She'd picked out the pattern herself, but was she falling for the ways of the world?

Faye stepped back. "Okay, Hannah, let's take a look at you."

Faye had promised to stay with Zabeth tonight, making arrangements with Richard to watch the kids, so Hannah and Martin didn't need to stay in Winding Creek for this occasion.

Hannah looked at her aunt's reflection in the mirror. Her complexion was ashen, and her lips and fingertips were slightly blue. The swelling in her legs and her physical weakness caused her to use a wheelchair these days. "How much did you pay for the material to make this?"

"None of that. It's your birthday, and you look beautiful, Hannah-girl, not much like the scrawny, pale girl of two years ago."

Hannah swallowed. "I feel just as out of place tonight as I did then."

"Well, of course. That'll fade with time and some experience, but you look like you could own the world. Enjoy it." She adjusted the tubing to her nasal cannula that fed her a constant stream of oxygen.

Faye winked. "I bet you'll be on Martin's top-ten list of best-looking dates ever. Now that's saying something."

"Thanks for the constant reminder of Martin's past dates, Faye. It's very . helpful. Really."

Faye rolled her eyes. "It's the way it is—or was before you came. Deal with it. But maybe you'll be the last. Who knows. One thing's for sure, he's not likely to ever hook up with anyone younger."

Zabeth held up her hand, letting them know she intended to say something. She drew several deep breaths of pure oxygen before trying to speak. "You just got a bad case of nerves. You'll have a wonderful time."

"Sit." Faye pointed to the bed and opened a small makeup kit. "We'll just use a touch of color on your lips, cheeks, and eyes."

Not sure she liked this idea either, Hannah sat and let Faye fill in as a makeup artist. Hannah wondered if Martin was the least bit nervous about tonight. She hoped he was.

As she'd learned over the last two years, Martin's heart was pure gold. He drew her, despite his occasional raised voice and sarcasm. He'd drop anything at any time when she called him. Even if he was in the middle of some important meeting when she called, he would make time for her. He had helped her with tutoring, with Zabeth's illness, and in hundreds of other ways, showing her how much he cared.

She knew the things she really liked about him were practical, but practical counted for an awful lot in her opinion. Paul had always needed her to wait. Wait. Wait. Whatever her needs were, they had to be put on hold to fit with his schedule.

And there was another side to Martin, one that caused her cheeks to warm when she found him staring at her from across the room. He wasn't as tall or broad shouldered as Paul, but she discovered she really liked that. With her being in heels tonight, he'd only be an inch taller than she was. There was something wonderful about being able to stare a man in the eye when walking or talking or…almost kissing.

His confidence mesmerized her. It seemed contagious, and she needed that, like a garden waiting for the spring rains.

Faye dusted Hannah's cheeks and eyes with a light rose-colored powder while Hannah wondered what it would be like to be kissed by Martin. Maybe even tonight.

"Man in the house." His voice startled her, and she gasped.

Zabeth chuckled. "You're going to need my oxygen tank if you keep that up."

"We're coming," Faye yelled, then reached for a tube and stroked the pink gloss across Hannah's lips. Faye grinned and backed away. "All done. I'll wait in the living room with Zabeth."

"Thanks." Hannah grabbed the matching pouch Zabeth had made as her purse and tucked the lip gloss inside it.

She drew air into her lungs, counted to three, and stepped out of her bedroom.

Martin whistled. "Man alive." He held a bouquet of roses and orchids toward her.

"Thank you. They're beautiful." She drew them to her face and breathed deeply.

Suddenly feeling more awkward than nervous, she hoped to get past this and find their typical comfort zone.

He held a vase out to her. "I figured you'd need one of these."

She shook her head. "I'll keep them with me for now."

Setting the vase on the table, Martin eyed her and smiled. He looked like he wanted to say something, but Hannah knew he would wait until they were alone.

Faye moved in front of her and rearranged a stray hair. "Well, this is one night you won't be sleeping with your date, right, little bro?"

Feeling as if she'd been slapped, Hannah staggered under the realization of what Faye had just said.

"Shut up, Faye." The words came from both Martin and Zabeth, but it was too late.

Hannah dropped the flowers and reached for her keys that stayed in a bowl in the center of the table.

In one fluid move, Martin snatched them before she had a good grip. "Hannah, wait. I can't change the past."

Faye scoffed, "But *she* can change your future."

He glared at her. "Stay out of this, Faye."

Zabeth's face furrowed, and Hannah knew she had no choice but to smooth things over and leave with him if she was going to keep her aunt calm.

Hannah forced a smile. "Forget the past and look straight ahead, ya?" She bent to kiss her aunt on the cheek. "I'll be in to see you when I get home, okay?"

Zabeth nodded and placed her hands on Hannah's cheeks. "Happy birthday, Hannah-girl."

"Thank you." Hannah allowed Martin to help her slide into her coat. With his hand on her back, she walked out the door, leaving the flowers. When he closed the door, she pulled away.

"Hannah." His smooth voice offended her. "I wanted to talk to you about this, at the right time. It's just absurd to talk about it before a first date."

She stared at the barn, refusing to make eye contact. "You sleep with your dates?"

"No." He paused. "Well, I did. In another lifetime, before church and half a decade before I met you."

Her heels tapped against the steps as she descended them.

When she was on the bottom step, Martin's warm hand took hold of hers. "Talk to me, Hannah."

She pulled her hand away. "I don't like it."

"Me either, times a hundred." He rubbed his forehead. "But there's nothing that can change what's been done. Nothing."

Hearing both desperation and resolve in his voice, she remembered the night Paul had discovered her secret. If he could have seen her heart in spite of the circumstance, he might have realized that the only thing that mattered was their future, not the past. If he'd chosen to deal with the events and decisions that made him uncomfortable, they could have moved into a deeper relationship. But instead he took a stand on one issue and ruined everything.

"The very idea of you…" She took a ragged breath. "It makes me feel insecure and…and jealous."

He moved in close, and she could smell his cologne. "That's because you think every relationship means something special. It has for you. But our friendship is the only one that's ever meant anything to me. I don't know where we'll land, but we don't have a chance if you cut me off because of my past mistakes. It's only between me and God at this point."

"No it's not. It will never just be between you and God, not for me. Can't you see that?"

Odd as it was, Martin didn't defend himself; he seemed to be waiting for her to judge him and make a ruling. A dozen emotions rolled through her before stopping on a single thought. If they could find peace and unity over this issue, they'd be able to overcome their sexual history—his through poor choices, hers by force. But both had to be reckoned with.

Suddenly his past seemed less of a threat and more like equal footing—like a trade-off of baggage to be dealt with. Beyond that comforting realization, Hannah wondered, if God had forgiven her for all she'd handled wrong in life, could she withhold forgiveness from Martin?

She slid her hand back into his. "I overreacted, and I shouldn't have."

He gently squeezed her hand. "You were sucker-punched, and I'm really sorry."

She drew a deep breath, ready to start the evening over. "I've never been on a date."

A soft grin eased the tension on his face. "How does a girl get engaged without dating?"

She shrugged. "Let's not talk about that." She felt a hair clip in her coat pocket. "I don't want to wear my hair down."

He laughed. "I didn't think you would."

She pulled out the clip and pinned up her hair. "Am I date umpteen hundred for the month?"

"No. We made a deal at Christmas, remember? Besides, I'll tell you a secret." He looked around the yard conspiratorially. "I haven't been on a date in more than nine months."

She felt calmer, knowing their time together had caused him to stop dating early last summer. Standing directly in front of him, she waited for him to look into her eyes, say something witty or sweet or even sarcastic, and make her forget everything but the moment.

But he didn't say anything at all. He just stood there, smiling at her.

"I'm no longer a teenager."

"Mmm, I know."

"If you almost kissed a teen, maybe you could come closer this time."

"Well, last couple of years my rule has been that I don't kiss until the fourth date. That way I don't freak out later when I realize I didn't like the girl. If someone lasts through four dates, she's worthy of a kiss." He caressed her face. "But I could make an exception."

He slowly brought his lips to hers, and every speck of loneliness that had remained with her for two years was swept away.

Chapter 27

Martin stared at the casket perched on the hydraulic lift designed to lower it into the ground. The green indoor-outdoor carpet under his feet covered the loose dirt that had been removed to make room for a woman he loved like a mother. The trees around them were in full end-of-May bloom.

People had gathered in droves. Most of them he went to church with. But none had brought any sense of comfort. It wasn't for Zabeth that he grieved; it was for Hannah most of all, and for Faye and her children, and then for himself. Zebby had died in her sleep at the cabin with Hannah right beside her. But Zabeth was free now. He knew that. Even so, it'd be a long year of grieving, with years of lesser grief. That was just the way it worked.

In spite of how taxing the last few days had been, Hannah had responded with a quiet reserve, doing whatever needed to be done. She'd put up a stoic wall, and for now he was allowing her to cope in whatever manner she chose. She'd provided Dr. Lehman addresses for all of Zabeth's family and asked him to send letters, informing them of her death. For reasons Martin would have thought she was past now, she'd asked Dr. Lehman to use his own name, address, and phone number as the contact person or to refer people to the funeral home. The burial had been delayed as long as possible to give Zabeth's family time to reply to the letters they'd received by overnight delivery. But no one had responded.

His sister's cries broke through the heavy silence, her uncontrolled grief a stark contrast to his own silence. For days she'd behaved as if nothing existed but her own pain, not even her children or Hannah. Faye had acted this way when their mom died, and it had been Zabeth who had comforted her then. Had that really been sixteen years ago?

Across from where he stood, Hannah sat quietly on a white folding chair.

He wanted to go to her, but he kept his distance. His sister was beside her, sobbing without control. As if losing Zabeth wasn't enough to sink Faye, Richard had walked out on her last week. He'd been coming home less and less until he finally told her he was seeing someone else. Kevin and Lissa didn't yet know their father had left them. They had enough to deal with this week, losing the only grandmother they'd ever known and bearing the pain of their mother pulling even further away from them. Leeriness at what life held for Faye, Kevin, and Lissa made Zabeth's passing even harder.

Delicate fingers shifted inside Martin's hands. He glanced down.

Lissa looked up at him, her dark brown eyes swimming in tears. "I want my daddy."

Martin knelt beside his five-year-old niece. While he tried to think of something to say, a small hand patted his shoulder. When he turned, he found six-year-old Kevin staring at him, desperate for comfort. Reflected in their eyes was an ache deeper than they could convey in words, and he didn't know how to fix it. They needed promises for their future, and he had none.

Hannah unlocked the cabin door but couldn't make herself go inside. The eerie silence would swallow her. It'd been this way since Zabeth died, and today, the day of her burial, it was even worse. She took a deep breath and pushed open the door. Stepping out of her shoes, she flicked on a light before sinking onto the sofa.

She wished Faye hadn't gone to the gathering after the funeral. Her speech was slurred and her movements clumsy. Hannah could only conclude she'd been drinking. Faye had made a spectacle of herself as she wailed about Richard leaving her. When the commotion started, Martin's eyes met Hannah's from across the room, and he hurried the children out of the house. Too weary to deal with one more thing, she had slipped out to her car and come home. She looked about the cabin.

Home. Even today, it still held some of the appeal it had the first day she'd seen the place.

She flipped through the mail. Still, not even one of Zabeth's family members had responded to the letters Dr. Lehman had sent. Laying the junk mail and bills to the side, Hannah rose from the couch and walked into Zabeth's room. She ran her hand over the old dresser and the bed and along the wall until she came to the closet. She went into the small room and pulled an armful of Zabeth's dresses to her face, breathing in the lingering aroma of her aunt—a wonderful scent of fresh air and the expensive soaps Martin gave her.

She wiped away a tear and whispered a prayer of thankfulness. She had found her aunt and had treasured twenty-six months with her. In spite of the hurt, she'd always be grateful for that. But she'd just buried the only person who'd ever known all there was to know about her and yet had loved her unconditionally.

A car horn tooted three times in quick succession. That was Faye's signal when she was coming up the drive—although it seemed odd that she'd drive here since her one saving grace was that she didn't drive while under the influence.

Too drained to deal with anyone, Hannah muttered, "Not tonight, Faye."

Car lights flickered against the bedroom window as the vehicle slowly approached. Hannah closed the door to Zabeth's bedroom and went to the front porch. It was hard to tell in the dark, but the vehicle that came to a stop didn't look like Faye's.

Martin climbed out. With his body between the open door and the car, he faced Hannah. "I just wanted to come by and check on you. You disappeared pretty quickly."

Hugging her arms tightly around herself, she didn't move closer to him as she wanted to do. "I'm sorry I left early."

"There's no need to apologize. Faye's enough to run anyone off."

Hannah ached to feel the warmth of his arms around her, but she kept her distance. Death and funerals were a part of life, and she refused to get all needy because of them. But it'd been a week of sidestepping Martin's comfort, and her resolve was growing weaker.

He closed the car door and walked toward the porch, reaching into his shirt pocket. He pulled out an envelope. "I wrote down the names of everyone for my own use, but I thought you'd want to keep all the cards that were on the flowers."

"Thanks."

He sat down on the top step of the porch.

"Who's watching over Faye?"

"She's asleep. I didn't think Nina should be responsible for her, so I asked her mom, Vicki, to keep an eye on her as well as Kevin and Lissa for a bit."

Hannah sat down too, feeling the oddity of being here alone with him. No one spoke, reminding her of the day he came here and apologized to her—two years ago.

Across the field, mist rose from the creek banks, looking purplish under the night sky. Crickets sang loudly, and an occasional bullfrog croaked. Peace seemed to slip right into the place where anxiety had been only moments ago. But it wasn't just the scenery. She could have that by herself. It was having Martin near.

He drew a deep breath. "It's nice here. Quiet and peaceful, and it suited Zabeth, but…I think it's a bit too lonely out here for you by yourself. Don't you?"

"You're going to bring this up now?"

"It's on my mind." He faced her. "Remember when you called me a beetle thing?"

She laughed. "I didn't mean to." She dared to finish her thought. "But had I known it was so befitting…"

His deep laughter filled the night air, and she wished he could stay and sleep on the couch as he'd done on occasions when Zabeth returned home after a hospitalization. Desperate for a reprieve from the loneliness, she rose from her spot on the porch and pointed to the step below where Martin sat. A gentle smile formed on his lips, and he shifted his legs. She sat down.

He wrapped his arms around her. "How are you, phone girl?"

She swallowed hard and shrugged, but the warmth of being in his arms made her grief more bearable.

Martin rubbed her shoulders. "So how about we find you a better place to live? You can sell the place in a few weeks and find somewhere not so isolated or quite so plain or—"

She stopped him. "It's home, and I'm staying."

"If you change your mind…"

"Yeah, thanks."

She turned her head, looking Martin in the face. He placed his hand against her cheek and neck and rubbed his thumb back and forth.

Slowly he lowered his lips to hers. "Mmm. I could have used that a week ago."

Enjoying his closeness, she nodded and kissed him again before turning back around.

Martin propped his chin on her shoulder, as if he needed the warmth of her touch as much as she needed his. "I always felt guilty about Zabeth."

"Guilty? Why?"

"It was my mother's influence in Zabeth's life that ended up causing a division between her and her people. Mom swooned over Zabeth's ability to learn music, lined her up in recitals and gigs. When her community learned what was going on, Mom offered her a place to live."

She pondered his words before answering. "Your mother was not what led Zabeth away from the Amish life. That came from years of living under rules that demanded one thing while her heart wanted something else. Your mother just lit a path that Zabeth's heart was already searching for."

"I needed to know that."

The tenderness of being held eased through her, giving her strength to face the night alone. For the thousandth time Hannah wondered how Faye had gotten so lost when she had two women of such high caliber trying to show her the way, but Zabeth never wanted the subject mentioned. "Zabeth loved your mother, especially for bringing music into her life. I don't think she ever regretted the sacrifice it took to have that joy. And I know she never regretted raising you, loving you like her son."

"Thank you." His voice wavered, and he cleared his throat.

"Martin," Hannah paused, wondering if maybe there was a better time to ask her questions.

"Just say it, sweetheart."

He'd never used that term before, and it stirred her like when he played her favorite songs, making her feel they were meant to be. "You shared a sketchy version when we met, but what really happened to get Faye on this substance-abuse path?"

He brushed wisps of hair off her neck. "And we were having such a nice conversation." He pulled back from her and pushed a button on his watch, making it glow. "I don't think now's the time. I'd better go, but if anything comes up, Hannah, anything at all, you call me."

Frustrated that he'd cut her off so quickly and that he'd rather leave than talk to her, she rose, making it easier for him to stand.

He pulled the keys from his pocket and headed for his car.

Hannah followed him. "I don't like that you're suddenly treating me like a kid sister who's too frail to live alone in her own home or too weak to get a straight answer. If something is too much for me, I'll let *you* know. And you're the one who uses the phrase *just say it*."

He stopped and studied her. "I've never treated you like a sister. That's just disgusting, Hannah. I do my best never to push you in this relationship. That's all."

"And I admire that. I really do. But there's a difference between respecting who we can be, given time, and refusing to talk about things with me."

He ran his hand through his hair and walked to the split-rail fence near where Ol' Gert was standing. Hannah followed him.

Ol' Gert put her head across the fence, and he patted her. "I was twelve when Mom accused Dad of using her like a maid, never having time to raise us, never being a part of our lives. She wanted him to stop working and traveling so much. I think she just missed him, but I'd never seen my dad so angry, accusing her of using him. He said she wanted his money and the house, the cars, clothes, whatever. He said she wasn't his maid because she'd suckered Zabeth into being one." Martin shook his head. "That wasn't true.

My mom loved and treated Zabeth like a sister, not hired help. But the fight unleashed years of garbage. It went on for weeks before my dad finally packed his bags and moved out."

Hannah rubbed his back. "I...I shouldn't have asked this question, not today of all days."

Martin faced her. "For being so close, there are still things we hold back, aren't there?"

Dread of telling him that she'd once carried a child and was unable to ever carry another one washed over her. "Yes."

"It's time to move past those things, okay?" When she gave a slight nod, he continued. "The separation went on for months before things got totally out of control. Faye and Mom were arguing one day—I'm not sure about what—but it ended with Faye telling Mom she didn't blame Dad for moving out and she didn't know how he'd stood it for as long as he had. Then Faye stormed out, got in her car, and left. You know the rest. Mom followed her and never made it back."

She took in several deep breaths. "I'm so sorry." She gazed at him, searching for some sense of how to piece together what she knew of the Palmers. "Did your father ever comfort Faye, ever talk to her and tell her it wasn't her fault?"

Martin shook his head. "They barely spoke. Then less than two weeks after Mom's death, Faye disappeared. She'd pop back up every couple of months, always more needy and less stable than before. I was just a kid, so I didn't realize how heavily she drank and used. Zabeth stayed, making things as stable as possible. Dad stopped traveling as much. He became all that Mom had wanted to begin with. He came to my baseball games, taught me all he knew about business and the stock market, and gave me birthday money each year to invest."

"And Faye, did she get any of these benefits?"

"She wasn't there."

"You said she was there some of the time. What did he do to—"

He put his hands on her shoulders. "It's really time for me to be going."

"But..."

He lifted his hand. "No more, please."

She nodded. "Sure, I understand."

Placing his hand on the small of her back, he slowly kissed her. "That's what I came here for." He smiled before pulling his keys from his pocket again. "Will I see you in church on Sunday?"

"I'm on call, so there's no way of knowing right now."

He opened his car door and paused. "I'm glad Zabeth had you with her for the last two years."

Without waiting for a response, he got into his car, leaving Hannah to wonder how Vince Palmer could abandon his daughter to her guilt—even if she were to blame. And she wasn't. It was an accident, an awful one that seemed too heavy for both Martin and Faye. Faye needed her father to look her in the eye and tell her it wasn't her fault.

She ran her fingers over her lips, the sweetness of Martin's kiss clinging to her. If he could so easily see his sister drowning and not reach out to her, would he do the same to her if she made a mistake?

Chapter 28

The sound of the phone shrilled through the open windows as Mary wrapped the freshly baked muffins with a towel. She hesitated, unsure whether to try to make it to the phone shanty or not. It was quite a jaunt from Mammi Annie's kitchen to the shanty, and she wasn't sure she wanted to run—not in her newly pregnant condition.

Deciding not to dash to the phone, she placed the muffins on the table and turned to rinse her hands. The call would be from one of her mother's sisters. When the phone did ring, which wasn't often, it was always one of her aunts.

Mary had long ago given up on Hannah calling again, but that wasn't all she'd given up on. If Hannah didn't call or write, she wasn't going to return. And life moved on. Although Mary wasn't sure it had moved on for Paul. He'd be finished with his graduate degree by summer's end, but that wasn't a sign he was making progress emotionally. She and Luke would go to his grandmother's and see him later in the day. She hoped for his sake that he'd stopped waiting. Hannah had been her good friend while growing up and while Mary was recovering from her injuries, but Hannah had made a poor decision when she tried to hide her pregnancy from everyone. That's where most of the troubles came in.

Mary brushed a damp cloth down her apron, cleaning off the flour. Mammi Annie entered the kitchen, wiping sweat from her top lip. "Is there a reason why you're baking instead of planting your garden?"

"Ya, but not one you want to hear."

Mammi Annie smiled and shook her head. "I'll tell you what, Mary. You're too excited about that upcoming baby to settle down and take care of this year's crop, but you'll regret that if Luke has to buy food come winter because his wife didn't do as she should."

"I'll get to it next week. Tonight we're going out visiting."

"Well, is that really what should come first?"

She knew Mammi was trying to gently prod her to settle her whirlwind emotions, but the garden held no interest whatsoever. It was already the middle of May, and she hadn't put a seed in the ground yet. As usual Luke was patient with her and listened each night as she prattled endlessly about being pregnant.

"Where are you two heading this time?"

"To Mrs. Waddell's."

"To visit with that Paul fella?"

"Yes. He came by E and L a few weeks back and made plans with Luke for us to visit him. Until he came by the shop, neither of us had seen him in ages."

"You're not going to tell him or his grandmother of your news, surely."

"No, of course not."

Keeping herself from shouting to the world that she was expecting come November was really hard. She knew it wasn't something proper families told, but Mary wanted everyone in Owl's Perch to know her good news. Fact was, she wanted to put the information in *The Budget* and let the whole Amish world read that she was entering her second trimester, according to the midwife. But so far, only the adults in her and Luke's immediate families knew. Thankfully, her days of nausea were behind her. Because Hannah had explained certain things to her and because she'd longed to conceive, she'd known early on that she was pregnant. She'd used one of those at-home pregnancy tests to confirm her suspicions. Well, actually she'd used a dozen of them over as many months, but finally one had given the positive sign.

After taking longer to conceive than any other girl who'd married during her same wedding season, she couldn't contain her excitement.

Nor her health concerns.

She pressed her hand down the front of her dress, unable to feel even the slightest bulge through her clothing yet. At night, when she undressed, she slid her hand over the slight bump. It was such a miracle. One day a toddler would play near her as she worked her garden or hung laundry on the lines. One day she'd have a child who had once lived inside her.

"Mary?" Luke was in the driveway sitting in the buggy when he hollered through the screen door. "You ready?"

"Ya." She grabbed the muffins. "Don't wait up, Mammi. Paul said something about staying and playing a board game or two."

Mammi Annie harrumphed. "If that don't beat all, you and Luke hobnobbing with the likes of that man. You know the gossip spreads like wildfire whenever he is involved."

"If you don't say anything about where we're going, then nobody will know. Ya?" Mary didn't wait for her to answer before walking to the buggy. "Seems Mammi Annie disapproves of us visiting Paul."

Luke slapped the reins against the horse's back. "I can give you a short list of things she does approve of: you and our baby."

Tingles of excitement ran through Mary. From the day she'd learned she was pregnant, she'd felt like she was soaring with the hawks. Once in a while her conscience still nagged at her, but she'd made it this far without telling Luke the things he didn't want to know about his wife. She would not share her secret now.

It was a long ride to Paul's place, giving them lots of uninterrupted time to talk.

"Did you invite Matthew to come tonight?"

"Ya. He's not in a sociable mood of late." Luke guided the horse off to the side, letting several cars pass. "All I know is Elle ain't kept her word that she'd be living here by now, but she hasn't asked Matthew to release her from her promise to marry him. And he just keeps hoping things will work out."

"Just like Paul. Waiting and hoping. I hate this for both of them."

"Yeah, I know you do, but it's not yours to take on, Mary. Matthew's building a good business, and if it don't work out with Elle, then it don't. I think Paul's moved on too. I think that Dorcas girl will be there tonight, so don't be upset if she is.

"I won't be upset. I can't blame the man, and Dorcas seems nice enough. I just never thought Hannah'd stay gone like this. Did you?"

Luke shook his head. "Not once."

She slid closer to him. "I never knew what to think of Elle returning or not, but I always thought Hannah would come back to Paul when her pain and grief eased." She wrapped her arm around his. "I'll always be grateful we made it though."

Luke pulled into the driveway of his old shop. "I wish Matthew would forget about Elle and find somebody worthy of him."

"Yeah, I do too."

He helped Mary down, and they crossed the weedy path between the Lapp and Waddell properties.

Paul strode onto the porch and opened the door for them before they had a chance to knock. "Hi."

"I brought you these." Mary held out the muffins, noticing how full of life Paul appeared. When Hannah first left, he looked pale, and he lost a lot of weight in the weeks that followed. But tonight he looked robust and self-assured.

"Thanks. These'll go perfect with the coffee I have brewing. Come on in." He gestured toward the back door of the house.

As Mary crossed the porch, she saw several people in the kitchen she didn't know and one she did: Dorcas. For Hannah's sake, Mary hurt for what her friend could have had if tragedy hadn't struck.

She covered her stomach with her hand, grateful for what her future held.

Hannah pulled into Faye's gravel driveway. Her place wasn't nearly as nice as her brother's, but then again Martin worked hard and invested wisely. Faye didn't work, had no investments, and now that she didn't have Richard to support her or the children, Hannah wasn't sure what Faye would do. Her need to find work while buried under the grief of losing Zabeth and Richard weighed on Hannah. More important, it weighed on Martin even though he didn't talk about it.

She got out of the car, crossed the concrete porch, and knocked on the door. Even though Faye was close to no one now that Zabeth had died,

Hannah hoped to reach her. She was sure it'd mean a lot to Martin if his sister could find her way free of substance abuse. Plus, Hannah wanted both children enrolled in school this fall. It was absurd for Faye to pawn them off on any available sitter and then refuse to send them to school until it was mandatory. Kevin's age demanded he go this year, but Hannah knew it'd be good for Lissa to enter kindergarten—mandatory or not.

It wasn't easy trying to befriend Faye. She used people rather than bonded with them. She never considered returning favors or chatting over a cup of coffee. Her attitude wore on Hannah, and if it wasn't for Martin, Kevin, and Lissa, she'd bail out of this relationship.

Lissa opened the door. "Hannah!" She squealed and jumped into her arms.

Hannah gave her a long hug.

Kevin came running into the room. "Did you bring us lunch?"

Hannah put Lissa on her hip. "Are you hungry?" She looked around the messy room. "Where's your mom?"

Lissa covered her mouth with her finger. "Shh. She's asleep."

Kevin licked what looked like peanut butter from his fingers. "I was tryin' to make peanut-butter sandwiches, but we just got one slice of bread."

Wondering why Faye hadn't brought the kids by the house, she held out her hand for Kevin. "I'll fix you something."

She took him by the hand and went into the kitchen. A quick peek into the cabinets and fridge said Faye needed a trip to the grocery store. She heated a can of soup and found some crackers to spread the peanut butter on. While they ate, she made a list of items to get at the store, making sure she bought plenty of foods Kevin could fix for them. When they were finished, she sent them outside to play and went to Faye's bedroom.

She knocked on the door. "Faye?" Calling to her again, she entered the room. "Faye."

The shades were pulled tight and were taped around the edges to keep out the light. "Faye." Hannah shook her.

Faye moaned. "What?"

"Get up!" Hannah shook her again. "You cannot leave Kevin and Lissa alone while you sleep. There's almost no food in the house. The door wasn't even locked when I arrived. You're a social services nightmare. Do you realize that?"

Faye took a deep breath and sat up. "Are the kids already up for the morning?"

"It's afternoon, Faye. I know it's hard losing Richard and Zabeth, but if you don't pull your act together, you're going to lose your kids too."

Faye pulled at Hannah's dress. "Don't turn me in. I'm a good mother. You know that."

"I know you want to be. There's a difference." Hannah jerked the tape off the sides of the black-out shades, peeling paint and fraying the shades at the same time. "Get up, take a shower, and let's go to the store."

"Yeah, okay." Faye staggered to her feet.

"If you ever pull this again, I'll take the children from you myself. Got that?"

She nodded. "I'm trying, Hannah. I swear I'm trying."

"Why didn't you bring them to me like you usually do?"

"I...I took a few drinks and..."

"Didn't drive."

"See, that's a good thing. You should be glad for that part."

"You don't drive because you don't want to get a DUI. What lame excuse would you like to give for not calling me? What you've done this morning is dangerous, Faye. Your children were hungry, and Lissa opened the door for me without even knowing who it was. Kevin was trying to figure out how to turn on the stove. He's six years old! Do you get that?"

Faye sank onto the bed holding her head.

"You're depressed too. You need help, Faye, professional help."

"Oh good grief, Hannah. That makes Zabeth a whole lot smarter than you. Open your eyes. I'm beyond help."

Hannah remembered well the feeling of being trapped, and she regretted sounding so harsh. "No one is beyond help, Faye—not unless they're dead. And you're not dead." She eased onto the bed beside her. "This is really hard to explain, but I'm convinced it takes two things to survive on this fallen planet. One is forgiveness, because when we forgive, we're saying what was done to us is not more powerful than God's ability to redeem us from it."

Faye stared at her as if her words might be sinking in.

Hannah put her arm around Faye's shoulders. "You need to forgive yourself. You need to believe what you did is not more powerful than what God can do from this point forward. I can't see that as I look around your life, and I know you can't either, but that's where the faith part comes in. Now you think on those things while you get your shower, and we'll talk some more."

Luke pulled the mail from the box and read the return address on each envelope. He looked around the property for his wife and spotted her in the garden.

Walking toward the garden, he opened the letter from her doctor's office. "Mary Yoder, please be advised that you have missed your last two appointments. We have concerns about your rehabilitation and wellness program and would appreciate it if you would contact our office at your earliest convenience." Luke mumbled the words and closed the letter.

When he came to the edge of the garden, Mary saw him and stood straight, holding her back. "I've been at this all day. But here's the deal, I'm doing the planting, and you'll do the weeding, right?"

Luke held the letter out to her. "What's this?"

She took it and glanced over it. "It...it must be a mistake."

"It still has you listed as Mary Yoder."

She nodded. "I saw that."

"You're keeping up with those visits and everything, right?"

"Oh, Luke, I'm seeing the midwife now that I'm expecting, and there's no reason to keep going to those expensive doctors for them just to tell me I'm healthy. Ya?"

"Well, it's different with you, and I don't know..."

"Luke, I'm fine. You know I am. The doctor has given me a clean bill of health over and over again. It's time to forget the days of the accident and live like they never happened."

"Mary Yoder?" He lifted the letter from her hand and read it again.

"Mary Lapp, thank you very much." She washed her dirty hands off in the pail she'd been using to water her newly planted crop. Wiping them on her apron, she gazed up at Luke. "Unless you care to change your last name instead."

Luke scratched his forehead. "It just seems they'd get the name right."

She grabbed the pail and stood. "It also seems you wouldn't walk around in wet clothes."

"What?" He looked up from the paper just in time to see his wife throw water on him. "Mary Yoder!"

She burst into laughter and ran from him. "Who?" She grabbed the hose and held it toward him. "Even my husband calls me by my maiden name?"

"It was a mistake."

"Ya, and so was this."

Water smacked Luke in the face, and he charged her and wrestled the hose from her, all the while enjoying her laughter. She'd shed too many tears afraid she might never get pregnant. This new joy was a welcome thing.

When he had control of the hose, he drenched her good before she slid down on the grass. He dropped the hose and ran to her. "I'm sorry. Are you okay?"

Laughing, she grabbed a handful of loose dirt and tried to rub it in his face. He pinned her hands to the ground, chortling before they both grew serious as he lowered his lips to hers. "It's definitely Mary Lapp," Luke mumbled. "I remember that clearly now."

Chapter 29

With Kevin and Lissa in tow, Hannah entered the church doors, returning a dozen greetings. She made her way to their children's church classrooms and signed them in before giving them hugs and heading for the sanctuary. The place wasn't very churchlike from the outside. It had once been a shopping complex, but that was impossible to tell once you were inside the renovated building. The praise music filled the air. A hint of unease clung to her as she maneuvered through the place without Zabeth.

She'd already arranged for Vicki and Nina to get the children after church and take them home. Either she or Martin would pick them up later. She took her seat in what had been Zabeth's and her spot. Martin was behind the keyboard, totally absorbed with the band. Although she missed a lot of Sundays due to her work at the clinic, she loved most parts of going to church here: the teaching, the music, the prayer time, communion, watching the altar calls, and the friendliness of the members. Other parts she could do without. Actually there was only one other part: the clothing worn by a lot of the women, especially the ones around her age. Jeans, short skirts, and tight tops seemed not to bother anyone but Hannah. But if men came here to worship God, why would a woman dress in such a way as to totally distract them? Wasn't God allowed one day, in His own house? She just didn't get it.

Then again, she figured it was her problem. She couldn't even manage to wear her hair loose, so what did she know? It'd taken her far too long to become comfortable wearing the mandatory scrubs when doing clinical rotations for nursing school.

Martin looked her way and raised his brows, showing his surprise. If he thought her making it to church when she was on call was unusual, she might need to get the ammonium carbonate out of her medical bag for the next shocker.

When the musicians moved to their seats for the preaching, Martin headed her way as he'd done every Sunday since last Christmas. As he took a seat, she could smell his cologne.

He placed his arm on the back of the bench. "I'm glad you made it. You doing okay?"

"Sure. You?"

"Yeah, I am. Listen, I'm having a memorial type gathering at my place this Friday. I can count on you being there, right?"

"For Zabeth?"

"Yeah, just a time with the band, singing her favorite songs."

"That should only take about three days."

He coughed into his hand to hide his laughter.

Howard, the man in front of them, turned around, smiling. "We know how to separate the *youth* when they get rowdy during service."

Martin pointed his thumb at Hannah, like it was all her fault. The man chuckled and turned back around. She folded her arms across her waist and frowned at Martin.

Pastor Steve opened the service, the PowerPoint slide behind him declaring the subject in bold, black letters. "Today's topic is intimacy and sexuality."

Hannah's breath caught. Martin leaned in, rubbing her shoulder sympathetically. "Breathe, phone girl. It's a five-part series," he whispered through his laughter.

She swallowed, wondering what all would be covered from a pulpit.

The pastor unbuttoned his bright red sports jacket. "Intimacy can be thought of as *in to me see*. And we let very few people really see who we are, but when we're a couple under God's direction, we long for that. But how do we get it?"

Hannah's cheeks burned mild to flaming as the service went on, but the teaching was insightful and filled with humor. As the pastor brought the service to a close, Martin got up to head for the keyboard. Before leaving the pew, he pointed at her. "You stay."

She gave a nod. When the service ended, she hung around in the sanctuary, chatting with people while waiting for Martin to finish playing the last songs. She was totally engrossed in answering some questions from a grandmother-to-be when she felt the warmth of Martin's hand on the small of her back.

"You about ready?" he asked.

The woman took her cue, thanked Hannah, and left.

He studied her, not looking his normal, confident self. "I'm starving, and you're not going to make me eat Sunday lunch alone, right?"

"Actually, no."

"Wow, can't say I saw that one coming."

Hannah straightened his shirt collar. "We need to talk." She patted his chest. "I brought us a picnic lunch."

He looked suspicious. "Where to?"

"Somewhere no one will hear you screaming at me."

"Hmm, I don't like the sound of this." They headed toward the exit. "There are picnic tables beside my office. No one will be anywhere near there on a Sunday." He pulled his keys from his pocket. "I'll drive and then bring you back here to pick up your car."

She dangled her keys. "I'm the one with the food. I'll drive and bring you back here."

He got in the car and made himself comfortable, punching the radio stations and making smart remarks about her driving. His sarcasm kept things lively from the time she got into the car until she pulled into his office parking lot. The manicured lawns and walls of windows gave the one-story, red-brick building a very classy look.

She put the stick shift in reverse and set the brake. "Nice place."

"Not bad." They opened their car doors in unison and got out. "I'm looking at leasing a new building next year since we're outgrowing this place, provided I pass my engineering exams in October."

"Have you turned in your board application forms?"

"Yep."

They chatted over little things while covering the table with a cloth, setting out the food, and eating lunch, only pausing to say a prayer before eating. The conversation meandered throughout the meal, but when he tossed his napkin onto his paper plate, an obvious transition took place.

"Okay, I'm full and completely satisfied, so what's on your mind, Esther?"

"Esther?" Hannah repeated before she realized he was referring to Queen Esther and her appeal for her people. "You're no king, and I'm not afraid anyone will lop off my head." She gathered the dirty plates and put them back in the basket.

He chuckled. "So what gives?"

After putting the rest of the items into the basket, she took a seat. "You do, I hope."

"What do you want?"

"You to get Faye into rehab and go to counseling sessions with her. Talk your dad into doing phone sessions on a regular basis. He's got the money. Get him to fly here for a few weeks. We need to help Faye get free of this unfair burden of guilt she carries. Shift the focus from her being the black sheep to the reality that she's a victim in this too."

He sighed. "Hannah, sweetheart, your motives are good, but Faye is a lost cause."

"I don't think so, but this isn't just about her. I mean, I've seen her at least three times a week since I met her. Under that veneer and deeper than her drug use, she's really sweet and hurting. I think you have enough influence on her that if you pushed in the right ways, she'd go into rehab, but—"

"No, she won't. Underneath it, she's an addict, Hannah. I'm sorry. That's just the way it is. She's not willing to go to rehab or counseling. And even if she would, I'm not going with her, and I'm certainly not asking my dad to get involved."

"Your dad wouldn't even call during a session to help his daughter?"

Martin stood, picked up the basket, and walked toward the car. "You'd have to know him."

She followed him. "What's he like?"

"Distinguished, filled with charisma, and bitter at Faye. Your plan isn't going to work. Faye has to want this, and she doesn't."

Hannah opened the trunk of her car. "But if you presented it..."

He placed the basket in the trunk. "No human can control another one's will. She doesn't want help."

"Sure she does. She just might not realize it yet, but if you—"

He slammed the trunk shut. "You're the one who..." His words came out mocking and condescending before he stopped. He walked away from her before turning. "I'm not willing to spend time and energy to land in the same freaking place with her I've been in for the past sixteen years—only to fail again. Do you know what it takes to be my age and run a business like this?" He waved his hand toward the building. "I have forty employees who all have personal issues, but at least they fight for success. Faye has no fight in her, and that's not our fault. The answer is no."

She stepped in closer. "And if you can do that for your employees, think what you could do for your sister. And you."

"Me? Are you saying I need help?"

"I...I'm saying if Faye gets help, it'll help you too."

He raked his hands through his hair. "There's nothing to help. I resent you implying that I need *Faye's* help."

He was yelling at her, and she knew he'd rather fight with her than for his sister.

"I'll keep Kevin and Lissa during every session. It won't be easy, but it's doable. You and your father haven't really tried. She's been left alone. You were a kid. It wasn't your fault, but it's time to—"

"You haven't been here but two years, and you have it all figured out—who's right, who's wrong, how you can fix it. Just butt out, Hannah."

"Fine." She opened her car door.

"Zabeth would never ask this of me."

"She was a mother to you. I want more. I want what you can't give me unless you can reach past your apathy and anger and help your sister." She angled her head, catching his eye. "Is that what you want from this relationship, for me not to ask more of you than Zabeth?"

An expression she couldn't read crossed his face. "No, of course not. Although a little of Zabeth's nondemanding ways would be appreciated about now."

"She wanted you and Faye and your dad—her family—to find a resolution to the nightmare that stole everything. All I'm asking is that you go with Faye and try to find some answers."

He shoved his hands into his pockets and walked off. "Why?" he shouted at the sky before facing her. "Why is jumping through hoops for Faye so important?"

In spite of his sarcastic tone, it was a fair question, but she could feel embarrassment burn her skin at the thought of answering.

She swallowed hard. "It's not just for Faye that I want this, or for you. *I* need this."

"You?"

Hating that she'd backed into a corner where the only way out was to share things she didn't want to, she made herself speak. "Look, I know this is unfair, but I need to know that when I make stupid decisions and you get caught in them, you'll reach out to me. Your sister made a mistake, and it feels like you just washed your hands of her."

He closed the distance between them. "That's ridiculous, and you're not making sense. You'd never do anything as—"

She placed her hand over his mouth, unable to hear his declaration of faith in her. "Everybody does hurtful stuff, Martin. I need this from you." Lowering her hand, she forced the next words out. "I never told you, but I became pregnant from the attack, and I tried to hide the whole thing from Paul." She crossed her arms, hating that her eyes were misting. "I knew if he ever found out about the rape, he'd end our relationship. He did, within two minutes of learning the truth. The baby died, and I came here." She shuddered. "Your sister made a mistake and has paid too high a price."

He took her hand into his. "I'm sorry Paul was a jerk. And I'm sorry for what you went through." He paused before giving a nod. "I see your point that it's easier to walk away than anything else." He sighed. "I'll see what I can do to get Faye into counseling, but you can't get upset when this plan does nothing to help her."

"It'll work. I know it will."

He rolled his eyes, took a step back, and opened the driver's door for her. "From now on, I'll know to beware of beautiful girls carrying loaded picnic baskets."

"Yeah?" She laughed.

He bent, giving her a kiss.

She caressed his face. "Thank you for doing this."

"Yeah, yeah, yeah, that's what you say now. Just wait until it all blows up in our face."

"It won't."

$\mathcal{M}$atthew read the letter one last time before scrawling his name at the bottom. He folded it and shoved it into the envelope addressed to Elle. Against everything he'd spent years hoping for, he went to the mailbox, placed it inside, and lifted the red flag. An early-morning summer breeze carried the burnt smell from the Bylers' barn. The memory of flames leaping toward the sky last night left a sick feeling in Matthew's gut. But that didn't compare to the twisting ache that breaking off with Elle was causing.

Trudging into his workshop, he couldn't help but rehash how little he'd seen Elle since she went to live with her father more than two years ago. Each trip back she was different, more of an Englischer and less of the Elle he'd fallen in love with. He'd seen the look in her eyes, the one that said she no longer admired who he was or what talents he possessed. He wasn't in the same class of people as she was, and her visits seemed only to confirm that for her.

She'd spent the last year driving all over the U.S. while snapping pictures, but somehow her car just couldn't make it down these familiar roads very often. She'd signed some sort of contract without realizing exactly what it meant, and Matthew had been patient as she tried to get in her hours so the contract would be fulfilled. When it was time for instruction to begin, she had to get special permission to finish out her contracts among the Englischers and yet still be allowed to take instruction classes. As a testimony to Elle's ability to talk people into things, her bishop agreed. At first her efforts to be here for instruction had given him hope, but she hadn't made it for the last two lessons, nor had she called or written him.

Her agreement with her father not to call Matthew had ended quite a while ago, but her letters and phone calls had dwindled to nothing, and it was time he accepted reality. Her father had won. Elle would never be baptized into their faith.

Pulling on his tool belt, Matthew ran down a mental list of what he needed to get done today.

Luke was traveling, taking a week to handpick supplies and stock up for this next year. This was the fourth buying trip in as many months. Matthew went on the last three. Luke had avoided going for a while because of Mary, but now he wanted to get his time in so he wouldn't need to travel as Mary grew closer to her November due date.

Sarah drove the half-loaded produce wagon toward Miller's Roadside Stand.

She was sick of her parents always whispering about her odd behavior. Her hand had a burn on it, and she didn't know why. So what? If the constant gray cloud that clung to her thoughts would go away, maybe she could explain how she felt. But it never did.

Weariness made her movements hard during the day, but the nights were even worse. Fires blazed everywhere, creeping across Amish land until they burned right through her home. She shuddered.

After pulling the wagon under a shade tree at the roadside stand, she climbed out and looped the horse's reins around the hitching post. The stand had a blue and white tentlike covering, lawn chairs for the vendors, and plenty of parking for customers. The Millers' home was at the high point of the property, just a couple of hundred feet from the street. They rented a portion of their stand to anyone who needed a good place to sell things. Since the Lapps' house was so far off the main roads, this was one place they had always come to sell the extra yield from the family garden.

Leaning over the side of the wagon, she grasped the handles of the bushel basket.

"Sarah," Lizzy Miller called from her front porch.

Setting the heavy container on the ground, Sarah figured the girl was helping her mother collect this month's rent for the roadside stand. Sarah waved, letting her know she'd heard her. Then she reached into the wagon and unloaded the rest of the baskets while Lizzy hurried down the hill toward her.

"Did you hear?" Lizzy panted. The girl had graduated the eighth grade with Sarah years ago.

"Hear what?"

"The Bylers' barn burned down last night, all the way to the ground!"

The words shot through Sarah, making her feel woozy. Was her nightmare coming true? She set the small baskets of raspberries on the ground and straightened. "You sure?"

"Go see for yourself."

Without answering Lizzy, Sarah climbed into the wagon and took off.

It was quite a jaunt to the Bylers', but within thirty minutes she was pulling up at their place. Smoke was still rising from a few spots. Lizzy was right; there wasn't a salvageable piece of timber anywhere.

Unable to remove her eyes from the damage, she got out of the wagon and edged up to the smoldering embers. The barn had been a full, strong structure. She'd been to singings and church meetings here throughout her life. Hannah had taught her how to jump from the loft into a pile of hay in this barn. Stepping around the smoldering parts, Sarah walked through some of the ashes. How could such a strong building, with thick timber running in all directions for support, be reduced to this?

The tongue is a fire, a world of evil…and sets on fire the course of life.

A shudder ran through her, and those words looped through her mind again and again.

Aiming to find where the loft had crashed from its high position to the ground, Sarah continued walking around the edge of the building. Sadness deeper than any laughter or joy she'd shared in this building twisted inside her.

Wondering if the tiny corncob dolls she and Hannah had made and buried under the ground in the tack room more than a decade ago were still there, Sarah went to the spot where she thought they should be buried. The area had been along the outer wall. No smoke rose from that area. She held her hands over the cinders. They gave off no heat. Soot covered her hands and dress as she moved a few burnt two-by-fours. When a portion was cleared, she grabbed a piece of burnt tin from the roof, knelt where she thought they should be, and began digging.

Matthew heard the door to the paint shop open. David had finished his other chores and had arrived to add another coat of shellac to the fifteen buggies that were close to being fitted to their undercarriages. Matthew worked another spoke into place on its wooden-hoop frame, hoping to get a dozen wheels done before nightfall.

As the morning wore on, sounds of the outdoors echoed through the open windows, allowing him to hear when the mail carrier approached. A desire to run to the mailbox and snatch back the letter gripped him. His palms became sweaty as he imagined the postal vehicle slowly heading, mailbox by mailbox, toward the Esh place. Ignoring his anxiety, he wrestled to line up the spokes that sprawled from the wooden hub with the hand-drilled holes in the circular frame.

He reminded himself that long before Elle's father showed up, her bishop had asked her to wait until she was at least twenty-one to join the faith. At the time he hadn't understood the reason, but the bishop had turned out to be right. Some Englischers had tried living Amish. It never lasted for more than a few years before they pulled out of the faith, sold their places, and returned to the easier ways of the fancy folk.

He'd thought it would be different for Elle since she'd been raised Amish half her life. As the mail carrier closed the metal lid on the Esh mailbox and drove off, Matthew went to the barn and bridled his fastest horse. He needed a few minutes away from the shop.

Holding on tight, he spurred the horse across his property, jumping every fallen log, trampling through the creek, and riding at breakneck speeds across the flatlands. The warm breeze whipped through his shirt, cooling the sweat against his body. His straw hat flew off, but he didn't slow. He should have known Elle wasn't likely to return to the Plain life. He tightened his grip on the reins and dug his heels into the horse, wishing he could outrun reality.

When Matthew spotted the profile of a female across the meadow, he slowed the horse to an amble. She seemed to be kneeling in the grass. He tugged at the rein and clicked his tongue, heading the horse in that direction.

As he came closer, he could make out a white prayer Kapp on her head. He thought it odd that the woman didn't seem to hear the approaching hoof-beats against the dry ground.

A childlike voice drifted through the air. "The tongue is a fire, a world of evil…and sets on fire the course of life."

"Excuse me." Matthew brought the horse to a full stop. The girl jumped up. "Sarah?" She was covered in soot, and the hems of her skirts were torn. "What are you doing out here?" He scanned the edges of the fields. "Is someone with you?"

She shook her head, looking terrified. Dark soil covered the green and brown grass beside her, and he realized she'd been digging in it. "What are you doing?"

"I…I was burying something for Hannah."

"Hannah?" He steadied his horse. "When did you talk to her?"

She turned her back to him, knelt, and put whatever was in her hand into the hole in the ground and covered it. When she stood, she stepped on the fresh dirt, packing it down. "I haven't spoken to her." After wiping her dirt-covered hands down her apron, she turned her palms upright, as if she were offering him a gift. But her hands were empty.

"How did you get this far from home without a horse?"

"I came to bur—" She didn't finish her sentence.

Matthew tried again. "Did you drive a horse and buggy to the Yoders and then walk to this spot?"

"I went to Miller's Roadside earlier, then drove the horse and buggy to the Bylers'. From there I drove to the back part of your property and walked."

Matthew was even more confused now. Sarah had always been skittish and odd, to his way of thinking, but this behavior left him more uneasy than ever. Her hands trembled as she tried dusting them off. He decided not to try to figure this out. He'd just talk to Luke about it when he got home. "Can I give ya a ride back to your buggy?"

She nodded, and he reached a hand down to help lift her onto the horse's back. She wrapped her hands around his waist. Not liking this one bit, he dug his heels into the horse. "Geh."

Chapter 31

Martin stared into his sister's almost-black eyes, weary of this conversation. He'd been at this session for more than an hour. Hannah was baby-sitting Kevin and Lissa at his house, and he'd told her he'd be home by five. It was Friday, so she didn't need him to relieve her for classes or the clinic, but she did have plans of some sort.

Faye needed to live at the rehab center for a few more weeks, but all the intervention had accomplished so far was schedule chaos for Hannah and him. Hannah arrived at his home by six in the morning, and she needed to leave his house by five in the evening, Monday through Thursday—except on Tuesday. Tuesdays were the worst. She had that quilting thing at the clinic and often ended up taking Kevin and Lissa with her and dropping them at the house before going to the crisis center. He had to leave work at four in the afternoon, cutting off at least three valuable hours of work time to care instead for his sister's children.

With Dr. Smith listening silently, Faye had gone through a whole box of tissues, but they'd landed in the same place they always did. She claimed that everyone in the family hated her because they blamed her for her mom's death. Martin denied it. He didn't blame her for that, but the drugs and alcohol abuse were her choices. She had to be accountable for that.

But not for the accident.

Still, what led to the shattering of their childhood made more sense each time he came here. Occasionally when she shared a recollection, it caused other memories to flood his mind, and in some ways he understood both Faye and himself more now.

When Martin talked to his dad about doing phone sessions, he refused. Flat out. Martin didn't intend to tell Faye he'd contacted their dad. It was hard enough to get her into rehab and counseling without reminding her how little their dad wanted to do with her.

She grabbed another tissue. "Can't you see how Dad manipulated me to fight with Mom and then, after the accident, he just abandoned me?"

"Dad's never manipulated anybody. You ran off, Faye. But even then, he kept giving you money, supporting you."

She sniffled. "Don't you ever wonder why he did that?"

"He's done nothing but try to help you."

The counselor shifted in her chair. "Okay, we've covered a lot today. I think this session has been extremely helpful."

The doctor continued talking, drawing things to a close, but Martin wasn't listening. He'd heard plenty, and none of it was new. Faye just didn't get it. No one blamed her but herself. She had destroyed her own life, not Mom or Dad or him. Surprisingly, on this trip he'd heard one encouraging thing: she was attending chapel services.

After the counselor closed the session with prayer, Martin left without another word.

Thanks to his sister, he had a mess of a life to keep up with, including juggling her two children—with Hannah's help.

Hannah.

Despite having built a good friendship beforehand, he and Hannah were being taxed by this stuff with Faye. Hannah had cut her hours at Dr. Lehman's clinic, but she couldn't cut her school, study time, or clinical rotation hours.

She worked harder than anyone he knew and continued to amaze him. For quite a while after first meeting her, Martin kept dating, looking for other possibilities—because of her age and background. But a part of him kept hoping that when she was older, she'd be the one he'd been waiting for. The one he'd been looking for since he'd realized the importance of God in his life.

When he was a kid, his mother had told him, "When you get old enough, date, date, date, but never settle for less than the one you know in your heart is right for you." He'd like to hear what advice she'd give him now.

But she was gone, thanks to his sis—

Oh God, please…

His stomach clenched in a knot, making him feel sick. He had to pull to the side of the road. Like a spray of cold water in winter, chills crashed over him.

Faye was right.

Dear God, I do blame her.

Memories of how he'd coped after Mom died seeped into his mind from somewhere he didn't know existed. He'd always believed he and his dad were good people caught in an awful situation, but where did that leave Faye? And why hadn't he seen any of this before now?

He turned the car around to go see his sister.

With Lissa and Kevin playing in the yard, Hannah sorted through another box in Martin's storage room inside the cottage behind his home, looking for items to donate to the women's shelter. Martin cared nothing about this stuff from his childhood and Lissa's and Kevin's infancy. It was time to put it to good use. Since Martin was late again, she continued digging through it. She'd already brought out a bassinet from the storage room, cleaned it, and set it up. The washer and dryer had worked all day on old blankets, sheets, and baby clothes.

Through the screen door, she could hear the children's voices as they made pies from outdated flour, eggs, and milk she'd found when cleaning out Martin's fridge and cabinets. Kevin and Lissa were mixing the items with sand and had a table set for a bake sale. Their childish excitement over old foods had made her smile.

Even though she was still living at the cabin, she spent more time on Martin's property than at home, and it was unexpectedly stressful. She'd discovered that the cottage behind his place was more her style than his house. His fully air-conditioned, electronically endowed, television-crazy home made her long for the cabin. Most of all she missed having time to enjoy her garden. Martin's manicured lawns, maintained by paid help, were picture perfect, but they didn't compare to the beauty of the landscape at Zabeth's place. As soon as Martin came home today, she'd head for the cabin and weed the garden.

In a few weeks both Kevin and Lissa would begin school. She'd updated their immunizations and taken care of the paperwork. Martin had enrolled them.

Remembering she'd seen one more box of items she hadn't gone through yet, Hannah went back to the storage room. She opened the box and pulled out folded sheets and blankets one by one. As she came to the bottom of the box, she noticed frayed edges of fabric under a store-bought blanket. She removed the top item, revealing a patchwork quilt that showed clear markings of being designed by Zabeth. Pulling it out and laying it in her lap, she noted the tiny black squares of material added to the defined pattern. Hannah smoothed her hand over the well-worn quilt. It was Zabeth's work all right, and it looked like someone had abused it before packing it away. The fabric patches—leopard skin, white silk, pink tulle, crimson satin, brown suede—were not Zabeth's usual choices, which meant she'd made it for someone special with fabrics from his or her personal life. It had to belong to a Palmer—Faye, Martin, or their parents. Whoever received it hadn't understood; a quilt was like a person, possessing strength and honor as well as frailties and needs. Right then, she decided to work on the quilt at the next quilting.

Hannah took it to her car. As she was closing the door, Martin pulled into the driveway.

She waved as he got out of his car. "Hey, you're even later than usual."

"Yeah, I know."

"The kids have eaten, and there's a plate for you in the oven if you want it."

"You're leaving now? Are you on call or something?"

"There are only so many hours of daylight, Martin, and it's hard to weed a garden in the dark. I have rotation this weekend. That makes this my only time to do something outside of school, work, and baby-sitting."

He scoffed and pulled his checkbook out of his back pants pocket. "Just let me write a check to cover what you'll make on that garden."

Hannah blinked. "What?"

"Oh, come on, Hannah. This is ridiculous." He filled in a check and held it out to her. "Forget the garden. We're both pulling double duty as it is, and this will more than compensate."

"Do you think money is the answer to everything?" She pulled her keys from her dress pocket and got into her car.

"Get out of the car, Hannah. Now."

She rolled the window down. "Excuse me?" She released the brake and pressed the clutch. "I resent being treated like a child. Moreover, I refuse."

Before she pressed the accelerator, Martin stepped behind the car. She slammed on the brakes, turned off the motor, and jumped out. "Are you crazy?"

"Don't get angry with me and just leave. Stay and scream until all the neighbors hear you, but don't ever do that."

In that moment she realized that a similar situation was how he'd lost his mother. She shut the car door. "You want me to stay and scream? Fine! Your all-air-conditioned, highly technical, very modern house is driving me crazy!"

"Yeah?" He screamed back. "Well, when you go off by yourself, you drive me nuts, and I have no cabin of refuge!"

They stared at each other.

Hannah propped herself against the car. "I drive you nuts?"

He shrugged. "Maybe."

Standing in front of her was her closest friend, a man who'd made himself vulnerable by reaching out to his sister because she'd asked him to. "I'm sorry."

"Yeah, me too. And I won't ever try to put a price on that stupid garden of yours again."

She laughed. "Deal."

Kevin ran from the backyard, carrying a pan of *pies* with him. Stress was etched on his young face, and Hannah realized the raised voices had him in a panic. Lissa was right behind him, looking as if she was about to cry.

Before she could say something, Lissa pulled on Martin's leg, her dirty hands leaving imprints. "Who's leaving?"

Martin put Lissa on his hip.

Hannah picked up Kevin. "Nobody. Not right now. I might go to the cabin later."

But the concern in their eyes said they'd heard the anger between the adults and didn't believe her. "Your Uncle Martin and I were playing. That's what you heard, but you know what I think? I think your uncle is hungry and needs a nap."

Martin nodded. "May I please have food and a nap?"

Kevin giggled. "Naps are for babies."

"Are not!" Lissa yelled.

"Whoa." Martin held up his hand. "Answer my question first."

Hannah pointed at him. "You may have food, but it's too late for a nap. So…after you eat, you, Kevin, and Lissa may come with me to the cabin."

"I'd rather have a nap."

Lissa shook her finger at him. "You better watch it, Uncle Martin. Hannah won't let you have a snack with your dinner."

Martin gaped mockingly at one and then the other. "What?"

Lissa giggled. "And even if you're good, she doesn't allow television."

He touched the end of her nose with his index finger. "Yeah, I've heard that before. But that means you're just happier when I'm home, right?"

"Thanks, Martin."

He chuckled as he set Lissa's feet on the ground. "No. I thank you, Hannah."

Hannah put Kevin down and took the *pie* from him. She bit her bottom lip and bounced the pan filled with gunk up and down.

Martin pointed at her. "If you start this, I'll finish it."

She stepped in close. "Promise?" she taunted right before smacking him in the chest with the pie. She took Lissa into her arms and took off running to get another pie.

Martin whispered something to Kevin, who ran into the house. Instantly they were divided, the girls against the boys. From the pie-making area, Hannah grabbed a handful of gunk. Kevin came back outside with a bottle of ketchup and mustard. He passed the ketchup bottle to his uncle. The two guys moved in close, and she flung the goop at Martin, missing completely. He mocked an evil laugh and stepped in closer.

"Don't you dare, Mart—"

He squirted the red sauce over her bare feet and across her dress. He then aimed the bottle at her face. He roared with laughter before aiming the bottle at Kevin.

"Yeah, get me, Uncle Martin. Get me!"

The next ten minutes were spent with Kevin and Lissa playing dodge ketchup. When the bottle was empty, the four of them were a mess.

Martin and Kevin went to one bathroom to get cleaned up, and Hannah and Lissa went to another. Twenty minutes later the kids were clean and dressed in warm clothes and sent back outside to play, with all yucky stuff off-limits for the night.

Martin and Hannah went into the kitchen. She pulled his plate of food from the oven and set it on the table. He grabbed a bottle of water from the refrigerator.

Hannah sat at the table, waiting for him to say something.

Martin stabbed a forkful of potatoes. "I got a little too angry."

"And too demanding. But I might have been a little testy myself and a bit desperate for the solitude of the cabin."

He took a bite of the grilled pork chop. "That's so good," he mumbled.

"Was it bad at work today?"

He shook his head. "The average hassles. But I had to put everything aside again to meet with Faye. The session with her was really long and difficult."

"Why didn't I know you were seeing her today?"

"I guess because I don't like to think about the sessions, let alone admit when I'm going to them."

"Do you want to talk about it?"

"Well, 'want to' might be pushing it, but I will." He winked at her. "Can I have a promise first?"

"I promise."

"Do you know what you just promised me?"

She nodded. "To not get angry and leave but to stay and work things out."

"Nope. You just promised to marry me."

She burst out laughing.

He set the fork down and covered her hand with his. "I need you to keep your word on that, Hannah. Since we first met at GymberJump, you've shown your tendency to turn your back and just leave. On our first date, I had to take the keys."

"I just get angry way beyond what's happening right then, and I don't know what to do with it other than get away."

He sat up straight and picked up the fork. "I really don't understand it from someone as levelheaded as you are, but you've got to give me your word—no more leaving during the heat of an argument."

"I promise."

He nodded. "It was a good session with Faye, the best we've had yet. Only it was draining and just made me feel nauseated. I faced some things I didn't know about myself."

He ate and talked. Later they moved to the chairs in the backyard. Lissa and Kevin climbed into the hammock and went to sleep to the sounds of adults discussing events in their week. When the children dozed off, Martin and Hannah began talking about deep things again. As Martin told about the progress Faye was making and the self-realizations they were both having, hope for the Palmers' future warmed her. Faye was coming home next week. They would still need to help juggle Lissa and Kevin so she didn't get overwhelmed, but she was coming home.

"Hannah?"

Her head was against the back of the chair as she watched the leaves of the sycamore sway softly under the glow of moonlight. "Hmm?"

"Do you feel like you know what you want in life?"

The sounds of crickets rode gently across the night air while she thought about his question. Voices from the past demanding she live by the *Ordnung* rose, then faded. An image lingered of who she once thought she'd become— in a caped dress and prayer Kapp, trying to live an obedient Plain life but determined to find enough freedom within to discover her real self.

Looking across the lush lawn to the electric lights shining through the windows of the stately home, she was again struck by the contrast of her life now. Then Hannah's eyes focused on Lissa and Kevin, snuggled under a blanket. They were so precious. She smiled at Martin, who watched her intently. "Most days."

"Think you'd care to take our dating more seriously? You know, make a verbal commitment?"

She laughed. "And ruin whatever this game is that we play?"

"It's called the game of growing up, and you've played it quite well."

"It's a shame I can't return the compliment."

"Cute."

"So, after accepting the challenge of committing to date just one girl, you want to step up that pledge?"

He took her hands in his. "Truth is, even though I went out with all those girls, I've always been looking for you, and then you landed here— entirely too young to do anything about it and from a different world."

Somewhere inside her, his words snuggled against her soul and the magnetic pull of being this close to him made her head swim. But she was in too deep already since she hadn't told him the one thing that might cause him to change his mind. "I don't really see a need to step up what we have. We're dating. We've agreed you won't see anyone else."

"Just me?" he mocked.

She gave him a kiss. "Yep, just you. I better head home. Good night, Martin."

Chapter 32

Matthew lifted off the back of the truck the last box of supplies from Luke's most recent trip to the wholesale stores.

Nate McDaniel, their truck driver and Englischer neighbor, who lived some fifteen miles down the road, clapped his hand against Matthew's back. "You got quite a stack of papers mounded in your old workshop."

Perching the edge of the box on the tailgate, Matthew chuckled. "Yeah, I know. We hired a cousin of Esther Byler to come in and help out. She starts later today, but a person might go in there and never come out."

Nate laughed. "Buried alive by paperwork." He pulled keys from his pocket. "Hope whoever you find is up to the task." He glanced at his watch. "I gotta run. It took me and Luke two days more than we figured on to get all that stuff. I imagine the missus has a honey-do list a mile long."

"Thanks, Nate." Matthew hoisted the box. "We should be all set for quite a while." As Nate pulled his truck out of the driveway, Matthew carried the load into the storage room.

With a clipboard in his hand, Luke stepped in front of Matthew and jotted down the inventory numbers off the side of the box. He then pointed to a section of boxes. "Let's put it over there."

Matthew slid the carton into place. "Where's David and Jacob?"

"Tending horses and lallygagging, in that order." Luke lowered the clipboard to his side and bounced it against his leg. "I know Jacob is Mary's brother and all, but we gotta do something about him."

Matthew nodded. "I know. But right now we need to talk about somethin' a lot more serious." Wasting no time, Matthew told Luke about finding Sarah covered in soot and burying things in an unused field.

Luke wiped his brow. "What do you think she was doing?"

"I have no idea. I took her to her buggy that she'd left near Mary's house, but I didn't go back to the field and dig up whatever it was she buried. That just seemed wrong." Matthew propped his foot on top of one of the boxes. "You know how bad she got right after Hannah left. Well, I hate to say this, but she seems really bad again. Maybe the Bylers' barn going up in flames made her slip right off that ledge again. It's the only reason I can figure why she'd be going through the ashes."

A car door slammed, causing Luke to go to the window. He turned to Matthew. "I think I'll go to the Yoders' and let Mary know I'm back. Then I'd best go to the folks' place and see what's up with Sarah. And, uh, good luck, Matthew. Looks like you're going to need it."

"Huh? What are you talk—"

"Matthew Esh!" Elle's voice vibrated the walls as she entered the front door of the shop.

Luke passed the clipboard to Matthew and slipped out the side door of the storage room. Matthew walked through the connecting hallway and into his old shop.

Elle waved papers in the air. "This is how you wait for somebody?"

He recognized the pages in her fist. He was surprised she hadn't been relieved by his letter and figured she was more insulted than disappointed. "Hi, Elle." He went to the file cabinet, which had more papers stacked on top of it and beside it than in it. "You mad 'cause I dared to do what you wanted to but wouldn't, or 'cause you actually care?" He removed the inventory sheets from the clipboard and opened a cabinet drawer.

She shook the letter at him. "This stinks, Matthew, and I'm disappointed in you."

"In me?" Unable to find the right file, he shut the drawer and added the papers to the large stack beside the cabinet. "I'm not the one running around like it's my *rumschpringe.*"

"That's ridiculous! I'm not using any freedoms to..." She didn't finish her sentence, and he figured her conscience had stopped her cold. He felt like a parent with Elle, the rebellious teen, sneaking around behind his back.

He pointed at her hair, which she was now wearing shoulder length with wild curls going every direction. He'd wanted to see her like this, no question, but he never thought she'd walk around for everybody, hair flying. "Nice, uh, outfit."

Pushing the sides of her slinky, printed green and sky blue skirt against her legs, she pointed to its length, which came just below her knees. "This is perfectly modest," she growled at him. "And it's a reasonable compromise while I finish up my contracts with that photography studio."

"Yeah, I know. Life is all about everyone making compromises while you half fulfill your part of the agreement."

"I signed a contract, Matthew. It was based on hours logged, not a set number of months. I told you all this." She shook the letter in the air. "So I found some interests out there and asked you to give me a bit of time. How is that not fulfilling my part of the agreement?"

"You know how to write, but I seldom receive a letter anymore. You own a phone, but I don't even remember the last time you called me. You own a car, but you rarely come to visit. You've missed the last two articles of instruction. You can lie to yourself if you want, but I'm tired of it. Your dad wanted you away from us, away from me, in order to break us up, and he's accomplished that goal. You wanted to go to that photography school, and I agreed to give you all the freedom you needed, but I never signed up to play the fool."

"I've been busy trying to get my hours done!"

"And I've given you lots of room and time. But this isn't about how busy you are. Your heart is no longer invested in us. You're supposed to be living here and dressing Amish to take your instructions, but you've sidestepped everything to fulfill this contract you shouldn't have signed in the first place."

Her gorgeous eyes fastened on him, and he was caught off guard by her moment of calmness. "The way I've been dressing is really just camouflage, if you'll think about it. I mean, in the real world no one thinks anything about dressing like this."

The real world?

Irritation ran hot as she avoided his points and then insulted him, but he chose not to take up an argument over her meaning of that phrase. He clasped his suspenders. "Look me in the eyes and tell me you're every bit as sure about us as you try to make yourself sound."

She hesitated, and Matthew thought his heart would sink into his shoes. "You been going out with someone while I've been waiting?"

"Of course not—"

"I'm tired of the games, Elle. Do you understand?"

The screen door swung open, and Esther Byler's cousin, the new hired help, walked in.

"Kathryn, we're in the middle of something here. Can you give me a minute to finish up before we begin on the paperwork?"

As Kathryn's dress swished out the door, Elle slapped him in the chest with the letter he'd written to her. "I can make up for missing the two article lessons. The bishop said so."

Matthew took the letter from her and shrugged. "No doubt you did a fine job of talking him into it."

"This isn't about how I'm acting or dressing or how busy I've been. This is about you. You've become this successful, wealthy man since I moved away. I bet girls are just flocking your way from all over the state. Maybe you don't want the embarrassment among your Amish peers of marrying some ex-Englischer, even if I were ready to take my vows."

Matthew folded the letter. "I didn't back away, Elle. You did."

She jerked the papers from his hand and ripped them in two. "Fine." She threw the torn papers at him and ran out the door.

He hurt all over as he watched her drive away, but his resolve hadn't been shaken one bit. She was no longer the Elle he'd fallen in love with, and she had no real desire to leave the ways of the Englischers and live Amish. She couldn't even be honest enough with herself to acknowledge the clear truth of her choices.

It hadn't been easy, but he'd ended things for both their sakes.

Luke moved through the dim house and up the stairs, looking for Sarah. He'd seen Esther with Rebecca and Samuel at the pond, but he hadn't spotted any of his other siblings yet. The green shades barely let the late-afternoon light in. As he topped the stairway, he saw the shadowy outline of his mom sitting in her rocker.

"Mamm, where is everybody?" When she didn't move, Luke eased into the room and removed his straw hat. "Mamm?"

Like cold molasses being poured from its container, she turned her face toward him. "Any word from Hannah?"

Since the community phone Hannah would call was at the Yoders', Mamm asked that question every time she saw him.

"Not for a long time." He squeezed the brim of his hat. "You okay?"

"Yeah." Mamm pulled her shawl tighter. "But Hannah would know what to do…if we could just contact her."

"Know what to do about what, Mamm?"

She rose from the chair and went to the chest at the foot of her bed. After kneeling and opening it, she pulled out something wrapped in newspapers. Closing the lid, she rose, removed the paper, and held the bundle in front of him. "Sarah came home in these a few days ago." Mamm took a corner of each side of the fabric and let it unfold in front of Luke.

It was the soot-covered dress and apron Matthew had told him about.

His mother took a step back and sat on the bed, looking worn-out. "She tried to hide them in the trash," she whispered. "You don't think she had anything to do with the Bylers' barn burning down, do you?"

"No." Luke took the dress from her and rolled it up. "No, Matthew saw her in a field behind his house the day after the fire. You must have seen her in these clothes the morning after the fire, and they weren't damaged then. Right?" He grabbed the newspaper off the floor and wrapped it around the clothes.

The lines across her face eased, and a half smile tugged at her lips. "Yes, that's right."

He put the wrapped clothing back in the chest and closed it.

Mamm drew a deep breath. "I should've thought about the timing of it all. She took some bushels of produce to the Miller's Roadside Stand that morning. She came home at the end of the day without any empty baskets or any money. According to Deborah Miller, Sarah just up and left everything there first thing that morning, but she didn't come home until nearly dark." Mamm fought tears. "I'm getting scared. I don't want to lose another daughter."

Luke eased onto the bed beside his mother, wishing he knew the answer, any answer that would bring comfort.

Mamm rubbed her head firmly. "Why didn't I stand up for Hannah when I had the chance?" A sob burst from her before she gained control.

Luke gave her a pat on the shoulder and tried changing the subject. "Where's Daed, Levi, and Sarah?"

"Daed and Levi are hauling pews to the Millers' for Sunday's service. I have no idea where Sarah is." Mamm wiped her tears. "Something's wrong with her. She's always been jittery and has spoken before she thought, but I was sure she'd outgrow her oddities. Now they grow like weeds in the garden. You've got to help me talk to your Daed about her."

Luke was fairly sure Paul could help Sarah or would know who could, but his Daed wasn't going to allow that. Luke and Mary saw Paul here and there. They'd had dinner with him at his grandmother's place a few times. He was nearly finished with his schooling and worked a fair amount of hours at a mental-health clinic not far from here.

Mamm searched his face before she rose to her feet and paced the length of the room. "Why didn't I speak up? I knew in my heart Hannah wasn't any of those things they accused her of." She stopped all movement. "I can't stand it any longer. My anger burns against—" She covered her mouth, as if suddenly aware of what she was saying.

"Against the church leaders?" Luke finished for her.

She shook her head. "They responded based on what they knew, but we betrayed her." Mamm stared into his eyes. "If I'd done Hannah right, Sarah wouldn't be having these problems."

"That's not true, Mamm."

"Yes, it is. And I've got to look my eldest daughter in the eye and tell her I'm sorry I failed her. I'm sorry her father and I turned against her."

"Ruth!" Daed's voice boomed from the foot of the steps, followed by his clomping up the stairway. "I'll not be talked about behind my back in my own home."

Expecting his Mamm to lower her head and apologize, Luke witnessed a shadowy image of Hannah in his own mother as she lifted her head and squared her shoulders. "Fine, then I'll say it to your face. I've not spoken of this with anyone before today, so don't think I've been sowing bad seed. I've held my tongue until my heart holds nothing but venom and anger. I followed you, Zeb Lapp, when I felt it was wrong to do so. And I'll swallow poison before I bow to your great and mighty wisdom again."

His mother wasn't just angry with Daed; she was bitter. And as Luke stood there, he vowed to always give Mary a voice. They were a team, and he might be the leader, but he'd not ever think Mary should hold her opinions while doing things his way. They'd talk and pray and decide together. Even if they made the wrong choice because he gave her too much say, they'd go through whatever happened in unity. Any bad decision made and worked through together had to be better than what his father had done to his mother.

Mamm pointed a finger at his father. "You despise Naomi Esh for speaking to you the way she did, but at least she was honest. Heaven forbid a female see something a man doesn't and tell him he's wrong."

"Ruth! You will get control of your tongue immediately."

"I won't. God gave me a mind and a heart, and you've trampled all over them. Rather than stand before the church leaders and tell them they were mistaken, you sided with them."

"Is it my fault Hannah snuck letters to that Mennonite boy and lied about why she was going to Mrs. Waddell's? How do you know that child she carried wasn't his?"

In spite of his fear, Luke knew it was time to speak up. "Daed, I know Paul. I met him the first week Hannah was gone. The baby wasn't his. They were secretly engaged, but he's as good a man as I've ever known. Even though he's got that education in psychology, he planned to work for you and win your approval. I don't doubt that he kissed Hannah, but it went no further. I believe that, and if he had any reason to think that was his child, he would have married her. Fact is, he came back for her and intended to marry her anyway, regardless of how she came to be pregnant."

His father stared at him as the clock ticked the seconds into minutes. Finally Daed's shoulders slumped, and he sat on the bed, looking up at his wife. "Do you hate me for this, Ruth?"

Mamm stared at him, and Luke thought she just might.

She knotted her hands into fists. "I want my daughter back—if only so we can stand before her and confess our sin. I think she'd know how to help Sarah. She's in a bad way, and she's only gotten worse since the day she learned of Hannah's troubles. Hannah would know what to do. I believe that."

Mamm went downstairs, leaving Daed without an answer to his question.

Luke's father ran a rough hand over his face, swiping his misting eyes. "I...I'd like to be alone for a while."

Luke closed the bedroom door as he left. He went downstairs, gave his mother a long, wordless hug, and walked out of his house. As he climbed into his buggy, a windstorm of emotions pounded against him. But he didn't know anything he could do to change the situation. Not one thing.

Chapter 33

*H*annah stacked the books into the crook of her arm and whispered a prayer as she locked the cabin door. Days of poring over pages of nursing care for each stage of a person's life would do her no good if she was late. Schooling didn't get easier as time went on, but in months she'd have her nursing certificate.

And probably run down the aisle to receive her diploma, at least on the inside. She opened the passenger door and laid her books on the seat. A car horn blasted long and loud three times. Even though she wasn't able to see over the knoll, she was sure it wasn't Martin. He arrived at work early and stayed until nearly bedtime—except on Fridays, when they went out.

But that wasn't the way Faye blew the horn either.

Faye's vehicle topped the knoll, spewing dirt in every direction before it fishtailed. The driver regained control and flew toward Hannah before slamming on the brakes. Faye climbed out of her vehicle. Her unkempt hair and dirty clothes turned Hannah's stomach.

"Faye, is something wrong?"

Faye didn't even look at her as she opened the backseat to her car and unbuckled Lissa. Kevin climbed out behind his sister.

"I…I have class tonight, but you know we planned for Kevin and Lissa to come here on Saturday after my rotation and to stay until Monday evening."

"No!" She slammed the car door.

Hannah started toward her. "Faye?"

Faye set Lissa's feet on the ground and nudged her away. "Go," she snapped at both children. Kevin and Lissa joined hands, staring at their mother.

Hannah stepped between Faye and her children. Hannah reached for her, but she jumped back and glared. Icy fingers of anxiety wrapped around

Hannah's throat, making it difficult to breathe. This was no tantrum or bad mood. Faye's pupils were dilated. She was using again.

"What have you done?" Hannah whispered through clenched teeth.

Faye pushed her backward. "I can't do this anymore. I just can't."

Hannah easily regained her footing and ignored the physical shove. "You *have* to be able to do it. We'll call Martin. He'll go with you, talk to the counselor with you."

"I'm done, Hannah."

"Done? You can't mean that!" She silently counted to three, trying to control her anger. "I know your life has been unfair and filled with a ton of grief. Our lives are a lot alike in that. But you've gotta keep fighting. I'll help you more. My schooling will be over soon." Hannah managed a smile, wondering how much of what she had said was getting through the drug-induced fog.

Faye backed away from her. "You know nothing about my life! You waltz in here and become Zabeth's hero. I'm the one who stole her dearest friend!"

"I…I…" Stunned at this viewpoint, Hannah struggled to find some words. "Faye, this isn't about me or Zabeth or Martin or even your mom. You've got to fight for your life, the one God gave you, regardless of anyone else—including your own past. I landed here and—"

Faye covered her eyes. "And you lived happily ever after." The hopelessness in Faye's voice sounded painfully familiar.

Hannah took Faye's trembling hand and looked into her eyes. "Oh, come on, Faye. You know where we met and how I changed my last name. Half the time I just manage to cope."

Faye's steely eyes looked a little softer for a moment. "That's all?"

Hannah sighed. "It's enough." She rubbed her throbbing head. "My drug of choice is absolute determination."

Faye shook her head, hostility returning to her expression as she opened the trunk of the car. She took out two large boxes filled with crumpled clothes and toys, tossed them on the ground, and shut the trunk. "Take care of my babies." Faye climbed back into the car.

"What?" Hannah glanced around, looking for something that made sense. "Wait. When are you coming back?"

She slammed the door and slung pebbles and debris as she sped off.

Hannah wanted to scream and run after her, but instead she smiled at Kevin and Lissa. "Hi, guys." She knelt in front of them. "Why don't you go get some eggs out of the refrigerator and some mixing bowls to make mud pies with?"

Kevin wrapped his arm around his sister's shoulders, as if to ease the weight of their mother's departure. "Sure." He turned his back on Hannah. "Come on, Lissa. You can cook those pies using some muffins tins, just like Aunt Zabeth showed us."

Hannah pulled her phone from her pocket and called Martin.

Martin laid the set of plans in front of the developer. "Your problem began when your graders read the stakes wrong. The field books and survey-crew equipment verify that we staked the curb accurately. We're not paying for your mistake, but what I can help you do is adjust the elevation of the building's foundation to match the existing curb. It won't be a super easy adjustment, but..." He felt his phone vibrate. "We won't charge for restaking the building. The engineering fees to rework the plans will be your responsibility."

The man stared at the plans, clearly needing a few minutes to digest the bad news.

Martin ignored the buzz of the phone hooked to his belt. The last four calls had been from Faye. He'd read the screen and continued with his business meeting. He'd call her later. Maybe in a day or two. He'd spent the last three days dealing with issues on this job site, and he wanted to stay on track so he could get out of Columbus by midnight.

"You say the construction crew read the survey stakes wrong?"

"Yes, that's what the surveyor and I showed you earlier on the job site. The elevations on the stakes do not match the curb that was poured, but—"

Without removing it from his belt, he shifted the phone to hit the Reject button and caught a glimpse of the screen.

Hannah.

She'd called him a total of four times since arriving in Ohio—the first three were when Zabeth needed to be hospitalized, the fourth was the night Zabeth stopped breathing. He grabbed the phone and pulled it to his ear. "Hey, what's up?"

The developer smacked the papers. "How much money are we talking about?"

Martin held up his hand, signaling for the man to give him a minute.

"She dropped off the kids with large boxes of their stuff and told me to be good to her babies. Martin, I...I don't think she's coming back."

"What?"

The developer rattled the paper. "Can we get back to this, please?"

Martin didn't miss the man's ill-tempered tone, but he walked out of the room and closed the door behind him. He glanced at his watch. "Call Nina and take the kids there. I know it's a school night and all, but this is sort of an emergency deal. Her parents will understand. Then you go to class. Tell her to put them down in sleeping bags in the living room and someone will pick them up in the morning."

"No." She elongated the word. "I can't. They know what's going on. They watched Faye leave them, and I'm not going to hurt them worse by dropping them elsewhere."

"Hannah, just do it. Attendance is ninety percent mandatory at all times. You can't afford to—"

"I didn't call for you to give me a list of orders, Martin."

The dull headache he'd had all day increased, sending a twisting pain down his neck. "I'm trying to keep you on track. That's all, Hannah. I can't just drop everything, and neither should you. Let me try to reach Faye, and I'll call you back later."

She didn't answer him.

"Hannah?"

"Yeah, I heard you. Bye."

Disconnecting the phone, he realized that whatever she'd hoped for when she called him, he'd let her down. He didn't understand certain aspects of Hannah yet, but this much he got: she hadn't wanted him giving directions like he was her boss or her parent.

He walked back into the room. "Dale, I have to go."

"You can't leave now."

He began rolling up the plans. "There's a family emergency, and I need to go."

The man pulled a leather billfold thick with cash from inside his suit coat, visually sending a reminder of his strength. "I believe in the Golden Rule. The man with the gold rules. Stay, and we work this out. Go, and I'll find someone else."

"A very smart woman once asked me, 'Do you think money is the answer to everything?' I have a family issue, and I'm going home." He slid the prints into the cylinder container. "I'm sure I'll be available next week. If that's not good enough, we'll send all the information we have to whoever you hire."

Martin walked across the parking lot wondering what Faye would have done with Kevin and Lissa if Hannah hadn't been home. He piled the plans and his laptop into his car. He wouldn't arrive in Winding Creek for nearly three hours, but it was the best he could do. He tried to reach Faye, and he tried calling Hannah back. Neither woman answered her cell. He called Dr. Smith to see if she'd heard from Faye or knew where she was headed. The doctor talked to him for over an hour, sharing pieces of encouragement. It all sounded nice, but the reality was bleak and heavy.

It had long been night by the time he pulled into Zabeth's drive. His frustration had grown with each passing hour. As the car lights hit the front porch, he saw Hannah sitting on the steps. He parked the car, wishing he'd come across as less of a jerk and more of a friend when she'd called him. Hannah stood, and he walked to her.

He smiled. "You okay?"

She shook her head. "I was so sure we could make a difference." She closed the distance between them. "I'm sorry."

He wrapped his arms around her. "You don't need to apologize."

She laid her head against his chest.

"We did our part, Hannah. That's all anybody can do." He laid his cheek on the top of her head. "How about we get you moved into the cottage so it'll make life easier while we get this mess sorted out?"

Without answering, she pulled away and turned toward the cabin. He saw a rustic cabin, a relic, and not something to regret leaving, but he doubted that Hannah viewed it the same way.

Martin stepped next to her. "I can help you pack. It's not like you own much, mostly clothes and books, right? After we get the cars loaded, we'll move Kevin and Lissa, hopefully without waking them. Then—"

She placed her hand on the center of his chest. "But it's my home."

He sighed and nodded. "I know, sweetheart. I do. But I don't know how we can juggle everything with you way out here. It's the school year, and their district doesn't bus this road. And even when I leave early, I can barely get home from work in time for you to leave for your classes. I certainly can't make it here."

Without a word she walked to the fence and patted Ol' Gert. He followed her. She had a passion for certain things, and he loved that about her—even if it meant working through their different, equally headstrong opinions.

He took her hand. "Talk to me, okay? Say what you're thinking."

She tilted her chin, looking resolved. "There's nothing else to talk about. Kevin and Lissa need a stable environment—for now that means living in a way that keeps them from being shuffled around like they're a burden."

"I agree, but that's just your decision, Hannah. I asked for your *thoughts*."

She shrugged. "Even without the *Ordnung* instructing me, I think desire comes second to doing what is right."

"You're pretty amazing, you know it?"

"I know you think so. Far be it from me to disagree."

Martin chuckled, running his fingers over her soft cheek. "I'm sorry for barking orders at you when you called."

"I know." She kissed him. "What are we going to do about Faye?"

"I've got meetings all day tomorrow, but then I'll start looking for her while you keep Lissa and Kevin, okay?"

She nodded. "Let's start packing."

With Lissa in her lap and Kevin sitting beside her, Hannah finished the last page of a picture storybook of *Heidi*. She hadn't sent them to school today. They were nervous about Hannah and Martin disappearing on them. She figured it was just one day, and they'd return on Monday.

Hannah closed the book and patted Lissa's pajama-covered legs. "Okay, bedtime."

Kevin jumped up. "I'm not going to sleep. I'm gonna turn out the lights and watch the stars glow that we put on the wall today. When Uncle Martin gets home, I'll show him all the constellations we designed."

Hannah set the book on the coffee table. She figured if he stayed in bed watching the stars long enough, he'd go to sleep. "Okay by me."

He hurried toward his room. Lissa stood on the couch, wrapped her arms around Hannah's neck, and held on tightly as Hannah walked upstairs. Lissa giggled the whole way.

Hannah set her on the bed and waited while she scurried to her sleeping spot. She tucked the blankets around her, sat on the side of the bed, and kissed her tiny hands. How could Faye just walk out on her little girl?

"Hannah."

"Hmm?"

Lissa gazed up, her big dark eyes absorbing everything. "What's *buoyant* mean?"

Hannah stroked Lissa's hair. "You want to run that by me again?"

"But I'm in my p.j.'s. Where do you want me to run?"

Hannah repositioned herself on the bed. "Nowhere, sweetie. That means I need you to repeat what you said."

Her face blossomed with wonder. "So you don't know what *buoyant* is either?"

A deep chuckle made Hannah turn toward the doorway. Martin leaned against the doorframe, looking as confident as ever.

Lissa giggled. "Uncle Martin!"

She started to get up, but Martin held out both hands in a stop-sign fashion. "Stay, Rover, stay."

She snuggled back under the covers. Hannah moved to the foot of the bed.

Martin sat down beside Lissa and patted her head. "Good girl."

She broke into giggles. "He pretends I'm a puppy sometimes."

Hannah nodded. "I see."

She sat up, encircling him with her arms. "I love you, Uncle Martin."

Martin gave her a gentle hug. "Back at ya. Now snuggle down, and let's say good night to God." He lowered his head and said prayers with her.

Suddenly Hannah was swept back to her own childhood. Her Daed used to tuck her in each night, lay his hand on her head, and say a silent prayer. In the silence she used to imagine he was begging God to make her be a good girl. She never quite managed goodness, but she missed the warmth of hearing his last words of the day as he tucked her in.

Martin whispered her name, drawing her out of her thoughts. The prayer was over, and he was standing next to her. He nodded toward the door.

He turned out the light and pulled the door almost shut as they left.

Hannah began descending the stairs. "Any signs of Faye?"

"None." He sounded tired. "I talked to every friend and acquaintance I could find. I visited homeless shelters, talked to Dr. Smith. I came up completely empty-handed." Martin touched her shoulder, and she stopped in midstep. "She might not come back."

There was no sense in asking him what they were going to do if that happened. He didn't know. And yet they both knew.

They heard a door open, and Kevin appeared on the landing.

Martin drew a deep breath. "Hey, sport, what's up?"

"Come look at what me and Hannah did to my room today."

Martin glanced at Hannah, not looking all that pleased that the guest bedroom was being transformed into a kid's room. "I'm in the middle of—"

Hannah tugged at his shirt sleeve and gave a slight nod toward Kevin.

Martin's body tensed with frustration. "I'll be right there."

Kevin went back into his room, and Martin sighed. "Listen, we need help this go-round. I know you think it's pawning the children off on someone who doesn't love them, but I intend to find someone who can come into the home. You've taken on more hours at the clinic, and you have school most nights. I already have a good list of candidates to fill either a full- or part-time position as nanny. I want to begin interviewing."

"I could take a leave of absence. Kevin and Lissa need stability and lots of it. I just don't think hired help is the answer."

"That's because you think if you work at something hard enough, you can fix it. You can't heal the damage Faye and Richard have done, and dropping everything in our lives to baby the kids isn't the answer. I want you to go on with your life as much as possible. Hiring part-time or full-time help is the ans—"

Hannah held up her hand, stopping him. "Maybe you're right."

Martin moved in closer. "I know I am."

"Of course. So do you have someone on that list you're already considering seriously?"

"Depends."

"On what?"

He took her hand in his and caressed it. "On whether you're going to get angry if the answer is yes."

"Are all men like this?"

"No. Very few climb to this level of honesty."

She laughed. "How do you have a list already? She left yesterday."

He looked at the ceiling and whistled innocently until she smacked his shoulder. "I started looking for someone when Faye was in rehab, but a certain young woman I know wouldn't even consider it."

"All right. You know my schedule. Just set up a time and date. Have whoever it is come here right after lunch one day. I'd like to see her in this environment, and she can have dinner with us."

"Uncle Martin." Kevin sounded exasperated.

Martin looked to the landing. "I'm coming. Go on back to your room." They waited for the door to close. He turned back to her. "This is a good decision, Hannah. It'll be just what we need so that Kevin and Lissa are taken care of but we get more time to date without kids in tow."

"Ah, so that's the goal, huh?" She went to kiss his cheek, but he pulled her into a lip kiss. She inhaled sharply. "Your plan sounds promising." She finished descending the steps. "See you sometime tomorrow."

"Hannah?"

She stopped and turned. "Yeah?"

"Is the cottage comfortable enough? Anything I can do or buy that would keep me from having to hear you complain about it later on?"

"Yeah, earplugs. Good night, Martin."

"Good night."

Chapter 34

With the aroma of new leather permeating the small shop, Luke sat behind the commercial-grade sewing machine, stitching a well-oiled piece of rawhide around the padding of a horse's collar. The gas-powered motor that provided the strength for the heavy needle to do its job sat outside, right behind the wall where he was sitting. His thoughts seemed to move in rhythm with the steady *flub-dub, flub-dub, flub-dub* of the machine's engine.

Joining Matthew in business and renting his old harness shop out to an Amish couple was the best thing he could have done. It seemed if Matthew put his hand to something, it became a huge success. Why, with the rent money he was making and the income he was earning as Matthew's partner, he and Mary would be able to build a home of their own soon.

Luke cut the heavy-duty strings, loosened the rawhide from the machine, and rose to assemble another collar.

A shadow fell across his workbench, causing him to look up. "Daed, I didn't hear you come in."

The man stood in the middle of the room, reminding Luke of a statue. "The fact that divorce is unheard of among the Amish does nothing for a man if his wife hates him."

Luke had no words of comfort, and now wasn't the time to try to get his Daed to see his fault in all this, so he remained silent.

His father walked to him and held out a piece of paper in his trembling hands. "I never meant to…" He shut his eyes. "I got a letter from a Dr. J. Lehman in Alliance, Ohio." His eyes watered. "My sister died, and a doctor sent me a note about it. The doctor mentioned that a relative had delayed the funeral to give any of Zabeth's other relatives time to come. If I had my guess, I'd say the relative he speaks of is Hannah. I don't know how she learned of my sister or her whereabouts, but none of my relatives had anything to do with my sister."

Luke took the envelope. The doctor's name was the only readable part. The return address looked as if drops of water had hit the ink and smudged it. He opened it, but there was no letter inside. "Daed?"

He gave a fatigued nod before pointing to the paper. "I know that's not much information to go on. I had shoved the letter in my pocket, and it went through the washer, but it seems the envelope fell out and wedged itself under the washer. Maybe you know someone who can help you figure out how to find her."

Luke shook his head. "Not unless I ask Paul. He'd know—or know how to find out."

His father pointed to the envelope. "If that's the only person, then that's who you should take the information to." His eyes reflected hurt so deep that a physical pain shot through Luke. A sob broke from his Daed's throat. "I've tried standing true to Sarah, like I shoulda done with Hannah. But her nervousness just gets worse, and she's mumbling to herself and turns up in the oddest places. Yet she doesn't seem to know why she's at those places. She's locked inside herself, and no one has been able to reach her."

Dismayed, Luke couldn't respond, and he watched his father turn and leave the shop.

Luke stared at the envelope, wondering what to do. Was it fair for his Daed to use Paul to find Hannah when he hadn't spoken a nice word to or about the man in the two and a half years Hannah had been missing? Besides, Paul seemed to have moved on, with Dorcas. And clearly Hannah still didn't want to be found. She hadn't written in a long while, but last he heard from her, she was going to school and felt good about where she was.

And although Mamm longed to see Hannah, she'd had her chances too, hadn't she? Instead she chose to let Hannah grieve in solitude after her baby died. She never went to her.

But Sarah—she hadn't been the same since the day she'd learned of her sister's plight. If there was a reason for Paul to help find Hannah, Sarah was it.

Unsure what was the right thing to do, Luke tucked the paper into his leather apron and returned to the work at hand. Figuring this out would take awhile.

Martin walked to the cottage. He thought Hannah might want to know how well the interview had gone with the potential nanny, Laura Scofield, a sixty-two-year-old woman with excellent credentials. More than that, he wanted a few minutes with Hannah. He tapped on the door. It was almost eleven o'clock, but she'd just pulled into the driveway a few minutes ago. The hour was the downside of taking night classes. The truth was he couldn't wait for her to get her diploma and end this continual rivalry he felt with her schedule.

She opened the door, looking gorgeous and tired. "Hey." Stepping back, she invited him in.

"I took all the laundry by the dry cleaners." He held out the basket of washed and folded clothes.

"Thanks. Care for a drink?" She set the basket on the table.

He grabbed two bottles of water. "I interviewed Laura Scofield, the nanny I mentioned to you. I'd like you to meet her as soon as you can, and perhaps you should set up that appointment. I think Laura is a perfect choice, but I feel pretty strongly that because of your age, you need to establish yourself as her authority concerning the children so no issues ever crop up in that area."

"Ah, leave it to you to think about such things. I'll call her tomorrow and schedule her visit."

He held up a bottle of water. "Want one?"

"Yeah." She stifled a yawn. "Kevin give you trouble going down for the night?"

He opened her bottle of water and passed it to her. "Has a cat got a climbing gear?"

"Taking care of two children is probably not how you'd like to spend your evenings."

Martin sneered. "Not hardly, but it's growing on me. It's not nearly as bad as I thought it'd be."

Hannah took a sip of water. "The Amish consider a baby the most precious gift on this planet. The People cherish them—just because they exist."

"Yet they don't seem all that warm and inviting once people are adults. My mom told me Zabeth's troubles were plenty. And you left at seventeen and changed your name. So what happens between infanthood and adulthood?"

She motioned to the porch.

"Sure."

They moved to the porch and sat on the steps. It seemed their best conversations took place outside, especially at the end of the day.

She pulled her legs in and propped her chin on her knees. When nothing but the gentle hum of crickets filled the air, Martin wondered if she'd answer him or not. It was never a given that she'd answer his questions.

She stretched her legs out and ran her hands down the row of buttons on the front of her dress. "I left because I refused to repent. I think the reasons for leaving are as varied as people themselves."

Wondering what she had needed to repent of, Martin asked, "Is Paul still the reason you've never gone back home?"

"For a while I didn't think I could stand seeing him with someone else." She paused and seemed to shudder. "My father saw me the night I'd been attacked, witnessed the trauma, and yet later on he chose to believe I'd had a fight with Paul or something that night. I don't really know how he twisted it in his mind, but he didn't believe how I came up pregnant."

"What happened between you and the rest of your family?"

She slowly explained each piece of the story until he understood things she and Zabeth had been silent about since he and Hannah met.

He moved in closer and put his arm around her shoulders. "Do you still miss Paul?"

She gazed at Martin, a smile crossing her lips. "I've found an unusual fish in the sea, a bit self-centered, but a remarkable man nonetheless."

He pulled her closer and kissed her cheek. "Well, this fish is pretty happy to be caught. But sometimes I get the feeling you're still unsure about us."

"It's not just a feeling. I am unsure, because I haven't been ready to tell you everything."

"This is everything, right?"

She shook her head. "I wish." She paused. "Because of complications after I gave birth, I...I can't have children."

In her voice he heard the depth of loss she felt for the children she'd never bear. "I'm sorry."

"I wasn't sure when to tell you. It seems presumptuous to bring it up too soon and wrong to have waited this long."

He removed his arm from her shoulders and slid his hand over hers. "No guilt over the timing."

She watched as he kissed and caressed her fingers. "Don't just rush in to make me feel better, Martin. You have dreams for your future, and maybe I don't fit as well as you'd thought."

"And maybe you fit better. I should have told you this, but I didn't want to scare you away. I don't want children. Even after getting serious about life and God, I stopped seeing some women because I didn't want children, and I realized they did."

"You'd put your hand on the Bible and confess that's true?"

"I've never told a girl something in order to sound nice or to soften the blow. Not that sweet a guy."

She pushed him back. "Yeah, but this is me. We're different together, more bonded for reasons I don't need to explain."

"True enough, although I didn't realize you knew that." He rose. "I know what I want, but I'll give the younger member of this band time to think and process. Good night, Hannah." He headed toward his house before stopping in midstride. "If we'd both known that being honest about who we really are would have helped rather than caused problems, we might have actually told the whole truth earlier on."

She shook her finger at him. "You're making that phrase circle inside my head again."

"The one missing the accurate adjectives *charming* and *intelligent*?"

"That'd be the one."

"So what is it?"

"Shut up, Palmer."

He kept a straight face, knowing she'd just answered him. "You're not going to tell me what it is?"

"I did."

He laughed. "Yeah, I know, but something with *charming* and *intelligent* would be much more accurate."

"I'm fully aware of that."

He chuckled and went inside his house.

Chapter 35

Inside protective services' small office, Paul clutched the phone against his ear as Luke shared that Zeb Lapp had information about Hannah's whereabouts and was hopeful Paul could help locate her. The day had started like any other, with a miserable longing for Hannah. And now…

"J. Lehman, Alliance, Ohio." Paul repeated Luke's words as he wrote them down. "Did your father say when he received the last letter from Hannah?"

"The letter didn't come from Hannah. It came from someone notifying him of his sister's death."

"He has a sister?"

"Did. And that was news to me too. She died in May." Luke paused. "Daed gave me this info in August, over a month ago, but I wasn't sure it was right to get you involved. Asking you to find Hannah isn't about what Daed wants or even Mamm. I'd not have called you if this was for them. But Sarah…"

"I've had a few encounters with her since Hannah left. She doesn't seem to be coping very well. Is she doing better?"

"Worse. From what Matthew and Mamm have told me, whatever you saw is nothing compared to what she's like of late. I think if Sarah could just talk to Hannah one time, she might get better. If you can find a way for us to reach Hannah, a phone number or address where we could send a letter, it'd mean an awful lot to me."

Paul wasn't going to tell Luke about his last encounter with Sarah, but there was no doubt she needed help. "Luke, I appreciate that you contacted me with this info. I'll do what I can and let you know."

They said their good-byes, and Paul hung up. He was done with waiting for Hannah to return on her own. If he'd ever thought she'd be gone for more than two years, he would have hired that private investigator before the trail became impossible to pick up.

But this way, she'd been gone long enough to find peace and healing on her own terms. Now she needed a reminder of the worthy things she'd left behind and of the gaps her absence had caused. Her sister needed her. Paul loved her. It was time for her to come home. And now he had enough information to find her and nudge her to do just that—come home. He began an Internet search for any Lehman's phone number in Alliance. It didn't take long to learn there wasn't a single Lehman listed. Paul widened his search to a twenty-mile, then fifty-mile radius of the place and jotted down all the possibilities.

Starting at the top of the list, Paul began dialing.

As the hours passed, he scratched through possibility after possibility. He'd skipped lunch, and his co-workers had left for the day. But all he could think about was hearing Hannah's voice again. He was unsure what his hopes were beyond that. For her to come home immediately? For him to go to her first and them talk for a month solid until they knew each other again? Too many thoughts and emotions hounded him to discern any of them with clarity. Only one thing he knew for sure: he longed for Hannah to be in his arms. Things were different from when she'd left. The gossip and anger had dissipated. She'd lived on her own long enough that no one would expect or demand she line up with their desires or repent of things that weren't her fault. It was all different, and he had information in hand to finally contact her and let her know.

He dialed yet another Lehman number.

"Lehman's Birthing Clinic. Midwife Nancy Cantrell speaking."

"Hello, this is Paul Waddell, and I'm looking for a Hannah Lapp."

"Is she one of Dr. Lehman's patients?"

"I...I don't think so. She's a friend, and I'm trying to locate her."

"This is an Amish birthing center, sir. You must have the wrong number."

Amish? On the contrary, he must have the right number. "Is Dr. Lehman's first initial J?"

"Yes, Dr. Jeff Lehman."

This was too much of a coincidence. Hannah had to be connected to this doctor.

"But there's not a Hannah Lapp who works for him?" Paul suspected the woman was leery, more interested in getting off the phone with as little said as possible than in helping him. "Does he have any other offices?"

She hesitated. "Yes. He has another clinic and a main office. But there are privacy laws concerning patients and workers."

Confidentiality laws. As a counselor, he dealt with them all the time. "I'd still like to have those numbers if you don't mind."

With the note in hand, Paul connected to the Internet. In less than two minutes, he had the man's main office address. This Dr. Lehman or someone on his staff might not be willing or able to tell him anything over the phone, so Paul's best bet was face to face. He grabbed his suit jacket and headed out. There was no reason to leave tonight since he wouldn't arrive until nearly midnight. But by lunchtime tomorrow, he intended to be in Ohio.

Leaning over the drafting table in his office, Martin tried focusing on his work. His thoughts were everywhere but on the set of engineering plans in front of him. Mostly they were on the brown-eyed girl living on his property.

But even with all their progress toward a lasting relationship, in Martin's ears echoed the sounds of prison doors clanking shut. Even if Faye returned and succeeded at living clean and being a good mom, as if that were possible, he'd still never be fully free of the responsibility to keep things stable for Kevin and Lissa. At least Hannah had agreed with him about hiring Laura. She'd only work part-time, but it would free them from some of the schedule juggling and give them an occasional evening off. Even if Laura became a live-in nanny, he and Hannah would never have the kind of freedom and bonding time he'd always dreamed of having. He loved Kevin and Lissa, but he chafed at the nonstop patience and effort it took to raise them.

He wondered what he'd be like in this situation without Hannah's influence.

His thoughts jumped to when he'd lost his mother. Zabeth had stepped forward and never once made him feel unwanted. On the contrary, she'd made him think he was the greatest thing to ever happen to her life. But was he? He'd been a bit hardheaded and rebellious at times.

As he allowed his mind to drift, a memory surfaced that he hadn't thought of in more than a decade. A few weeks after his mother's death, he got off the school bus to see Zabeth in the driveway, talking to a man. Whatever was going on was intense, because they never even noticed him. Looking back now, he realized how young Zabeth had been—single and in her early thirties, only a few years older than he was now. Funny, she'd always seemed like someone's mother.

The man had put his arms around her. "Take a few months and get the boy past the worst, but you have a life of your own, Zabeth. A future with me."

"Can't we find a way to blend our lives? Must it be a choice?"

"My ranch is in Wyoming, Zabeth. You've known that all along, said you'd move there come summer."

"I know, but—"

Martin had dropped his book bag, causing Zabeth to notice him. He couldn't really remember much more, other than being introduced and feeling that the man hated him. He never saw the man after that day. Obviously, Zabeth had made her choice, and she chose Martin. Fresh grief for Zebby rolled over him, and before he even realized it, he was praying that he'd become the type of guardian she had been. One who sacrificed without grumbling, loved without resentment, and gave freely, making the kids in his home feel like treasures. When he opened his eyes, he ached to hug Kevin and Lissa. It wouldn't hurt anything if he checked them out of school a little early.

If Hannah wasn't too busy today, maybe he could pick up all three of them, and they could go for ice cream or something where they could talk and laugh, and he could let them know he truly did care. Whether he had planned it or not, these children were a part of his life, and he intended to make sure they knew they were a part of his heart.

He picked up the phone and hit the speed dial. A rap on the doorframe interrupted him. Amy Clarke held up a blueprint tube containing a set of plans.

He pushed the disconnect button. "What's up?"

She stepped inside and moved to the leather chair in front of his desk. He placed the receiver in its cradle. Amy was a couple of years older than Martin and rented space in the adjoining office for her landscape-architect business. This kept Martin from needing to hire and run a whole different department under his engineering firm. Even though she thrived on spontaneity, she maneuvered through the orderly business world with a cool savoir-faire.

"A land plan was sent to McGaffy that I didn't approve." She thumped the tube against the palm of her hand. "And it shows more lots than the county will allow on that parcel."

"Send a corrected land plan back to McGaffy that the county will approve, and the developer can take it or leave it. I'm not willing to work the extra hours to get a variance with the county to make the developer happy." He placed his hand on the receiver, ready for this conversation to be over. "I'm heading out for the weekend. If anything else comes up, it'll need to wait until Monday."

Her blue eyes opened wide, and she tucked one side of her blond hair behind her ear as she rose. "Okay, if you say so."

"We can talk about this more next week if we need to." He picked up the receiver and punched the speed dial for Hannah's cell phone. "Amy, please close the door on your way out."

Paul parked his car in front of a clapboard house with white columns, black shutters and trim, and a gray porch and steps. It sat on a tiny plot of ground, flanked by dilapidated homes on both sides of the street. The large wooden sign with fancy black painted letters said this was a women's clinic, with doctors on site Mondays and Wednesdays only. Even though today was Tuesday, an Open sign hung on the glass door.

Paul glanced at the cellophane-covered bouquet he'd bought at the local florist shop, lying on the passenger seat beside him. He knew he shouldn't have bought these. Such a move was premature and undoubtedly out of place, but he couldn't resist.

Climbing out of his car, he prayed that this place could lead him to Hannah.

As he opened the door, a bell jangled, making him cringe at the noise. A grandmotherly woman behind a desk to his right glanced up and smiled. "Can I help you?"

He eased up to her and held out his hand. "Paul Waddell."

"I'm Sharon. Nice to meet you, Paul. What can we do for you?"

"I'm looking for a friend of mine."

"Is she a patient?"

"I…I don't think so. I believe she's a friend of Dr. Lehman's. Is he here?"

The woman chuckled. "Dr. Lehman is almost never here. He has a couple of doctors on staff and a slew of community-service volunteers. Maybe the friend you're looking for is one of his volunteers. What's her name?"

"Hannah Lapp."

The woman slowly shook her head. "No. There's no Hannah Lapp. He has a Hannah Lawson, who works really closely with him."

Paul's heart leaped. Would she use a different last name? Of course she would. Changing her last name was probably one of the first things she did.

"Is she here?" he asked, his voice trembling.

"She doesn't work out of this office. She helps Dr. Lehman at the Amish birthing clinics and counsels at the rape crisis center."

"That's got to be her!"

The woman's eyebrows shot up.

He took a breath, choosing to sound calmer. "Can you tell me where his clinics are?"

"Sure. But she's on leave right now, taking care of her new family." She shrugged. "I don't know her, but I heard Dr. Lehman saying that the man has two children and that Hannah took some time off to help them get settled."

Feeling a bit unsteady, Paul dropped into a chair.

Maybe the woman was mistaken. Or perhaps this wasn't really his Hannah after all. "Do you have an address for her?"

Sharon hesitated. "I'm not sure I should…"

Paul pulled a business card out of his billfold. It wasn't an ethical thing to do. If this got back to the board of the Better Path, he could be in serious trouble since the card could be misleading, but he gave it to her anyway. "Her father is trying to get in touch with her. He asked me to—"

She took the card and read it carefully. "I do remember overhearing Dr. Lehman tell his wife that Hannah had moved away from home rather abruptly and something about they'd tried to reach her family…" The woman spun her Rolodex to the Ls, then pulled out a card. "Let me jot this down for you." As she wrote Hannah's address, she asked, "Until she moved, she lived in Winding Creek. Her new place is just south of there. Do you need directions?"

"That would be very helpful. Thank you."

Following the directions the woman had printed out for him, Paul drove toward the south side of Winding Creek. Within twenty minutes he pulled up on the street across from the home bearing the address Sharon had given him.

It was a nice two-story, slip-form stone house with stacked-stone columns. He even caught a glimpse of a cottage behind the house. Everything about the place spoke of a comfortable lifestyle. If this was where Hannah lived, it was no wonder she hadn't given up on surviving in the Englischers' world and come home.

Leaving the flowers in his vehicle, he strode up the sidewalk. He rang the doorbell and waited. His mouth was so dry he wasn't sure he'd be able to speak if someone did come to the door. When no one answered, he returned to his car.

Laughter and silliness rang out from the three of them as Martin pulled into the driveway. Lissa was sound asleep. He and Hannah got out of the car. Kevin unbuckled himself and jumped out. Hannah unfastened Lissa's restraints and lifted the sleeping girl from her seat. When she stood, her eyes met Martin's. In the silence, her eyes told him everything he wanted to hear. She was happy. While the kids had played in the sandbox at the park, he told Hannah what he'd realized about himself and why he'd come home during the middle of the day.

Lissa mumbled. "Where are we now?"

Martin smiled. "You're home." The words were simple enough, but they stirred him.

Hannah eased Lissa's head onto her shoulder. "But you can stay sleeping." Walking toward the house, Hannah whispered, "I'm going to lay her down. Keep the house quiet, okay?"

Martin nodded and opened the trunk of the car. He grabbed the Nerf football he'd bought earlier today. "Okay, go out for a long one."

Kevin took off running.

Martin chortled. "Not that far. Come back." They tossed the ball back and forth, and Martin tackled him a few times before Hannah bounded back out the door and into the yard.

He tossed her the football. Surprisingly she caught it.

"Tackle!" Martin yelled.

Kevin came running at full speed. Hannah put her hand in front of her. "Whoa, guys. Girl on the field."

Martin took the ball from her, tossed it to Kevin, and wrapped his arms around her, facing her. "Yeah, I know. Cute one too."

She pushed against him, but he didn't let go. He glanced at Kevin, who was throwing the ball into the air and catching it.

Martin touched her soft face and gently guided it to his. He lowered his lips almost to hers, but she backed away.

"Hannah." He gazed in her eyes and stroked her cheeks with his thumbs, waiting.

When she relaxed, he eased his lips to meet hers and was again struck by the powerful physical and emotional reaction he had to her.

After an intense kiss, she put a bit of space between them. Her lips curved downward, and she shrugged. "Not bad."

He laughed.

She snickered. "I love your sense of humor."

"Good. Because I haven't found anything about you I'm not in love with."

"You lie."

"Do not." As he brushed loose curls away from her face, he resisted her push against him. "So how do I move past not bad?"

She pressed her palms against his chest, clearly ready for him to let her go. "I…I think you should throw the football with Kevin."

"Uh-huh, and I think you should kiss me."

Frowning, she stood on her tiptoes and barely touched her lips to his, as if that would be sufficient and he should go play with Kevin now. But in the instant after touching her mouth to his, something in her seemed to shift, and she ever so lightly kissed him again. Once, twice. Her hands no longer pushed against him but balled into fists that held his shirt as she barely skimmed her lips over his—four times, six times—before he received the tenderest, most powerful kiss of his life.

Martin took a step back and drew a deep breath, trying to pull his stare away from her. "Uh, you know, it's really not necessary for us to wait any longer before we get married."

"What kind of a proposal is that?"

He clasped his hand around her neck and looked into her eyes. "A desperate one."

She laughed. "Good grief, Palmer. I feel like you're trying to close a business deal."

"It'll be the best deal I ever made." He took a few steps toward Kevin before turning back to Hannah. "I love you, phone girl."

Knowing she needed time to process every new curve in life, he jogged to the middle of the yard and clapped his hands. "All right, buddy, put one here."

Watching Hannah from inside his car, Paul sat speechless, his hopes shattered. The optimism that had kept him hopeful for the past two and a half

years was destroyed. There was no reason to get out of his car and see her face
to face. She had a new life: a gorgeous home, a husband, even a family. She
worked closely with that Dr. Lehman.

Englischers. All of them.

Well, he hoped Mr. Lapp was pleased with the outcome of his strictness.
If his goal was to keep Paul out of her life, he'd certainly accomplished that.
Unable to stomach blaming someone else, he closed his eyes and tried to center himself. He was the one who'd walked away while she was begging him to
listen. He was the one who didn't return for her until days later. There was no
one else to blame.

But somewhere beyond the growing ache he felt, he was grateful she
seemed happy.

After all the years of praying for the best to happen for her, God had hon-
ored his requests.

And yet he felt betrayed.

He'd been so sure she would find wholeness and then return. Well, she
had found it—without him. Pouring more salt in his wounds, no one in the
happy family even noticed him sitting in a parked car across the street from
their house. Suddenly unable to imagine what it would be like to look in her
eyes knowing she was married, he started the engine. He had the information
the Lapps needed to contact her, and he'd take it to Mr. Lapp himself, but it'd
be best if Paul left here unannounced.

He put the vehicle in gear and drove away.

Chapter 36

*M*atthew dipped up a bowl of his mother's hot-fudge cake and slid a spoon in it. His brother had been having lunch with him when the shop's phone rang out across the yards. David had taken off running since it was his day to field calls. Sometimes keeping up with the growing business was a hassle, but they managed. Now Matthew figured he at least owed David a bowl of dessert. He pulled a clean dishtowel out of a drawer and placed it over the bowl. He'd trained Kathryn to take orders and handle most of the office stuff, and she was good at it, but her sister had given birth, and she'd gone to help out for a few weeks.

His mother sank the lunch dishes into the sudsy water. "Keeping some of that separate so I can't eat it all while you're gone? Or you got someone else in mind?"

"The horses," Matthew answered with a grin. "We're low on hay, and I didn't figure they could tell the difference."

"Uh-huh. That's why you ate a bowlful of it yourself." She looked up at him with those tender mom eyes.

He poked her with his elbow. "You're a really good Mamm, you know that?"

She gave him his routine hug before he returned to work some hundred feet away. "You're not such a bad son either."

"Not bad? Me? I'm terrific. Yep, nothing like the rest of my family." He tried to keep a straight face, but he grinned anyway.

She pointed to the bowl. "Take it and go, or you can stay and wear it."

Chuckling, Matthew went out the front door and across the yard. He'd take this to David and then go back to working in the carriage shop, where he was attaching the underpinning of a buggy to its body. His Daed, along with six other men and two wives from the community, would soon be back from the carpentry they'd been doing in Maine. The women helped do the cooking and kept an eye on the men, so the wives back home never felt unsure of what their husbands were up to.

Although it was September, the summer's heat had yet to break. He wondered if David had dared to run the three-inch, battery-operated fan he'd bought for him or if his whole face would be glowing with color and sweat. As an employee, he was nothing like he was as a brother. He was diligent and willing—even to leave the rest of his lunch to catch a phone. As much as it surprised him, he liked having David work with him. If his obstinate brother was this good, he wondered what Peter would be like when he graduated this year. If things continued as they were going, there'd be enough work to go around.

Gasoline fumes rode the humid breeze, stinging his nostrils. He lifted his head, sniffing the air. The dimness of his shop made David's job of reading and filing all the paperwork harder. It had been built to hold in heat in winter and keep out the sun in summer. Unfortunately, that made a kerosene lamp necessary to read and file the receipts and orders.

But the odor he smelled now wasn't kerosene. And the closer he drew to his old shop, the stronger the smell became.

A car pulled into the shop's driveway, and its horn tooted.

Matthew paused, waiting for the car to come to a stop. The driver came into view.

Elle.

She got out, looking a lot different from the last time he'd seen her, a month ago. Her hair was pulled back, and her dress was every bit as modest as the caped ones the Amish women wore.

She had a rather guarded smile on her face. "Matthew." She closed the car door. "Could we talk a minute?"

His first impulse was to say yes, but reservations mounted by the second. It had taken him too long to end things between them. He wasn't interested in opening his heart to her again. The jagged scent of gas cut through his thoughts, and he decided to get this over with and check on the source.

Her eyes found his, and she smiled again. "You don't have anything to say about the new attire?"

"It's your life, Elle. However you choose to dress and act no longer mat‐ters to me." He turned away from her, looking toward the motorized engine at the back of the shop as the possible cause of the fumes.

"You know, after the way you stood by Hannah through everything, I thought you'd stand by me."

His body flushed with heat at the shadowy accusation, and he stepped closer. "I helped Hannah carry a load that should not be put on anybody, and I helped her follow through on her choice to leave. Seems to me I've done the same for you, Elle Leggett. If Hannah had been my girl and asked me to wait indefinitely while she whooped it up among the Englischers, I woulda re‐fused. I'm tolerant, not stupid."

"Matthew, we need to talk. I mean really talk. You're too distracted around here. Let's go for a ride and—"

"I...I need to check on something." He strode toward the shop and had nearly reached the door when Elle caught his arm.

"I've come here in humility and honesty, and you walk off? Has every‐thing about this business of yours changed the man I fell in love with?"

Her words about loving him cut through his resolve. The very thing he wanted to avoid had happened. Traces of who they'd once been stood be‐fore him; memories of kisses tempted him. Through the screen door he could see David sitting at the desk. He glanced up, his face frowning at Elle's presence.

A breeze ran through the open windows of the shop and whisked through the screen door, filling the air with fumes. "David?" Matthew slung the door open. "Any idea where that—"

A flash of orange light exploded from the attic overhead. Something fell from the ceiling, knocking David out of the chair and to the floor. Burning fumes and smoke pushed Matthew down and scalded his lungs.

"David!" Struggling to keep his eyes open, he worked his way back to the door and into the smoke-filled room.

His eyes felt seared, as if they, too, were on fire. Staggering, he held his hands out in front of him to feel his way to the file cabinet. "David!" He surged around him. Through the murkiness of his vision, he could make out flashes of orange light.

"David!" Remembering what he'd always been told about smoke, he dropped to his knees. It was impossible to keep his eyes open. They burned too badly, and the stinging smoke made it worse. Grit from the floor buried itself in his palms as he crawled toward David. At least he hoped he was going in the right direction.

He felt papers and a piece of wood. "David!" he yelled over the sound of creaking timbers and lapping flames before the smoke choked him.

Outside the shop he heard Elle and his mother screaming. Luke was barking orders. "Stay back. The ceiling's about to collapse."

"Do something!" His mother's voice pierced the crackle of fire. "Do something!"

"Matthew!" Elle called.

"Someone ride bareback to the Yoders and dial 911. Hurry! Jacob, find every hose you can and conn—"

"I've got a cell phone in my car," Elle cried.

Matthew's hand landed on a thick piece of coarse material. He grasped it and tugged. When it didn't budge, he followed it, patting the floor in front of him as he went. His fingers landed on something soft, like flesh. Running his hands over the lump, he realized what it was. His lungs felt tighter than even a moment before.

David.

He tried to lift him, but he didn't have the strength. Unsure which way the door was, he wished he could still hear the noises from outside. Grabbing David by the arms, Matthew shuddered. There seemed to be no life in his brother. Tugging on him, pulling him across the floor inch by inch, he felt his own strength draining. Blackness threatened him as he tried to backtrack out of the building.

A faint popping sound came from above. Specks of smoldering embers fell from the ceiling. A crack sounded. He moved to cover David's face and torso. Something crashed to the floor a few feet from him. Pain seared his back as burning splinters landed on him. Matthew forced himself to hover over David, protecting him.

When the noise from the ceiling stopped, Matthew struggled to his knees, unable to catch more than a shallow breath.

Noises from outside became clear again. His mother continued to scream for David and him. He dragged his brother in the direction of her voice. Water from somewhere drenched his back and legs, making it even harder to tug on David.

"You're out of the building, Matthew." His mother sounded as if she was right beside him, but he still couldn't focus his eyes. "You're out. You can stop now." Mamm whispered the words, but she didn't touch him, and he couldn't see her.

"Matthew? Can you hear us?" Elle called.

"David! No!" His mother's sobs filled the air.

Matthew reached for David's shoulder, wanting reassurance he'd gotten them both out of the building okay, but all sense of his surroundings slipped away, and there was only darkness.

~~⚬~~

"Shh. Stay here," Sarah told Esther and the rest of her younger siblings, who were already seated at the kitchen table. In her bare feet, Sarah tiptoed through the living room and to the front door. Their home had been like a bus stop lately. Day before yesterday Hannah's Paul had arrived during meal time. Just moments ago it was Jacob Yoder who'd knocked on their front door, right in the middle of dinner, and Mamm and Daed had gone to the porch to talk to him.

Sarah stood beside the open window. She'd managed to hear the conversation with Paul this way. He'd given Daed a piece of paper. Paul said it had Hannah's address and phone number on it. He said he'd come to pass the information on to them, but he wasn't going to contact Hannah, and he didn't say why.

Now Jacob was here, and Sarah didn't intend to miss one word of what was said.

"I-I," Jacob stuttered and then paused. "I came to tell you…there was an explosion and fire at Luke and Matthew's place."

Sarah thudded against the wall as Jacob's words swirled inside her, tearing at her. "Oh, God, please, this can't be happening." She whispered the half prayer, half accusation.

The tongue is a fire, a world of evil…and sets on fire the course of life.

First the Bylers' barn, now Matthew's shop. The flames were getting closer and closer. Her house would be next, and it'd be all her fault. She'd said things about her sister she shouldn't have said. She'd started the gossip on purpose.

God is not mocked: for whatsoever a man soweth, that shall he also reap.

She moaned. Matthew's shop had caught fire. She couldn't believe it. According to Jacob, David and Matthew had been injured and were on their way to a hospital, the extent of their injuries unknown.

Silently she screamed for God, but if she didn't confess her sins before the bishop, God wouldn't help her. If she did confess her sins, God Himself couldn't save her—not from her father.

But Hannah could. She'd faced their father whenever he discovered one of Sarah's wrongdoings, and she had not let him lay a hand on her until he calmed down. Daed had grown to appreciate that about Hannah, although when they were younger, she'd taken a switch in Sarah's stead on many occasions.

Jacob's quaking voice interrupted her thoughts. "The bishop is calling for a community meeting at his place. There's talk that someone in the community is starting these fires."

Her tongue had set the fire. Unable to breathe, Sarah closed her eyes and silently begged for God or someone or something to help her.

An idea struck her, and her legs wobbled at the excitement of it. For the moment confusion melted away.

Hannah's phone number. She hadn't dared look for it after Paul brought it by and Daed took it to his room. Fear that he'd burn it, too, had kept her from even trying to find it. But now she had nothing to lose.

She rushed through the living room, darting to avoid being seen through the windows, and up the stairs. Sweat dripping down the back of her neck, she went into her parents' room and closed the door behind her. She went to her Daed's dresser and began opening drawers.

"It's in here somewhere," she mumbled to herself as she pushed T-shirts and socks to one side and then the other. After searching through each drawer, she was empty-handed. Scanning the room, her eyes stopped when she came to the chest at the foot of the bed. As she knelt in front of it and opened it, a stomach-turning smell of scorched material made her gag. She dug through the stuff until she found a piece of burnt material. Unfolding it, she realized it was the dress she'd worn the day she went to the Bylers and poked through the ashes. Her parents must've found the dress she'd thrown away.

They were collecting evidence against her. Did they know?

Tossing the dress back into the chest, she figured they probably didn't *know* anything or she'd have been confronted by now. Beaten. Thrown out of the house. Disowned forever.

Her chest hurt, and she could hear Hannah telling her to slow her breathing and picture herself sitting on the pier, dangling her feet in the pond. There wasn't time for that. Sarah pulled quilts and old baby clothes out of the wooden box until a piece of paper floated to the floor. It'd been tucked in a quilt, safe from prying eyes during the warm month of September.

"Sarah?" Her father was in the room.

She froze, too frightened to look up. She clutched the coveted piece of paper in her fist.

Her father wrapped his hand around her arm and lifted her to her feet. He took the paper from her and unfolded it. "You will tell me what you're doing going through things that do not belong to you."

She couldn't even catch a breath. How was she supposed to talk?

"Right now, Sarah." His words came out purposeful and hard.

She fought for air. "I...I've got to call Hannah."

"Why?" He barked the word at her.

She shook her head, unable to think with him in the room.

Daed clenched his jaw before he wrapped his hand around her wrist. He slowly turned her hand over, palm side up, and stared at it. He looked into her eyes and pressed the paper into her hand. "The decision is yours."

$\mathcal{P}$aul walked the rows of yellow squash in his mother's garden, twisting ripe ones from the vine and tossing them into the bushel basket. His attempt to break free of his disappointment and pain wasn't working. Over two years of believing Hannah would return and they would reunite was hard to let go of. He'd convinced himself she was somewhere mending while gaining maturity, that by the time she came home, she'd no longer be too young to marry. He swallowed hard. Clearly she wasn't too young to marry.

He'd held on to the dream of her return for so long that he felt ridiculous. And yet he still loved her. His life would never be what he believed it could have been with Hannah.

Nevertheless, it went on.

He'd known from the time she was fifteen that she'd tug on many a man's heart. There was no way around it. He twisted another squash off its vine. Five years of his life had been devoted to waiting on Hannah to love him the way he loved her.

But she'd grown to love someone else.

An Englischer. An upper-middle-class one at that. He could hardly believe his Lion-heart would fit into that lifestyle. It was his fault, really. He'd led Hannah to desire a lifestyle beyond her community. He'd always talked about the freedoms of electricity, computers, education, and cars. He'd put idealistic views into her head, thinking he was helping her see the value of stepping out of the Old Order ways. In many respects he'd acted more like a fancy Englischer than a Plain man, and he'd done so in front of an impressionable young woman.

Paul's family and community weren't like Hannah's Old Order Amish life, with no electricity or high-school diploma, but his roots were in the simple ways. When she left, he'd had one foot in each world. If he hadn't, she might not have found it so easy to leave the Plain life.

His regrets wouldn't solve anything. He'd lost his temper when he learned she was pregnant, and he'd always pay the price for that, but it was time he let go of his guilt and turned toward home and the roots he believed in. He refused to handle his loss the way his Uncle Samuel had. He wouldn't grow a heart of stone and live out his days single, pining for what might have been. He'd taken the paper with Hannah's phone number and address to the Lapp home yesterday. Her family could contact her or not as they saw fit, but he was finished longing for Hannah Lapp.

Completely finished.

The dinner bell rang. He grabbed the bushel basket and headed for the house. His sister and her husband, William, were here with their two boys and new baby girl. The Miller family was visiting too. Dorcas had brought the ingredients for homemade ice cream. It was a celebration in honor of his securing a full-time position at the Better Path and finishing his graduate program—although he planned to skip the commencement ceremony this time. Working at the Better Path wasn't much of a job as far as pay or benefits, but he could do more preventive work as a counselor for families than as a caseworker.

Placing the basket on the back porch, he peered through the window. Dorcas was laughing with his mom about something while arranging candles on an oversize cake. She'd been feeling really ill lately, even having days where she could barely get out of bed, but she seemed fine today.

She glanced up, spotting him. Her eyes grew wide, as if he were spying on what she was doing. She wagged her finger at him before joining him on the back porch.

"Hey." She nodded toward the house. "You gonna be able to stand all the family ruckus over you?"

"I always do," he teased back, focusing on her. She wore the clothes of her People. He'd never seen her without a prayer Kapp. Her heart was as respectful of the Mennonite ways as any he'd ever seen. She'd remained his friend throughout all his pining for Hannah. They didn't have the same level of camaraderie as he and Hannah had shared, and they rarely laughed together, but that could change with some effort.

He went to the edge of the porch and studied the horizon. "She isn't coming back."

Dorcas came up beside him. "I'm sorry."

He turned to face her. "No, Dorcas, I should apologize to you. You've been patient and hopeful for me that she'd return. But you didn't really want her to come back, did you?"

She closed her eyes, and her face twisted with emotion. "No. You're not angry at me, are you?"

He watched the fields, trying to let go of his desire for Hannah's return. "No, not at you." He willed himself to give attention to the present, but like a hurricane gaining strength, bitter emotions churned inside him. "After dinner, would you care to go for a walk?"

She looked surprised. "You know I would love to. But I thought you were going to Gram's to take care of the garden after dinner."

Hannah's garden.

The one he'd tended for three summers, waiting on her to return. "It can grow weeds." He motioned toward the house. "Let's go celebrate."

While the band held the last note of a song, Hannah laid the microphone down. Ready for a break, she walked into the kitchen. Placing a coffee filter into its basket, she heard Laura upstairs playing games with all the kids. Laura was just working part-time for now, giving Kevin and Lissa time to bond with her while Hannah and Martin were close by. Nina was glad for the reprieve and hadn't even come over with Dave and Vicki tonight. Hannah filled the basket with fresh grounds and poured water into the coffee maker, then watched fresh brewed coffee immediately begin to fill the decanter. The band sang a song by Rascal Flatts about forgetting the past and moving on.

Memories of life with Zabeth circled through Hannah's mind. How grateful she was for the chance to have been a part of Zabeth's life, but she missed her.

The musicians began another song. Laughter and loud voices echoed through the house. She grabbed a grape from one of the prepared trays and popped it into her mouth. Life in Martin's house was amazingly easy, and most day-to-day problems were solved in the time it took him to write a check.

"Hey." Martin strode into the room, all smiles. Whiffs of his cologne followed him as he placed his hand on the small of her back.

She couldn't help but smile. "Hi."

"Any chance I can talk you into us going away for the weekend with Vicki and Dave?"

"Ah, chaperones, huh? And you think that'll cause me to at least consider this rather brazen request?"

"Exactly." He grabbed a mug and poured himself a cup of coffee. "Come on, Hannah." He filled her cup and set the decanter back in place. "We have Laura now, and we need some time without Kevin and Lissa." He drew the cup to his lips.

She added sugar and powdered cream to her coffee. "Okay. It's probably time I learn to trust your judgment more."

He choked on a sip of his coffee. "You're going to kill me being so agreeable about things without warning. But since you're in such a generous mood, maybe we could catch a movie during this weekend outing?"

"A movie?" The bottom of her mug scraped against the countertop when she wrapped her hand around it. "I've never been to a movie theater or watched the DVD thingy here at the house."

"Good. Makes it easier to work out what movies you haven't seen yet." He smiled.

She giggled. "True enough. If I agree to this, do I get the infamous expensive popcorn and candy to go with it that I hear people talk about?"

"You can have anything you want, Hannah. Date night or not."

Hannah believed that. She just hoped she never took advantage of it.

Lissa ran into the room, laughing. "Me and Kevin's being good tonight, huh?"

"Yes, you are," Martin answered. Hannah nodded in agreement.

"Can I have some soda?"

"How about either juice or water?" Hannah asked.

Lissa brushed strands of hair off her face. "Apple juice."

Martin took a cup and lid from the cabinet and opened the fridge.

Looking from Martin to Lissa, Hannah couldn't imagine ever living a solitary life at the cabin again. The adjustment to living on Martin's property had taken some time, but now this is where her life took place—where schedules were juggled, where any and every thought or emotion was welcome to be freely expressed. She smiled to herself. Where music reigned supreme and lights flicked on in one room and off in another without a care given to it, where friendships were built and opposing opinions were listened to with respect.

Martin poured the drink and snapped the sippy lid on it.

Warmth and gratitude radiated from deep within her as if it were Christmastime and she were sitting in front of a roaring fire.

Wrapping her hands around the mug of coffee, Hannah watched him interact with Lissa. He'd changed a lot in the time she'd known him.

Kevin and Lissa still had times of crying for their parents, especially for their mom. Hannah had little doubt they would continue to miss their parents, but they knew they were loved, and surely that would cause abundant life to grow.

Lissa took the drink. "Thanks."

"You're welcome." Martin patted her head. She leaned against him, hugging his legs, and he rubbed her back before she ran out of the room. He returned his attention to Hannah. "Care to tell me what's on your mind?"

She shrugged. "Nothing."

His green eyes fastened on her, making her feel like everything about her mattered to him. "I think there is."

She smiled. "You're right. There is."

"Come on, phone girl, talk to me."

"I've just been thinking…" She shrugged. "That I'm very glad. That's all."

He moved in close and slid his arms around her. "Ah, are the words *charming* and *intelligent* coming to mind much these days?"

She put her palms against his chest. "You just can't not tease, can you?"

"Nope."

"Well, just for your information, those words are included. And more."

He kissed her forehead. "I like the sound of this. Those brainwashing tapes rigged to play in the cottage while you're asleep must be working." He brushed her lips with a kiss.

She felt safe and warm, loved and respected. In his arms, life never seemed as heavy.

"Any other words you want to share? There are children and friends in the house, so, you know, keep it decent."

She laughed. "That's enough for now. I wouldn't want you to be tempted to sin by thinking too highly of yourself."

"Oh, come on. Just one more thing?"

Her cheeks were burning, and he was fully amused. "Shut up, Palmer."

Laughing, he hugged her tighter. "I'm pretty thankful for you, Hannah. You probably have no idea."

"That's exactly what I wanted to tell you."

"That you're thankful for you too?"

She smacked his arm. "You're difficult. You know that?"

"And you have trouble telling a person what you're thinking and feeling. You know that?"

"Well, duh." She pulled him close, and he responded by brushing her lips with kisses, slowly and gently. "I…love you."

He stopped kissing her and stared.

"Well, breathe, Martin. If you pass out,"—she took a step back—"you're on your own." She tapped the floor with her foot. "Thump."

They shared a laugh before the phone interrupted them. She glanced at the caller ID, then looked at Martin. "It says it's John Yoder. You think that could be the Yoders from Owl's Perch?"

Martin reached for the phone.

She stopped him. "I'll get it."

With her pulse racing, Hannah grabbed the phone. "Hello?" She pushed her finger against her free ear, trying to block out the music and voices in the background. She walked out the back door.

"Hannah?" A young female voice wobbled and screeched.

"Yes?"

"You gotta come back, Hannah. You gotta." Her sister sounded rattled.

"Sarah, what's wrong?"

"Matthew's shop burned down, and the bishop's looking for who did it. It's my fault, Hannah. Me and my tongue, we did it."

"Matthew's shop?" She looked at the back door, hoping Martin had followed her. He was right behind her, watching. "Did anyone get hurt?"

"Matthew and David are in the hospital."

"How badly are they injured?" She felt Martin's hand on her back, comforting her already.

"I don't know." Sarah cried harder. "I'm sorry for the stuff I spread, Hannah. I…I'm sorry."

"Hush now, Sarah, hush." Hannah almost choked on the words. Of all the people she'd missed since moving here, Sarah was not one of them. She had betrayed Hannah too many times.

Sarah drew a ragged breath. "It's my fault. Because of what I did to you. The fire's coming for our house. Don't you see? First the Bylers' place, now Matthew's. It's moving closer. It's coming for me."

"Oh, sweetie." Hannah reverted to the tone she'd used in their childhood when Sarah would get so nervous she couldn't catch her breath. "I'll head for home by midmorning. Everything will be okay."

"Really?"

Hannah's breath caught. The idea of going home didn't hold near as much terror as it once had, but it was far from appealing. "Yes, I'll be home by tomorrow night."

Through broken sobs, Sarah whispered, "Thank you."

A dial tone buzzed in her ear. After a moment, she pushed the disconnect button.

Martin grabbed a lawn chair and pulled it up behind her. "What's going on?"

She sat. "That was my...my sister Sarah. There was a fire. I...I need to go home."

Concern flickered across his brow. "How long?"

"Just a few days."

"How did she get my phone number?"

"I don't know."

Martin knelt in front of her. "Will you be back before school on Monday? If you miss, with their policy of mandatory—"

"I don't know, but I'll be home by Wednesday for sure."

"I'll take time off from work and go with you. Laura can keep Lissa and Kevin here."

Hannah shook her head. "You don't understand, Martin. My family may not even allow me in the house. The community will be cold, to say the least. If I take you, I'll be treated worse than an outsider. If I have any hope of doing what needs to be done or of helping Sarah, I've got to do this alone."

"But I can make this easier on you."

"Not this time. You're more likely to lose your temper and make things worse. I'm not treasured in Owl's Perch like I've been since I landed here. You'll have to trust me about this."

He gave a reluctant nod. "What's wrong with Sarah?"

"She's a lot like Faye, only she doesn't need the addiction to be an emotional wreck. She said her tongue set the fire."

"Her tongue?" Disbelief etched across his face. "Is this the same Matthew you told me about?"

Nodding, she caressed Martin's cheek. "Yes. He stood by me, helped me leave, and gave me money. I've got to go to him."

Martin placed his hand over hers and rubbed it. "Hannah." He stood and guided her to her feet. "Once you're there, you'll be faced with figuring out all sorts of things."

"I think I'll be figuring out how to get back to you, Kevin, and Lissa quickly. I'm coming back just as soon as I can." She snuggled against him. "This isn't going to be enjoyable, Martin."

He kissed her forehead. "You'll question what you really want, where you really fit in—that kind of stuff. I love you, Hannah Lawson. Don't forget that."

"I won't, not for a minute. And I'll return as quickly as I can." She took a step back. "We need to explain this to Kevin and Lissa. And I need to pack."

"We need to go over directions of how to get on the Ohio Turnpike."

She took him by the hand and led him toward the cottage. "Before all that and before we talk to the kids, I have something I want to give you. It was supposed to be for your birthday in two weeks, but now's a better time."

Martin tugged at her hand. "I need to get something too and let the others know where we've gone."

"Sure." Hannah went into the storage room and lifted the repaired quilt from a box. She unfolded new wrapping paper across the kitchen table and laid the quilt inside. She still wasn't sure who it had originally belonged to. The only thing she knew for sure was Zabeth had designed and sewn it. And since Hannah and her Plain friends at the quilting gatherings had repaired it, she was going to give it to Martin.

When she heard the knock on her door, she hurriedly put the last piece of tape in place and turned the package over. "Come in."

Martin popped open the door and walked inside.

"I've been working on repairing something for you, so it's not new."

He took the gift from her. "May I open it now?"

"That's the idea."

He unwrapped it, tearing the paper at will. His face drained of emotion for a few seconds before he looked at her. "Where…did you find this…and how did you find the time?" He ran his finger over a corduroy square in the blanket.

"It was at the bottom of a box in the storage room. The Tuesday afternoon women's group at the clinic always sews quilts for charity." She grinned. "You'll be glad to know you qualified."

Martin chuckled. "Thanks." His green eyes lingered on her before admiring the quilt again. He spread it out over the kitchen table. "I've missed this thing for years. Zabeth and Mom made this when Faye and I were children. Zabeth placed it over me at night every winter for years after my mom died, so it became mine."

"Don't put it in the washer, or it'll fall apart again."

"I didn't know that." He gazed at the multicolored patches. "This was from my mother's wedding gown," he said, pointing to a square of white satin. "And this," he said, his finger moving to a patch of faded-blue denim, "is from my grandfather's overalls. Did you know he was a dairy farmer?" His fingers skimmed each section tenderly. "This is from my first pair of cowboy pants, when I was four. This quilt is a patchwork of Palmer life—before it became a train wreck."

"You're doing the best anyone can to make things right."

He laid the quilt on the chair and took her hands. "Hannah, I have something for you, but maybe it's not appropriate as you head back to your Amish community." He reached inside his jeans pocket and pulled out a small box. "It's a birthstone ring."

She opened the box to see a gold ring with two stones nestled in an S-shaped loop.

Martin removed it from the box. "It's sort of a strange gift. One is Kevin's birthstone, and the other is Lissa's." He chuckled. "Lissa's stone is a diamond, and Kevin's is a ruby—well, actually his is a garnet, but I think the ruby is the same basic color, right? And it's a higher quality stone." He lifted her left hand. "I know you haven't said yes to anything, but if you'd wear this on your left hand, it'd mean a lot to me."

Hannah watched as he slid it onto her finger. "Ah, so it's an honorary mother's gift, yet somehow it tells everyone I'm spoken for even though I've not accepted your rather brazen, albeit romance-free proposal. Have I missed anything?"

Martin kissed the finger that now wore the ring. "You know me entirely too well. But you skipped the fact that I am in love with you."

"Oh, I never skip that part. I think about it all the time." She slid her arms around his shoulders and hugged him. "Thank you for everything. I wouldn't want to face Owl's Perch without knowing I have you here waiting for me."

"There's one more thing." He pulled some papers from his pocket and passed them to her.

She opened them. "A trip to Hawaii." She glanced up. "Over Christmas?"

"Before you say no, consider this: Dave, Vicki, and Nina are going too. As are several top employees from the company. Kevin and Lissa aren't near as likely to miss their parents as badly over Christmas if they are in a whole new setting. You'll be finished with school, and we should celebrate. And my idea is perfect."

She couldn't deny the idea was exciting—to get on a plane and fly, to see a beach for the first time in her life, and in Hawaii. "That's you, isn't it? Thinking through every angle of something and then going for it." She folded the papers and passed them back to him. "I'll look forward to it every day between now and then."

Martin kissed her, sealing her determination to get back to him as soon as possible.

Luke paced the floor of the hospital while the Esh family talked with the doctor at Matthew's bedside. The orangy smell of cleaning products was all too familiar, and it brought back awful memories from Mary's time at a medical facility.

Elle waited at the end of the hall, looking like an outcast.

Mary came to his side and took his hand before laying her head on his shoulder. Luke turned and wrapped her in his arms. They'd survived their accident three years ago and recovered. But this time was different. There'd been a working cell phone and a car. Luke had the power and the means to make decisions.

Yet David hadn't survived.

Matthew's parents, Naomi and Raymond, came out of the room. Luke and Mary went to them, but Elle hung back, listening. Naomi stared straight into Luke's face and spoke flatly. "He was awake and asking for you, but the pain medicine must've taken over, and he's asleep for now. When he wakes, just know his eyes are covered with bandages, so he won't be able to see you. None of the burns will require a skin graft." She brushed her hands down the front of her apron.

"Does he know about David?"

Naomi nodded. "Yes."

"And that the business is gone?"

She nodded again. "We told him everything."

"Will he get his eyesight back?"

"Ash and soot from the ceiling fell into his eyes, but the doctor thinks that when the bandages are removed in a couple of days, he'll be able to see."

Grief was etched on Naomi's and Raymond's faces. They'd lost one son. Hopefully just one. Luke feared the weight of what had happened might break Matthew, even if he regained his eyesight. Raymond led Naomi to a chair and sat beside her.

Elle went into Matthew's room.

Ignoring the ways of his people, Luke placed his hand on Mary's protruding stomach, so thankful she hadn't been near the shop when the explosion occurred. Everything dear to him was right here in his arms, but Matthew had lost his business and his brother. And if anyone asked Luke, the man had never had Elle to begin with, certainly not since her father returned.

He dreaded the realities that would beat Matthew without mercy for a long time to come. He walked to the doorway of Matthew's room. An IV was attached to one arm, and he was lying on his stomach. Aside from the temporary problem with his eyes, nothing but the skin on his back had received burns. Elle stood beside the bed.

Matthew stirred. "Luke?"

Elle placed her hand over his. "It's me—Elle."

Matthew pulled away from her. "Go home, Elle. Just go."

"Matthew, please. I'm so sorry—"

"Get out."

Elle glanced up, spotting Luke. He nodded toward the door, confirming Matthew's words.

Anxiety over Matthew and facing her father wore on Hannah as she drove across the Pennsylvania state line. She'd been foolish and desperate when she'd left home two and a half years ago, thinking freedom could be found in running away.

She'd arrived in Alliance broken; nevertheless God had given her Dr. Lehman, and he, in turn, had found Zabeth. And Zabeth had brought Martin, Lissa, and Kevin into her life, and Hannah loved them.

Her freedom had been found in the love they offered her.

But was anyone ever completely free?

She didn't think so. Never free of troubles or of human need. But she was free to make mistakes or get caught in a trauma and still be loved. That was something Owl's Perch couldn't give her.

In spite of her reluctance to return, she looked forward to seeing the friends she'd left behind. And Paul? Well, it should be easy to avoid him. If she had to face him, she wouldn't share how badly he'd hurt her. It wasn't any of his business. He might be married to that Dorcas by now, or at least engaged, but Hannah had moved on.

Thoughts of Martin filled her mind. She'd done more than just move on, and even though her nerves said otherwise, Paul Waddell was simply someone she'd once thought she loved.

Nevertheless. For the first time in years, the word spoke softly in her spirit.

She'd face her father before leaving again.

Nevertheless.

She'd take these few days and find peace with her past. Then she'd return to Martin, Lissa, and Kevin.

Content with those thoughts, she drew a deep breath.

She didn't know what would happen in Owl's Perch, but she trusted the One who held her heart. The One who'd taught her that He was more powerful in her life than any injustice—past or future.

Acknowledgments

With deep gratitude I thank those who've faithfully helped me with this project.

My dear husband, your love and support make this possible.

Miriam Flaud, my dear Old Order Amish friend, who opens her home, reads each manuscript, and answers questions via her phone shanty because she has a heart of gold.

Eldo and Dorcas Miller, whose expertise about the Plain Mennonite community mixed with their willingness to teach me have been a tremendous blessing.

Joan Kunaniec, a wonderful Plain Mennonite who willingly shares her love and respect of the Plain ways.

Rick and Linda Wertz, whose readiness to help with research, photos, and accurate navigation of the Pennsylvania roadways is a gift in my life.

Jeffry J. Bizon, MD, OB/GYN, and his wife, Kathy, who make time to keep the medical information correct; I couldn't have done this without your help.

To all the awe-inspiring people my husband and I met while spending a week in Alliance, Ohio. Your warmth and openness lingers with us still.

Mrs. Rhonda Shonk, Office Manager, Alliance City Schools Career Centre and the Robert T. White School of Practical Nursing, whom I relied upon to keep Hannah's schooling experiences accurate.

Don and Jean Aebi and Sue Feller, residents of Alliance who shared information via e-mail after I returned home to Georgia. You made the nuances of being an Alliance resident come to life.

Steve Laube, my agent. I'm forever blessed to be one of your authors. You're everything I'd hoped for in an agent. You have calmed my nerves and answered my newbie questions with the patience of Job. Thank you.

And a special thank-you to my editor extraordinaire, Shannon Hill, who is clearly skilled at molding lumps of clay. And to Carol Bartley, whose keen sense of story balance never ceases to amaze me. And to everyone at Water-Brook Press, I'm very grateful for all you do.

Glossary

aa—also or too

ach—oh

alleweil—now, at this time

da—the

Daadi Haus—grandfather's house. Generally this refers to a house that is attached to or is near the main house and belongs to a grandparent. Many times the main house belonged to the grandparents when they were raising their family. The main house is usually passed down to a son, who takes over the responsibilities his parents once had. The grandparents then move into the smaller place and usually have fewer responsibilities.

dabber—quickly or at once

Daed—dad or father

dei—your

denk—think

denke—thank you

des—this

draus—out

du—you [singular]

Dummkopp—blockhead or dunce

Englischer—a non-Amish person. Mennonite sects whose women wear the prayer Kapps are not considered Englischers and are often referred to as Plain Mennonites.

es—it

fehlerfrei—perfect

geh—go

gut—good

hatt—difficult or hard

Heemet—home

hilfe—help

ich—I

in—in

iss—is

Kall—fellow

Kapp—a prayer covering or cap

kumm—come

kummet—come

letz—wrong

liewer—dear

loss—let

loss uns geh—let's go

mach's—make it

Mamm—mom or mother

Mammi—shortened term of endearment for grandmother

mol—on

muscht—must

net—not

Ordnung—The written and unwritten rules of the Amish. The regulations are passed down from generation to generation. Any new rules are agreed upon by the church leaders and endorsed by the members during special meetings. Most Amish know all the rules by heart.

Pennsylvania Dutch—Pennsylvania German. The word *Dutch* in this phrase has nothing to do with the Netherlands. The original word was *Deutsch*, which means "German." The Amish speak some High German (used in church services) and Pennsylvania German (Pennsylvania Dutch), and after a certain age, they are taught English.

rumschpringe—running around

schnell—quick(ly)

schpring—run

schtobbe—stop

schwetze—talk

seller—that one

so—so

uns—us

verhuddelt—confused

was—what

Welt—world

will—will or wants to

ya—yes

---

* Glossary taken from Eugene S. Stine, *Pennsylvania German Dictionary* (Birdsboro, PA: Pennysylvania German Society, 1996), and the usage confirmed by an instructor of the Pennsylvania Dutch language.

About the Author

CINDY WOODSMALL is the author of the best-selling novel *When the Heart Cries,* the first book in the Sisters of the Quilt series. Her real-life connections with the Plain Mennonite and Old Order Amish families enrich her novels with authenticity. Cindy lives in Georgia with her husband, three sons, and one daughter-in-law.